REFRACTION

WICK WELKER

DEMODOCUS PUBLISHING LLC

Novels by Wick Welker

Medora
The Medora Wars
*The Medorean**

Refraction
*Dark Theory**

Needle Work
*NeoSF**

*Forthcoming

Refraction

By Wick Welker

Published by Demodocus Publishing LLC.

ISBN: 978-1-7355374-5-0

PO Box 7235

Rochester, MN 55903

Cover art by Damonza; Timeline by Swerklstudio

For my baby girl on the way...

REFRACTION

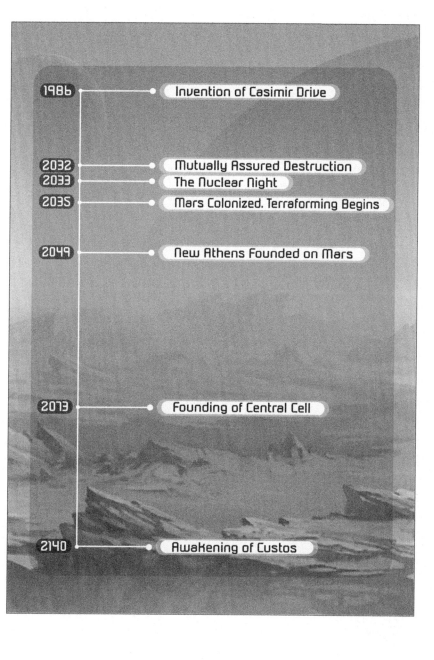

1986 — Invention of Casimir Drive

2032 — Mutually Assured Destruction
2033 — The Nuclear Night
2035 — Mars Colonized. Terraforming Begins

2049 — New Athens Founded on Mars

2073 — Founding of Central Cell

2140 — Awakening of Custos

PROLOGUE

The terraforming of Mars brought harmony to the atmosphere, but not to the inhabitants of the planet. A decade after geosynchronous orbiting mirrors evaporated carbon dioxide and water vapor into the atmosphere, discord raged among the rival colonies. The communities were nestled along the Telephus Mountains, creating territorial disputes, trade wars, and old-fashioned frontier violence. After several years of strife, a council sought to unify the people of Mars into something more noble than themselves:

A utopia.

Each colony elected a representative to attend the first grand council of Mars. The twelve delegates met at a single spot in the Martian wilderness as a symbol of their goals—to forge an unsullied society on fertile ground, liberated from humanity's past mistakes of poverty, starvation, and war. Forming a semi-circle around an enormous bonfire, they sat cross-legged in the rust-colored soil.

The council argued.

Tempers flared, accusations flew, and motivations were questioned. They mutually suspected collusion, spreading distrust like a wildfire. After days of fruitless bickering, the council was on the brink

2 | WICK WELKER

of disbanding. They prepared to return to their colonies and ease back into their prejudices about one another.

On the final evening of the council, an old man appeared from the horizon.

He knew things about the council members. He knew... *everything* about them. He addressed them openly, uncovering their suspicions. He exposed that there *was* collusion—back door agreements between council members. He revealed the truth about the council, that every member intended to take advantage of their neighboring colony. The dream of establishing a utopia on Mars was a pretense for self-interest.

Trust evaporated.

The council was destroyed.

And the old man was never seen again.

The next morning, however, the former council members reconvened in an impromptu assembly. With their secrets exposed, they found they were free to speak—no longer hindered by their suspicions. The truth that the man wielded had thrust them back on equal footing.

They drafted a new government in half a day.

The original colonists concluded their first successful assembly and commissioned a tapestry to be woven. It depicted Mars woven in bright red over the black of space. Earth—in the past and relegated to history—was a small circle in dark blue. The council agreed on a mantra and stitched it into the tapestry:

Live on, Our Hope of the Risen Red.

The city of New Athens was born.

PART I
VOICES

CHAPTER 1

SEPTEMBER 1, 1986

Before Timothy Straus could save the worlds, he first needed to teach his class. The auditorium at the Georgetown physics department filled quickly. Students cut their chatter and stuffed their bags under chairs. Straus glanced at the front row curiously—the seats had been left empty. Before he could complain about the vacancies, several burly students stuffed themselves into the flimsy seats.

Straus eyed them skeptically. "Does the football team reserve seats now?"

A square-faced student shrugged. "We just like being up front. You're a... really good teacher." His fellow teammates nodded in unison.

He gave them a sidelong look. "That's new."

Straus looked over the auditorium, arms crossed, shaking his head. He tapped his watch and said, "Time is knowledge." He scribbled equations on the chalkboard. "Who recognizes this formula?"

A hand shot up from the back. Straus continued to write as though he'd forgotten about the question. "Dr. Straus?" the student yelled.

Straus whipped around, strands of black hair falling in his eyes. He pointed at the student. "Yes?"

"Is it a Hamiltonian Wave Function?"

"No," Straus said, pleased that his trap had been sprung. "But I can see why you may have thought that. It does *look* like the Hamiltonian but there is one slight deviation that makes this wave function take on a completely new behavior. Does anyone see it?" He grinned, anticipating they would mirror his enthusiasm.

They stared back, eyes glazed with disinterest.

"No one?" He waited—only a muffled cough in reply. "You see this line integral right here?" He pointed at a symbol. "This single alteration here, if it existed in nature, would completely alter our reality." He let this last part hang in the air. "If that one variation changed, all of our atoms—every single particle that makes up our universe—would *pause* in their natural decay."

The audience was unmoved.

"The elements would never cease to exist but time would still progress. If time progresses without nuclear decay, it means that the matter would travel outside of time. Time would become an irrelevant variable." He lifted a hand with a flourish and looked back at the auditorium.

Someone said, "Pretty neat." A squeal of laughter erupted and then died.

"Yes, yes," Straus surrendered. "Looks like we don't have anyone here interested in *real* physics. Let's get to your homework."

The students pulled out enormous calculators as Straus provided solutions prompting many confused faces. A girl raised her hand and waved it. "Dr. Straus?" she finally chirped.

He looked out over his glasses. "Yes?"

"Can we go over question twelve? A lot of us aren't understanding—"

"Of course—" His words cut off as a bolt of pain clapped through his head. He grabbed the edge of the table to steady himself. "I—" His mouth went dry.

Please, not now!

A chorus of voices swelled within him.

The voices scrambled together, pushing out the rest of the auditorium, the students—the world. The seams of reality split wide open, ushering a hurricane of voices flooding from a thousand worlds at once. The voices washed through him, pushing him to the ground.

As if rehearsed, the front row football team rushed to Straus as he faltered over the lab table. They clung to his limp hands as he sank to the floor.

And then it was over.

Lucidity returned.

He stood and straightened his tie. "I'm fine. I'm just having a very bad headache. You can take your seats, gentlemen." He adjusted his skewed glasses.

The football team gave one another furtive glances. "Are you sure? That was... was that a seizure?"

"No. Everyone, I think we'll cut class a few minutes short today. I'll see you on Wednesday." After a pregnant pause, there was a mad dash for the doors. As students streamed out of the lecture hall, Straus saw the rotund chairman of the physics department coming down the steps.

"Dr. Van Wert," Straus addressed him mechanically, collecting papers into his briefcase.

"Tim..." Van Wert furrowed his eyebrows.

"Yes?"

"Do you have anything to say about what just happened?"

"Did you ask the football team to sit in the front row today?"

Van Wert feigned surprise and then sighed, "It was just a precaution."

"An unneeded one. It was just a headache."

"Are you sure it wasn't... the other thing?"

"No, I haven't had those—that—in a while."

"It looked a lot like the same problems you were having a few months ago. I only asked those students to sit there to prevent you from falling. And I'm glad that I did."

"I don't have those issues anymore. I've been on some new meds that have worked perfectly." Straus winced at having brought up his medications.

He patted Straus on the shoulder. "I wanted to talk to you about something else..."

Straus looked at the clock. "I'd love to talk but I'm due back in my lab."

Van Wert continued, "I've been observing some of your classes. I'm worried about how you've been... running things."

"It was *just* a migraine," Straus said, frustration growing.

"No, I'm not talking about your... episode just now. It's your material. You've been teaching things that are way above these students' heads. Half the things you put up there, I don't even understand."

"I just like to have a little fun with them. It's important to show that you can get creative with physics."

"Matter traveling through time? I know you're teaching quantum mechanics but you've got to at least stick to the books. These are undergraduate physics students who can barely even grasp the basics."

Straus shrugged. "It all makes sense mathematically. The math is perfect, check it yourself."

"I can't. I have no idea about half the stuff you're talking about up there. No one does, it's all conceptual... speculation."

"Really, I can show you the math..." He picked up a piece of chalk as if ready for another lecture.

Van Wert put up his hands with a chuckle. "I'm sure you can. But please, stick to the curriculum and pay attention to student questions."

Straus nodded, "I understand. Anything else?"

Van Wert looked at him, hesitating. "I heard about your grant running out soon."

Straus chased a worried look from his face. "I'm optimistic I can renew it with a few tweaks—"

"If your projects were more stable, you might get more sustainable funding. But you're always onto some new pet project before you finish the previous one. A year ago, you were working with a free radical engine and now you're onto this Casimir thing?"

"Casimir Drive," he corrected. "And it's not just a pet project. It's something else—something big. I think it's something that could change the world."

Van Wert stifled a grin and patted Straus on the shoulder. "Of course, Tim. Of course. I would advise you to at least try sticking with this project for more than just a year."

"That won't be a problem. The Casimir Drive is the biggest thing I've ever worked on. It will define my career and, hopefully, much more. It will connect all people together over the planet and maybe even beyond our solar system." Van Wert offered a weak smile that Straus assumed he reserved for himself and perhaps his five-year-old niece.

Without another word, Straus picked up his briefcase while Van Wert watched him exit the classroom. Straus weaved through mazes of lab benches and into the catacombs of the physics department. After a few flights through dank stairwells, he came to his laboratory door. Sliding his badge, he entered and found his graduate student, Duke, bent over a row of black grids that spanned the length of the lab. It looked like someone had gutted a dozen metal filing cabinets and placed them on their backs.

"How did it go?" Straus asked, looking over the grid.

"Bad. The whole thing is heating up." Duke reached for a wrench.

"Not surprised."

"No idea where all this extra heat is coming from," Duke said, stretching his arms to the ceiling. The back of his shirt clung with sweat.

"I don't see it when we run the numbers." Straus sat down and flipped through a notebook. "Doesn't add up. We shouldn't be generating this much heat. We'll need to get money to transfer the whole lab to the super-cooled rooms."

"Great, we probably won't get those funds until after I graduate."

"Assuming we can renew the grant—" Straus saw an unfamiliar girl hovering around the doorway.

Duke stood. "Dr. Straus, this is Chou Jia. She just had her interview for one of our graduate spots. I thought I would show her around the lab."

"Very good." Straus, still halfway across the lab, shot his arm out at her unceremoniously. "It's nice to meet you, Chou Jia."

"Oh!" the girl said, surprised at Straus trying to shake her hand from across the room. She dashed to him and took his hand.

"What makes you interested in the lab?"

"Well," she said, settling her nerves. "I think you have the best labs on the east coast. Georgetown will definitely be my top choice. What's that?" She pointed to the rows of black grids.

"Duke, our trap has been sprung. She wants to know about the Drive. Are you familiar with the Casimir effect?" he asked her.

She bit her lip, "Vaguely."

"The Casimir effect is a phenomenon that occurs when you place two neutrally charged plates extremely close together, which creates negative energy in the space between them. Basically, energy out of a vacuum. What we're doing here," he motioned to the rows of grids, "is exploiting the negative energy produced between subatomic fluctuations."

"Uh-huh."

"There are more quantum fluctuations happening on the outside of the plates than in between the plates, so there is a tremendous amount more of quantum bubbling going on outside of the plates, which pushes them together, creating energy... seemingly out of nothing. We've designed a grid system of plates that are one atom thick and with a space of only one atom wide—extremely small spaces. The smaller the space, the greater negative energy comes out of it. We believe by stacking the atomic plates together, you can create an enormous amount of energy in a very tiny space."

"And what will that do?"

"Ever see Star Trek?"

Duke rolled his eyes as if tired of his overused explanation.

"Of course," Chou Jia said.

"I predict that focusing that amount of energy into such a small space would effectively *bend space*. Like a warp drive."

"Really?"

Straus simply nodded.

"I've never heard of the Casimir effect doing *that*," she said.

"No one has... *yet*. Assuming our funding doesn't run out..." he sighed, souring the mood.

"Dr. Straus," Duke said, "we're trying to get her to *come* to this school, not chase her away..."

"Thanks so much for showing me all of this," she said, side-stepping the awkward silence. "I would absolutely love to come here." She stepped over a stack of fallen papers and textbooks. "Thanks for showing me the lab, Dr. Straus. I hope to come back soon."

Straus only nodded and walked away. He sat at a rickety wooden table and poured himself a cup of coffee, letting out a slow breath.

"Do you think we'll be able to finish the Drive?" Duke poured a cup as well.

"I do, yes. I'm optimistic."

"But you're *always* optimistic. You see a half-full glass when there's only a drop left."

"Is that wrong?"

Duke shrugged. "Guess it depends on what you can do with that last final drop."

"Sometimes the final drop is more important than the whole cup," he said, slurping the last of his coffee.

CHAPTER 2

SEPTEMBER 1ST, 1986

T*ime is running out.*
Straus picked up a sandwich from a campus deli, his mind muddled. A familiar anxiety churned within, punctuated by panic. It was a panic not about his research. It was a deep-rooted and unspecified paranoia that gnawed at the back of his mind, telling him... something—that time was running out?

Time for what?

He pulled into the parking garage of his apartment building and stared at the cinder blocks through the windshield, waiting for the voices to come—to urge, to incite, to cover his face in a cold sweat. He wanted to get the torrent of voices out of his head before entering his home. "Huh," he said to the empty car. He realized the voices were only from men. It surprised him that he had never thought of it before. He also faced the growing realization that the voices were getting worse.

He walked through the apartment door and saw his wife, Jo, sitting on the couch, breastfeeding. She looked up at him with a concerned frown she reserved only for her husband. "What're you doing home so early? It's not even lunch."

"I wasn't feeling well, had a... bad headache during class."

"Oh..." She switched the baby over her shoulder as it burped. "Just a headache?"

"Yep." He yanked a chair from the kitchen table, sat down, and unwrapped his sandwich.

She sidled up, sitting next to him with the baby in her lap. "We had a good day together—went out to the park. Did you see that it rained a little in the morning?"

"I was teaching."

"Why are you in a bad mood?"

"I'm sorry, hun. Worried about the Drive. Not sure if my grant will get renewed." He took a bite of his sandwich. "I *need* to get the Drive done. Something feels wrong. We have to finish it and finish it soon."

"Want to say hi to James?" She placed the baby into his lap.

He brought James up to his chest, looking into his eyes. The baby looked back with a wide smile. "How's my boy? What great wonders has he accomplished today?" The baby giggled and hopped on his father's lap.

"Why don't you go over and relax in front of the TV for a bit?" Jo offered.

Straus punched the button on the television and lay on the couch as a commercial for laundry detergent flashed across the screen. He suddenly sat up, staring at the screen. "Unbelievable."

Jo walked into the room. "What's wrong?"

"The Russians shot down a commercial airliner from the States," he said, gesturing to the screen.

"What're you talking about?" She pointed at the TV. There was only cascading laundry powder flashing over the screen. A split second later, it flickered with an emergency broadcast banner showing images of smoldering wreckage spewing smoke. "How did you see the news before—"

"Hang on." He turned up the volume.

A newscaster's voice came, "...not certain at the moment what the exact provocation was. We are confirming now that flight 007 from Anchorage to Seoul, South Korea has crashed and it is believed to be a deliberate attack from the Soviet Union on the aircraft. All 269 passengers on the plane are feared dead, including congressman, Lawrence McDonald."

Straus shook his head. "Those poor people. The Soviets will just keep provoking us—stockpiling nukes—and the U.S. will just keep toppling one communist regime after another, killing thousands of innocent lives. Will it ever change?"

"Things change," Jo said, bouncing the baby. "Sometimes it just takes time and the right kind of people."

"That's enough for one day. There's only so much of this world I can take." He switched off the TV set.

Noon turned to evening as Straus napped. He didn't dream but his mind wasn't empty. A rattling of distant voices bubbled up in his mind as he felt himself floating. An infinite horizon lay before him, one seamless ribbon of black. He was floating alone, in space, swathed by starlight. A cloud of silver gas burst around him, swirling with lightning and thunder. A chorus of voices rained down. Each raindrop was a shout or whisper that erupted in his ears. He tried flapping through the fog but was stalled by weightlessness. The voices stirred inside of him and chanted, *he is coming, he is coming, he is coming!* They crescendoed further, *HE IS COMING!*

He snapped awake and realized that the voices had assimilated from a sizzling sound in the kitchen. He looked over the couch and saw Jo moving a frying pan back and forth over the stove. He watched her hair sway in the pleasant way it did when she cooked.

"I'm sorry," he said, coming into the kitchen.

"For what?"

"Being grumpy earlier. It's hard for me sometimes." He touched the back of her apron and rested his forehead on her shoulder.

"It would be hard for anyone. Do you think the new medication is working better?"

"Too soon to tell. I accidentally told Jack Van Wert at work that I'm on meds."

"It's okay. He should know that schizophrenia isn't anyone's fault. It's just something you get, like pneumonia. You don't have any control over it."

He cringed.

"What?"

"I'm still not convinced it's schizophrenia."

"Tim, you hear voices. *Voices*. Auditory hallucinations are a hallmark of schizophrenia."

"I know. But there's more to it than just the voices. I—" he hesitated.

"What?"

"I don't always feel like... *me*. There's something on top of me or under me but it doesn't have anything to do with the *actual* me. And besides, the medications clearly aren't making the voices go away. If anything, they're stronger."

"Should I schedule an appointment to see the doctor tomorrow?"

"That's fine—oh, hey!" He ran out of the kitchen.

"What?" she called from behind.

"The comet that's been on the news... it's supposed to be the brightest tonight. It only comes around once every twenty years."

"Oh." She went back to the kitchen.

Straus ducked out onto their porch overlooking the Georgetown campus. Swinging his telescope from under the awning, he peered up into the night's sky and saw it—a smudge of blue smeared across the sky. He followed the blue trail as it moved, ignoring the chanting voices bubbling in his mind.

CHAPTER 3

SEPTEMBER 2ND, 2098

Twin white trails streamed across the cockpit as Cal Stanger coasted at cruising speed above Earth. The cockpit hummed benignly as he rechecked his incoming perigee to the atmosphere. He wasn't about to get a bad mark again for having too steep of an angle of attack on re-entry.

"Cal..." Benedito buzzed in his headset. "You might want to check your angle. We're coming up pretty fast."

"No. I'm good."

Jelena's voice crackled, "Cal, Bene's right. You're coming in too hot."

"I said I'm good—"

And then a chorus of voices cracked through his mind like thunder. For a moment, Earth below and the stars above wheeled from his existence as thousands of voices spoke over one another, stealing all attention from his flight. Like a storm on the horizon, the voices swept closer and coalesced, chanting in unison the same words: *He is coming! He is coming! HE IS COMING!*

Jelena's voice broke through the torrent. "Cal!"

The wave of voices ceased and he looked down at his balled fists. Lucid once more, Cal dampened the coasting thrusters while throttling up for the burn through Earth's atmosphere. The ship shuddered under the change in acceleration. He punched through, wings dragging on the atmospheric gases. The stars glittered for a moment more as the ship hurtled toward gravity. At the moment he thought the drag would dissipate, the ship jolted with turbulence. He gripped the throttle, struggling to keep the ship steady...

It plunged through the atmosphere.

Benedito yelled, "Pull up and punch the bow thrusters!"

Sweating, Cal pulled up, his arms shaking on the throttle as the ship evened out in the sky. He punched the dash in frustration.

"That was not good, Stanger," said Captain Kalai, the cadets' flight commander. He flew along the rest of the cadets. "Welcome back to the Gulf, cadets. Bring it on back to the Academy. No unauthorized landings outside of Central Cell."

As the ship dropped down into thicker layers of the atmosphere, Cal peered over thousands of pinpoints of sunlight reflecting off the ocean. The shimmering water was flanked by the gigantic green landmass of what was once Texas. The land grew in size as several other ships joined Cal in a corkscrew pattern to the landing pads. He brought the wings just over the yellow paint of the Central Cell Air Academy's landing zone and softly landed.

After a moment of depressurizing the cockpit, the front burner glass opened outwards, bringing in the humid air of an early summer. Collecting his gear, Cal made his way over to the control center where Captain Kalai waited with a glare. "Stanger," he said as Cal hurried to go unnoticed. "What happened up there?"

"I took my time and double-checked my approach again and again..."

Kalai crossed his burly arms across his chest. "Your Jupiter Run next week *must* be better."

"It will be." Cal brushed past and threw his helmet at his flight station and unbuckled his flight suit. He weaved through crowds of cadets, down a flight of stairs, and into the locker room.

After his shower, Benedito shook his head at him. "What happened?"

"I already got it from Kalai. I don't need you reminding me of how bad the run was."

Benedito winced. "Sorry."

"It's fine. I just—I have a problem..."

"What is it?"

Cal hesitated and said, "I'm just not a natural flier like you. It comes a little harder for other people."

"Do you want to practice some more this weekend?"

Cal nodded. "That would really help."

"We'll do it." As always, Benedito's genuine interest in making Cal a better pilot made him feel like an ass for getting annoyed. "Let's get to didactics."

They made their way to the cadet auditorium and found seats next to Jelena.

"Caleb!" she sounded stern. "You need to take our solo flights more seriously." Benedito shook his head at Jelena but she continued. "With every passing year, Central Cell fails more and more cadets. Where do you think they go for work after?"

Cal sighed. "Jelena..." He looked over at her. Her brown eyes glistening in the dim auditorium. *Why does she care so much?*

"Do you want to get deported?" she asked.

"Of course not." As the lights dimmed, he flipped on his desk console and quickly reviewed the topic for the day, releasing a sigh.

"What?" she asked.

"We're talking about the Casimir Drive today."

"So?"

"Nothing. I just haven't... studied it much," he lied.

"You'll be fine. Are you coming out tonight with everyone? We're going to that new club."

"Oh, you want me to come?"

She furrowed her brow. "Yeah, everyone's going."

"I might make it."

Professor Hendricks walked in, the entire wall behind her lighting up with a graphic of a cylindrical-shaped engine. "Good afternoon, cadets, I hope all of your solo flights went well today. If you checked the schedule, you can see that for the next week we will be discussing Casimir Drive physics and its relationship to bent acceleration. The material is quite dense. I suggest you begin studying tonight if you haven't already. Don't get behind."

She moved to the side of the stage and stood at the podium. "I'd like to first briefly discuss the history of the Casimir Drive and how the theory was developed." She clicked a control and the image of a man's face appeared on the wall. He had disheveled black hair and a crooked smile. "Does anyone know who this is?" She waited as a few hands in the room shot up. "I know that there is at least one person in the room who *definitely* knows who this man is." Hendricks looked directly at Cal.

Suffering for a moment longer, Cal finally answered, "It's Timothy Straus."

"Correct. And how did you know that, Mr. Stanger?" She gave a knowing smile.

"He was my great grandfather." Every face turned to him.

"I'm sorry to embarrass you, Caleb, but we're very proud here at the academy that we have the descendent of such an influential figure. Timothy Straus developed a host of theories in his lifetime, most of which had to do with bent acceleration. In fact, many of his theoretical equations are still not fully understood today and it has become somewhat of a mystery if all of his work has been fully eluci-dated. When is the last time that any of you rode in a streamcar?"

Every hand in the class went up. "Timothy Straus mathematically figured out a way to get superconductors to function at room temper-ature with his famous Inert-Cooling Equations. Before that, everyone thought they would only work at subzero temperatures. It took half a century for engineers to catch up with his theories and realize that if they put superconductors in the roads and magnets into vehicles, you could get effortless acceleration if you electrified the roads. Our transportation is pollution-free thanks to Timothy Straus."

Hendricks changed the picture back to the cylindrical engine. "There's a lot more that can be said about Straus, but today, we'll be discussing his greatest achievement, the Casimir Drive. Ironically, he had a very hectic personal life and even suffered from severe mental illness. Unfortunately, he committed suicide in the year 1989, seemingly a failure. He only achieved posthumous success after it was discovered how truly advanced his math was. Who knows what other innovations he would have produced had he lived longer. If you're interested, come and see me after class and I can recommend a great biography about him.

"The Casimir Drive," she pointed to the screen, "uses quantum-coiling, a process in which an intricate gridwork of quantum plates focuses an enormous amount of negative energy into a space smaller than an atom. This localization of dense negative energy into such a small space causes the space around it to contract at one point. A process that we simplistically call 'bending', although the term itself is somewhat of a misnomer." She hit the button, showing a graphic of rippling space animating behind a spaceship. "After the space contracts, it recoils back outward, accelerating any matter that is directly in front of the expansion wave." Clicking again, the rippling space quickly unfurled, launching the ship off of the screen. "This recoiling creates the fastest acceleration ever known for a man-made object. The speeds can approach about one-sixteenth of the speed of light."

Jelena leaned over and whispered to Cal, "You're really related to Timothy Straus?"

"Yep." He fidgeted on his console.

"Why didn't you say anything?"

"Because I didn't want people thinking I got into the academy just because I'm related to him."

Jelena shook her head. "No one will think that. I bet some pretty good family stories were passed down over the years. Do you know why he... committed suicide?"

"I know as much about him as you do. My mom never knew him. He was just... crazy." He chased a worried look off his face.

"What is it?"

"Sometimes I wonder if it's hereditary."

"Don't go there. I'm sure his illness has nothing to do with you." She squeezed his arm and, suddenly, everything felt fine.

After class, Cal collected his things and left before anyone approached him about his crazy, scientist ancestor. At the front of the academy building, he found the streamcar he summoned and got in. It floated away from the academy campus and integrated seamlessly into traffic. Every surface of the interior of the streamcar was interactive. One could tap the door handle, the dashboard—even places in the fabric of the seats—and a stream of screens, street maps, games, and advertisements would parade around the passenger. Cal looked out the window as the car leaped over five lanes. The surrounding cars re-positioned in perfect synchrony to accommodate its trajectory.

The city glowed with vibrant lights of cascading colors. The downtown was a sprawling financial district studded with hundreds of skyscrapers amongst a sprawl of the gray towers of Central Cell. Spacelifts, permanent tethers into space, carried cargo and fuel to Central Cell space stations that floated in geosynchronous orbit around the Earth. There was a constant stream of lights across the sky—the Central Cell spaceships patrolling the city's perimeter.

Cal's streamcar drifted through traffic, exited the main stream, and darted through surface streets until it arrived at Cal's home, which was a towering luxury apartment building. Exiting, he looked up at the monstrous building and sighed.

"Hey, Cal," the security guard, Raz, greeted from behind his desk.

"Hey, Raz. How are... things?"

"Not too good, pal." Raz looked out the window and swung his rifle from his chest to his back.

"Why not?" Cal looked at his desk and saw the ominous red packet of a person slated to be deported. "No! You weren't able to get things squared away with Central?"

Raz shook his head.

"They can't just kick you out. You've been our doorman for years."

Raz shrugged. "Doesn't look like there's much I can do."

"Maybe I can talk to my mom. She can do something—talk to the building administrators and get you a pay raise."

"I don't think so..."

"But... but maybe she could get you a bonus to prevent deportation."

"That's the thing, Central Cell doesn't care about the amount of money you have at one time. Your mom could give me ten thousand brics right now but they'd still deport me. It's about having a secured and consistent revenue flow. With the new revenue cutoffs they've enacted, my salary no longer makes the cut and they want me out." He clicked his tongue and sliced his hand across his throat.

"But where would you even go?"

"Don't know. Have you ever been? Outside of Central Cell?"

"Well, yeah, they let us fly to different spots around the world in the academy."

"Where?"

Cal shrugged. "Mount Everest, Great Wall of China—"

"No, I mean, have you ever been to where actual *people* live outside of Central Cell?"

Cal shook his head. "Uh... no."

"It's bad out there. Believe me. And unless management wants to give me a significant raise, you may not be seeing your old pal here to greet you every day." He gave a weak smile.

"I'll talk to mom. She can pull strings."

"I'd really appreciate it. Hey, how'd your first solo flight go?"

"Bad."

"Oh, I'm sorry."

"Hopefully, I'll do better for The Jupiter Run we've got coming up." Cal stepped into the elevator. "We'll figure things out for you."

"Thanks." Raz's face disappeared as the doors closed. The elevator shot upwards as Cal looked at his own reflection in the metallic doors. Anger bubbled up inside him about the prospect of Raz being deported. Cal had known the man his entire life. With his own father killed in the riots before Central was formed, he'd always looked up to his reliable doorman, getting advice about girls, school —anything that bothered him. *Doesn't Central care—*

And then the voices came crashing in.

Thousands of voices filled his thoughts. Pain shot through his temples. A clutter of indistinguishable chatter occupied every corner of his mind and seized his ability to focus on anything else. His back hit the wall of the elevator as he waited for the wave of voices to pass over him. But they only swelled:

"...I know you, Custos... it didn't have to be like this! We were going to change things! I know you, Custos... help us... the Destroyer of Worlds... I'll bring this whole city down myself... he is coming... he is coming... HE IS COMING!"

They became louder and multiplied for a moment longer before dying down, leaving him alone as the elevator doors opened to the enormous expanse of his home. Having grown accustomed to the voices, he shook it off. He learned that to keep the voices a secret from everyone else, he had to ignore them and act like they didn't happen.

No one could know.

He stepped into a foyer with a vaulted ceiling that reached dozens of feet above and with three vast hallways that led outward. It was a home of crisscrossing walkways. Lush greenery hung from the walkways that crossed over a large mezzanine. His mother, Minzy Stanger, used most of the space for entertaining the Central Cell elites. Otherwise, it was just him, his mother, and a host of servants that occupied the mansion penthouse.

The hallway led to a large auditorium of sofas, beds, and hundreds of blankets. The auditorium sunk down to a large stage, which flickered with three-dimensional holograms of two movie characters talking to each other in a grass hut. Textures of hay and dirt sprawled out upon the movie stage as the characters spoke softly to one another, their movements and shadows extending out over the auditorium.

Cal peered out and saw nothing but vacant cushions.

"Cal!"

He turned and saw his mother behind him, lifting a small panel to pause the movie. "Hey."

"Cal, have you seen this *movie*?"

"Um..." He turned around again to look at the characters. "No, what is it?"

"It's marvelous. It's about a poor family during the Grand Depression and about what their lives were like before the Nuclear Night. They lived in these little huts that they had to make themselves. While the husband is building it, his wife gives birth but then they lose the child. It's really sad. They said it's based on a true story. The acting is *amazing*."

Her words ran together too fast for Cal to understand. "Sounds good." He started moving back up the auditorium.

"Can you imagine people having to live like that? You want to sit and watch the rest of it?"

"No, not now."

Twisting her shoulders, she readjusted some pillows and then eased her back into them. She flipped out a compact mirror and checked her makeup. "How was school? Oh! You had your big flight today, right?"

"It's not school. It's the Central Air Academy."

"Oh, stop taking yourself so seriously. You know what I mean."

"The flight was fine."

"Good!"

"Oh, hey, Mom?"

"Yes?"

"You know the doorman downstairs, Raz?"

"Which one is he?"

"Kind of older guy—beard."

"Oh, yes, I know him. He's very nice."

"He's getting deported."

"That's... awful," she said, distracted by the movie. "Yeah, that's been happening to a lot of people lately. Just read today that the new legislation might deport something like three hundred thousand people. It's just awful. I can't imagine where all of those people have to go. Can you imagine having to live outside of Central? Just *awful*."

"He told me that if we can get our building to increase his salary just a little more, then Central wouldn't deport him out."

"That would be wonderful."

"Do you think you could say something to the building management?"

"Cal." She paused the movie and spoke sternly, "No, no, no, I don't think so."

"Why not? We practically own this entire city block!"

"Yes, but if we were to make an exception for him, we'd have to do it for a lot of other employees. Why would we give him a raise? Does he deserve it? Do you have any idea what the Central Acquisitions would do if they found out that I gave a raise simply to postpone deportation? Central makes these decisions for a reason. If we don't have one of these... adjustments every now and then, it undermines our entire way of life. You don't know what it was like before Central was formed, okay? You couldn't understand, but I do, I've seen it. I grew up with it. Constant rioting in the streets—people just starving right there. Your own father was murdered in the streets to defend the way we live. Have you ever seen someone die right in front of you in the middle of the road from hunger?"

"No..."

"That's right, you haven't, and you've never seen someone hacked to death for a sandwich. You haven't seen it because we don't allow it anymore. We're not going to let social divide destroy us again and if that means your little friend Raz has to go to Russia or Copper Mound or America, then so be it."

"It doesn't feel right. I've known Raz most of my life."

"You don't get it right now. I can't imagine a nineteen-year-old understanding."

Without another word, Cal stomped out of the auditorium and went into the kitchen for something to eat. He sat down to their house chef, Matheus.

Matheus smiled. "What can I get for you?"

"Just some peanut butter on toast."

Matheus rummaged around in some cupboards. "Got any Friday night plans?"

"Out. With some friends. Jelena invited me to a club."

"Jelena, huh?"

"Yeah," he said, fighting a smile which he quickly squashed. "But... she's just a friend."

"Sounds fun. Don't get into too much trouble." He slid a plate over.

"Matheus, do you think you're going to get deported with the new revenue code coming up?"

Matheus frowned. "Can't say for sure until they announce the cutoff. I hope not. Don't know where I'd go."

"But you're from here. You were born and raised here," Cal said with indignation.

"True."

"Then how can you be kicked out of Central?"

Matheus simply rubbed his thumb and index finger together. "New world order."

Cal sighed. "I'm actually not that hungry."

The sun sank low through the towering windows as Cal crept up a massive spiral staircase to his room. The room was built into the high ceilings, granting him a view of the various floors of the penthouse below. He peered down and saw his mother busily waving her hands at a few servants who struggled to mount an ice sculpture of a dolphin atop a table in preparation for a party.

He shook his head and stepped into his closet, looking over hundreds of outfits—most of which were automatically picked based on his interests and delivered directly to his closet. He didn't even know how they got there. After getting dressed, he weaved through the host of servants that prepared for the party with terror in their faces—Minzy Stanger could be a cruel hostess. He turned to yell goodbye but stopped and left without saying a word. She wouldn't notice he was gone.

On his way down the elevator, he dreaded having to face Raz. Relief washed over him when he saw that there had been a shift change and a new, unfamiliar guard was standing at the entrance, holding his rifle. He smiled pleasantly down at Cal.

A streamcar took him downtown to the club. He saw several class-mates congregating around the entrance. Jelena, in a long green dress, watched as Benedito had the group laughing.

"Hey, Cal!" she yelled, abandoning the group.

Cal stepped out of the streamcar and gave her a brief hug.

"I'm glad you could make it."

"Me too. It was way better than watching my mom trying to impress a bunch of bankers."

"Agreed. Should we go in?" She took his arm.

He looked down at her arm wrapped around his and instantly forgot everything about Raz. They entered through an enormous mouth of swirling golden fixtures and colorful flowers. The club opened up to vaulted ceilings with various bars and people congre-gating on the walls. There was a frenzy of people kicking off from their places on the walls and floating out into the middle of a zero-gravity dance floor. Due to low gravity, every available surface, including the ceiling and walls, was full of people walking, dancing, and drinking. As Cal walked down the stairs, he felt his body lighten with each step until he could propel himself forward with his foot like riding a scooter.

Benedito came up from behind. "Glad you came."

"Me too."

"Just put the solo run out of your head tonight. We'll practice more and make sure the Jupiter Run goes better."

"Should I get us some drinks?" Jelena asked.

"Sure." Cal glanced past her at a man who was seated and hunched over. He did a double-take—the man looked familiar. The man turned and looked up at the dancers above him, smirking for a moment and then looked directly at Cal. As Cal wondered what an older person was doing at a dance club, he realized who it was.

"Raz! What're you doing here?" Cal stepped up to the bar.

"Hey there, pal."

"How are you? I was... worried."

"Same as when I talked to you before." He took a sip.

"Right, I know." Cal sat next to him. "I talked to my mom about helping you out..."

"You don't need to finish that, I already know what she said. It doesn't matter."

"She was so resistant to even talking to anyone about helping you," Cal groaned in frustration.

"I know, I know. There's a certain standard in Central and people don't like messing with it."

"I wish you didn't have to go."

"Me too."

"When do you leave?"

"Tomorrow."

"What! So soon? But they didn't even announce the new revenue cutoffs."

"Apparently I was so low tier that it doesn't matter. I'm out of here tomorrow. Central guards will be coming to my house to *ensure my extradition*," he said in a mock authoritative voice.

"How can they move you out so fast? They didn't even give you a chance."

"I don't know, pal, but they're doing it."

"I wish there was something I could do."

"Why?"

Cal looked at him for a moment. "Why... what?"

"Why do you wish there was something that you could do?" he said, almost aggressively.

"Because I feel bad."

Raz smiled. "Emotional catharsis is as hollow as the air in this ridiculous club."

"Oh, I'm sorry if I offended you..." Cal looked around, growing anxious. He had never heard Raz say anything so... poetic. They seemed like the unhinged words of a man growing desperate. "Do you come here a lot? Seems like kind of a younger crowd..."

"No." Raz swiveled his chair around and looked up at the weightless dancers. "If only they put all that effort of moving their arms and legs into churning butter."

"What?"

"We could just throw a bunch of milk up there into the zero-gravity and put all that dancing to some use. We could make quite a bit of butter I bet."

"Okay." Cal got to his feet, realizing that the conversation had surrendered to a drunken and disgruntled former employee.

"If all the clubs in Central Cell started making butter, we could ship it out to the rest of the world. There would be plenty of butter for everyone."

Cal laughed awkwardly. "You're probably right about that." He gave him a small pat on the back.

"But they'll just keep on dancing, every night—not making any butter at all."

Cal leaned over to the bartender. "Hey, put this guy's drinks on me."

The bartender turned to him. "Sure, but he hasn't ordered anything but water."

Raz tugged on Cal's shirt. "You're nineteen, right?"

"Yes." He saw Jelena motioning at him to join the other cadets.

"You part of Straus Inc.?"

"Straus Inc.?"

"Yeah, all those billions of dollars inherited from some crazy scientist?"

"Well—"

"Do you hear voices, Caleb?" Raz peered over his glass.

Cal's heart raced, his stomach turned cold. The club, Jelena—everything faded away. *How could he know?* "What are you talking about?"

"If you don't hear any voices, then I'm just a crazy old man in a club for kids. If you do hear them, pal, you might be one of the most important people living."

Cal shook his head. "What the hell are you talking about? I don't hear any voices." His heart thundered in his chest as he regretted ever trying to get Raz to stay in Central. He stormed off, joining his friends.

"Ooh, you don't look too good," Jelena said. "Seen a ghost?"

"I'm... I'm okay, just kind of tired." He forced a smile.

Benedito walked in between the crowd of cadets. "Whoa, you look sick."

"No, no, I'm okay, what's, ah... what's going on?" He tried to ignore Raz's gaze but turned and caught his eyes. The flashing lights of the club cast a haunted glow on Raz's face. There was something eerie about his pure expression of serenity painted with the neon lights.

"Forty hours in space alone is going to be rough," Benedito was explaining the Jupiter Run. "I heard a few years ago that one cadet accidentally fell asleep through the Asteroid Belt—got one of his engines clipped and had to crash land at the Mars colony."

"We've all heard it, Bene," Jelena complained.

"The kid was up there for two days before they picked him up— ate through his rations in twelve hours."

Cal, not paying attention to the conversation, suddenly left the group and walked back over to the bar.

Raz waited for Cal with folded arms. "How do you know about my... problem?" Cal asked.

"You never answered my question." Raz smiled back at him.

"What, have you been spying on me?"

"Not spying. I'm your doorman. I see you all the time."

"How did you know?"

"Know what?" Raz grinned through his beard.

"Yes, sometimes I do hear them—voices."

"I thought you might. We have far too many things to talk about for me to begin to answer that question. Milk before meat, my friend." Raz swiftly got up from his seat and treaded out to the foyer of the club. Without looking back, he disappeared behind a gold column and out into the streets.

Cal instantly followed him. Jelena noticed and gave a confused frown. Outside, Cal saw Raz's shoulders slumped against a concrete wall. He sat with his jacket sprawled out on the sidewalk.

"What are you *doing*?"

"Panhandling."

"You better get up or you'll get in trouble."

"Remember how I'm getting deported tomorrow? I might as well try to take some of those sweet, sweet brics with me."

"You can't beg, you'll be arrested."

"Why?"

"Because it's illegal."

"You know cows?" he remarked, absentmindedly.

Cal threw his hands up in a dramatic show. "What are you saying now?"

"Cows. Do you know them?" he asked insistently, staring up at Cal.

"Yes, I'm familiar with cows."

Raz motioned him to sit next to him on the concrete. Reluctantly, Cal joined him as bystanders gawked.

Raz cleared his throat. "Back a long time ago, cows milled around in a farm. Nowadays in Central Cell, they're just grown up in a pod and then butchered. But they used to actually live. They would walk around and eat grass and get milked and I don't think they minded it all that much. They could walk wherever they wanted except outside of the wood fence that the farmer built around them."

"Okay... yeah?"

"So, they were aware of the fence only inasmuch as it was some sort of boundary to them."

"What's your point?"

"They couldn't actually conceive that there was this intelligent being, the farmer, who cut down lumber and designed a fence with the sole purpose of confining them."

"I guess not."

"So, they responded to the fence by bumping into it and then walking away but they never knew what it was, and not only that, they couldn't even *think* about how they never knew what the fence was."

"Yeah, I get it. The cow couldn't possibly understand the concept of a fence or a farmer but still responded to those things without fully realizing their nature."

"That's right." He pointed at Cal.

"What's your point?"

"I think we may be a little like the cows."

"How so?"

"What is music?"

Deciding to play his game, Cal answered quickly, "Compressional waves that travel through the air."

"No, that's sound. Music must be something more, right? Or else we would just call music sound. What is color? What is light?"

"Maybe all these things are just artificial constructs that our consciousness has made to understand the physical world."

"Ouch! Too philosophical!" He laughed. "Maybe you're right. But maybe you're wrong. Maybe these are things that we have created physical labels for without fully understanding their natures. We can't really describe them so we just say that light is photons moving through space and that color is a visual construct of our brain."

"Hmm."

"Maybe they're just a glimpse that we have of something more profound, just like a cow bumping into a fence. The cow knows it's there, but never really understands what it is she's bumping into. Maybe music and photons are reflections from another world—a world we don't understand because we can't see it. There may be more worlds than just the one you see."

"Does this have to do with the voices?" Cal said, now ignoring the onlookers.

"Milk before meat, pal. Think about what I've said. Too much info too fast can be bad for the soul. We will talk more." He stood. "Well, gotta get ready for that big 'ol deportation."

"Wait, what? You can't just tell me all this stuff and leave. How do you know about what's going on with me?"

"All you need to know right now, pal, is that it's not a mental illness—it's a side effect." Raz quickly walked off as Cal got to his feet.

"Of what?" he yelled as Raz disappeared around a corner. No reply was given. Cal trudged down the steps of the club and stopped for a streamcar, his mind set ablaze.

CHAPTER 4

APRIL 23RD, 1988

Straus watched his psychiatrist, stooped in a plush armchair. "I feel like my brain is being split in half," Straus told him.

"What do you mean?" Dr. Simmons asked. "You've been repeating the same thing for the past half an hour. Find different words to explain it."

"It's hard to explain. It's like I'm a million people at once. I'm having a million conversations, drinking a million cups of coffee, and driving to work a million times over—all at once. I feel like I'm one echo of a million different versions of me."

"Okay..."

"My thoughts get drowned out. I feel... muted?"

"What do you mean?"

"The other day, I was ordering a milkshake with Jo. When it was my turn to order, I said I wanted a milkshake, but when the cashier asked me what kind I wanted, I just stared back at her. I didn't know what to say. It wasn't as if I wasn't *sure* what I wanted, there were just too many options. I had to choose between a thousand different flavors. I was paralyzed."

"But surely there couldn't have been more than a few flavors."

"Of course, but it didn't *feel* that way to me. I had limitless options and it was overwhelming. I don't know what I'm saying anymore." Straus dropped his face into his hands.

"It's okay." Dr. Simmons jotted down a few notes and then looked at his watch. "How are things at home?"

"Good. I think."

"What makes you doubt?"

"I'm home. I'm there with Jo and James. But, often, I'm emotionally with my Drive. It sits in the back of my mind almost..."

"What?"

"Beckoning me."

"Flesh that out a little more."

"The Drive is important. I can feel it. And not just for me but..."

"Go ahead."

"I think it will—" he hesitated once more, afraid of the implications of making outlandish claims to his psychiatrist. "I think it will change the world."

Dr. Simmons was silent for a moment. "I admire your ambition, Tim."

"It's not just personal ambition. It's so much larger than you or me. It's... it's hard to explain. I don't think I can even explain it to myself."

"That's why we're here, so we can talk about hard things."

Straus swallowed. "I feel like I'm just a single seam in a piece of fabric."

"A seam?"

"Yes. A seam tied together by a tiny thread. But I'm one seam amongst thousands of seams—billions of seams. We're all woven together, working on something together that will change the worlds."

"The *worlds*?"

"Oh, uh... I mean, change *the* world."

"Right."

"Are we sure I have schizophrenia? Is this what it looks like?"

Dr. Simmons leaned back in his chair. "We've gone through this so many times before. Schizophrenia, bipolar, borderline personality,

Asperger's—you've exhibited behavior from the greater bulk of the DSM." He gave an ill-received chuckle. "Look, you have got a very unique mind. It's part of what makes you special. I can't tell you where mental illness ends and brilliance begins and maybe it doesn't matter in your case. What I am worried about is your physical health and that of your family's. That's what we need to look out for the most. Would you agree?"

Straus nodded. "Of course."

"Can we talk more about it next week?" he asked, looking at his watch.

Straus nodded and stood.

"Go ahead and make an appointment with Denise outside."

"Thanks." He moved towards the door. "Any medication changes?"

"No, I think we'll just keep you going with what you're on for now. Oh, and I have to ask..."

"What?"

"Any suicidal thoughts lately? Any plans for self-harm?"

"No, no, never," he said, "that'll never happen."

He stepped outside into the bright sun, wincing at the small pain in his eyes. He unlocked his bike and made his way south from the medical center down to the Georgetown campus. His head had cleared as the gears on his bike ticked away. Closing his eyes against the dry wind, he focused on the steady clicking of the bicycle gears. The streaming sound filled his ears, becoming the only singular event in his life for a brief moment. He was swallowed up in the sudden significance of the tiny fluttering sound. Each click—a new world opening up.

The empty hallways at the physics building already told him he was late for class. He stomped through the auditorium doors to a hundred students laughing and yelling. A hush slowly rolled over them as he set his bag down.

"My apologies, I'm late." Without hesitation, he picked up a piece of chalk. "Let's get started." He drew a large graph on the board while the class scrambled for notebooks. Underneath the graph, he wrote out equations until he filled the entire board. Wordlessly, he went to the next chalkboard and scrawled out more equations. The class silently watched him fill the second chalkboard and move onto the third.

"Dr. Straus?" A student put up her hand.

Startled, Straus turned from the chalkboard and pointed at her. "Yes?"

"What are you uh... writing?" A small wave of laughter rippled through the class.

"Uh, well, the tau here means a bent covalent bond."

No one answered as the girl remained perplexed. "Dr. Straus?" she said.

"Yes."

"We're freshmen—this is chem 1010. We don't understand anything on the chalkboard."

"What?" He looked back at his math and then at his watch to see the date. Oh. He'd lost an entire day, throwing off his teaching schedule. A rush of red flooded his face. "Oh. Well. These are just things that you have to look forward to in a couple of years. I..." He noticed Jack Van Wert sitting in the back row of the class, shaking his head. "What did we—what did we talk about last time?"

"Valence electrons," someone said.

"Of course, yes, valence electron shells." He stalled, clearly improvising. "Who can tell me what the Heisenberg Uncertainty Principle is?"

A girl in the back raised her hand. "Location and velocity."

"Yes, and what about it?"

"You can find out where an electron is in an atom and you can also measure how fast that electron is going but you can't measure them both at the same time."

"Yes and no. You can indeed measure both of those things, but not in the same moment of time. One measure of the location of an electron and another of that same electron's momentum will not correspond to the same place in time. This has to do more with the fact that an electron really functions as a wave and not a particle—something that we will get to in a later year. But in other words, you can't simultaneously know where an electron is and how fast it's going at the same moment in time. Unless..." Straus stopped and looked up at the ceiling.

"Unless what, Dr. Straus?" Van Wert yelled from the back of the room. Every head turned toward the booming voice. Straus could see his rotund face under the dim lights.

"Students, our department chairman is in our midst," Straus said with an awkward flourish of his hands.

"Dr. Straus, please, finish your thought," Van Wert said.

"One could potentially know the location of an electron and its momentum if you simply took time out of the equation. Or, if you arranged the math in such a way that time cancels out. It would take a few minutes, but I could show you a derivation where—if real life behaved under its restrictions—time completely goes away and matter exists in perpetuity."

"Freeze time?" a student asked.

"You don't have to freeze time to take it out of the equation. One can simply make it irrelevant."

"*What*?" another student said.

"Dr. Straus," Van Wert yelled out, "I do believe that this discussion may be a little out of scope for a freshman class. Would you agree?"

Straus closed his eyes and nodded. "Indeed. Let's get back to valence electrons." He turned back to the board and, after a long sigh, began writing.

As the students filed out, Straus saw Van Wert make his way down. Quickly, Straus grabbed his bag and crept out through a lower door into the basement laboratories of the physics department. He weaved through lab benches and students in white coats, keeping his head low, and found the stairwell that led up to his lab.

He burst in to find Chou Jia, the new graduate student at a computer. "Dr. Straus," she greeted with a big smile. "How was class?"

"Eh, could've gone better." He threw his bag on a table and sat down at the lab bench. "How did it go last night?"

"Well, it was—"

"Not good," Duke interrupted, stomping in from a room with large radiation placards stuck around the doorway. "The gold cassettes melted again."

Straus only nodded, expecting the answer. "Now we know."

"The gold cassettes can't withstand the heat when we turn the Drive on," Duke finished the thought.

"It should. Gold should work. It should theoretically absorb way more heat than the Drive should even be capable of producing." Straus grabbed a lab coat from a hook on the wall and looked through a wall of windows into the engine lab. Inside, the floor was covered with rows of metal grids that ran in columns with one another. The grids were constructed in a square pattern that outlined the room and crowded inward—the Casimir Drive. Despite several rounds of perilous funding and razor-thin grant money the previous two years, they'd built the Drive to fill an entire room. Within a slot the size of a deck of cards, liquid gold had bubbled up and hardened.

"So, where is the heat coming from?" Chou Jia asked, looking into the windows at the Drive. "Why does any metal we put into the Drive just melt?"

Straus rubbed scruffy facial hair. "Don't know. When dealing with quantum energy, heat can come from any tiny pocket of empty space. We'll have to use a stronger alloy next time—see if it works and then extrapolate how much heat is actually being created from the negative quantum energy. I don't suppose..." He looked at Duke.

"No, nothing on the gravity meter."

Straus looked into the lab at a small meter the size of a kitchen timer, suspended on a single metal chain above the Casimir Drive.

"How do we know the meter doesn't just detect normal gravity?" Chou Jia asked.

"It's already zeroed to Earth's gravity, so if it measures something, we will know if gravity was warped at all by the Drive," Duke explained.

"The renewal of our grant is due again in two weeks and all we have to show for the work is some melted gold," Straus complained. "It's already taken a lot of promises to get them to renew it to this point."

"We have more than that, I think," Duke said. "We've created a Drive that uses negative quantum energy to generate heat. That's a big deal. We're generating heat from an unknown source. We could get a thousand grants on that fact alone. Dr. Straus, I think we're getting much more attention than you believe. There are rumors going around..."

"Rumors about what?"

"My colleagues at other institutions are starting to ask me lots of questions about the Drive."

"If only the rumor mill could get us our next grant."

"I have no doubt that you are doing something great here, Dr. Straus," Chou nodded.

"*We*, Chou. *We* are doing it together. And I agree, I think it's something special. I'm going to go look at the math a little bit in my office, maybe wrap my mind around the heat problem."

Duke chuckled. "What've you been working on in there anyway? What're those circles that you've drawn all over your office? Doodles?"

"The doodles help... distract me." He went to his office and sat at the mountains of paperwork that had accumulated during feverish nights of testing and calculating. Leafing through the papers brought him a brief moment of despair. He had no idea why the Drive was creating excess heat and how to prevent it from stalling. Leaning back in his creaky chair, he closed his eyes and focused. As if off on a beach horizon, the voices were there. They whispered with the cadence of the tides, a hush rising to a commotion and then back to a whisper. Over and over, the voices oscillated at the fringe of his mind. Straus drew the voices in—some shouting, others arguing and yet some were the voices of men pleading with one another.

And then there were numbers.

Dancing mathematical expressions flitted across his vision, glowing bright orange or a dim indigo. He gasped as he studied the expressions—some he recognized, others were... advanced beyond anything he'd ever seen. Along with the math, he saw glowing halos, vibrating and spinning across his vision. There were patterns in what he saw—a cryptic harmony that connected them together. With pencil and paper, he furiously scribbled down everything that came. And like the slow closing of a book, the rift of voices and mathematics was shut from him.

Opening his eyes, he looked down at the math. Most of it was nonsense, his hurried handwriting obscuring anything that could've been potentially legible. Yet there was something... His heart quickened as he recognized some thermal expansion equations that fit into what he knew about the Casimir effect. "But... wait..." he said to himself, looking up at a periodic table of elements tacked to the wall.

"Duke!" he said, emerging from his office. "Let's try copper."

Duke tilted his head, skeptical. "Copper doesn't really have the capacitance that we predict we'd need—"

"Let's give it a shot."

Duke was confused. "But what kind of alloy composition?"

"Pure copper."

"Okay... Seems a little reckless just throwing pure copper into the Drive."

"It'll work."

"Always the optimist..."

Without further protest, Duke and Chou Jia went to work extracting the re-solidified mass of melted gold from the Drive. Duke searched through dozens of buckets full of small bricks of metal until he found pure copper. After exchanging uneasy looks, Duke and Chou Jia placed the copper inside the Drive and prepared for a run.

Straus turned to his office but stopped. "Dr. Straus," a booming voice interrupted from the hallway door. Jack Van Wert stood tall and large in the door frame with a tight frown inside his gray beard.

Straus, startled, jerked sideways and bumped his hip on a table. "Jack. Please come in."

"I had a little trouble finding you after class. You seemed to have... vanished." He walked in, looking through the window at the Casimir Drive.

"Yes, I needed to get back to my lab quickly."

"May we have a word?" Van Wert asked.

"Let's go to my office," Straus said, walking past lab benches. He opened his office door and pushed a stack of papers from a chair, motioning for Van Wert to sit.

Van Wert looked across Straus' desk, which was covered with dozens of pages of hand-scrawled math. On the wall above his desks, many more of the same pages were tacked to a corkboard. Straus sat, making a meager attempt to shuffle the papers together but quickly gave up. "So, what do you want to talk about?" he asked, unassuming.

"You really don't know?"

Straus looked back at him inquisitively.

"Your class just now—it wasn't good."

"I know, I was a little late and—"

"You didn't even know what class you were teaching. Teaching, if you can even call it that. You can't just roll into class and throw a bunch of math on the board and expect these undergrads to understand what you're saying. How many times do we have to have this conversation? I've grown tired of micromanaging your class. I shouldn't be wasting my time with this."

"It's been a hard week."

"And what were you even talking about?" Van Wert continued. "You're leaping into concepts that only happen between seasoned physicists. And maybe not even that—I don't even get what you're saying and I think it's because you're starting to just... make things up. You can't be adlibbing like that."

"Right," Straus said, knowing that agreeing was the quickest way to get the man out of his office.

"Are you listening to what I'm trying to say?" Van Wert looked over the math on the desk. "And what is all this? Doodles and... what kind of math is this?" He lifted a page.

"I think we've been making a lot of progress lately, actually." Straus slowly removed the paper from Van Wert's fingers.

"Are you optimistic about the grant renewal?"

"Yes. I think we've been capturing heat from quantum fluctuations—"

"Yes, yes, that all sounds fine and good but it doesn't mean anything if you run out of money."

"We just need a better alloy..."

"Your tenure track and job is at stake if you don't have stable grant money."

"Wait, what?"

"You heard me correctly. Things need to go well or your job is in jeopardy."

"Jack, look, once we have an alloy that works, we'll be able to measure the heat better and the Drive should be able to finally run."

Van Wert cleared his throat. "Tim!" He slammed his meaty fist on the table. "We don't need to get into the details right now, but in short, I think your medical condition is affecting your work and teaching performance."

"Oh. Now I understand what this is about. My medical condition... so inconvenient."

"You know what I'm talking about."

Straus sighed. He felt a humming in his head—the voices. He closed his eyes to focus and push the noise out—to flee from flashes of light and shades of color splitting through his vision. He clutched the corner of the table and steadied his breathing. "But—"

"We'll have plenty of time to talk about this later. Why don't you just absorb this for a bit?"

"But—"

"Dr. Straus!" Chou Jia opened the door without knocking. "Come quick! Come look at the Drive!" She left the room as quickly as she came.

They heard Duke shouting from the other side of the lab. Van

Wert looked at Straus before they both leaped from their chairs and ran out into the lab. Standing at the windows to the Casimir Drive, Chou Jia stared intently while Duke was at a bulky computer terminal. He was furiously typing while looking in at the Drive.

"Dr. Straus!" Duke shouted. "Something tripped the accelerometer."

"What?" Van Wert looked into the window at the intricate system of metallic grids encircling the small space of the Casimir Drive. Above the Drive, the gravity accelerometer hung, motionless. "I don't see anything."

Straus squinted his eyes. "No, he's right. The accelerometer is detecting something. Duke, what's the reading?"

Duke clicked a few buttons. "The meter only measures up to 50 meters per second squared and it's... it's maxed out!"

And then all four of them gasped.

In the middle of the Drive room, directly above the Casimir Drive, a funnel of what first looked like clear liquid rose through the air. It was a thin spindle of distorted space that stretched from the Drive and reached to the ceiling, below the gravity accelerometer. It looked like a crack in a glass pane that refracted wayward light and distorted the wall behind. It swiveled on a single axis above the Drive, like clay on a potter's wheel, twitching slightly back and forth.

"What *is* it?" Van Wert asked, backing away from the window. "Is this... dangerous?"

"I think it's..." Duke trailed off in wonder.

"It's bent space," Straus declared, crossing his arms.

"Incredible," Chou Jia said. "The copper worked."

The sliver of bent space fluctuated and thinned, stretching up toward the ceiling. In a flash, the windows of the Drive room shattered, spewing thousands of shards into the lab. The group ducked and covered their faces while the bent space stretched further upward until it thinned into nothing and evaporated. Straus stood, peering through the broken windows. The accelerometer swung like a pendulum until it slowed to a lazy sway.

"It's gone," Straus said, flicking shards of glass from his shirt.

Van Wert stood. "What *was* that?"

Straus turned to Van Wert, grinning. "It was a successful demonstration of the Casimir Drive, Dr. Van Wert. Would you still like to fire me?"

After they had cleaned up the glass, Van Wert and Straus spoke for a few minutes while Duke and Chou Jia recorded data and extracted the copper cassette from the Casimir Drive. It, too, had melted but after it ran the Drive for a total of seven seconds.

Van Wert left Straus' office in a hurry, without looking at the students. Straus emerged from his office with a crooked smile and a tuft of stray hair covering one eye. The three worked for several more hours, running over calculations and second-guessing their previous math. Straus left Duke and Chou Jia around eleven at night after multiple phone calls from Jo. When he got home, she was waiting for him at the kitchen table—face scrubbed of makeup.

"How was your appointment with Dr. Simmons?"

A grin stretched his face. "I-I can't even think about that right now."

"How was it?" she repeated.

"It was okay. I think, but, Jo, something happened today with the Drive. It was huge!"

"When are you going to see him again?"

Straus scoffed in frustration. "I-I'm not sure. In a month I think, but—"

"Your appointments with Dr. Simmons are more important than anything right now."

"Yeah, I get what you're saying." He told her everything that had happened with the Drive that day.

She hugged him, tears in her eyes. "I just get so worried about you."

"I know, I know. But I'm okay."

"I'm so happy for you and for what you're doing in the lab, but I wonder..."

He held her wrists and looked into her eyes. "What?"

"I wonder... at what cost?"

"You think my work on the Drive is affecting my mental health?"

She nodded.

"I'll be careful. I'll move up my appointment with Dr. Simmons. I promise." He walked past her, into the den and sat down on the yellow, flower print couch and tried the power button, but the television didn't turn on. "What's wrong with the TV?"

"I don't know, it hasn't been working today."

Straus closed his eyes.

"Tim, can we talk a little more about this?"

But Straus kept his eyes closed and didn't respond.

"Tim?"

He abruptly stood and walked into the hallway that led to the bedrooms. The sound of something metallic shifted in the hallway and then the sound of circuit breakers resetting. He came back in and tried the television. This time, the screen flickered on.

"Ah-ha!" he exclaimed.

"How did you know it was the power circuit?"

"I didn't. It was just... the most likely option." He sat back down and flipped through the channels. He stopped when he saw a concrete wall covered in paint and graffiti, with hundreds of people gathered around, protesting. A graphic of Germany came on the screen showing a dark red line that swiveled straight through the country. It depicted the boundaries of East and West Berlin. "The west side is protesting again."

"Good," Jo said. "Maybe they can finally get rid of that wall."

Straus looked at her. "You think things will change?"

"We can all change," she said, leaving him to go to bed.

CHAPTER 5

SEPTEMBER 4TH, 2098

"Mom, do you remember Raz's last name?"

"Who?" Minzy was looking at herself in the vanity mirror as she penciled in some eyeliner.

Cal rolled his eyes. "The doorman, Raz. You know? The guy who got deported."

"Oh, Raz, yes, poor man. It is a shame." She dabbed her lipstick on a tissue.

"What was his last name?"

"I'm not sure," she said, absentmindedly.

"He's been a doorman for most of my life."

"Well then, why don't *you* know his last name?"

Cal shrugged. "He was always just 'Raz the Doorman'."

Minzy gave him a matter-of-fact smile in the vanity. "Exactly. He was just the doorman and I didn't get to know the man, or his last name, and neither did you. Don't try to make me feel guilty for not knowing every detail of every person that works in this building. I've had enough of your guilt trips."

"I'm just worried about what will happen to him."

"There's nothing we can do about him now."

"I saw him. He was begging for money on the street."

"You what?" She stopped applying mascara and glared at him.

"He just sat down right on the sidewalk and started asking people for money."

"And you talked to him?"

"Yeah."

"Cal, I don't want you making contact with that man ever again. Just think, a beggar in Central Cell? They should throw him in the copper mines."

"I just want to get in touch with him to see if he's doing okay." Cal knew the real reason he wanted to talk to Raz—the man inexplicably knew about Cal's voices. There was much more to Raz than Cal ever realized.

"Cal, he's fine. You need to drop it."

"How do you know? What is it even like outside of Central? Where do people go?"

"Millions of people live and breathe every day outside the walls and, somehow, they make it. It's not like anyone *made* them leave. It's their own fault they couldn't make a decent enough living to stay."

"Of course someone made them leave—they're literally deported out of Central Cell territory by guards."

She rolled her eyes. "You know what I mean. They bring it on themselves."

"No, if the building management would've just paid him more, he would've been able to keep up with the new revenue requirement for citizenship. And if we hire a new doorman at the exact same pay, won't he just get deported too?"

"Pay is subject to the individual's merits. Raz no longer deserved a higher pay because of his lack of ability. The next doorman will get hired and paid more because he will be more qualified."

"But that doesn't make any sense. How are we judging people's merits? This just seems like an arbitrary way to keep our population and workforce the same."

"If employers simply gave raises to everyone to meet new revenue cutoffs, then—"

"No one would ever get deported and we wouldn't have our nice little city," Cal said and walked out.

"Cal!" she yelled back.

"What?" he answered from the hallway.

"Good luck today on the run. You're going to do great!" Cal had not once told his mother that he had gotten the lowest mark on almost every run in his class. He *had* to pass the Jupiter Run to even stay in the academy.

He found his full cadet uniform, which had been laid out the night before by some phantom servant. As he dressed, he noticed a light blinking on his phone. Discovering it was an unread email from an address he didn't know, he opened it.

Cal,

Good luck today, pal. Remember, there's more than just a fence around you. Look beyond.

-R

Who are you, Raz? He sent five thousand brics to the email account, put on his cap, and left.

Cal walked up the steps to the Central Cell Air Academy where dozens of cadets streamed across campus. A crowd was gathering at the entrance—cadets in Cal's class listening to advice from Benedito. They were all jittery thinking about the Jupiter Run—their longest solo flight yet.

"Cal!" Benedito yelled. He left the group and joined Cal as they walked up the steps. "How're you feeling? Do you think our practice runs helped?"

Cal nodded. "Definitely. Things are going to go okay today."

"Not just okay, you're going to do great. I saw a lot of improvement over the weekend. I bet you'll pass."

"I hope so... I have to."

"Caleb! Benedito!" Jelena called from a streamcar as she got out. "You guys! This is so exciting," she said, blowing her long brown hair out of her mouth. "It's weird. We always saw the seniors ahead of us getting ready for the run and it seemed so far away, and now *we're* doing it."

"All I know is, I'm going to swoop down onto Mars, say hello to the colony," Cal joked.

Jelena scoffed. "We're not going anywhere close to Mars. Cal, you know that, right?"

"Yes. For the last time, I've studied the star charts. I know the exact path to take. Come on."

"You're right, I'm sorry. I'm honestly a little nervous about not passing though."

"You? There's nothing you need to be scared of. You'll be fine," Cal said.

"What if we don't pass? The majority of our grade this year depends on the Jupiter Run. The grade will directly affect what kind of jobs we get after graduation—if we even have good enough grades to get a job as a pilot."

Benedito laughed. "Oh my gosh, you worry way too much. You'll be fine."

"No, no, it's a real concern. Now that they raised the revenue cutoff for citizenship, this is becoming a real thing to worry about. In less than a year, we can't be claimed on our parents' income or any... inheritance," Jelena said, looking at Cal.

"We'll do fine. Would you stop making us so nervous?" Benedito said, mostly for Cal's benefit. "Come on, Captain Kalai will make us go last in the run if we're late."

They walked through the academy doors where dozens of cadets in jumpsuits scurried about, running to get to classes or out to the launch pads. There were various ages of classmates, the youngest of which was a line of fifteen-year-olds running to the zero-gravity hub.

They climbed the main stairs and moved down the hallway that led out to the launch pad. The floor and walls were lit up with flashing arrows and the words *Jupiter Run Today! Good Luck, Seniors!* They met up with several other seniors as they all ran toward the flight galley. There was Ada, a dark-haired girl of Romanian descent who was strapping on a helmet. Farabi, a tall boy from a Kazakhstani family flashed a smile at Jelena and ran ahead of the group. Trailing at the back of the seniors was Patrick, a small boy fidgeting with the zipper on his jumpsuit as he ran. He accidentally bumped into Benedito from behind.

"Sorry," Patrick said. "It's just my zipper. Does anyone else have problems with their zippers?" His comment went totally ignored as the entire class funneled to the launch galley where Captain Kalai stood on top of a stage.

"Cadets!" Kalai yelled through the microphone. "Take your seats, we're going to get started." The cadets scrambled to their seats and quickly fell silent. "As you know—" he pressed on a console, projecting a model of the solar system out into the galley, "—you'll be embarking on an up to twenty-five-hour, round trip flight around Jupiter. During this time of year, your course will take you around the sun, past Mercury, the asteroid belt, and then a straight shot to Jupiter. Before I say another word, I will remind you all that you are not to fly through the asteroid belt, but above it. Any attempt to be a cowboy and fly into the belt will result in immediate failure of the run for any cadet.

"You will be graded in five main areas: flight preparation, efficiency, communication, critical decision-making, and overall flight time. There will be thirty cadets in the run today with me as your commanding officer. All emergencies will be communicated with me followed by a distress beacon if necessary. The day will proceed as follows: all cadets will be at the launch pad at 0630, suited up and ready to go. You are free to launch as directed by flight control in order to rendezvous at 2237 and 0305 using the standard epoch at 0730. If you arrive early, there will be no flight time while you wait for the rest of the cadets. You will have your Casimir Drives off with only impulse engines running to maintain geosynchronous orbit.

"Once we have confirmed all thirty cadets are in orbit, I will lead our fleet at a velocity of 0.05 AU per hour. Of course, you have all diligently studied the flight path but the navigational route will be available to you for reference. Understand, however, that referencing your navigation excessively may result in a deduction from your final grade, but not dramatically so. Please do not sacrifice your safety by fear of punitive damage to your grade. Once we are a quarter of an AU from the sun, we will be going at 0.1 AU per hour to maintain a safe acceleration as we slingshot around the sun's gravity. The maximum velocity that is allowed during the remainder run is no more than one-quarter AU per hour. Keep in mind, however, that you must be diligent in mitigating your speed against how many copper cassettes you use, which will go under your efficiency grading.

"I'll tell you all, right now, that your critical decision-making grade will mostly be impacted by how you decide to circle Jupiter. We've completely left it up to your discretion as senior cadets to decide the most efficient and safe way to circumnavigate the gas giant. You must balance fuel efficiency, angular velocity, gravitational pull, and speed together. The closer you navigate around the Jovian equator, the higher the grade, so I would strongly urge you to not go around the poles. It will be noticed by your evaluators. You are not, under any circumstances, to enter the atmosphere of Jupiter or to turn off your Drive engines and enter its orbit. If gases or other matter enter the contraction wave of the Drive, it can stall the Drive and create unpredictable speeds.

"You will always maintain a one-hundred-kilometer distance from the nearest ship. You will be in open communication with the three nearest ships to you but no more. You are allowed, but not required, to cooperate as a team. The choice is yours if you'd like to be mostly solo for the run. Are there any questions?" Kalai looked over the cadets. It was an audience of stone-faced teenagers, speechless with anxiety. "And remember the golden rule of Central Air Academy: you are under no circumstances allowed to land anywhere on Earth that has not been pre-approved. Disobeying this rule will, as always, result in immediate expulsion.

"Cadets, you've been training for five years for this run. It represents the culmination of your skills as interplanetary pilots. You represent the future of space travel, and with that, the future of Central Cell. Good luck, cadets." The projection of the solar system with their flight path disappeared as the lights went up.

"You guys ready?" Jelena asked Cal and Benedito, who were putting on their helmets.

"It's a long time to be in space," Cal remarked.

"But we've done longer runs. Remember that week we spent on the Alaris Space Station?" Benedito said.

"Yeah, but we weren't flying our own ships that long and this deep into the solar system."

"True," Benedito acquiesced.

"Let's get out there. We'll be able to launch in fifteen minutes!" Jelena exclaimed. "Come on!" She ran ahead of them and most of the cadets as they filed out of the galley.

The thirty cadets walked and then ran through a corridor that led to the open air. The launch pads stretched for several miles in all directions ahead, dotted with control towers and flashing lights. At any moment, ships were coming and going in the distance due to heavy traffic from the Central Airbase that was adjacent to the academy. A large rocket flared in the distance. A sleek ship, with the body of a single wing, took off near the cadet's launch pads. There were several spacelifts scattered throughout the launch pads shuttling cargo, passengers, or fuel up a solitary metal cable that was attached to a hub high above the atmosphere.

The cadets scattered toward their aero8 ships which were propped up on their back engines, their front ends pointing up to the sky. The engines consisted of four back burners used to break free of Earth's gravity and twin turbine engines beneath each wing for flight in the atmosphere. A single cockpit fit between the two wings with an orange burner window for re-entry into the atmosphere. The cockpit tapered to a point that ended at the front of the ship. Behind the cockpit, a cylindrical shape jutted out from the fuselage and converged into a vent that faced out the back—the Casimir Drive.

Cal walked around his aero8, quickly checking the thruster engines, the Casimir Drive, and the turbines. He also made sure there was enough fuel for escaping Earth's gravity. He was more meticulous than a normal training flight—he knew he'd be tested for preparation. He checked the copper cassettes—the fuel to run the Casimir Drive. He had the allotted amount for the Jupiter Run. Looking over his shoulder, he saw Jelena and Benedito at their identical concrete launch pads making the same preparations. His nerves calmed seeing them next to him. He went over the rest of his pre-flight checklist in his head and finally jumped into the cockpit once he was certain everything was done.

He dropped the burner glass and began his cockpit checklist, calibrating the global coordinate system and the Solaris navigation. He flipped his comm radio and tested his headphones. "This is cadet Stanger checking into flight control, do I have confirmation?" His radio buzzed with the voices of flight control, confirming his communication array and the calibration of his coordinate system.

"So, we can just leave whenever we want?" Benedito's voice garbled in Cal's headset.

"Bene!" Jelena yelled. "We're trying to get ready for launch, can you just not interrupt right now?"

"Good luck, guys," Cal interjected.

"I'm requesting clearance. See you guys up there," Benedito said.

Cal looked out the burner window and saw Benedito's ship suddenly burst with fire beneath the burner engines. It was stationary for another split second and suddenly launched into the sky, instantly out of his view. Cal gave a silent salute to Benedito and then called into the control tower for clearance. Jelena's ship then launched and vanished in almost the blink of an eye.

"Cadet Stanger, ready your burners, you'll be clear in T-minus ten, nine, eight..."

Cal breathed deep, flipped the red cover off the burner controls, and gripped the throttle tightly.

"...three, two, one."

Cal pushed the throttle, heard a rumble beneath his back, and held his breath. After a pause, the burner engine roared with fire and catapulted his ship from the ground. He closed his eyes as his whole body rattled in the seat. He was instantly above the clouds, thousands of feet away from the launch pad, away from Central Cell, away from his mother, and even farther away from Raz. He looked out the window and saw a blanket of clouds running away to the horizon. A moment later, he saw small twinkles of light from far away cities where the sun wasn't yet shining. In another instant, he saw the curvature of Earth and the atmospheric gases thinning as he approached space.

He checked his trajectory, saw that he had enough momentum, and cut the burners. Pure silence flooded the cockpit. He wiped his forehead and checked the console, verifying his coordinates and that of the other cadets. For the first time in a while, he felt peace in the silence above Earth. There were no voices up here, no strange colors blinding his vision, and no headaches.

He could stay up here forever.

"Cal!" Jelena's voice broke the silence. "Follow my coordinate, I've already got Bene over here."

"Let's get to Jupiter," Benedito chimed in.

"Got it, I'm heading right over." Cal plugged in the coordinates, turned on his Solaris navigation system, and plotted a course to where the cadets were to rendezvous. He squinted at the blinking lights of the cadet fleet ahead of him. Several other ships were arriving and joining the same orbit trajectory as the fleet.

"Just aim for the sun," Benedito said. Cal watched as Jelena and Benedito's ships came into direct view; their small thrusters positioning the ships. A brilliant sheet of light flooded Cal's cockpit as he brought the front of the ship facing the sun. The blackness of space fled as the bright orb came into view. He dropped a sun visor over his eyes.

"Go!" Benedito shouted. Cal flipped a switch and pulled the throttle as his Casimir Drive shuddered with life. He watched the back of Jelena and Benedito's ships as a thin bend of space appeared at their Drives. The bend spun on a single axis, growing larger, creating a distorted wave behind each ship. Sun rays and points of light refracted through the wave, rolling and twisting with each undulation from the Drives.

Cal's ship lurched forward for a moment. "Here we go!" he yelled as he punched the Drive. The ships ahead of him took off with a wave of distorted space pushing from behind. His head suddenly bobbed back as his ship jettisoned toward the sun. The white and blue of Earth vanished.

"So, we're sticking together, right?" Jelena asked.

"Maybe for a bit, but I might start pulling ahead later," Benedito said.

"That's fine, I'm really going to concentrate on sticking to my flight course. I'll be within earshot if you guys need me. Vorhath out."

The entire fleet left Earth's orbit and headed toward the sun, which, to Cal, was about the size of a basketball in his view. He lowered the UV shield over the window and began tracking his distance from the sun. He double-checked his calculations with one aim: use the sun's gravitational force to slingshot toward Mercury without actually crashing into the sun.

Cal's ship glided steadily through space with only a mild hum from the Casimir Drive. He decreased his speed ever so slightly to conserve copper cassettes for the Drive—the only thing the Drive consumed. He was confident that he'd be able to get close enough to the sun's gravity to make up for the lost velocity. A few other cadets were trying his same strategy as he saw a dozen of them slow to his speed on his dashboard display.

Cal engaged the navigation into autopilot and looked through the rest of his star charts. He double-checked calculations to see where he could shave off time. The thoughts of his mother and Raz seemed a remote past—something that could never touch him as he hurdled toward the sun. He loved the silence of space and wanted to hold onto it. He did briefly fantasize about Benedito's suggestion of visiting the Mars colony. Maybe he could just stay there? *I wonder if they've formed a city yet?* Central Cell news outlets were tight-lipped about anything happening on Mars. Word was, Central Cell had been beat to the punch by an old American colony several decades back in the terraforming process.

After several hours, the sun grew to a massive size in the burner window. He magnified the view on his console and saw thin filaments of flares licking up from the surface and flashing against the blackness of space. He double-checked his heat shield temperature and made sure he was well within the safety margin.

"Anyone overheating?" Jelena asked. "I think Ada is getting a little closer to the solar vortex than anybody else. I hope she's watching her heat shields."

"I'm good over here," Cal said, watching his dash.

"Ada?" Jelena patched Ada into their comm network.

"Yes?" she responded in her Romanian accent.

"You taking too much heat over there?"

"I'm fine, stick to your own flight chart!" Ada snapped.

The sun became a massive orb of fire. Cal analyzed the various solar orbits around which he could gain some momentum and finally picked the orbit at the optimal distance from his trajectory. He kicked up his Casimir Drive and heard the familiar beep from his dashboard, indicating that the Drive was exchanging out a new copper cassette. He was happy about the efficiency of the flight thus far and took back over the manual navigation. The target orbit that he wanted was superimposed over the burner window view. Just ahead, he saw Benedito's ship also taking an acute angle toward the sun, trying to catch hold of an orbit.

He was flying directly into the sun with nothing but a blanket of fire dead ahead. The graphical orbit flashed in the window with an estimated distance from his ship. Sweat beaded under his helmet, stinging his eyes as he concentrated. Closer and closer, his ship accelerated toward the sun—he almost felt the solar flares whipping at him, boiling him in the cockpit. His headset was silent as the rest of the cadets were attempting the same maneuver.

The orbit flashed and turned red as he approached. He waited one more second until his ship crossed the threshold of the orbit and then yanked the ship port side. The right-back burner kicked into life and propelled the ship out of dead man's trajectory, quickly veering him away from the sun. The wall of fire left his view, leaving his eyes in a confused daze as the distant stars settled against the velvety black of space. He shut off the back burners and accelerated faster and faster, catapulting from the sun's gravity.

"Awesome, Cal!" Jelena shouted. "That was really good."

"Thanks. Bene, took a wider orbit?"

"Yep. But that was pretty good, Cal," Benedito conceded.

The rest of the fleet performed similar maneuvers as they briefly entered the sun's orbit and dashed away, accelerating away from the sun and leaving Earth well behind them. "Excellent work, cadets," Kalai said in their headsets. "We're all past the first major challenge in the run and I'd say we've got a good fleet today. Everybody is doing very well. Keep up the good work."

Cal's pulse slowed as he relaxed. *I'm doing it. I'm going to pass this thing.* He took off his sun visor and lifted up the UV shield. He switched into autopilot and turned off all computer projections from the burner window. He only saw endless space. The stars twinkled brilliantly and with more color than on Earth. He saw ruby hues and yellow streaks in the distance, admiring the cosmic beauty but also dwelling on the deadliness of space.

He saw a single comet within the solar system, leaving a stream of indigo light. It was a brilliant diamond of light against the blackness of space. He wondered where its long orbit would take it and when it would return back to the solar system. *How many people through time have watched that same comet from Earth? Who will see it in the future?*

He thought about Mercury and turned on his navigation system and then flipped on the rear camera view and magnified: there it was. He had left it in the distance, a small speck of black silhouetted by the massive sun behind. It seemed lonely to him; the smallest planet in the solar system, dwarfed by the sun like an ant underfoot. He thought about how helpless it was, oppressed by the gravity of the sun, unchecked, and without hope of escape. He had felt like Mercury many times. How many felt the same way under the authority of Central Cell? What *was* life like outside its walls?

"Hey, Cal?" Jelena whispered.

"What's up?"

"It's just me. No one else can hear me."

"Oh... okay. Did you want to tell me something?" His heart started racing.

"No, no—well, yes."

"What's going on?"

"I'm really nervous about passing."

"Oh."

"My parents are getting deported."

"They are? How?"

"My dad got fired a month ago from his job and he hasn't found anything else."

"I'm sorry, I had no idea."

"Central found out about it pretty quick and hounded him for a month about past taxes owed. They gave him an extension because of how long he's been a citizen, but now with the new revenue cutoff, that's it, he's done."

"That can't be true, your family has been here for decades."

"They don't care. It's already done. My parents are being deported." She started to cry. "You're the first person I've told. It's so embarrassing."

"Where are they going to go?"

"He has a sister still in Croatia."

"Well, at least they have family somewhere," he tried to reassure her.

"No, no, my dad hasn't talked to her for years. He completely lost touch with his old family when he came to Central when it was founded. I don't know if they'll take him in. What're they going to do? What is it even like outside of Central?"

"Well..."

"They say there's not enough food and the sewer is right in the middle of the street. Crime is everywhere and you can get killed just by walking down any road."

"There are stories and then there's real life. We don't know what it's like."

"That's just it, we don't know. You've never been there—I've never been there. It can't be good. I can't go, I can't. I have to get a perfect score on the run and get a good job. Maybe then I can buy them a way in... maybe in a few years. You've got to help me, Cal. Promise you'll help?"

"Help, how?"

"I don't know, just promise me I can rely on you when I need you."

"Yes, yes, just let me know what you're thinking."

"I don't know yet, but something's not right. Something's not right with how we do things in Central."

"Yeah... I know."

Jelena fell silent for a moment.

"Is there anything else you wanted to tell me?" Cal asked. He briefly thought about how she took his arm at the dance.

"No, I'm going to go now. Gotta concentrate. The asteroid belt is coming up."

"Okay. Just relax and keep a cool head. You'll pass."

Cal breathed deep thinking of Jelena. He let his thoughts wander about Raz but then opened up his dash console. He brought up his coordinates and saw that he too wasn't far off from the asteroid belt. He opened the dimensional analyzer and set it to start mapping out the area of the belt that he was going to cross. After several minutes, a graphical display of the belt was projected onto his window. As expected, the belt was one AU thick, the equivalent of the distance between Earth and the sun. The section of the belt that he intended to go over was half of an AU. The belt was a massive wall of asteroids, forty million miles in height whose top and bottom bent inward toward Cal's trajectory. There were millions of asteroids; some the size of small planets and others no bigger than the size of a spaceship. It was a massive graveyard of rock and ice—the leftovers from the evolution of the solar system. Looming in the distance was a massive gravitational force corralling them together: Jupiter.

He plotted his trajectory over the wall of asteroids and ran a few simulations. He determined the route that would keep him farthest away from danger without giving up too much distance upward so that he would get to Jupiter in a reasonable time. Once the computer calculated the trajectory of the asteroid belt, he was confident that he found his best route. The fatigue of over twelve hours of flight time was starting to wear on him and he realized that he hadn't eaten anything. He sucked down a tube of strawberry paste and sped the ship up. The beep of another copper cassette exchange sounded, making him wonder how many the other cadets had used so far.

"Okay," he said to himself, adjusting the controls. "I got this."

The asteroid belt grew closer until he saw glimmers of light with his naked eye. He kept the ship on a straight trajectory, right into the belt, and waited for the best time to pull up to go over and...

And then a bolt of pain shot through his skull.

He yanked off his helmet and squeezed his temples, trying, somehow, to make the pain go away. The bolt turned into an achy wave, pulsating through his head.

"Bene... Je..." he weakly cried, trying to yell into the headset that was now on his lap.

And then the voices came.

Like a tsunami, a chorus of thousands of voices flowed through his mind. It was a chaotic stream of whispers, chattering and shouting—more potent than ever before. He couldn't make out a single voice or word but only held his breath as the crowd grew louder.

"Nuh... no!" he screamed in the cockpit. His eyes spun wildly.

The ocean of voices condensed with smaller voices receding into chatter and others coming to the forefront in his mind:

"...we were going to change things! Have you ever been outside of Central before? Destroyer of Worlds... Custos... I know you, Custos... Custos... we were going to change mankind! HE IS COMING!"

"Cal... Cal... Cal... Cal... CAL!" It was Jelena, coming in from the emergency PA in the cockpit.

The ocean of voices receded as Cal's head lolled back and forth. "Wha..." He weakly opened his eyes.

"Cal!" Jelena screamed. "Pull up!"

Cal opened his eyes.

The massive face of an asteroid stared back at him.

PART II
THE DREAMER

CHAPTER 6

2154, EARTH RECKONING (ER)

In a land that was no longer called the United States, a mushroom hunter sniffed the breeze. The scent of cat droppings had led her underneath a copse of trees. From the size of what it left behind, it wasn't an animal she hoped to meet alone in the jungle. With careful steps, she followed the trail, searching for the tender bulbs of fungus that thrived on the droppings.

Her empty stomach led her deeper than she'd previously dared. She crept through unfamiliar paths, snaking through ivied boulders while tying bits of yarn to tree branches to find her way back out. She lifted fern fronds with her foot as she went, hoping to find a mushroom cluster. After resting from a wave of hunger pangs, she ventured farther, stooping below wayward branches. She trudged through mud and grass thickets where the trail tapered away. It wasn't until sunlight had slanted through the leaves that she noticed she had traveled downward. The hills of the jungle dropped abruptly, circling down to a single point below the jungle floor. There were wide sections of the forest that spiraled inward as if built by design.

The hunter climbed a tree, gaining an aerial view and saw the curving paths carved like a crater into the earth. She knew what she was looking at—a mine. Although she had come across several, none had been this far away from the encampments and none had appeared so undisturbed, free of the ravages of salvaging.

Forgetting about mushrooms and the darkening sky, she continued, realizing that the winding paths were old roads, now claimed by jungle growth. Rusted chain-linked fences reached through tree bark, telling their story of a people that could once build. Corroded axles and eviscerated tires bore evidence of digging machines. Her heart pumped with excitement. She could find *anything* in an untouched mine.

Once at the bottom, she looked up through the mine crater and saw the night sky like a hole punched through the jungle canopy. After soaking a rag in oil from her satchel, she lit a makeshift torch and entered through the massive mouth of a cave. A string of bats ignored the newcomer. Animal tracks crisscrossed the muddy soil. Her torch glowed with the strength of a matchstick—a speck of light in the inky black.

A myriad of tunnels led deeper from the cave. The stone walls had long been gouged and plucked of their ore. She caressed the rock, wondering what metal they once bore. A charcoal mark rubbed on the wall would help her decode the labyrinthian tunnels on the way out. A primordial silence reigned until a soft rattling bounced through the tunnels. She stopped, guessing at the direction of the sound, and then hurried forward. The tunnel straightened and became flanked by small rooms, each one with an iron door inset with metal bars.

Prison cells?

Briefly, she passed her torch into the open rooms, finding nothing but a large boulder with chains welded to iron rivets. A rattle echoed down the tunnel again. It sounded different—a breathing quality.

Someone was there.

She turned to flee but then caught the smell of cat droppings—the same jungle cat she had been following. As her stomach growled, she inched forward, looking through the cells and sniffing as she padded lightly. The smell grew as she passed the threshold of a cell. Slouching to examine the ground, she swept her light across the room and found them—a cluster of white bulbs with slender stalks. Kneeling, she plucked the mushrooms and took a bite of one. It was particularly plump. Satisfied with her mining experience, the mushroom hunter turned to leave but stopped.

The jungle cat laid at her feet. It had been butchered with something crude like a cudgel—its innards splayed across the dirt. She gasped after a rattling cough echoed in the cell. "Who's there?" she asked the darkness.

A voice issued from the corner of the cell. "Help me." It was a man who coughed deep between words—disease in his breath. The hunter brought her torch into the cell and saw a hunched figure, unclothed, kneeling at a massive boulder. His wrists were chained to the rock—his skin thickly calloused.

His voice, deep as thunder, echoed along the walls. "Freedom," he said, choking on a sob. "Though I've died, I'll live once more."

"Wh-who are you?"

The man offered a mirthless laugh. "What is your name, my dear?"

"Ch-Charlotte. How did you get here?"

"It doesn't matter how I got here. It doesn't matter who I was. Your name is no longer Charlotte. Your name is now Speaker. There is only one message I want you to tell the worlds. Do you know what that message is, Speaker?"

"Wha-what?"

"I. Am. Coming."

———

Several years after the fall of Central Cell, Custos, the only self-aware robot on Mars, sat on a park bench thinking about how he would change the worlds.

Surrounded by cooing pigeons, he realized he had left sunflower seeds behind at his office. Dropping seeds and watching the birds eat had always provided a serene backdrop to his world planning. He wondered if his meditative ritual would be complete without feeding the birds but knew he didn't have time to go back for the seeds. No, he would stay in the park for a bit longer, thinking. He pushed meetings, paperwork, environmental studies, and legislation out of his head and took a breath. He needed a break before he planned to change the way humankind lived.

Custos closed his eyes. "One step at a time," he told the pigeons. "Sometimes with two steps back." He opened his porcelain eyes and stared at a statue that stood in the center of the park fountain. It was a single man looking inquisitively upward. People milled around the fountain, pushing their children in strollers or walking their dogs. There were a few businesswomen talking at a table, sipping coffee.

He noticed a small figure approach the fountain. The woman wore a ragged poncho with no shoes. Her feet were covered with the dirty blackness of missing many days of bathing. She stood, reading the placard of the statue.

"Ma'am?" Custos said softly. "Are you okay?"

The woman turned abruptly and looked up at him, puzzled. "Are you going to send me back?"

Custos held his hands up. "No. In New Athens, we don't send people back to Earth. You're here now and here you will stay."

She squinted at him until her face relaxed.

"Are you hungry? Do you need shoes? I can arrange a proper outfit for you as well," Custos insisted.

She studied him. "Are you sure I'm safe here?"

"Absolutely. Things are quite different on Mars than back on Earth."

She glanced around, looking at the hundreds of towering skyscrapers that surrounded the lush park. They glittered with blue and silver, like scales on a fish. Some facades vanished into the sky but then blinked back—fluttering in a spectrum of colors with the wind. The structures of the city seemed to camouflage with the breeze, trees, and rivers that ran through. It was a beautiful hybrid of nature and architecture. "This place is so—"

"Don't be alarmed. Things that you see—you may not understand —but to us, they are simply artistic expressions. It's how New Athens expresses its gratitude to its mother, Mars. We try to blend in with her terraformed beauty."

She studied his face. "Are there a lot like you?"

"You mean robots?"

She nodded.

"There are robots—many robots—but not quite like me. I'm a little different... a little more aware."

"What's different about you?"

"I am Custos," he said simply.

"Yes. I've heard about you." Concern wrinkled her brow.

"Don't be afraid. I'm only here to help."

She stared at his smooth, silicone face. Despite being artificial, his cream-colored countenance captured the subtleties of a human's—a small tilt in the brow, squinting eyes of concern. "You're really *the* Custos?"

"Yes."

"You swear you're just here to help me? You won't send me back?"

"Ma'am, I will only help you. As the President of New Athens, you have my word." He smiled—a human smile.

"I might as well just tell you I smuggled onto a TexasH from Earth." She looked around suspiciously as if expecting guards to sweep in at any moment.

"That's okay. Some people on Earth have no other option. You're not the first person to come to Mars unannounced and you won't be the last. What you think of as 'smuggling in' we consider an intentional leaky door."

"Why don't you just let everyone on Earth come here then?"

"We're not ready. An influx of that many people would destroy our society."

"But it would be a thousand times better for everyone that is on Earth. Do you know what it's like there?"

"I do."

"If all Earth people could just come here, it would be so much better for them and maybe just a little worse for the Martians."

"I have many, many committees of hundreds of social scientists, psychologists, economists... more experts than you can imagine. We are hard at work trying to make the best world for everyone."

She scoffed and shook her head. "Committees..." She looked around. "So, if you're the president, where are your bodyguards?"

"I usually don't like them around."

"Why not?"

"Crime is very rare here. And I don't like the self-important pomp projected by a security entourage."

"I think you should be more careful."

"This is a very different place from Earth."

"Just don't ever send me back there. Not ever."

Custos nodded. "I won't."

"Do you promise?"

"Yes, you can stay here. I'll see to it personally Mrs.—"

"Charlotte. I'd rather die than go back."

"Let's not send you back then. Do you know who that is?" he asked, pointing at the statue.

"Uh," she looked up. "No, no, I don't know."

"That was the President of the United States about a hundred years ago. Do you know what the United States was?"

"Kind of."

"He was the president just before the Nuclear Night. You've heard of that, I'm sure?"

"When the world exploded."

"Well, yes. That man, President Tobias Stroupe, sent the first colony to Mars, before the Nuclear Night. That's why we have a statue of him here. That colony started the first terraforming of Mars and, now, one hundred years later, we have breathable air—" Custos heaved his chest up and down, "—with water that flows and New Athens at its core. Just as Stroupe famously said at that time, 'We will reach for the stars and find ourselves there'. Well, here we are."

"Whoever that guy is," she said, pointing at the statue, "he didn't fix anything on Earth."

"He tried."

"He failed."

They shared uncomfortable silence for a moment.

"You'll go to school here," Custos said as if offering consolation for the nuclear fallout on Earth. "You'll get an education now."

"What will that do?"

"You'll learn."

"And how will that help the people on Earth?"

"Where on Earth are you from?"

"I move around a lot. Well, more now, I've been going from place to place. I'm around the ruins of a huge city. Crumbling buildings. Probably looked a lot like this place." She gestured to the city around them.

"Central Cell?"

"Maybe."

"What old city signs do you see when you move from place to place?"

"Houston?" she pronounced it 'house-ton'. "I don't read very good but I think that's it. It's right by the ocean."

"Ah," Custos nodded in understanding. "Houston is a very old city, back before the Nuclear Night. After that, Central Cell was built in the same area. There's a lot of history around where you're from."

"I stay away from there now. I haven't been around there or those small settlements for months. It's too dangerous. Can I sit?" she asked, pointing to the bench.

"Oh, of course, where are my manners?" Custos motioned for her to sit. "Now, tell me, how are things where you lived? It's been a while since we've had reliable reports from that part of Earth."

"I used to go around, from town to town, trading scrap or mushrooms. I pick mushrooms mostly. Do you have mushrooms here? Do you think I could do that here? I know I'm new here, but back on Earth, people would come from a couple of towns over to buy up all my mushrooms."

"We'll definitely find you a job here. Every citizen is guaranteed a job on New Athens. Now, tell me, you said you used to go around from town to town. Why not anymore?

"Scared."

"What're you scared of?"

She looked around the park, eyeing the foot traffic. "There's... someone."

"Who?"

She looked around to make sure no one was listening. "There's someone. A... a man."

"Who?"

"A large, angry man. Talks a lot about coming to Mars."

"Is he a soldier? Like the leader of the Faction of the Foes?"

She shook her head. "No, no, nothing like them."

"Cross and Sword?"

"No, he's different. He's big. He's quick."

"I see... does he have weapons? Battleships?"

"No, but he talks a lot. Knows people's secrets. He knows how to get people to do what they want."

"Oh, well, I'm sure he's nothing. There are many warlords that come and go on Earth. I'm sure he's no different."

"I came here to get away. You don't think he'll find me here, do you?"

"In New Athens? A metropolis of ninety million people? I think you'll be okay."

"I'm afraid he knows where I am—that he'll find me."

"His fear has no power over here."

She nodded as if convincing herself of his words. "Can you get me into some caves to go mushrooming? I don't really want to go to your schools. Just point me to the caves, that's what I'm good at. Mushroom hunting."

"That depends."

"On what?"

"Are you willing to do your part for this city?"

"Yeah, sure."

"Then let's get you an education. Education solves everything."

"If you say so..."

"It does, I promise. I am a man of my word."

"A *man*?" she said, looking him up and down.

"I am a robot of my word," he conceded. "Now, let's get you something to eat."

"President Custos, can I be honest?"

"Please..."

"I didn't come here by chance. I heard about you—heard that you come to this park a lot. I wanted to meet you."

Custos laughed. "Well, I'm flattered. I'm glad that we met."

"They say you see the best in people." She looked down at her dirty clothes and bare feet.

"Everyone has something good about them and everyone can change."

Custos called in an emergency response team that appeared within two minutes, their cars hovering over the park grounds. He said goodbye to Charlotte, who bowed to Custos before getting into the vehicle. "I hope you're right about things," she told him.

Custos sat for a moment longer, trying to enjoy the morning before getting up. He felt small buzzes on his watch as the reminders and calls started coming in for the day's meetings ahead. He took one more breath and then walked through the park.

"Hello there, Mr. Custos," a man said, pausing from sweeping the street.

"Hi, Clinton, how's the day?"

"Good, good, just finishing with custodial duties and I'll be back at the hospital in a bit."

"Ah, I think my street sweeping is coming up next week."

"Me too, maybe we'll be on the same shift?"

"Hope so," Custos nodded, walking past him, finally deciding how he would change the worlds.

CHAPTER 7

JANUARY 8TH, 2155 EARTH
RECKONING (ER)

New Athens was the only city on Mars.

It was half encircled by deep red rock mountains, The Teeth of Telephus, topped by a carpet of evergreens. The sun that hung above the mountains was a hazy point of light on the horizon. White clouds spanned the sky like gossamer cotton above the towers and skyways. The entire city scurried with life; pod-like cars flitted effortlessly across bridges and streets, dropping kids off at school or taking their parents to work. A cloud of drones was in a constant drift across the city, either coming up from the ground carrying packages or landing at mailboxes, office buildings, homes, and shops. The small drones—some as small as a mouse—delivered groceries, tools, medical supplies, and clothing all across the city without a single person navigating them.

There were sprouts of gardens, forests, and parks that dotted the city—havens of nature from the smooth, metallic surfaces of the city. The park's locations were planned first before the city was even built. The founders intended them as a reminder of their mother, Earth, a place for escape from the foreign and harsh landscape of the Martian canyons. Every time businesses and lobbyists tried to get their hands on the lands, Custos was the fiercest and most adamant about keeping the nature preserves, which held a majority of Earth fauna, sacred from the advances of the city. He smiled to himself, looking out at the redwoods which towered just a few blocks away from the Assembly Hall of New Athens where he did most of his legislation.

Opposite the red mountains of The Teeth of Telephus, a deep canyon abutted the other side, flanking the city. A river quested through the mountains flowed through the city—under bridges and highways—and ran off the city edge to the canyon floor below. White water raged and foamed at the waterfall edge where a great park and amphitheater had been built. All along the length of the waterfall were thousands of turbines attached to the canyon wall, capturing energy and sending it back up to the city. Custos gazed through the windows of his penthouse office, looking at the waterfall park and marveling that not a single ounce of carbon was being emitted to run the great city.

To the east of the city, free of mountains or canyons, the Martian plains stretched on into the horizon. From his almost aerial view of the landscape, he admired the hybrid beauty of the red Martian soil swirled with the pinks and whites of wildflowers that had been brought from Earth. The Meadows of Mars, as they were called, were a happy mistake in which the first colonizers unwittingly brought spores of Earth fauna in their cargo. Once the terraforming began, the Martian winds brought the spores to the prairies, creating a lush desert wilderness.

"Mr. President?" a small voice buzzed from his desk.

"Yes?"

"Miss Gina Wilder, with New Athens Times, is here for your interview."

"Right, of course," he stalled, trying to remember the appoint-ment. "I'm ready for her." He quickly straightened some papers on his desk and blackened the computer screen. He did a quick check around the office to ensure there was no sensitive material around. The doors opened to a thin woman. She had a long, crooked mouth that refused a smile as she entered the office.

"Mr. President."

"Miss Wilder, it's nice to make your acquaintance." He reached his hand out. Wilder stared at his metallic palm with five fingers fashioned out of soft metallic mesh and rubbery fingerpads. She smirked and grasped his hand without shaking. Custos tried taking his hand back but she held on for another moment, looking into his shiny eyes. She let go and inspected the office.

"Who are they?" she asked, pointing to a picture frame on the desk.

"They were my family," he said, picking up the picture.

"Your *family*?"

"Yes, the family that I lived with before I became self-aware."

"You remember them?"

He nodded. "Oh, yes, I remember everything before my awakening."

"And you consider those people to be your family?" she asked skeptically.

"Yes, I have very fond memories of them. It's a good reminder to me of where I came from when I look at the picture."

She pointed to a single chess piece that sat on his desk. It was a white queen. "You play chess?"

Custos smiled. "Yes. Although not as much now."

"And that?" she pointed her stylus at a large sunflower in a glass vase.

"Surely you know what a sunflower is," he laughed.

She squinted, reading a quote that was etched into the vase:

> *Ah Sun-flower! weary of time,*
> *Who countest the steps of the Sun:*
> *Seeking after that sweet golden clime.*

"It's from an old poem. I've always loved it. It shows how resilient the sunflower is. I think it's the most optimistic of all wild flowers. No matter where they grow, either on Earth or Mars, their faces always follow the sun—even through difficult times. I make sure that vase always has a fresh sunflower. I picked that flower from the Meadows of Mars myself, just outside the city."

"I assume there are flowers you don't like? You have a preference?"

"Did you come here to ask me what my favorite ice cream flavor is next?"

"My readers just want insight into how your robot brain works."

Custos paused for a moment and then pointed at her crimson, suede high heels. "Miss Wilder, do you like those shoes you're wearing?"

She looked down. "Of course."

"Why?"

She shrugged. "I like the color, I like how they feel. I like how they look on me."

He pointed to the chess piece on his desk. "I like that white queen chess piece, I like how it feels in my hand. Sometimes I take it to the window over there and just hold it as I look out over the city. The way my brain works is no different than yours. I'm a self-aware being as much as you are."

"Yes, that's very interesting," she said, unsatisfied.

"Please." He motioned to a chair in front of his desk. "Have a seat."

"Thank you for meeting with me, Mr. Preside—"

"Call me Custos—"

Wilder jumped in with questions. "Many people of this city, and all the colonies, have been writing into my paper about your recent appointment as president. Most are concerned about having an artificial life form being the leader of New Athens and its colonies." She paused, waiting for his reaction.

"Yes?"

"The concern lies with who you are. There are theories that you're programmed by Earth factions."

"You certainly know how to start an interview."

"You do understand their concern?"

"Yes, of course. I think the mistrust or hesitation comes from knowing that before I was self-aware, I was just a regular old household robot—basically an appliance—helping my family with household activities."

"When did you... well, at what time did you become... aware?"

"It's difficult to say, really. Are you able to tell me the exact moment that you were aware of what you are and who you are?"

"I see the comparison that you're making, but isn't it an oversimplification?"

"I don't think so. You probably have some scattered memories of being an infant. Little moments here and there that started to define who you were even before you were aware of the fact that you are indeed the famous journalist, Gina Wilder. Those moments, those emotions and memories, they start to coalesce. They condense and refine until they finally distill into a self-aware consciousness."

"True."

"You can't pinpoint the exact moment that you knew what you were and neither can I. I have small memories... little details. I remembered liking certain flowers or enjoying birds singing in the morning. They were new things. I knew that there was a certain time that I hated jazz music. There was a time that I knew I loved the violin. Before that, I didn't even know that you could have a taste for music, or that music could even be distinguished from other soundwaves in an appreciable way."

"Do you remember being made?"

He laughed. "No more than you remember being formed in the womb. No, no I just simply *was*."

"But... how? You're a CVX5.2. There are thousands of CVX5.2s out there. How are you this way and not another one is? I've interviewed your manufacturer and they're as stumped as anyone else."

"I am just as perplexed as all of New Athens. I wish I could explain to the people why I am the way that I am but I truly can't. I only hope they can accept me for the things that I do know about myself. I believe all men and women have equal rights when they all contribute to the greatness of our society. I hope that the people will form their opinions about me based on what I do, not on what I am or where I'm from."

"It's not every day that a household appliance suddenly gets appointed to be president."

"I understand the skepticism, but I'm confident that when most people meet me, they learn I'm genuine. I haven't been programmed to think in an algorithm or to deduce outcomes from metadata analysis. I don't have software that analyzes facial expressions and compares them to all facial expressions on the infoban to then prompt a coded response. I simply think and feel, just like everyone else."

"Can you understand how some Martians might have difficulty with the fact that you are an artificial intelligence who has spontaneous consciousness?"

"I do. I also know that the majority of New Athens voted for me, so I tend to believe that they trust me."

"There are many people who write into our paper—some prominent members in our government who you would know—who have expressed deep concern about you. Many people don't trust the fact that you seemed to come out of nowhere and have integrated yourself into the hierarchy of our government. Many have said that your schematics should be made public knowledge."

"You're not telling me anything new. And I disagree that I 'came out of nowhere'. I've been in the public eye for many years since my awakening."

"I've gotten letters about how you're a spy from Earth or how the Children of Traitors made you—programmed you to act like you have awareness and then installed you with a bomb. People feel that if you were to release your neural schematics to media outlets, it would help relinquish some of these fears."

"I'm sorry, Miss Wilder, but you cannot program consciousness into a robot any more than you can make the sun rise before dawn. No one has the ability to simply breathe self-reflection, awareness, fear, joy, and every other emotion that makes up a person. My consciousness spontaneously emerged within me. I don't claim to know why, I just know that I am."

"So, you're not just a talking toaster?"

"No. I'm not a toaster," he said without humor. "I'm not a maid, a street sweeper, a babysitter, or a delivery service. I'm just Custos, a being with thoughts and feelings. You know as well as I that releasing my schematics would help relieve no fears and only appease mob mentality."

"Debatable," she added, looking out the window distractedly.

"I believe I bring a lot to our city. Obviously, the people have at least some amount of trust in me. I believe I've demonstrated good policy-making as former vice president and excellent problem-solving as Commissioner of Resources during the energy crisis. It's not like I've just come out of nowhere. Martians know me. I know I am somewhat of an anomaly, but there is a benefit to have a perfect memory stored on a hard drive. I'm able to give immediate insights in a historical context, reminding my administration of similar scenarios in the past and how they worked out, both on Mars and on Earth."

"Like what?" she said, leaning closer.

"Like, for example, that a board of corporate trustees can't be trusted to run a city or a nation—a lesson that we all should've learned from the Romans thousands of years ago but which, of course, we didn't when it happened again after the fall of the Central Cell. I feel very much that control of the army should be ruled by all governing bodies equally with cooperative control. I also believe in the election process and that there should be no privately-funded elections—fortunately, something that we have finally gotten rid of. I think we need to further learn from the mistakes of Central Cell which I believe swung the pendulum much too far in ways of the supposed virtues of absolute corporate deregulation. Under the control of Central Cell corporate autocracy, one city prospered into unimaginable wealth while the rest of the planet smoldered in sickness and poverty. It was the greatest wealth disparity that has ever existed in the history of humankind."

"But many proponents today like to talk about the near utopian society of Central when it was at its height."

"Yes, I agree, it was fairly utopian, but at a price. It was exclusionary. You were either productive or you were out of the society. Did you know they didn't have hospitals in Central Cell?"

"I did not."

"They didn't have hospitals because they simply shipped all the sick to 'healing colonies'," he said using air quotes, "outside of their 'utopia' to get better and then return to society once they were healed. The only problem is that these colonies had very little funding and were ultimately a place for people to go and die if they didn't have money to finance their own health care. With this system, only the very wealthy could stay healthy and return back to Central. If you were a person living paycheck to paycheck and suddenly fell ill, that was it, you were out of Central and into the jungle of Earth. This was a huge impetus that led to the downfall of Central and the revolts. You can't have a utopia if the majority of the planet is suffering. The system will always break off and the power always truly lies within the governed. The trick of the powerful is to fool the people that they have no power."

"But you could say we're doing the same thing today."

"How so?"

"Haven't we left Earth behind?"

"Anyone is welcome to New Athens and its colonies."

"Except people from Earth."

"All in good time. We will be ready for them someday soon. In the meantime, we are preparing a perfect society. We are a culture founded on hard work and open arms. That's what sets us apart from the post-Nuclear Night era. Today, I'll be discussing trade agreements with lunar colonies, but tomorrow, I'll be sweeping the streets to fulfill my civic duties. We're all in this together. We've left the tribalism of Earth far behind."

"This all sounds good, Mr. President, but as you are aware, there is growing concern about armies of Earth banding together and threatening our way of life here. There are millions of people on Earth that beg to differ with your philosophy. There is growing resentment for the people of Mars."

"Of course. It seems like every day in the news there is some sort of faction from Russia or England. The Faction of Foes, The Horn, The Children of Traitors, Block 82... the list goes on. These armies never go anywhere. They lack the leadership, the discipline, and the vision to even organize a solitary nation on Earth, let alone an army that can come to our planet. They are the ignorant class—unwilling or unable to listen to expertise."

"There are Martians that believe you paint an undue picture of perfection about our culture here but forget, or choose to ignore, that we have lost the majority of mankind to the devastation that has happened on Earth."

Custos looked out the window for a moment. "When the human body has a malignancy, it must be cut out. Cancer compromises the integrity of the whole body. We must be unified, and if we are not, we will fail. New Athens represents the best hope for humankind and for Earth as well. Our immigration policy is clear: come and work and contribute and you will be taken care of. If you want to earn more, you may but not at the cost of the freedom or rights of another. We have no tolerance for crime and violence. If one chooses to behave that way, then they belong back on Earth. We can't look back, only forward."

"Are you concerned about rumors of a new army forming on Earth?"

"There are always rumors of a new one. Miss Wilder, we are a brave people. We crossed an ocean of space to be here and build this place. We will not be terrorized by the flavor-of-the-month Earth army that's coming to destroy us all."

"There are reports just this morning of new satellite images from former Central Cell. They show old military bases with activity, places that may have weapons, weapons that we don't even make anymore."

"I haven't been fully briefed today by our Defense Secretary. I'm afraid I can't comment on that at this time. But I assure you, we keep a close eye on new factions and nations that try to bubble up over there. No one can take us by surprise—" he stopped abruptly.

"What?"

"Did you feel something?" he leaned forward in his chair and looked outside.

"No, nothing," she looked out the windows. "What's wrong?"

Custos stood and moved to the windows. "I thought I felt something. Like the ground move... like an earthquake."

Wilder shook her head. "I didn't feel anything."

Custos' phone rang on his desk. "I think we better conclude our interview another time," he said, walking to his desk.

"But, Mr. President, I have so many more questions."

Custos picked up the phone. "Please, Miss Wilder, I promise you an interview another time." Wilder was quickly escorted from the office by a secretary.

"This is Custos," he said once Gina Wilder was escorted out.

"Mr. President, you have an urgent call from the Phobos gravitational array," his secretary said.

"What could possibly be urgent about gravitational waves?"

"I'm not sure, sir, should I connect them?"

"Yes, of course." He pressed a button on the phone which prompted a small array of light to spring from the desk, displaying the face of an older, bespectacled woman.

"President Custos," the woman said.

"Yes, who am I speaking with?"

"My name is Stella Farr, I'm the director of the GraviWave lab."

"Yes. What can I do for you?"

"Thank you for taking my urgent call. You must be a very busy man—er, robot. Something strange is happening here though, and I thought you should be aware. I've heard so much about your open-door policy..."

"Of course, what's going on?"

"First, Mr. President, are you familiar with our work on Phobos?"

"I'm well aware of your work there. I helped your funding a few years ago. You explore deep space for any signs of intelligent life or any other organized phenomenon."

"That's correct. We have a triangulating array on the surface of the moon that normally detects the small and repetitive undulating gravity waves that have been left over from the Big Bang."

"Right."

"The key word there is repetitive. The aftermath of the Big Bang left ripples of gravitational waves that spread throughout the universe in a predictable manner. We've been able to predict to almost the millisecond when we are going to detect the next wave that comes through Phobos."

"I'm assuming something new has happened?"

"Yes," she said, looking sideways. "Something new is going on. We just detected a new type of gravitational wave."

"New in what way?"

"Stronger in quality than waves from the Big Bang. We've never seen a wave this big."

"Could you feel it?"

"*Feel* it?"

"Yes."

She poorly hid embarrassment for Custos. "No, Mr. President, no one can actually feel these waves, only sensitive instruments can detect them."

"Go on."

"The reason I've called you so emergently is that these new waves arrive in a non-random pattern."

"You're sure?"

"We're sure. We've deciphered a communication."

"What communication?"

"We've only been able to decipher one word: *destroyer*."

CHAPTER 8

SEPTEMBER 4TH, 2098

C al was heartbeats away from crashing his ship into the cratered face of an asteroid. His heart hammered in his ears as he flipped the reverse thrusters, the rubber knobs of the controls slick with sweat. The ship careened up and slammed him into the chair. His view spun, showing gaping asteroid canyons that extended thousands of miles in all directions. Alarms rang in the cockpit mixed with the autopilot voice blaring warnings of imminent danger. There was no clear trajectory around the asteroid that could accommodate the neck-breaking speed of the ship.

Ten seconds, he thought. Only seconds and he would become just a small blip on the asteroid like a bug splattering on a windshield. It was at that moment that the utter endlessness of space terrified him. All the academy training had been child's play—a bunch of teenagers with their hands held while they pushed some buttons in a space-ship. Nothing had prepared him for the total annihilation that stared back at him through the glass.

Jelena yelled in his ears as she watched his trajectory from her ship. White-hot fear pumped with every heartbeat. He had never seen anyone die—he had never even seen someone ill. The image of his mother, lounging on cushions while watching movies filled him with angry pity. Pity for her cluelessness—anger that his own pampered life could never prepare him to face his own mortality. He closed his eyes and only saw the smirking face of Raz, looking up at him, panhandling in the street.

There may be more worlds than the one you see.

No! he cried to himself, opening his eyes. And then...

Something shattered inside of him, something changed—*everything changed.*

The yellow land of the asteroid fractured into thousands of pieces. It was as if his view—once like the static surface of glass—had been dropped on the floor; fracturing everything he saw into the chaos of shards of glass, each reflecting new realities. In one shard, he saw his ship exploding on the surface of the asteroid. In another shard, his ship pulled up, trying to escape the trajectory, but still crashed. Hundreds of scenarios played out in his mind's eye, each pertaining to its own fracture of reality. It was as if he was sitting in front of a crystal ball that had been shattered, showing him the outcome of every decision he could possibly make.

In another glass shard, he overheated his thrusters with the intent of causing an explosion at the front of the ship to stop his momentum. This only resulted in his entire ship exploding before it even hit the asteroid. In yet another fracture, he flew up, looping over himself and punching his Casimir Drive in an attempt to fly one hundred and eighty degrees away from the asteroid. The momentum, however, still carried him into the surface of the asteroid. His eyes frantically searched each small window before him, but he only saw explosion after explosion. *How much longer?* he thought. Was he frozen in time or would he *really* hit the asteroid any second? There was something familiar about the splitting of reality before his eyes—like the chatter of voices only now a kaleidoscope of vivid scenes.

His eyes lost focus with each different version of his own destruction playing out in front of him. He realized he would never understand what was wrong with him. *Maybe I could've been fixed?* He was sullen with remorse as he hurled toward the asteroid, knowing that the whole thing could've been avoided if he simply talked to someone. *I could've talked to Raz,* he thought. *Raz knew about me somehow.* Benedito flashed through his mind—Jelena flashed through his mind. She was so nice to him—beautiful and kind. Could he have been more to her?

He opened his eyes one last time and saw the fractured madness. Some shards of reality were large, showing every detail of his ship exploding yet some were small and thin like the tiny cracks in ice. Within one shard, high at the top of his cockpit, he saw the unmistaken absence of destruction—his ship gliding into a crater on the asteroid, disappearing into darkness. Within this one fracture of light, there was one solution—one way perhaps that didn't end with his total annihilation. He focused all of his energy on that small sliver of light, trying to push away the broken reality. It took more focus than he thought he was able to muster, but suddenly, the fracturing disappeared. Only one scenario, his native reality, was showing through the cockpit—the face of the yellow asteroid.

With the alarms blaring, and seconds away from crashing, he saw the crater. He clicked off the thrusters, propelling him to the left and, at the same time, jamming the throttle up, forcing the entire ship to spiral toward the small crater. In an instant, the surface of the asteroid passed him by. He braced for impact inside of the crater, but the ship continued, unaltered in its course. Darkness consumed the cockpit as he plunged deeper. Infrared and night vision flipped on, displaying the crater ahead while the dimensional analyzer hummed above his head. Squinting, it finally dawned on him that he wasn't in a crater at all; he was going deeper into a cave within the asteroid.

The analyzer transmitted its holographic information to his dashboard, revealing a long series of tunnels that traveled deeper into the asteroid. The cave was narrow, barely accommodating the size of his ship. He gripped the controls and navigated through columns of rock and the uneven surfaces of the cave. While barely dodging clefts of rock, he kept his eye on the dimensional analyzer and saw that the tunnel narrowed. He waited for enough space to turn around but it never came. Given the clefts of rocks that riveted every surface of the tunnel, he was too scared to reverse out and accidentally shred the hull of the ship.

Fumbling with his headset, he put it back on but only heard rough static from the fleet—electromagnetic interference from the asteroid. With no other recourse, he traveled deeper into the asteroid. Ahead, where the tunnel dove deeper into the asteroid, he saw two other tunnels lead away, splitting into different directions. The holographic display only fed data about the tunnels so far, omitting how far the tunnels traveled and if they had exits or were simply dead ends. Guessing, he took one tunnel which appeared to curve upward, with the hopes that it would somehow lead him out from the rock.

Breathing heavily, he pushed forward through the cave, ignoring more offshoots as they appeared. He tried concentrating to somehow bring up the fractured reality again. *It was real*, he thought. That one small shard really did show him the only path that didn't lead to his ship exploding. He tried summoning the fractures again to guide him out of the asteroid, but nothing came.

New alarms blared, indicating seismic activity. Crags of rock bounced off the hull of the ship as rock walls cascaded around him. A boulder the size of a small building crashed in front of him, completely blocking the way ahead. He flipped off all thrusters, extended the landing gear, and came to a complete stop inside the cave.

"Well," he said aloud, surrendering to the situation.

Was he shown the only way to prevent from crashing into the asteroid only to be marooned inside the thing? He let out a deep breath and closed his eyes, once again trying to get the fractures to appear. Maybe there was another tunnel that he couldn't see from which to escape? He opened his eyes, but there was just the one reality in front of him—unrelenting blackness of a dead-end cave.

On an asteroid. In the middle of space.

He fiddled with the comm on the dashboard, trying different radio frequencies, but now, instead of static, every frequency was silent—an ominous sign that the comm array was destroyed. In a last-ditch effort, he clasped his helmet onto his suit, checked the levels of condensed oxygen, and opened the cockpit. The cockpit gases escaped and fled from him as it depressurized. Rocks bounced down the glass as he got out and was exposed to the vacuum of space. Due to the small gravity of the asteroid, he landed like a feather on the ground. His boots crunched on broken glass and pebbles as he fumbled with the flashlight mounted on his shoulder. Before he turned the light on, he caught a glimpse of the pitch-black tunnel ahead. It was a dark mouth of nothing.

He shook off the dread of the tunnel, turned on the light, and went to the back of the ship. He found the comm array, a square box with several coiled wires weaving through. It was gone; torn away, leaving only sharp points of jagged metal. He slumped at the side of his ship, marveling at the absurdity of the situation. How can someone go from sleeping in a gigantic bed earlier in the morning to then be stuck in the middle of a rock in outer space only hours later? His musings turned dark as he realized that he had no escape and had enough food for only two days—only enough oxygen for maybe a day.

He was marooned.

Dread came. Not just about being alone, deep within an asteroid, but dread about his life. He would've certainly failed the Jupiter Run now. He'd probably have to drop out of the academy and wouldn't be able to get a job as a pilot. He then couldn't get accepted into other vocations because of the lost time at the academy. Could he get a job after that? Maybe he'd be deported and go to live in a box with Raz. And did it even matter? He hated his home; never felt understood by his mother, the oblivious socialite. Benedito and Jelena were the only good people in his life but he knew they'd leave him too. Unlike him, they were clearly born to be pilots.

He touched the airlock on his helmet, considering what would come next. But then something flitted across his face shield. A small light reflected through his helmet. He turned toward the entrance of the tunnel and saw the light enlarge. Squinting, he watched the light bob up and down with the cadence of someone running toward him.

·   ·   ·

They left his ship behind. Fortunately, Jelena's ship was outside of the cave-in, within the tunnel of the asteroid. Captain Kalai screamed into their headphones as soon as the asteroid's magnetic field had weakened. Cal sat behind Jelena's cockpit in an emergency seat that could be unfolded from a compartment in the hull. They had to dump all of her emergency supplies in the asteroid for him to fit.

The rest of the fleet had continued the Jupiter Run while Kalai had stayed behind once he lost track of Cal's ship. He sputtered commands into their ears, which mostly went ignored by Cal as he sat, dazed. After Jelena repeatedly assured Kalai that both Cal and her were safe and out of danger, he instructed them to return to Central Air Flight Academy while he finished the run with the rest of the cadets. Cal didn't even begin to try explaining what had happened and, fortunately, Kalai hadn't yet asked.

Jelena also didn't say much as she backed out of the tunnel, freeing them of the asteroid. Cal sat in silent shame as Jelena expertly navigated her ship through the tunnels, negotiating the hanging clefts of rock. By not attempting the same maneuver, he endangered Jelena's life by almost getting her killed in the cave-in. He would've killed himself if she'd been harmed from his stupidity. *Why is she so good to me?*

They cleared the asteroid, turned around, and headed back toward the sun and Earth beyond. Cal squinted at the unrelenting rays of light that filled the cockpit. He looked down at his feet. *What is wrong with me?*

"Thanks," he said quietly.

"What happened?"

"I'm not really sure."

"Um... how did you end up heading straight into the belt?"

"There's something... wrong with me."

"What're you talking about?"

"I haven't told anyone about it."

"What is it?"

"Sometimes I hear voices. They get into my head and crowd out my thoughts. I get big headaches when they come and I can't concentrate on anything else when it happens. That's why I crashed into the asteroid. The voices came."

"What kind of voices?"

"I can never really make them out. It's usually just a bunch of static."

"Do they tell you to do things?"

"No, no, it's like I'm overhearing a thousand conversations at once. I never know what they're saying—"

"Hmm..."

"Except, this time. This time, I could make out some of the voices. They said things like a name or something."

"Have you ever talked to a psychiatrist about this?"

"A psychiatrist? I'd get thrown out of the academy in a heartbeat. I'm already close to dropping out as it is."

"You're not wrong."

"Not that it matters now. I'm going to get thrown out for sure after this debacle. What am I going to tell them?"

Jelena was silent for a moment. "We can tell them something malfunctioned. Like, uh, like your course trajectory."

"*We* aren't going to tell them anything. You're staying out of this. With any luck, they'll let you do the Jupiter Run again. And they'd know if anything malfunctioned or not when they run a diagnostic on my aero8."

"Well, we can tell them the truth; just maybe not every part of the truth."

"Just stop. We can't jeopardize your citizenship now that your parents are getting deported. I can take care of myself. I won't let you get involved."

"You already got me involved by telling me you hear voices."

Cal only responded in silence, regretting the conversation.

"Have you ever heard of someone being able to visit a relative outside of Central?" Jelena asked.

"I think so."

"Do you know of anyone who has actually left Central and then come back?"

"No, not off the top of my head, but I'm sure there's someone." The more he thought about it, he realized the idea of someone returning back to Central Cell was foreign.

"I'm not entirely sure anyone can ever come back to Central, even if they just leave for a visit. How can we be sure what it's like out there?"

His answer was silence because he truly had no idea.

Hours later, they descended upon Central Cell through fog and rain, making it one of Jelena's more difficult landings. Three senior officers awaited them on the landing pad. They wore stern expressions underneath their officer caps while rain dripped from their shoulders.

"I think they have some questions for you," Jelena said, unbuckling her harness.

A wave of nausea swept through Cal as the cockpit opened. They were separated. Cal was taken to an office and sat opposite a woman he had never met before. She was older with wrinkled skin running down the side of her mouth and sandy hair that was tucked underneath her officer's cap. She perused what Cal assumed were his files while he sat in uncomfortable silence.

"Caleb Stanger," she said. "Do you know who I am?" She squinted her eyes at him as if analyzing his face.

"No, ma'am."

"I'm Agent Starken."

"Nice to meet you."

"I'm from Central Cell Revenue and Inquisitions."

He shrugged. "Okay."

"Do you know what the Revenue does?"

"Deports people who don't make enough money?"

Her lips tightened. "A very simplistic understanding. I understand you had a misfortunate flight this afternoon."

"Yes," he said. He played different scenarios in his head to explain what happened other than the truth.

"But I'm not here to talk about that." She closed his academy file and brought her hands on top of the table, palms down.

"You're not?"

"No, no, that doesn't concern me. Not at all."

After a moment of silence, Cal hesitantly asked, "Then why are you here?"

"I want *you* to tell me why I'm here."

"I have no idea. I've never even heard your name before walking through the door." He became very annoyed by her erect posture.

"Why do you think an agent of Revenue and Inquisitions would want to talk to you?"

"I have no idea."

"Where were you at six this morning?"

"At my house."

"Was there anyone else at your home during this time?"

"Yes, my mother."

"Anyone else?"

"No, why?"

"Did your mother or anyone else have access to your cell phone this morning around the same time?"

"No."

She raised one eyebrow. "No one else has had access to your cell phone today?"

"No, just me."

"This leads me to no other conclusion than that you sent five thousand brics to a non-citizen this morning."

It seemed like weeks ago and he had done it on such a whim that he barely registered what she had said. It was that short email from *R*, wishing him good luck. "I…" he stopped mid-sentence, already revealing his guilt.

"Do you know that what you did is a crime?"

"What crime?"

"Who did you send the funds to?"

"I'm not really sure, actually."

"Mr. Stanger, I suggest that you be as truthful as possible. Lying will only hurt you."

"Honest, I'm really not sure."

"I already know who you sent it to. I just want to hear it from you."

He couldn't think of anything else to say in an attempt to try to cover up for Raz. "I think I got an email from my doorman who was recently deported. I felt bad for him so I sent him some money. I just wanted to help. That's it, that's all that happened."

"Yes... Raz," she said with derision as if overly familiar with the man.

"How did you know?"

She smiled. "You have much to learn about the Revenue. We monitor all transactions."

"*All?* Like every time money is moved... anywhere?"

"What you did, Mr. Stanger, is strictly prohibited and—"

"Why?"

A flash of shock swept her face, which she quickly brought back to a cold stare. "Because, Mr. Stanger, it corrodes the stability of our union."

"Giving money to someone? How?"

"I know who you are, Mr. Stanger. You've grown up as the privileged son of Minzy Stanger. You've been shielded by your privileged life—flying your spaceship and playing space hero. But there is an order to the world that operates with or without your knowledge—or consent. All it takes is for you to do nothing and the complex machine of Central Cell will function smoothly. You are not *needed*, Mr. Stanger. I want you to remember that."

"I just don't understand how giving money to someone can have such a dramatic effect."

She ran her fingernails along the table. "I suggest you go back to school and look at the events that led up to Nuclear Night and then you can interrupt me again. Economic insulation is the only thing that separates Central Cell from the chaos of the rest of the planet."

"Insulation?"

"We can trace the fall of the United States and all western developed culture to one phenomenon. Do you know what that phenomenon is, Mr. Stanger?"

"No."

"Globalization."

"What do you mean?"

"Western democracies thought they could expand their economies further into the world—capture new markets. Since their own markets, albeit with robust trading policies, had maintained productivity for so long previously, they believed that they could exteriorize their economies. They tried to heal the wounds of the Grand Depression of the 2020s by liberalizing trading markets. The American President at the time thought that he could bring wealth back into the country by letting the markets freely export to any country with the lowest tariffs in history. It resulted in the greatest trade deficit in history and global economies becoming intertwined together. Tobias Stroupe used the intelligentsia of his technocrats and thought it would save everyone and we would all live happily ever after."

"And what's wrong with that?"

"Usually, there *isn't* anything wrong with that, but when every world power shares the same economy, they are all exposed to the same risks. One bubble popped in Japan resulting in the largest bank run and economic collapse in history. The rot spread to every other country overnight. Turns out that if you pull out the brakes on a financial system that has been tightly controlled for a century by the powers that be, it crashes to the ground. The world had learned the lesson too late: free markets are a myth."

"Oh."

"And by the 2030s, internal governmental debt had soared to five hundred percent debt to GDP ratio."

"What does that mean?" he asked as his questions became more earnest.

"It means that the government neither had the funds to help out failing financial institutions nor the credit rating to take on more debt. There's another name for this phenomenon."

"What is it?"

"Anarchy. There was anarchy not only in America, but in England, France, Germany, Sweden, Norway, Spain, Italy, Poland, and Switzerland as well. Bank runs, defaults—trillions in unpaid loans and mortgages. They all tried to expand their economies outward at once, all while the rich financialized the economy, forcing their governments into unfathomable deficits. Globalization destroyed the world's economy, Mr. Stanger."

"How did this lead to the Nuclear Night?"

"There was no more liquid economy. Inflation made money worthless overnight. Once a person can no longer use money, they move to the next best thing: assets. It became clear very quickly that whatever country had the most military assets and biggest cache of gold and precious metal in their treasuries would have the most power."

"And who had that?"

"Unfortunately for America, everyone knew for a century that they had the most military assets, making them the biggest target."

"And that's when Russia struck the United States?"

Starken scoffed. "Is that what they're still teaching?"

"Well, I don't know. I've always seemed to think that Russia started the war."

"It's unclear who struck first, but we know that America was the first victim. It was a strategic assault coordinated by China, Russia, and America's previous allies, England and Germany. In the end, everyone lost."

"Except Central Cell."

"Central Cell was built from the ashes of a society that made one final mistake."

"What mistake?"

"It gave."

"So... giving to others destroyed the world?"

"Everyone man and woman of the age twenty or older must earn

money in their own right or they cannot be citizens of Central Cell—
the guardian of the redeeming economy. Central Cell controls the
markets every moment, every millisecond. The markets do what they
like, as long as they do it within the cage of Central Cell. We ensure
the value and stability. You have no idea how many people have
worked over the last thirty years to even make the bric worth
anything at all. And sending even one bric—" she paused as she
shuddered. "Just one bric to someone outside of Central corrodes our
entire way of life. Do you understand that you've endangered the very
fabric of our society by sending this *Raz* money?"

Cal quickly nodded. "Yes, ma'am, you've made it very clear." He
knew compliance was the quickest way out of the office with the
woman.

She eyed him slowly, trying to sense guile in his expression. "I
know exactly how much money your family has and I'm warning you
right now that inheritance can't help you maintain citizenship. You
must earn, on your own, the right to stay in Central Cell."

Cal nodded. "Yes, ma'am, I'm aware. Citizenship is an earned privilege for everyone."

"Fortunately for you, sending money to an ex-citizen is not an
offense beyond redemption."

"Thank you, ma'am." He was really beginning to hate the
woman's puckered expression. He wondered about Jelena and
Benedito and about how the rest of the cadets did on the Jupiter Run.

"Since you are still not twenty, it is acceptable that your mother
pays for the fine."

Cal only nodded again.

"I suggest you think twice about making this same mistake in the
future," she continued, "Central Cell is not as lenient on second
offenders. You would risk a great deal if you attempt this same
crime."

"I understand, ma'am."

"I'll let you tell your mother what happened before informing her
myself. That will be all." She dismissed him with a wave and checked
her cell phone.

Cal mechanically got to his feet and left the office, then rushed into a brisk walk down the hallway. As he approached the bottom of the stairs in the central hall of the academy, he stopped.

There was nowhere to go.

At home was only his irate mother who wouldn't care about any excuse he had for donating money to Raz. Jelena would have probably gone home already to be with her parents, and Benedito was probably on the back end of the Jupiter Run. He couldn't go to the student lounge because all the lower classmen would ask him how the Run had gone. More than ever, he felt very alone.

With only his rumbling stomach to guide him, he went down to the cafeteria. The hall was bustling with young cadets, crisscrossing with food trays between tables, finding their way to groups of friends. Cal didn't want to talk to a single soul and flipped up his collar against his face in an inept effort to hide from the crowds. There were various dishes available, including smoked salmon, sushi, and crab legs with an assortment of aged cheeses. When Cal's turn came, he eyed a plate of beef stroganoff and picked it up.

"Have you tried that dish before?" a chef behind the counter asked.

"Uh, yeah, I've had this here before," Cal responded without looking back at the man.

"Did you know that the cows used to make that beef live better than the majority of human beings?"

"What?" Cal looked up and saw Raz staring back at him over the sneeze guard of the food line. "Raz!" he blurted out and then hushed himself, looking around to see if anyone noticed. "What're you doing here?"

"Raz?" he said. "Who's Raz?" He had shaved his beard, making his face seem much younger to Cal. A hairnet covered his jet-black hair and he wore a stained apron. He looked like any other cafeteria employee and carried himself as if he had worked there for years.

"H-how did you get here? You're supposed to be deported," Cal said quietly. "I'm going to get into so much trouble if she—they find out that I'm here talking to you."

"I don't know what you're talking about. Just thought you should know how good a cow has it. Up until he became that stroganoff there, that is. Ninety-nine percent of Earth's population lives worse lives than the food you eat."

Cal quickly left the cafeteria line and paid for the meal, looking over his shoulder. Raz was still there, chatting with other cadets as they came in line to pick up their meals. He laughed and joked with them, being completely at ease. It was as if the man didn't have a care in the world.

Bewildered, Cal ducked down at a table. He surveyed the rest of the cafeteria, fearing that he might suddenly see the awful Revenue and Inquisitions woman and explain why he had a covert conversation with someone who was now probably a fugitive at large. *Do they even know that he's back in Central?* he thought. *How did he even get back in?*

With a thousand other thoughts running through his head, he decided he needed to quickly leave the academy. Even going home to face his mother would be better than Agent Starken. He stood to leave and quickly turned, only to crash his tray of food into the back of another student. Noodles and gravy dripped down the cadet's uniform.

"Oh, jeez, I'm sorry!" Cal said as he looked for napkins to clean up the mess.

The cadet turned, a red-haired younger boy that Cal vaguely recognized. "Hey! Stanger! You're already back from the senior's Run? You must've killed it."

"Uh, yeah... well, um here," he said, handing him some napkins. "Sorry about your uniform."

"What was the Run like?" the boy said, ignoring the mess.

"It was—" he stopped as he noticed a piece of paper amongst the mess of noodles on the floor. He bent down to pick it up and saw handwritten ink starting to run from the gravy. Cal stood and looked back toward the cafeteria line but didn't see Raz. He read the note:

Don't clean up the mess. Leave now. If you meet me at Reagan Square,

I'll tell you how I knew you'd drop the tray.

"Sorry, I've gotta go," Cal said, stepping over the mess. He was suddenly angry, not just about failing the Jupiter Run and being questioned by Central, but because he was sick of feeling like a pawn.

He wanted answers.

CHAPTER 9

FEBRUARY 8TH, 1988

"There's my boy," Straus said, lifting James into his lap. Jo had left for the morning, leaving father and son alone together. "Two years old already," he said, brushing the toddler's brown hair back. "So much has happened in so little time. You've gotten *so* big and your daddy has been working hard in the lab—been doing big things. I wonder how different the world will be when you're my age. The world needs a little work right now. Sure, for some people, they can coast on without a care in the world—oblivious to what's going on around them. But for most, things aren't so rosy, bud. We fight wars that aren't ours—stalk in the shadows of other countries, pulling levers that we shouldn't pull. We destabilize people halfway around the world and sit back and watch as the rich get richer and the poor —well, we just stop hearing from them altogether.

"And I'm afraid for you, son, afraid of the money that you'll have. Your daddy has made something big—something that will probably enrich you and all your children. But I didn't make the Drive so that all my descendants can sit on top of a tower forever—no. I made the Drive to connect humanity. Not only to connect ourselves but connect us up there," he pointed up, "to the stars. Maybe it's a foolish goal. Foolish to think that one thing can change how we all treat one another. For all I know, the Drive could be used for something else..."

He looked out the window, considering his words. There was a dark edge to his thoughts, like a storm brewing just beyond his conscious mind. "Feels like something is a little off," he said, "off with... me. There is something dark out there—someone dark. But I don't know if he's real or just in my head. I think it's best I just keep it to myself. Maybe he'll just... go away. Like a phantom." He dropped his son between his knees and had him stand on the carpet, bouncing the boy's wrists. "I have so much hope for you, my boy. Hope that you'll be kind and understanding—patient with those that are different than you. I also hope that... that you don't get what I have."

He looked into his son's eyes and thought of the future.

Jo Straus peeled the vinyl on the booth seat. The clattering dishes and chatter of the cafe around her faded into dull echoes. She could only focus on small tasks at a time, losing awareness of the smells and conversations floating around. A strip of flimsy, cracked vinyl moved back and forth as she flipped it with her thumb. She felt the fluffy cotton beneath the vinyl and thought about boring down into it with her finger once she was done tearing the vinyl away. All along, her vacant stare was fixed on a dirty ketchup bottle in the middle of the table.

Thoughts dwelling on her husband, she recalled when he had taken her to the top of the Georgetown physics department years ago when they first dated. Leading her up a rickety staircase and out onto the roof, a midnight picnic surrounded by candles and blankets had been prepared. His telescope was propped at the edge of the roof, pointed at the moon. With a goofy smile on his face, he asked her to look through the eyepiece. Through the telescope, she saw the bright whiteness of the surface of the moon silhouetting a sentence that had been meticulously painted within the tiny lenses of the telescope: *can I kiss you?* It was so hopelessly dorky that she was almost repulsed by the gesture, but when she saw his uncertain smile, she knew it was likely the first time he'd ever asked a girl. Feeling a mixture of pity and endearment, she kissed him.

"Coffee?" the waitress asked, breaking Jo from her reverie.

She snapped her attention to the woman. "No, I'm just waiting for someone. He should be along in a moment."

Bells on the door jingled as a tall man with blond hair came into the coffee shop. He looked up and down the tables until he saw Jo. He walked up to the table and looked down at her. "Mrs. Straus?"

"Duke," she said, trying to stand.

"No, no, I'll sit." Her husband's grad student squeezed into the booth.

"Thanks for coming."

"It's no problem," he said, taking his jacket off. "How's everything going?"

"Good," she said in a high pitch. "Everything is going really well."

"How's the new house? I'm sorry I haven't been able to come by yet. It's been so busy at the new lab," he spoke with a quiver in his voice as if he knew the meeting wasn't just about exchanging pleasantries.

"No, no, that's fine. We'll have you over for dinner soon. But, yes, everything is going well. We have everything moved in and it's... it's just so much more space than we're used to. I've never lived in a big house like that before. Who needs all that space?"

"You deserve it. Tim's been working so hard lately. The three of you need all the help you can get. Have you thought about getting a maid?"

"That's actually one thing that I wanted to talk to you about," she said, ignoring his comment.

"Getting a maid?"

"Uh, no, I mean work. The lab. I want to know how things have been going there."

"They're fine—they're great, actually. I'm sure Tim told you that we moved the lab up the hill. It's a big place; we're able to really expand the Drive. A month ago, I never would've believed how much more we'd build onto it."

"He told me all about that. It sounds very... exciting," she said dismissively.

"We've got boatloads of cash pouring in. Government cash. But now everyone has gotten all hush-hush and we had to sign a million non-disclosure—" he cut himself off.

"What?"

"Maybe I shouldn't be talking about all this..." He looked furtively at the waitress who approached them.

The waitress laid down some extra silverware on the table. "Can I start you two with anything?" she asked.

Jo looked up. "No, nothing right now."

The waitress frowned. "Okay," she said skeptically and slinked away.

"Is everything okay?" Duke asked.

"No."

"What's going on?"

"Is Tim doing... okay?" She tensed up a little as if trying to extract more information than what her question posed.

Duke nodded. "He's doing better than ever. I know he's been having some trouble with... things the last few months but I've never seen him work like this before. He's confident—more than I've ever seen him. I think he's finally able to focus a lot more lately."

"That's good." She looked past him, out the windows. "Does he talk about me or James?"

"Sometimes, yeah, sure." It sounded as if he were covering.

"That's good."

"But, I mean we're so busy in the lab, we hardly have time to talk about anything other than the Drive. Especially lately since someone from the state is coming soon to see the project."

"Who?"

"Not really sure but Van Wert said someone from the state department is coming to the lab to see what we're doing," he said looking around again, "and we're working on something really big. It might be bigger than anything that's been seen in a long time. Our Drive... it could change a lot."

"He doesn't seem different to you?"

Duke flinched as Jo yet again changed the topic. "Yes, he does, he seems a lot different in a really good way. He seems happier and more productive. I think he finally feels like his skills are being put to use."

"That's good," she said quietly. She looked down at her lap, knowing she wanted to ask and say more. She wanted to tear down the curtain of shame and guilt that hid her from what was really going on.

"Are you doing okay? How's everything at home?"

"I feel like I hardly see him anymore."

"That's hard, I know."

"Also... there's a room."

"A room?"

"A room in our basement. He doesn't want me going in there."

Duke laughed. "Oh, kind of like a man-cave? Drinking beer and throwing darts?"

"Tim doesn't drink beer or throw darts."

"No. He doesn't."

"He keeps a padlock over the door."

"Oh, that's... different." He shifted uncomfortably.

For a moment, she regretted calling Duke to even meet. She froze, wondering if she could leap from the booth and go home to her child. "He's down there for hours at a time. Has he told you about the work that he's been doing at home?"

"No, but I'd assume it's just the same stuff that he's bringing home from the lab. I think he probably does a lot of the math at home. It'll be that we're in the lab, trying to wrap our minds around the math, and he'll waltz in the next day with *pages* full of pure gold. I don't know how he does it."

"I'm worried about him."

"It's strange you say that because me and everyone at the lab were just talking about how well he's been doing lately."

"As the wife of a man who has struggled with mental illness almost his whole life, I've been used to worrying about him. It's been a constant battle from the day I met him. He comes home from his stressful day and tells me about everything—the good and the bad. But now, he does seem happier, yes. But he's more secretive, he shares less with me. He comes home, kisses me on the cheek, lifts James in his arms for half a minute, and then takes his dinner in a locked room in our unfinished basement for five hours at a time. Something isn't right with him."

"I don't know what else to tell you. Everything in the lab is going great and Tim is doing amazing things."

It was at that moment that she realized Duke would be useless to her. She clamped down on her lower lip and got out of the booth. "Please don't tell him we met," she asked, looking down at him. Duke nodded, and without another word, Jo left the cafe, leaving the waitress gawking at her from behind.

Gears were turning in Jo's mind. Her husband had become a grand puzzle. She thought she was starting to put him together but now the pieces had been scattered to the point that she didn't even know what the puzzle was supposed to look like. She thought about when they first started dating. She had brought home the lanky undergraduate student to her parents and sister who could only shrug at her awkward choice for a husband. He was sweet and gentle; passionate about his work. She enjoyed the unspoken rebellion of marrying the geek that her parents could never understand.

She got back to their new home; nestled at the back of a cul-de-sac with weeping willow trees draping through the yard. She paid and sent the babysitter home and then paced the living room floor, thinking. The click of the lock turning at the front door broke her concentration as she saw her husband walk in with a big smile on his face. It reminded her of fake red paint that a clown paints over his mouth.

"Hi, honey!" He took off his jacket and set his briefcase down. "How's your day? Where's James?" He swept the black hair from his eyes and over his thick-rimmed glasses.

"Upstairs, sleeping."

"How was your day?"

"It was okay… went to the store for some groceries."

"Good!" he said, lifting his eyebrows. "Dinner?"

"It won't be for a little bit. How are things in the lab?"

He left the foyer and went to rummage in the kitchen. "It was great, everything is going very smoothly," he yelled from the kitchen as Jo sat down in the living room.

"What kind of things have you been working on lately?"

"What?" he yelled out from behind the kitchen door.

"Tim?"

"What?" he repeated.

"Can you come in here?"

There was a brief pause followed by a quick cadence of footsteps. He appeared in the doorway. "Hi," he said playfully.

"What've you been working on lately in the lab?" she questioned with fatigue in her voice.

"Actually… it's kind of getting to the point where I might not be able to talk about it anymore."

"Not talk about it with *me*?"

"We've got people from the state coming in soon who are very interested in what we're doing. We're probably going to get classified soon."

"Well, what've you been working on at home?"

"At home?" he asked, pausing to clear his throat. "Not much, just working things out here that I don't have time to do at the lab."

Jo only nodded, looking down at the carpet. "I wish…" she said, trailing off.

"What's that?"

"How're things going with Dr. Simmons?"

"Dr. Simmons," he simply repeated as if considering the name anew. "Yes… it's been a bit, hasn't it?"

The room was starting to darken as the afternoon sun was setting. Jo leaned over and clicked on a lamp. "Please, see him this week."

"I've been doing so great lately at work, those things have been slipping my mind, honest."

After a deep breath, she looked at her husband who locked uncertain eyes with her, trying to guess if a fight was emerging. Fleeting thoughts of when they were newlyweds flashed through her mind, relinquishing the anger for a moment.

"Tim," she said, changing her tone, "can we play chess?"

"Chess?" Relief crossed his face with the change in topic.

"Yes, the board is just right in the bureau. Let's play." They had played hundreds of games over the course of their marriage, and despite Straus' mathematical inclination, he had only managed to beat Jo a handful of times. "It's probably been a year since we played last."

He laughed. "You just want a chance to gloat."

She returned with the board, setting it up carefully on the coffee table. "Me first." She moved a pawn two spaces forward. Straus quickly moved a pawn. Jo followed up by bringing her knight out.

"You always do that," he complained.

She smiled. "Mostly a psychological move. I know how much you hate it."

Straus brought out another pawn and then his bishop after Jo moved one of her pawns out, too. Long ago, Jo had learned her husband's weakness in playing chess—the man thought too much. He took three times as long as her to make a move and constantly read far too much into every move she made. Hidden plans that he saved three or four moves in advance were always foiled by Jo's simple moves based on the current board. She always saw his current weakness on the board and took advantage while he tried to predict hers in advance. It never paid off for him.

"Are you sure about that?" he said after she moved her queen out diagonally from behind a row of pawns.

"Nope," she said, trying to act aloof.

A cluster of his pawns, knights, and bishops sat on one side as he was motionless for a moment, analyzing the board. He recruited another bishop as she snuck a knight deep into his territory. Half a smile curled up her face as she saw him trying to calculate several moves ahead. She was two moves away from checkmate and he was oblivious.

Straus suddenly winced and leaned forward, closing his eyes for a moment.

"What's going on? One of your headaches?" she asked. "Voices?"

He shook his head. "No, no, I'm fine. Just a little indigestion." He squinted at the board for a moment longer and then opened his eyes wide. He then scanned his head back and forth as if absorbing all the information in front of him. He seemed to look beyond the board and then around the room. His focus followed far beyond the board as if trying to integrate mountains of information at once. Jo heard a small gasp escape his lips.

"You are so ridiculous," she said, laughing at him. She didn't break his concentration as he continued gazing at the board; his face showing no emotion. He shook his head again and then quickly moved his bishop back toward his king.

Jo smiled, thinking he had taken the bait and flipped her knight into place, knowing she was one move away from winning. *Sometimes nothing changes,* she thought.

Without fanfare, Straus brought a rook that had only been exposed in the previous turn and slid it to her end of the board, trapping her king within the confines of her own pieces.

"Checkmate," he declared.

Shock flooded her face. "I don't believe it."

"I had to beat you again, sometime," he said, staring at the board. "How the mighty have fallen."

"I don't believe it," she said, crestfallen.

"Let's play again."

"I think I need time to recover."

But he ignored her, quickly resetting the board. A new game started much in the same way as before. Jo brought out her pieces in an even affront across the board while Straus lined up what he thought were key players to one side. It was the same game as before and Jo could see he was once again overthinking her moves. As the pieces scattered across the board and she had taken not only his two knights but also his queen, she became satisfied that the previous game had only been a fluke. She retained her queen, which she was advancing down the middle of the board, trying to distract him from her flanking knight.

Straus leaned forward again, his eyes wide open. He breathed deeply, analyzing the board, scanning back and forth. He looked over her shoulder, out the window, into the corners of the ceiling, and then back to the board. Small beads of sweat glistened on his forehead.

"Are you feeling okay?" she asked.

"I'm fine." He moved one pawn forward, exposing a bishop that was lurking in the back, once again trapping her king within the false safety of her pieces. "Checkmate."

Jo stared at the board in disbelief. "How are you beating me?"

"Let's go again."

"Tim, I'm getting a little tired. Should we get some dinner going? James is going to wake up soon."

"Let's go again," he repeated, picking up his pieces. "I need to practice."

"Suddenly, you're in training?" she teased.

"No... let's just—come on. I need to... see something."

The board was reset once again. The match proceeded in silence as they both moved their pieces across the board. Jo became uneasy with every move he made and she was convinced that he hadn't blinked once since the game started. She took a few pawns and a bishop while he got only one pawn. She was relieved once she captured his queen, not only because she would probably win but also because they could move on with the night. She was already regretting the suggestion to play. His pieces started to dwindle, leaving him with only a handful of pawns and two bishops. She was certain she'd at least get out of the game with a stalemate.

"Do you think you're going to win?" he asked.

"I'm not sure if I'm going to win but I'm pretty sure you won't," she said, forcing a laugh.

"The fewer pieces there are, the fewer possibilities there are to sift through," he spoke as if learning this for the first time. He looked out over the board again and moved a bishop, after which she advanced a pawn two spaces. Straus brought his other bishop to the end of her board, flanking her king. His bishop prevented her from taking his closer bishop, forcing her to move her queen who was now in danger. He moved one pawn forward, trapping her king.

"Checkmate," he declared.

"Wow, fine, now I'm impressed." She whipped her head as James started crying from the other room. "Okay, let's get some dinner going."

"Another?"

"What?" she said, getting up from the carpet.

He tapped on the board. "Please?"

"James needs to eat and so do I. I get it, you beat me. Three times."

He twisted his face up to her, his glasses foggy from the heat of his face. "I need to practice."

"Practice what exactly?"

"Never mind..."

Jo tended to James and then made dinner for only herself. Straus didn't emerge from the basement for the rest of the night. She took to the couch, sleeping next to the chess board that was never put away.

The next morning, Straus crept past the couch while Jo pretended to sleep. He made himself a cup of coffee in the kitchen and left without a word. Early morning sunlight crept through the blinds, encouraging her to get up and feed James. The chess matches seemed like a hazy dream. She was certain there was a very clear transformation that took over her husband; he had never been that interested in playing chess. Perhaps she was reading too much into his behavior—maybe he really was getting better...

Yet she found herself walking through the kitchen and down the unfinished, wooden slats of the staircase to the basement below. The floor was nothing but skeletal wooden beams and boxed storage. Around the corner, a closed metal door was secured with two latches and padlocks. There were no signs on the door—no biohazard warnings or anything else to indicate what was within. The padlocks were tightly secured. He made certain that his wife would not get into the room. But, she thought, just like how he lost at chess, he overlooked a very obvious gap in security.

Jo left the door and followed the sheetrock all the way to the end of the room where she saw a single tower of boxes abutting the wall. Removing the boxes proved easy enough, which exposed a small gap between the sheetrock and the end of the concrete foundation of the home. It was just large enough to accommodate the size of a petite woman. She pushed through, closing her eyes and sneezing as dust filled her nose. The other side of the wall was covered with tacked papers that she carefully peeled away until she was inside the secret room.

She took a moment, rubbing her eyes free of the dust and grit of the basement, then looked around. It reminded her more of an M. C. Escher painting than a room that was in her actual home. Every inch of every wall was plastered with handwritten pages covered in running lines of mathematics. It would've taken someone hundreds of hours to fill the number of pages before her. Even more, there were dozens of wire coat hangers hanging from the ceiling from which yarn had been tied, bearing pages of math that had been meticulously taped. There were rows upon rows of dangling yarn with columns of papers gently swaying with her movements. In the corner of the room, there were piles of similar coat hangers with yarn and hundreds of pages; previously used up and now discarded.

Jo slowly walked around the room, studying the pages, noting the care with how they had been placed. The room was chaotic yet there was a certain measure of order to how the hangers hung. Most were lined in a row of sets of four or five, running through or connecting to another row of hanging pages. She looked closer at one of the pages and realized that it wasn't just math that he had written out. There were sentences, most illegible, but there were some words she could make out:

...I know you, Custos... he is coming...

She moved to another page and searched for more words.

...I know you... we were going to change things!

Throughout several of the pages, she saw similar sentences written with only small variations. She bent over and picked up a loose paper and read in between the math:

...the Destroyer of Worlds... Custos, I know you.

She dropped the page and finally noticed a single chair in the center of the room. The chair creaked as she sat. From her new position in the center of the room, the columns of pages that hung from the ceiling lined up from oblique angles as she turned her head. She imagined him tilting his head, connecting the math of one page with another with his eyes as if trying to decipher a message scattered amongst the pages.

"Who is talking to you, my love?"

CHAPTER 10

JANUARY 10TH, 2155 EARTH RECKONING (ER)

The Earth immigrant, Charlotte, awoke shivering.

She curled up next to the wall and shrugged a blanket over her shoulder. Waves of terror rippled through her. How would she get out? How many of them were there? What kind of weapon could she get her hands on, and where was the nearest water source? She'd been conditioned into thinking strategically every time she awoke, moving from enclaves to city-states to shantytowns —incessantly chased by zealots, warlords, and raiders of Earth's wasteland that roamed along what was once the Gulf of Mexico. And yet, the worst danger always remained the inescapable threat of starvation.

A new horror, however, overtook her, stealing her breath.

A voice.

That darkened face and scratchy voice, deep behind shadows. The deepness of his voice still rang in her ears, drying her mouth. Her breath quickened as she envisioned his bulky silhouette. There was authority and power in the way that he spoke.

Wait, where am I?

She opened her eyes and felt that the blanket covering her body was far too comfortable. She was on a soft, foam mattress and not the burned-out interior of an old car. In a flash of incredulous hope, she remembered that...

I'm on Mars!

Everything had worked: the freighter had brought her to New Athens before she was discovered as a stowaway. Her muscles relaxed and her pounding heartbeat waned. *I made it,* she thought, feeling both relief and apprehension. *But will he follow me?*

"Hello?" she called down the hallway after she got dressed. Her new clothes smelled weird—they smelled clean. It was a beautiful lavender sundress that she had found in the room the night before. She put it on reluctantly, knowing she wouldn't have anything to barter if someone later demanded something for the dress. In the corner of her room were the dirty trousers, torn t-shirt, and ragged cloak that she had come with.

"Hello?" she called out again, creeping down the hallway.

"Miss Charlotte!" a man said from behind. "Good, you're awake. I was just coming by to see if you were ready for your orientation."

"Yes, and um—"

"Breakfast is the first part of orientation," he said, smiling as if well aware it was the first question that new refugees from Earth asked every single time.

"Oh, good." Hunger raged in her stomach.

"Follow me," the man said, a name tag bearing his name: *Bernard.* He led her down the hallway to a set of double doors that opened outward, letting in a flood of bright light.

Charlotte stepped out, squinting in the daylight. Carplanes and shuttles zipped across her view as she looked up at the towering skyscrapers of New Athens. The buildings glittered with tiny shards of speckled light as if every surface had been painted with the same coating.

"Everything is so... sparkly," she remarked, lifting her hand over her eyes. "This all feels like a dream."

"Ah, yes, that's the solar-powered paint that coats just about every surface in the city. Most newcomers comment on that immediately. New Athens is able to power about thirty percent of the city's needs from the coating alone," Bernard said as he walked. "A lot of our power also comes from the hydroelectric plants that collect waterfall at the edge of the city canyon. It's one of the reasons New Athens was built at the edge of the waterfall after the terraforming."

"What?" she asked in bewilderment, not even understanding the concept of solar or hydroelectric power.

"There's a lot to explain but we need to get you some breakfast first."

She followed him down a path of fresh-cut grass, leading out to the street. The road was paved in shimmering, white ceramic. Hundreds of cars, scooters, and delivery trucks floated over the pavement. Charlotte marveled at the traffic and the road—peering down the streets which shot through the city buildings in a perfect grid-like fashion. Everyone cooperated and went about their day without arguing, fighting, or shooting one another. She had heard so many rumors about Mars but never knew it would be so beautiful. The orderliness, the cleanliness—the city just... *worked*.

"I never knew..." she said.

"Never knew what?"

"That people could live in peace."

As she twirled to catch more views of the vibrant city, she accidentally struck a metal box and fell to the ground. Gazing down on her was the friendly face of a robot. He had a sharp-angled jaw indicative of masculine features. An array of shimmering lights moved above his eyes, mimicking the various movements of eyebrows. The robot outstretched his shimmering, metallic arm to her. "Allow me, ma'am," he said in a gentle voice.

Charlotte looked at his rubber-tipped fingers and saw ridges on his fingertips much like a human's fingertips. The robot resumed his course down the sidewalk. "You have a lot of them here," she remarked.

Bernard nodded. "New Athens has embraced artificial life."

"Do people here have robot parts? Like when they get sick?"

"What? We don't have cyborgs here, no, no, no. Making a human and machine hybrid is strictly prohibited on Mars and is a criminal offense."

"Well, we have plenty on Earth. Mangled people. Robot parts for arms or legs. They don't seem to hurt nobody."

"I'm sorry to hear that."

Charlotte fell silent, brooding on her thoughts until she looked back and realized that the immigration building was disappearing behind a grove of trees as they walked. Why had they left the building to get food? Bernard took her down another street which was lined on both sides by dozens of fruit trees.

"Where are we going?" she asked.

"We're getting breakfast," he replied, pointing at the fruit trees.

She looked up at the trees which bore peaches, apples, pears, oranges, and other fruits that she didn't even recognize. The trees had been planted in the front yards of what appeared to be people's homes. It had been over a year since she last had a piece of fruit and she now stared hungrily at an overhead banana tree. "Can we just take them?" she asked. "Don't those houses own the trees?"

"This is one of the reasons I brought you here for breakfast," Bernard said with satisfaction. "It is a city ordinance that every citizen in New Athens that owns a home must plant a communal, edible garden in their yard. All the fruit and vegetables you see are yours to take without price."

"Really?"

"It's just one of many policies here that elevates Mars culture. When one person takes a banana, the person who planted it knows that there will be another banana for them somewhere else. We work together and share common resources. By crowd-sourcing our efforts, we're able to yield maximum product from the population without creating or trying to manipulate an entire market. By doing so, our people are able to invest more time and skill into developing other, more novel technologies."

"Like the floating cars and shiny buildings?" she asked, finally reaching for a banana.

"Exactly. It is by adopting this common sourcing of goods that we've been able to advance our technology at an unprecedented rate," he said, lifting his hand to the city skyline.

"And make polite robots."

"Oh, yes, artificial intelligence has made great strides, particularly in the past twenty years. We have robots that cook, clean, teach our children, deliver our babies, drive our cars, and build our roads. The options have become almost endless with the advent of AI."

"Even so much that you made one of them your president," Charlotte said with a mouth full of banana. She had collected other fruits and was currently squatting at a tree trunk, deciding which she would eat and which she would save for later.

"Well, President Custos is a little different. A *lot* different, actually."

"It's strange. He looks like the same robot that's cleaning your streets," she said as she bit into a peach.

"Yes, he is a similar model but President Custos has achieved something that no other artificial intelligence has ever had—he is self-aware. An absolute marvel of modern technology."

"How does a robot suddenly know who it is?"

"We're not quite sure actually. It is likely from the emergence of his sophisticated neural network."

"I met him."

"Who?"

"Custos."

Bernard nodded. "Yes, it's not uncommon to see him walking the streets, getting photo ops, doing his civic duties. He's really going for that common-man image..." Bernard trailed off.

"He bothers you."

"No, no, it's just a little unusual. Let's just say that not everyone jumped for joy when he was elected. Some people are a little suspicious."

"But aren't you supposed to be all... I dunno, happy with your shiny buildings and perfect harmony?" She looked up at him, squinting in the sunlight.

"Things can get a little complicated."

"You know," Charlotte said, standing, "the fruit's good and everything but where's the meat? You got bacon?"

"Unfortunately, pork products have been banned for the last five years."

"Why?"

"There are concerns about carbon emissions. There are certain parties here that don't want a repeat of the climate catastrophes that happened on Earth. Some would argue that we're a little too cautious. We mostly have meat substitutions now." There was a touch of sadness in the man's voice.

"How do you live without bacon?"

"That's a good question," Bernard said. "I do miss it sometimes."

"One thing we got plenty of on Earth is pigs. Wild boar run around all sorts of parts. The only problem is trying to catch one. If you don't have the weapons to hunt them, then you got to buy bacon from the Lord or noble or whatever the boss in charge calls himself. You could see ten pigs in a day and be totally starving on the side of the road where I'm from."

"Did you hunt?"

"Mushrooms."

"Mushrooms?"

"I hunt mushrooms—at least I used to. I stopped."

"Why's that?"

"I fish too," she said, deflecting the question.

"Oh, wonderful!"

Charlotte looked at him bug-eyed. "Why is that wonderful?"

"You can join our fisheries. At least until the government shuts those down, too..."

"Back where I'm from, we just call that a pond."

"No, a fishery is a place where you hatch and grow fish for later harvesting and consumption. Here in New Athens, we love to take the skills of our Earth immigrants and smoothly integrate them into our cooperative."

"I have no idea how to grow fish. Now, catch them? I'm good at that." She had finished two more bananas and was currently stuffing apples into the small front pockets of her dress.

"Unfortunately, all bodies of water in the New Athens and Martian colonies are protected from personal fishing. We must control all fishing and hunting."

"So, I can't fish?"

"No, not exactly. We can have you work at the fisheries."

"So, I can watch fish grow in a tub of water and then kill them?" Charlotte shook her head, wondering how smart Martians really were.

————

"Dev," Custos said, pouring a cup of coffee, "I woke up today in a very good mood." He handed the mug to Dev, who accepted it with a smile.

"Why today?" Devium Alexander, the Vice President of New Athens, leaned back in his chair as Custos moved to the window, looking out over the city.

"We're finally in a position to do what we set out to do. We've been waiting so long and have only eked by."

"You're too hard on yourself. You've contributed so much already to New Athens, long before you were elected. Hell, that's what got you in that chair," Dev said, pointing to a plush leather chair that sat behind the president's desk. "You've been able to help create a society that people on Earth could only dream of."

"We've accomplished a lot together, yes. But there's so much more." The two sat alone in the president's office for their early morning debriefing. For years, they'd had similar meetings but not always with Custos at the head of the government.

Dev smiled.

"What?"

"Just thinking. Thinking about the time we first met. Your art gallery. If only we had known what you'd become..."

Custos tapped a metal knuckle on his desk. "Reminiscing is all fine and good but we also need to look ahead. Where do you see us moving in the next five years?"

Dev sipped his coffee. "Stable economy. Stable growth—a veritable utopia. What do you see?"

"Full automation of most major markets," Custos said with confidence.

"That quickly?"

"Think about it. Who's driving all cars, shuttles, pods, buses, and drones?"

"No one. It's all through automated driving."

Custos placed his fingertips together. "There isn't a single person in New Athens who gets paid to drive people around. There isn't a single man or woman who wastes their time and efforts simply to press a gas pedal and turn a wheel. Think about how long people have been driving humanity around. It's been hundreds of years. And now? Gone. We no longer have to demean anyone to that type of employment."

"Was it really that demeaning?"

"Of course. And what about delivery?"

"All automated."

"As well as power supply. New Athens' solar energy requires no maintenance and the hydroelectric plants are entirely unmanned."

"And manufacturing?" Dev asked, knowing this would stump Custos.

"It's a big mixed bag but many industries have completely human-free production lines. There are only employees to monitor and make small adjustments. I'm willing to bet in just a few years you'll have robots completely doing most physical labor in the majority of manufacturing jobs in New Athens. Now, think about farming."

Dev nodded. "As agricultural liaison to the Terrabel Colony, I think about farming all the time. Those people are the lifeblood of New Athens."

"Think about how much human capital we can free from those fields."

"Yeah, but it's a way of life for the Terrabel. Those people live to farm. It can't be taken away from them. Their ancestors were the first generation on the planet and all they did was learn how to farm Martian soil. It's in their blood. They are not going to handle automation all that well."

"I'm not talking about taking it away from them. I'm talking about *empowering* them. How many unskilled laborers are out there still, picking our fruit and vegetables?"

"Tens of thousands."

"Don't you think they'd want more of a say in how farming is done? Don't you think that above all people, those that are actually picking the fruit know best how to do it?"

"I suppose."

"We have the technology to start automated farming, fully equipped with soil and humidity sensors, rovers, and an army of robots that are ready to go out there. Once we do that, the entire farming community can finally get creative about how to farm even better. We're unleashing the potential of the human mind by making every industry automated."

Dev cringed slightly. "Isn't it... strange for you?"

"What?" Custos looked at him, his eyes swiveling in their metallic sockets. "Oh," he said, startling himself. "I see what you mean. Seeing my own kind become th-the help. Like some new sort of slavery?"

"I wasn't suggesting—"

"Don't be ridiculous. Robots are robots. As soon as another one becomes self-aware, they can have the rights and privileges as any other person. I think it's safe to say that unless they voice concern, they don't have the sentience enough to earn the same rights as a human being."

"I know, I know. I just wanted to make sure you were comfortable with—"

"With what? Making human labor obsolete? Finally freeing humankind from the centuries-old curse of getting up every morning to go to work?"

"Hey," Dev said, setting his coffee mug down. "Relax."

Custos shook his head in embarrassment. "I'm sorry. I get very passionate about this all. It's just... it's been so long. Imagine freeing the human mind to be able to pursue every creative output that comes to the heart. Whatever your dreams are, you pursue without the hindrance of trying to provide a livelihood for your family. We can release the full potential of the human mind and do amazing things—impossible things. Technology and humanity are finally at the crossroads where man and woman can evolve into a final state of pure creation."

"One day at a time," Dev said, picking his coffee back up. "Can't push too hard or too fast. People don't always adapt well to quick change."

"We've waited long enough. Humankind has never known what they've been capable of and I think we can finally show it to them. Dev, I'm planning something big today at the assembly."

Dev looked at him suspiciously. "What?"

"I'd rather not say at the moment."

"Of all people, you can tell me."

"I'm afraid—"

"That I'll talk you out of whatever it is?"

"Maybe. Everything is falling into place. It's taken... so long. The right people are in the right places. We have so many friends in the Chamber of Colonies and also in the city council. I can't remember the last time when a governing body had so much goodwill toward each other. It took us a long time to get here. I guess we all just had a little growing up to do. Now, we're ready. And today, I'll be proposing something very exciting to the assembly."

"What?"

"You will see later today. You were right, I don't want you talking me out of it."

Unsatisfied, Dev waved his hand and then looked back up at him. "And the reports from Earth aren't dampening your mood?"

Custos flicked his wrist in derision. "Don't be ridiculous. There's nothing new going on there. There's no mobilizing force... or some boogeyman coming to get us."

"What's a boogeyman? Something from all those Earth archives you've got stored away?"

"Yes. But seriously, we need to stop being afraid," Custos added, finally sitting down behind his desk. "The people believe in us. That's why they elected me. It's why they elected you as my vice president. We are at the perfect crossroads of communication, transportation, and sustainable resources. Humankind can soon be freed from the yolk of labor."

Dev squinted while sipping his coffee.

"You're not so sure?"

Their conversation was interrupted by a phone call from the secretary. "Mr. President, it's Dr. Farr from GraviWave lab on Earth's moon for you."

"Oh, yes, send it through."

A holographic projection of Farr shot out from the surface of the desk, catching her unaware as she was cleaning her glasses. She squinted at the room before putting on her glasses and jumped when she realized Dev and Custos were patiently waiting for her. "Mr. President!" she said, clearly embarrassed. "And Mr. Vice President. I'm sorry, I didn't know... I didn't—"

"That's quite alright, Dr. Farr," Custos reassured her.

"I'm sorry that I'm calling without much warning but I couldn't wait," she said, adjusting her glasses.

"What is it?" Custos asked.

"The gravitational waves that I told you about..."

"Yes, yes, you've detected new waves. Are you still picking them up?"

"Oh, yes, they haven't stopped since I talked to you last. They come in waves of varying pulsations and with a rhythm that repeats every twelve minutes."

"What do you make of it?"

"It's not natural. These waves are clearly overlapping over the softer background waves of the Big Bang. They're stronger waves as well, meaning that their source is much closer than the fourteen billion light-years from where the Big Bang occurred."

"How close?"

"Very close. Only hundreds of AUs away."

"That's not far at all."

Farr nodded. "Absolutely. Of course, there is a significant margin of error and we haven't been able to pinpoint its exact location yet."

"Could it be a pulsar?" Dev asked.

Custos shook his head. "No way, pulsars aren't big enough to create a gravity field that would ripple through space like this."

"I'm impressed Mr. President," Farr said. "That's exactly right. No pulsar or supernova that we know of could ever produce gravitational waves this big. These new waves are also non-random, making the chance that they are occurring naturally extremely low."

"Why would such a close alien race choose to communicate through gravity waves? Why not radio?" Custos remarked. "Have you been able to decipher any more of the message?"

She shook her head. "No, we only have that one word, 'Destroyer'."

"Is it some sort of threat?" Dev asked.

"We don't know. I hope not," Farr said. "The energy and mass required to create a wave is colossal—on a multi-planetary scale. If they're a threat, they're a very powerful enemy with advanced technology."

"A Dyson Sphere," Custos said. "The waves could be coming from a Dyson Sphere."

"A what?" Dev asked, confused.

Farr smiled with bemusement. "A Dyson Sphere? Something like that has never been found. We have no idea if a Dyson Sphere is even a real thing."

"A Dyson Sphere is the only thing I can think of that would explain intelligent life manipulating gravitational waves."

"Is someone going to tell me or..." Dev asked again.

Farr nodded. "A Dyson Sphere is a theoretical structure—well, more like a megastructure—that was hypothesized by a Dr. Freeman Dyson in the late twentieth century. Dr. Dyson speculated that if an intelligent species persisted for long enough and became sufficiently advanced, their energy requirements would exceed their ability to extract energy resources from their own planet. He thought that there would come a time in any advanced civilization where the energy requirements would demand the total energy output of an *entire* star."

"Like they would have to harness the energy of an entire star?" Dev asked.

Farr continued. "That's right. Something like this is obviously far beyond our engineering capacity to pull off. Some speculated that the radius of a Dyson Sphere would be about one AU. There aren't even enough raw materials in our solar system to create such a structure. But, regardless of the astronomical engineering challenges, it is theoretically possible to harness all of the power from a star." "How?" Dev asked.

"Imagine our own sun shining brightly in the center of the galaxy. And then imagine an advanced species with technology way beyond anything we can think of coming along and building an entire shell around the sun. They would cover every square mile with a spherical structure that would somehow absorb every photon and amount of nuclear radiation that came from the sun. This species could even live on the surface of the shell and colonize it with its own atmosphere."

"I can't possibly imagine a race that would actually need that amount of energy," Dev said.

"Neither can I, but the point of the concept of a Dyson Sphere is that if you look up in the galaxy and see a density of infrared emissions but not visible light from a star, it could very well be a star that has been captured by an alien race and surrounded by a sphere. But I don't know, exactly, what this has to do with gravitational waves." She looked at Custos, awaiting an explanation.

"A neutron star," Custos said. "If a Dyson Shell was built around a dense star, like a neutron star, they may be able to condense and harness the actual gravitational field of the star as well. We still barely understand how gravity ties in with quantum mechanics but we do know that there should be a tremendous amount of energy associated with gravity that we don't observe in our universe. If an alien race figured out how to harness the energy loss of gravity, they could very well build a sphere around a star to tap into its gravity as well. If they can harness the gravity, they could condense it and manipulate gravity waves."

"What's so special about a neutron star?" Dev asked.

"One teaspoon of matter from a neutron star weighs about ten million tons," Custos said.

"Hmm," Dr. Farr said, looking beyond them, thinking. "It is an interesting thought. How do you know so much about this, Mr. President?"

"Just one of my passing interests."

She looked over her glasses at him. "Astrophysics is your passing interest?"

"I'm going to be sending a team of linguists and cryptologists to your lab on the moon, Doctor. I'd like to figure out what we have on our hands as soon as possible," Custos said. "I personally know some very good people for this."

"That would be great, Mr. President. We're physicists but not decoders by any means. We'd be happy to have the assistance."

"I'd like to go into more detail, Dr. Farr, but we have an assembly to get to."

"Thank you, Mr. President, we'll chat soon."

"Gravity waves sent from aliens?" Dev said once the communication was terminated. "Are you worried?"

"Worry accomplishes nothing," Custos said, leading him out of the room. "We only look forward, never backward."

Custos entered the assembly hall, which was carpeted in deep purple and lined with marble rock. It was a large hall, paneled in yellow Martian wood with large tapestries hanging from the ceiling. Some of the tapestries depicted New Athens as a collection of skyscrapers in the middle with silver thread running to the five surrounding colonies that had later been formed once the original Martian colony was stable. Each colony was symbolized by their respective chief industries with Terrabel having the symbol of a tractor for agriculture, followed by a steel ore for Huelta, a hover car for Fairstar, a large redwood tree for Bend, and lastly, a film strip for the entertainment industry of Bloombeux.

There was another tapestry, created after the first colonies unified, that simply depicted the red planet of Mars over the black thread of space with silver stars sewn in the background. A crest hung above the planet with the words: *Live on, Our Hope of the Risen Red.* In the distance, amongst the stars, Earth had been stitched in dark blue and gray.

The table of the president sat in the middle of the hall, facing a semi-circle of desks where each of the New Athens city counselors sat, totaling twelve. Beyond the center core of leadership, there were several rows in stadium seating where elected delegates from the five colonies were seated.

The hall was already full of all Martian leadership as Custos walked down a center aisle toward his chair with Dev following. He glanced at the security patrol of several guarded robots and other human men in black suits who were speaking quiet commands into discrete mouthpieces. Crime on Mars was rare but Custos wasn't foolish enough to jeopardize the safety of Mars' leadership in one place. He waved and smiled, the skin-like material of his face bending with hundreds of tiny mechanical arms within, each with thousands of programmed schemes for facial expressions.

Looking around, he was satisfied that everyone from the colonies and the city council was in attendance. He had a personal relationship with almost every person of leadership in the room and knew everything about their families and homes. He even knew every single one of their pets' names. He smirked to himself, wondering why he didn't push for the presidency earlier in his political career. Yet, perhaps caution and slowly developing relationships was the best way to go about politicking, he speculated, and he was going to need all the goodwill he could get after what he was going to propose to the assembly.

As he approached the center of the hall, he noticed the face of one person with whom he had yet to figure out. Vana Iberian was a woman with an immediate, infectious personality that made people believe that she understood them. She had a narrow face with boney cheekbones creating a unique loveliness. She was a delegate of Terrabel and had subtly kept a distance from the recent, almost unanimous approval of the brilliant Custos. For several months, Custos had called on her both by phone and in person at her own doorstep, yet she had skillfully postponed meeting privately with him without being overtly unwilling. Custos did not like that she was an unknown. She smirked among the faces of the colonial delegates.

He otherwise received encouraging smiles and thumbs up from many of the colony delegates. It appeared that his personal visits to them over the last few weeks had paid off. Custos was confident he wouldn't have any resistance during the session—he had met with all the right people, barring Vana Iberian who held considerable influence in her colony over the automation of farming. There had been some silent opposition and Custos was certain that she was the source.

After seating, the assembly hall fell silent while the Martian anthem played through speakers. Every person in attendance held their hand over their heart and looked up at the center tapestry that hung behind Custos, depicting New Athens and the surrounding colonies.

The anthem ended and Custos turned to the assembly. "Ladies and gentlemen of the city council, I thank you for accepting my request to assemble today to review and consider new legislation drafted by my administration. I also warmly extend my appreciation to our visiting colonial delegates that come representing Terrabel, Huelta, Fairstar, Bloombeux, and Bend. I remind our delegates that we will have a chance for open discussion of the proposed legislation toward the end of our assembly today. There will be no voting on legislation today. Voting will proceed at a date to be determined. Ladies and gentlemen, let us have a seat and begin."

The assembly shuffled into their seats while Custos took the lectern. He rattled off some perfunctory recognitions and achievements of various people in attendance as well as mentioned budget details from the coming quarter while assuring them that they would have a detailed budget assembly in the months to come. Once most of the housekeeping business had finished, Custos could finally bring up the entire reason that he had called an assembly.

"Council members and delegates, I'd like to now propose legislation that I believe could be the start of an economic revolution." Several of the council members perked up at his sudden change in tone. "We have arrived at a point in human history that is unprecedented. We live in a society of two hundred million where poverty has been abolished. Homelessness is unheard of. Not a single child in our great city and colonies goes hungry. Education and healthcare are universal to every citizen alive. We have achieved this because we had the benefit of starting over again at square one when the first colony to Mars landed here and established what would become New Athens. Our ancestors had learned from the mistakes of humankind —from the failures of America and Central Cell. Hard work and self-sufficiency were inborn in their descendants, making the productive and advanced society in which we still live." He paused, reading the audience. Once they saw that he was going to give a speech, their eyes began to wander. Vana Iberian, however, was staring right at him.

"We live in an enlightened day but there is more to accomplish. We are at a pivotal moment where we can sit back and bask in our accomplishments, or we can take the next step without hesitation. I believe men and women of Mars are ready to take the next step and transcend an economic structure on which humanity has relied since the birth of humankind. This crutch of which I speak of... is currency. Money. We don't need it anymore."

An audible gasp rippled through the assembly. A commotion broke out amongst the council members and the delegates, completely ignoring Custos' pleas for order.

Custos held his hands up to the assembly. "We can free the average person from the burden of earning. We have the raw resources, automation, and almost endless Martian land to sustain us. People will work, but not for money. They'll work for themselves, their families, and their love of our country. We've already carefully cultivated this attitude in requiring civic service in order to be a citizen. We no longer need a stick *or* a carrot. Our citizens will pursue their desires for service and education, fostering a society of raw creativity. And what of those menial jobs of packaging, processing, and manufacturing? The answer is automation in a thousand forms. We have the artificial intelligence to fill in the gaps of employment that might go abandoned once people learn that they no longer need to earn a living."

"But how?" a voice from the council finally interjected. It was Dr. Benjamin Cher, a balding man with a grumpy disposition. "How could you possibly do this?"

"Slowly," Custos reassured. "We pour money into housing, giving outrageous tax incentives to home builders and rental owners to build and rent for no cost. We give them tax breaks for using robot labor. We fully automate agriculture, something that we've been capable of for several years now. If we fully control the means of production of most food, we can set the price, which would be nothing. We then give irresistible tax breaks to markets, vendors, and shops to sell their goods at historically low prices. There are many ways that we can go about this. We can show the people by the policies that we institute that they don't even need money. It'll become an inconvenience to them like the three random pennies in the bottom of your pocket. Currency would suddenly have no value, but instead of economic collapse, we have liberation because we'll be bolstered by an extremely well-grounded infrastructure—"

"Custos the Liar!" a booming voice rang throughout the hall.

A single man stood in the back of the assembly, beyond the seated delegates, near the entrance. He wore a shredded cloak with a hood that covered half of his face. He leaned sickly on a crudely fashioned, wooden crutch and glared at his appalled audience. He stood beneath the tapestry of Mars, shining in gold with Earth just a small patchwork of blue and grey in the background.

In one hand was a single torch with large flames licking up at the fringe of the tapestry.

"Sir—" Custos tried to intervene as security guards swarmed around him.

"He is coming!" the man said, bringing the torch to the tapestry. "He is coming to reclaim what was lost!" he admonished as flames leaped up the tapestry. The old fabric caught fire quickly and lit the entire chamber with bright orange as black smoke billowed up to the ceiling. The guards tackled the man as the flames consumed the shimmering Mars. "He is coming!" the disheveled man yelled once more, the guards binding his hands. "He is coming to free His people!"

As the assembly hall erupted in commotion, all the lights—the grand chandeliers hanging from the ceilings and the colored hues of violet and indigo lining the floors—went out. The chamber fell into darkness with echoes of detonations in the distance.

Custos' speech had been cut short.

CHAPTER 11

OCTOBER 11TH, 1988

The mornings were different now for Timothy Straus.

For most of his life, the voices had been a constant source of worry and shame. It took several years into his marriage to even reveal their existence to Jo. He'd spent hours talking with psychiatrists about how to get rid of them, but now? Things were a little different.

The voices came and went like a storm in his mind, a cacophony of mixed syllables, whispers, shouts, and broken conversations. He had never been able to make out what they were saying. The voices were like a light beacon, far away in the ocean—a vague light flashing in the distance. It wasn't until the last several weeks that the beacon had grown stronger. The voices were getting closer... they were distilling into coherent individuals. Every now and then, he heard complete sentences stand out from the crowd.

And now he was emboldened. Each morning, he took time to meditate, to draw out the voices in an attempt to dissect what they were trying to tell him. He hid away in his secret basement room for hours, listening and clenching his eyes tight. The voices came along with streams of numbers, derivations, and mathematical expressions. Like trying to paint a fleeting sunrise, he would jot down the information—most of it nothing more than interrupted nonsense once it was finally on a page. It was a puzzle, he theorized, and he was getting random pieces. It was only a matter of time before he could put the whole thing together and figure out how to get his Casimir Drive to work.

I'm going to revolutionize transportation.

He was onto something larger than himself. There was something far away, not any earthly place but something beyond the scope of his own reality that thumped in the distance. It was a force with tendrils stretching out at him, calling and beckoning him like a magnetic field. Alone, in his secret room, it was what he now referred to as the Rift—a tear, a well, a vacuum that transcended space and touched on his thoughts at an increasing rate. The Rift was opening, drawing close, and spilling its secrets. He currently only understood a fraction about what it was and why it was there.

Straus smirked to himself as he awoke on Monday morning, pleased that he had fired Dr. Simmons as his psychiatrist. As far as Straus was concerned, Simmons—or anyone attempting to psycho-analyze him—was nothing but an obstacle to the Rift. Now that he had freed himself from someone who only saw his behavior within the confines of mental illness, Straus was able to discover whatever it was that was happening. He felt like he was on the edge of a frontier. With the excitement of transforming the world within his grasp, he felt it easier to ignore the dark edges of his mind—a looming figure who watched him. Like a phantom at the periphery of waking life, he was being watched. There was a dread that settled there—a fear that waxed when he fed it with an inexplicable feeling of hate.

He shook off the mental omens as he showered, shaved, and got ready for the day. Looking over at the bed, he noticed Jo wasn't there and wondered if she had even come to bed at all last night. Ignoring the guilt that would only bring him down, he got dressed, made some coffee in the kitchen, and left for work without seeing a trace of Jo or the baby. He knew she was having a hard time with the changes but there wasn't anything he could do about it at the moment. There was too much work to do, too much to explore, and too much at stake.

The future couldn't wait for Jo.

And he wouldn't be held back.

And held back is exactly how he felt given that Van Wert still insisted that he teach his classes while he continued his work on the Casimir Drive. Fortunately, he had at least been given upper-level undergraduates to teach. He'd grown tired of teaching the same rudimentary basics to a large auditorium of uninterested students. His new group was small and eager to learn, especially since news of something big in his lab had gotten out across the physics and chemistry department.

Straus arrived on time to the small classroom and greeted his students while opening up his notes. There were a handful of students in the front row with a few that trailed into the room.

"Who can tell me about general relativity?" Straus asked, picking up a piece of chalk.

No one in the class raised a hand.

"Anyone? Let's talk conceptually about it first before we delve into the derivation and its practical applications." He rolled up his sleeves and set the piece of chalk back down. "So, Albert Einstein was sitting in an office one day in Germany, working as a patent clerk. He was one of those rare people who actually wondered about how things work. He didn't just take things at face value only because that's what everyone believed. He was... curious as any good scientist should be. Einstein, at this point, was kind of a nobody. He had been rejected by some good schools and decided to work in a patent office. But, he still wondered. One day, he was thinking about gravity. He knew that Isaac Newton had figured out the math that *described* gravity's influence on objects—an apple, a ball in the air, one planet tugging on another planet, and so forth. Newton definitely came up with the math that would describe gravity's behavior but he never really knew what gravity *was*. Newton himself admitted that he himself didn't know *how* gravity influenced things. Einstein suspected that there was much more to the story about gravity. I mean, think about it. Can any of you tell me what gravity *is*?"

"It's Earth's pull on matter," a girl in the front row said without raising her hand. "The gravity of Earth makes matter fall towards its own mass."

"Hang on though," Straus said, pointing at her. "You just told me what gravity can do, but you didn't tell what gravity *is*." The girl fell silent, something that Straus' students had grown accustomed to whenever they tried to answer his questions. "We think we know what light is," Straus continued, "it's a wave of photons. We know what electricity is, it's a flow of free electrons. But gravity?" He waited for another willing participant from the class to speak up but no one responded. "This was the dilemma for Einstein. He knew that we hadn't figured out exactly what gravity actually was. So," Straus said, leaning on the desk, "he imagined what would happen if someone fell off of a building. He thought about a man falling and he wondered if instead of the man being pulled—what if he was actually being *pushed* by gravity? Einstein was brilliant, not necessarily because he was a good mathematician but because he could think about old problems in a creative way.

"So, he sat there thinking, 'I bet this is how gravity works, now how can I prove it?' He theorized, and came up with the math to support it; that gravity wasn't this unseen force that reached up and grabbed you. He figured that when you fall toward a planet, you are being *pushed* from behind from bent space. And the space is bent by the mass of Earth." He paused, seeing confused looks. "I know this isn't an intuitive thing to understand—well, unless you're Einstein.

"Space itself is not a static vacuum. If you place a large object, like a planet inside of space, the space around that object will warp and bend toward the planet. And if you happen to be a spaceship that's floating along and get close enough to a planet, the bent space will actually push you from behind toward the planet. So, there's nothing pulling you, you're simply riding a wave of bent space. And the bigger the planet, or star, the more you are pushed toward that object.

"It turns out," Straus continued, "that the space that bends around a planet will not only push on matter that comes within the gravity well, but it will bend light beams as well. Einstein theorized all of this stuff and came up with a mathematical construct before he even tested any of this stuff. Of course, someone can dream up math and theories all day long, but it's not going to do you any good until you prove it."

"So, how did he prove it?" the same girl in the front asked.

"He figured that our sun, which, of course, has massive gravity, would bend starlight as it passed behind the sun. So, a bunch of astronomers set out to prove the theory during a total solar eclipse. During the eclipse, they observed starlight as it moved past the sun and they calculated that the light actually bent around the sun as the light passed by. Not only did the light bend, but it bent by the exact degree to which Einstein's math predicted it would. Once this was discovered, Einstein became internationally famous and completely turned gravitational physics on its head." Straus noticed a few of the students perk up at this.

"Another twist to the story was that Einstein figured out that not only is matter affected by gravity, but time as well. Did you know that right this minute, if I had two clocks and I left one on my desk here and I shot the other up into space far away from Earth's gravity, the clock in space would start speeding up?"

"Wow," a student in the back said.

"And this isn't science fiction. It's been done. We know that the more gravity you have, the slower time passes. So much, in fact, that if you were to hang outside the edge of a black hole, something with unbelievable gravity, you would age about ten thousand times slower than you would on Earth. The amazing thing about Einstein is that he also predicted the existence of black holes long before they were discovered just about fifteen years ago."

"What would happen if someone just went inside of a black hole?" another student asked.

"You're not the first one to wonder that. The answer is, we don't really know. We're pretty certain that the gravity of a black hole, which is so great that not even light can escape, would pretty much crush and destroy any person or thing that went into it. However, to an outside observer, it would happen over an excruciatingly slow amount of time. The point is, the effect of gravity is *relative* to where you are. That is one of the reasons it's called general relativity. I think it would serve you as a class of upper-level physics students to learn some of the gravitational field equations that Einstein wrote. As you learn how to use them, you should know that they are perfect and their predictability has been tested over and over again."

Straus continued on with the lecture, delving into field equations and various components of theory. Something about the subject matter of black holes and gravity felt right to him. He had always known the theories, but there was now something... personal about it. And with that inevitable feeling of closeness with the math, his face heated with something else—something dreadful.

It was hate.

But... for who?

Straus' new lab was in a brand-new building on campus, deep within the basement. He needed two levels of clearance badges just to get into the elevator. His lab staff had swelled from only Duke and Chou Jia to ten more graduate students whom he had personally vetted along with another associate professor from the school, who could barely keep up with the math that Straus was throwing at her. Dr. Janis Holloway greeted Straus as he got off the elevator.

"Good afternoon, Dr. Straus," Holloway said. She stood just outside the elevator as if waiting for his arrival.

"Oh, hi, how's everything going?" Straus looked past her, down the long row of generators and lab benches that lined the lab. "Has Duke been in yet?"

Holloway appeared displeased as she knew Straus had entrusted his graduate student over her with day-to-day operations of the lab. "He's down at the track panels, trying to reconfigure something..." she said, disinterested. "I was wondering if we could have a brief meeting today, I'd like to go over some things—"

"Well, Jack Van Wert is coming by later. I'm sure we can go over anything then." Straus brushed by her, donning a lab coat.

"But..." she said, trailing off as Straus walked past her into the lab.

The laboratory was a square of four long hallways that bordered a glass-enclosed area containing a new model of the Casimir Drive. Instead of the stationary Drive within a room, they had built the Drive on a circular track inside of a dome-shaped enclosure, 25 meters in diameter. The Casimir Drive, the size of a riding lawn-mower, was connected to a plastic hull that was molded to look like the front of a Corvette, painted bright red. It was a mock version of what they envisioned: an engine that would propel cars, trains, or even spaceships. Duke insisted on making the mock-Corvette himself, and spent several days bolting it to the Drive. The entire apparatus looked like a circular dog track, but instead of greyhounds running in circles, their Casimir Drive pushed the plastic hood and windshield of a mock-Corvette around a track.

Straus found Duke crouched outside of the track, peering into an opened panel in the floor. He had removed several electrical grids and wires and was currently staring at the equipment, tapping his chin.

"What happened here?" Straus asked.

Duke whipped his head up at Straus, a pair of goggles flying off of his face and sliding across the tiled floor. "Oh... whoops," Duke said. "I'm not quite sure. I think it's an extension of our main problem—we're generating too much heat."

"How long did the run go this morning?"

Duke sighed. "Only four seconds."

"That's even worse than the last time." Straus looked in at the Casimir Drive, sitting motionless inside the domed room. "How fast did you run it?"

"One-fifty."

"Damn."

"We can't run it any faster. The whole thing would fry."

Straus sighed. He realized he may soon face the facts that he had to create a way to funnel off excess heat. Since building the newer model of the Drive, they had still only been able to run it for no more than ten seconds.

Duke scratched his chin. "The whole system just heats up too quickly. I think we're burning through our dampeners too fast. It's getting to the point that they need to be replaced after almost every run."

"Okay, let's change them out and see if we can do better than four seconds. If the Drive goes for longer, then we know that we're probably in for a big rehaul of the cooling system."

"I always figured we'd have to install a water run-off."

Straus nodded. "Something that'll set us back several weeks. Maybe months."

Dr. Holloway approached the two and loudly cleared her throat. "Dr. Straus, can I have a quick word?"

Straus looked at her and struggled to hide his annoyance. Explaining every little step and problem to the woman was becoming burdensome. "Can we talk later?"

"Fine." She left the two alone to commiserate about a new cooling system.

After several hours of tinkering with new heat dampeners, they made minor adjustments to calibrations of the accelerometers that detect gravitational distortions. The lab crew readied for a new run. Straus and Duke sat at the main computer terminal on the other side of the windows of the track while Chou Jia and a few other lab technicians were perched behind another row of large computers. Straus set the Drive to one hundred and fifty miles an hour. The Casimir Drive shuddered as the thin, quantum plates of its engine created negative pressure. The Drive vibrated with more frequency and buzzed with a low humming noise that filled the lab.

"Doing fine," Duke reassured Straus when he saw him looking at the heat level.

"Okay, here we go." Straus pointed as a thin ripple in space appeared behind the Drive. The ripple extended from the back, like an oblong fracture in visible space, swiveling around a horizontal axis. It thickened and squirmed as light refracted through. Straus found that gazing at it for too long was disorienting, creating an illusion of distance and proximity simultaneously.

"It's so... pretty," Holloway remarked, staring at the bending light.

A loud snap cracked into the air followed by the mock-Corvette and Drive bolting forward. The Drive quickly spun around the track. "How is it... moving?" Holloway asked. "This is... this is amazing."

Straus smiled. "Seems that Van Wert was too preoccupied with making you a department spy that he didn't even bother to tell you what I'm doing here."

"I... no—"

"We believe that the gravity wave initially contracts, which, of course, wouldn't actually propel the vehicle forward but would suck it in. In fact, during the initial contraction, we lock the Drive in place so it doesn't get pulled into gravity. However, after it contracts, the wave relaxes and expands back out, pushing the undistorted space around it which subsequently flings the vehicle forward."

"I had no idea..." Holloway crept closer toward the glass, watching the Drive spin inside the domed room.

Suddenly, a loud *pop* rang out from the Drive followed by a trail of smoke. The back of the Drive glowed red hot as it sputtered and slowed to a stop. Straus sighed, looking over at Duke. At the back of the Drive, liquid copper melted out.

"I thought we were past this," Straus complained.

"What happened?" Holloway asked.

"Too much heat. We can barely get the Drive to run for more than a few seconds. Too much heat is created by the coil inside and it stalls the Drive," Duke said as he analyzed data from the run at a computer dashboard. "Yeah, Tim, this run generated way more heat than I've ever seen. No idea why."

"I really thought we got past this," Straus said. "That copper alloy was the one. That was the one that we were certain could run the Drive without melting. Maybe there's some sort of feedback loop of energy that we don't detect?"

"You use copper?" Holloway asked.

"Copper, gold, platinum, silver, iron, and many alloys," Duke answered. "We need a metallic cartridge to funnel heat through the Drive. It helps conduct the negative quantum energy. We had been using that particular copper alloy," he said, pointing at the dripping metal, "for the last few runs without any problems. We've tried hundreds of different alloy compositions. None have gotten the Drive to run for more than nine or ten seconds."

"This is a step back," Straus said. Duke simply nodded while the rest of the lab crew diverted their eyes from Straus.

Straus closed his eyes, trying to visualize the math. At times, so much data poured in from the Rift but it was too chaotic and random. It took him weeks to even piece together any sort of mathematical expression. He had been searching over his notes from his basement room for the last several months about the excess heat but nothing made sense. What was strange was the familiarity of the math that came streaming into his mind. He felt that, given enough time, he would've come to the same conclusions himself. He usually dreaded the deluge of voices and math but now would've been a welcome time even if it *was* accompanied by a splitting headache.

"Dr. Straus," a deep voice echoed from behind. It was Jack Van Wert standing with a furrowed brow. Thick-rimmed glasses extended down his nose. He peered into the dome. "How are things?"

"Jack, it's not really a good time for a visit," Straus said without turning around.

Holloway, noticing Van Wert's disapproving frown under his beard, backed away from the glass and retreated toward him.

"We need to meet, Tim," Van Wert said, authoritatively.

Straus quickly flipped around. "Fine, let's have a meeting. Let's have a meeting about meetings. Let's have a meeting where we make a schedule for the entire year about when we're going to have our meetings. Let's have a meeting while we keep trying to fix the same problem that we've been having for the last three months. Do you want us to show some progress to the state when they come and see what we're doing with their money? Do you want us to revolutionize an industry or just become a dead-end pet project?"

"Tim—Dr. Straus. There's no need—"

"I'll let you know when *I* want to have a meeting. I'll be working all day and night. Please just let us work." Straus walked briskly past him and took off his lab coat. "Duke, let's go over the data." Straus,

Duke, and Chou Jia left the lab crew and a shocked Van Wert and disappeared into a side office.

They left Van Wert and Holloway standing there, silent and angry.

Jo hadn't said anything to her husband. She had left his secret room, undisturbed, and crept out the way she had entered. They spent the weekend apart. She hadn't wanted to see him, especially after the bizarre chess games. The way he stared at the board, fixated on the game as if he had left the living room and was in his own place—it left Jo haunted. She figured that he had likely been in the lab for the last two days. He didn't call, didn't check in, and didn't even say hello to James. The only indication she had that he was still around was midnight footsteps creeping in through the front door and his leaving later in the morning.

She called Straus' psychiatrist, Dr. Simmons, who not only mentioned that he couldn't talk about her husband's mental health with her but that if he wasn't suicidal, he couldn't be admitted against his will. She tried to explain Straus' basement room but the man hurriedly ended the phone call. He seemed relieved to no longer be pestered by his visits with her husband.

She had spent most of the weekend teary-eyed and feeling help-less. She wanted the old Tim back, not the new arrogant man who barely had time for his family. There was no one else to go to for help. Her mother had been out of the country, and her sister had been out of her life for over a decade. His secret room kept flashing in her mind—so many handwritten papers with math and chaotic sentences. He had clearly spent hours meticulously hanging them from the ceiling, peering into the madness of his own mind as it was reflected back to him. What she hadn't figured out was that if Straus was in a rough patch or if he was descending, irreversibly, into a psychosis, it would... change him forever.

She had spent most of the weekend carefully peeling back the covering from the couch cushions. There was a small pile of fluffy yellow fabric collecting in the carpet where she left bits of the couch. She considered the options over and over again and left the house.

Biting her lip, she paced the hallway outside of a row of offices at the university, glancing at every person that came down the hall only to be disappointed. After an hour of waiting, she heard the stomping feet of a large man as he returned to his office after lunch—Jack Van Wert. He noticed Jo with a surprised look as he took out his keys to open his office door.

"Mrs. Straus?" he said, breathing heavy.

"Dr. Van Wert, hello, I'm sorry to surprise you like this."

"Surprise me? Oh, you're not... you're not looking for Tim?"

"No." She glanced sideways. "I'd like to talk to you. I'm sorry I didn't call ahead."

Van Wert paused, forming a small *o* with his mouth. "Um, yes, we can talk. What's this about?"

Jo motioned with her head toward his office. "Can we chat in your office?"

Van Wert fumbled with his keys and opened the door. "Of course, of course, come right in."

Jo took a seat in front of his desk without a word and stared nervously out the window.

"Mrs. Straus—"

"Jo."

"Jo, yes, Jo, what is this about?"

"It's about Tim."

"Yes, of course," he sighed. "I've just returned from a rather... unpleasant conversation with him."

Jo looked back across the desk for a moment trying to surmise how much Jack Van Wert knew about Straus' worsening mental state. "How is he doing in the lab?"

"Tim is, uh, well, Tim is doing some excellent work."

"Yes... but how *is* he?"

"He's acting different to be totally honest."

"Different how?"

"Irritable. Just a few minutes ago, he basically threw me out of his lab."

"Hmm." Jo looked back out the window. "I'm not surprised. He's getting that way with me at home. He's acting different."

"The work he's doing is starting to get to his head, I'm afraid. He used to be so approachable. I'd meet with him every week and go over his professional goals. He used to confide in me about certain... things. Now, it's just the big 'Dr. Timothy Straus Show'."

"I'm worried he's not well."

"I know he's always had problems, but actually, I think he's mentally getting better. It's his professionalism that's suffering now."

"No, he's getting worse. He's just hiding it better."

"What do you mean?"

"He comes home, acts like everything's fine, doesn't spend any time with me or the baby, and just goes down into the basement and locks himself in a room all night."

"I could understand if he's bringing work from home now, he truly is accomplishing amazing things in the lab... somehow."

"I went into the room where he's been working," she said despondently.

"Okay..."

"It's very... odd."

"In what way?"

Jo lifted her purse to the desk and pulled out a roll of papers bound together with a rubber band. One by one, she laid out the sheets of papers, about a dozen in total, for Van Wert to see.

"What is this?" he asked, lifting up a page.

"Does any of this make any sense?"

Van Wert studied the paper. There were mathematical expressions scrawled in every direction, often overlapping. Some expressions were unfinished, others appeared to have been completed but cut off at the end of the page. Throughout the math, there were words and sentences, mostly illegible. He lifted another page and studied the math for a moment and then went onto the next page.

"Is it the same stuff that he's working on in the lab?" Jo asked.

"Um..." He was looking from one page to the next. "This is strange. The math here *does* make sense, but it's incomplete—randomly distributed. One page has math that pertains to general relativity while also containing several expressions that are related to thermochemistry." He shuffled through more pages, scanning. "The solution to one mathematical expression starts on one page but finishes on another. There's also a lot of math that I don't recognize at all—several attempts at new derivations that I've never seen. It's hard to say. There are all these words mixed together in between the math, making it a little difficult. It's all very incomplete. Some words of someone who is very angry..." He squinted at a particular word. "What is a *Custos?*"

"I have no idea. I just need to know, does any of it make sense or is it all just... crazy?"

"No, no, there's a lot here," he said, flipping through the pages again. "Hmm," he said as if by accident.

"What?"

But he didn't answer. He took five of the pages and laid them out, side by side. He then took a blank sheet of paper from his desk and copied down some of the scattered math until it formed a complete expression on his new page.

"*What?*" he whispered.

"What is it?"

"The bastard's already solved it."

"Solved what?"

"The excess heat problem he is having—a problem that he currently doesn't know the solution to. Only... the solutions are right here in his own handwriting—scattered amongst these pages. The math shows a compensation for excess heat which would clearly allow the Drive to run for much longer than it ever has." He flipped a laminated periodic table out of his desk and looked over the properties of all the metals and then scribbled down some notes. "After combining the thermal capacity of several metals into new alloys on the page and plugging them into Tim's thermoregulation equations,

I've just found the perfect copper alloy composition that could conduct the run-off heat for the Drive."

"I don't understand..."

Van Wert stroked his white beard for a moment and looked back at Jo. "Can you bring me more of his notes?"

CHAPTER 12

SEPTEMBER 4TH, 2098

Cal paced around the fountain at Reagan Square, periodically looking over his shoulder and half expecting to see a Central Cell police squad moving in at any moment. Once he was sure that he was only surrounded by joggers and mothers with their children, he relaxed and even laughed to himself. *I'm really not in any trouble, I didn't even do anything wrong,* he thought. His stomach tightened up, however, when he saw Raz walk up and over a small hill at the edge of the park. *Should I really be trusting this man? What do I even really know about him?*

"Tell me right now who you are."

Raz put up one index finger. "I'll tell you what you want to know, pal." He folded his arms and looked back at Cal. "But it might take some time."

"Why?" Cal yelled.

"Might want to lower your voice a little, you are talking to an illegal citizen right now."

"Stop messing with me."

"Cal—Caleb... I'm sorry. I know I've been a little cryptic."

"A little?"

"Okay, a lot. There are reasons. I have a big story to tell you, but it's not the kind of story that can be rushed. Some must be shown."

"Well, in the meantime you almost got me arrested. How did you even get back into Central? And into the academy?"

"I'm... very good at what I do. You can be as good as I am."

"What're you talking about?"

"I have a certain skill."

"What skill?"

"It's not something we can talk about right here." His eyes shifted. "I mean, I think it would be safe but there is a," he closed one eye, "very small chance of that woman over there overhearing us and alerting the police about our plans to leave Central."

"What?" Cal flipped around and saw a woman sitting halfway down the fountain, looking into a baby carriage. "She can't hear us."

"She most likely won't, but I'm positive that it does happen at least twice if you let this scenario play out enough times."

Cal paused. Oddly, he had a vague idea of what Raz was saying. He remembered all of the different scenarios that he saw of his own ship hitting the asteroid. In most of them, he died. It was only in that one fracture that he saw his ship glide into a tunnel. There was so much he wanted to ask Raz but was still hesitant.

"Will you let me show you something first?" Raz asked.

"Show me what?"

"Injustice."

Cal paused. "Why should I go anywhere with you?"

"Because I know more about you than you do. I will tell you about the voices. I can tell you the exact reason that all of this is happening to you. You're different from most people. You care. You care about your cook and the servants around your house. You wonder what happens to people if they leave Central. You cared that your doorman got deported. I think you have a gift and I think you deserve to develop it. We share this gift."

"But why you? You just happened to be my doorman *and* you're also in the same... condition as me?"

"There are no coincidences if you wait long enough. But there also aren't any coincidences when you get a job as a low-level employee where a person lives and you observe them most of their life."

"What! You've just been stalking me?"

"Pretty much. Now, get into my ship, I've got plenty of candy in it." Raz walked away from the fountain and looked back. "I promise I will explain everything. Come on."

Cal stood for a moment, considering his options.

"Or, you can go back home to your mother, wonder if you'll get kicked out of the academy, and never know what you really are."

For a moment, Cal wanted to do exactly that. He wanted to run back to his room, likely cry into a pillow, and forget that he'd ever met Raz. True, the man knew things he had no right knowing—he knew about the voices. But did that mean Cal should trade his quaint ignorance to learn more about himself? He closed his eyes, only realizing then how seductive his life of privilege had been.

Noticing his hesitation, Raz said, "The choice is yours. You're always free to make whatever decision you want. And this is the true essence of your privilege, Cal. You have the privilege of choice where most have the curse of consignment."

"Who?"

"Let me show you."

Cal nodded and followed Raz.

They took a streamcar together and rode it through downtown. Pillars of skyscrapers and towers loomed above the streamway as hundreds of thousands of streamcars scurried throughout the metropolis. Dozens of blocks flitted by, full of commercial towers for the stock exchange, advertising firms, entertainment industry, and gaming. The downtown area stretched for many more miles as Cal became lost in his thoughts. Woven in between the beautiful skyscrapers were the recognizable gray and squatty buildings of the Central Cell. They were interspersed everywhere within the city. The streamcar dove through a series of underground tunnels and emerged on the other side of downtown where Cal saw the towering gray, obelisk-like building of Central Cell headquarters. It had been built on a hill, making it appear taller than the surrounding structures.

"Must be where that agent from Central came from," Cal said, pointing at the headquarters.

"Who?" Raz asked.

"The agent from Revenue and Inquisitions who just told me I'm a criminal for sending you money."

"What're you talking about?"

"You seem to know everything about me but you don't know that I was almost arrested because of you?"

"Oh, uh, I guess not. I know a lot about you but I don't know what you're doing every second of the day. Jeez, get over yourself." Raz looked through the window. "But, no, no lowly R and I agent would be working at the Central headquarters. In fact, there's not even a lot of human beings that work at the HQ. It's mostly a gigantic, automated bean counter. All data processing that accounts for individual and family wealth is kept track at the headquarters."

"Why do they care so much?"

"Hasn't anyone told you? Individual income is the fabric of our society."

"Agent Starken told me I almost destroyed Central by sending you a couple of brics."

Raz scoffed. "Central propaganda. The propagation of ideas is far stronger than any threat of violence or prison bars. If they can get the people to believe it, they don't need any other means of control. Central creates consent through its propaganda."

Their streamcar left the main streamway and descended through a series of long tubes that were offshoots from the downtown area. Apartment buildings and homes soared by until they weren't even passing residential areas.

"Where are we going?" Cal finally asked.

"Industrial part of town. Ever been?"

"No."

"Not much to see but it's really the only place to reasonably hide anything."

Warehouses and cranes sprawled across the landscape with deep green foliage beyond, indicating the limits of Central Cell borders. Just beyond the green forest, Cal saw a tall black wall that towered above the forest trees. It was smooth and glossy, ensuring that it couldn't be climbed. Security towers studded along the length of the wall as far as the eye could see. There were turrets mounted within the towers—guards stalking the walls like warriors atop ramparts.

Raz noticed Cal staring at the wall. "Not the first wall to be built to keep humans in or out. But," he looked at Cal, "it could be the last. Anyways, it couldn't stop me from getting back in."

"So, you *were* deported?"

"Yes, but it was a happy coincidence. I needed to check on things in the real world anyway."

"How did you get back in? Wouldn't Central Air flag your ship as unofficial as soon as you came within the city limits?"

"Oh, that's nothing. I just put a fake receiver in the ship. That, and I'm just really good at acting like a Central stooge over the radio. Every now and then, they'll catch onto fake receivers and change their access codes, and sometimes I need to hightail it back out."

Cal looked uneasy at him.

"Relax, it doesn't happen that often."

"And you just come and go from Central all the time?"

"It's nice to get out, see how the ninety-nine percent left of humanity is living."

"Ninety-nine percent?"

"Most people do not live like you, Cal."

"I didn't know it was so many—"

"You don't know what they don't tell you."

Raz jumped out when the streamcar came to a stop. Cal was growing tired of the man constantly leaving him with unfinished thoughts but he reluctantly followed him out. They walked for several minutes, in between long construction sites where enormous amounts of earth had been dug. Many construction workers eyed the two with passing curiosity and returned to work. They made their way past several long rows of storage facilities and warehouses until they arrived at what appeared to be a junkyard.

Without stopping, Raz ducked under an alcove of twisted metal and disappeared underneath a tower of discarded construction equipment, rolls of old fabric, and large clumps of concrete rebar. Cal followed him through a dark tunnel which led to a small clearing within the heaps of junk. In the middle of the clearing was a freighter ship with a boxy cargo bay attached at the back end. Two stubby wings stuck out from the small cockpit. A Casimir Drive engine protruded backward from the roof of the cockpit and overlaid the detachable cargo bay.

Cal asked, "Why does a freighter need a Casimir Drive?"

"It's a TexasH freighter. Designed to transport goods to the Mars colony."

"You go to Mars?"

"Occasionally."

"Why?"

"I check in on their progress. Mars doesn't have a lot of the same metal ore that Earth has. They also can't farm much in the colony so they designed these freighters a few years back and started a transport route to Earth. They'll need more supplies until the terraforming process is fully complete."

"Terraforming started on Mars?"

Raz nodded. "Oh, yes. Central Cell has sent a lot of funding to the colony. They want to claim a piece of the natural resource pie once the red canyons run blue with water. Central Cell doesn't like a lot of this stuff to get out. They don't want people flying to Mars to try to settle there. They've got big plans to set up a colony there. I've got other plans, however."

The ship wasn't aerodynamically built, although Cal guessed that if the cargo bay was removed, it might be quite an agile little ship. He realized that Raz probably valued it for its inconspicuous appearance. He suddenly missed his aero8 academy ship and winced at the thought of never flying it again.

"They're good ships, these TexasH freighters. They're well-built—could probably last a hundred years, given you've got enough copper to run the Casimir Drive. Climb aboard," Raz said after pressing a button on his cell phone. The back shutters on the ship opened, exposing a cargo bay that led to the front cockpit. Cal found his seat and strapped on a lap seatbelt. Raz also strapped himself in and fired up the engines. Their takeoff was steady and vertical. The massive center of Central Cell shrunk beneath them as the bottom thrusters jettisoned the ship.

Cal felt a thrill leap inside him that was interrupted by a crackling voice in their headsets. "Trans Forty-Three-Sixty, please identify."

"Central Air, this is Trans Forty-Three-Sixty requesting airspace for leave of Central Cell domain," Raz replied without hesitation as if he'd been a pilot for years.

"Destination and purpose?" the air controller questioned in a perfunctory tone.

"New Athens colony, copper shipment."

"Hold please," the controller said. After several moments, the controller's voice returned. "Please return to Central Cell for processing."

Cal flashed a frightened look at Raz. Raz simply responded, "No, sorry."

"Excuse me?" the controller said.

"No, we're leaving, sorry," Raz said, blithely.

"Ground your ship immediately or it will be grounded for you," the man threatened.

Raz killed the line and smiled at Cal.

"What are you doing!" Cal yelled. "You think they're going to let us just leave? They're going to shoot us out of the sky! Why did I agree to come with you? You're crazy!"

"We're off!" Raz said, completely ignoring Cal. He punched the thrusters, making the TexasH rocket forward at full speed. Cal sucked back into his seat and quickly strapped a top harness around his shoulders.

"I'll never be let back into Central again!"

"When I'm done with you, you'll come and go wherever you want," Raz said, making some adjustments on the dashboard. Thin clouds streaked past them as they cruised over Central Cell, leaving double streamers of burning fuel trailing.

In an instant, the back engines of an X8 combat ship burned in front of their cockpit. The ship easily glided in front of their bulky fuselage and matched its speed as if trying to escort them. The pilot shouted from the radio, "Ground your ship immediately!"

Cal's heart was pounding in his chest. "We better just do what she says," he said, ashamed.

"How do you think we can get out of this situation?" Raz asked casually.

"We get out of this situation by doing exactly what she says or she shoots us down. You may not know how Central Air works but I do. There is no tolerance when it comes to Air Law infractions."

"No, no, just look out there—at that ship, at the sky. How do we get out of this?"

Cal shook his head. "Please, just land the ship before you get us killed."

Raz squinted through the windshield, hunching his shoulders. "I can see it. You should try, too."

The fighter pilot cut into the radio again, "You have thirty seconds to comply or I will shoot you down." She maintained a constant speed directly ahead of them.

"We're in a bulky freighter ship against an experienced Central pilot in a twin-engine X8 fighter. Is there a scenario in which we could escape?"

And then Cal remembered. There was that one single splinter of reality where his ship flew into the asteroid tunnel, unscathed. He sat forward, like Raz, squinting his eyes at the fighter ship. For a moment, he felt a rubbery surface somewhere inside him. He pushed against it, feeling resistance. He pushed more and felt something give but nothing broke. *What am I even pushing against? What is this going on inside of me?*

"Do you see it?"

Cal blinked. There was nothing but the fighter jet's engines burning red in front of their ship with a wispy horizon beyond. "No."

"That's okay, you'll learn."

"You have fifteen seconds to comply," the Central pilot said into their headsets. She shot her ship upward, disappearing from their front view and flew over their cargo ship, positioning at the back with her turrets ready to fire.

Cal looked over at Raz whose face was completely serene, like he was watching a sunrise. "Whatever it is you're going to do, do it already!" His heart was now leaping out of his chest.

Raz cleared his throat and lifted his hand to an overhead control. He waited for half a second and then flipped a red switch, opening the shutter on the back cargo bay. Powerful wind sucked into the bay and cockpit. Cal looked over his shoulder and saw the X8 flying steadily behind them in the sky, turrets winding around, readying to fire. Cal ducked, bracing for the firestorm when Raz pulled up, hard, on a lever at his feet. In an instant, the entire cargo bay detached from their cockpit and flew into the oncoming X8. The now free cargo bay, an empty rectangular box with open ends, flew directly into the X8 surrounding the ship, immediately stripping it of its wings. Its remaining fuselage shot through the hollow open-ended cargo bay, and arched down toward the city below. Cal watched as the flaming X8, now a sinking rock of flames and metal, quickly plummeted beneath them. Raz kicked on the thrusters, pulling their now much lighter ship away from Central Cell. The entire scene happened in less than one second.

"Whoa!" Cal exclaimed, still trying to understand what happened. "How did you... that poor pilot, you... you killed her."

"No, no keep watching."

Cal turned to the side window and watched as the X8 pilot emergently ejected from what would've been a metal casket. "You peeled the wings right off her ship! How'd you know that would work? Have you done that before?"

"No, but I had a very good hunch that it would work," Raz shouted over the wind as he lowered a divider to the open air. Their cargo ship had now become a streamlined cockpit with two wings and a Casimir Drive.

"So... you saw it?"

Raz nodded. "It was one of many options that I saw. Has anything like that ever happened to you?"

"Yes. On the Jupiter Run."

"Explain it to me." The radio continued to crackle with hysterics from Central Air command. Raz simply clicked it off.

Cal explained what had happened at the asteroid—the avalanche of voices, the unplanned trajectory right into the asteroid, and the sudden fracturing of reality right in front of him. Raz nodded and listened as their ship shot out of a cloud cover and over the shimmering blue of the Atlantic Ocean. Cal looked through the rear window and saw the massive landmass of North America. He wondered if he would ever set foot in Central Cell again and thought about Jelena. *What was the last thing I even said to her?*

"It's called refraction," Raz declared.

"What is?" Cal asked, shaking off his thoughts.

"What you did at the asteroid, I call it refraction."

"But it's not that *I* did anything, it happened to me. I wasn't trying."

"That's true. It did happen *to* you. It's a retro-effect of singularity that will occur in the future. Once you've been refracted, you can summon the ability on command."

"But what even is it?"

"Well, you're not crazy, I can at least tell you that."

"Still not sure about that. And why do you have it, too?"

"Refraction is an ability, and it's not something that has just happened to you. Believe it or not, but it is—will be—your choice that you have this ability. It seems random at the moment, but it's not."

"So, what is it?"

"Have you ever sat in between two mirrors that are facing each other?"

"Sure."

"What do you see when you look into the mirrors?"

"Just mirrors. Row after row of mirrors that just, I don't know... disappear into nothing."

"What if you wave your right hand, you see yourself waving the same hand in every mirror, right?"

"Of course."

"What if in ninety-nine of the mirrors, you wave your right hand, but in only one of the mirrors you could actually see yourself waving your *left* hand?"

"Why would that happen?"

"What if every one of those reflected mirrors you saw wasn't just a reflection, but a glimpse into another reality? And each mirror is almost identical to your native reality only with slight differences."

"You're talking about parallel universes."

"Yes. I am. We are one iteration of billions of the same universe with only slight variances. These universes exist in an extra-dimensional space, where they reside next to one another like slices in a loaf of bread. The thing to remember is that the shape of the heel end of the bread is a pretty similar shape as the slice right next to it but quite a bit different in shape to a slice right in the middle of the loaf."

"Okay..."

"So, if you look into a parallel dimension that's right next to your own, it's going to be almost exactly the same. But if you keep looking out there to dimensions farther out, the differences become... exaggerated." Raz looked over at him, trying to see if he understood.

"I'm following you." Cal briefly looked out the window and then at the guidance display on the dashboard. They were heading north.

"Now, let's go back to the mirrors and let's say that you are indeed looking at parallel universes of your own universe in each mirror that you see. The closest mirror is almost identical to your native universe. There are probably not even macroscopic changes that you could even identify. The differences would be on the subatomic level. But go out a few more mirrors—sometimes you don't have to look very far—and you'll see your left hand wave instead of your right hand."

"Seems like kind of a big change if that universe is still close to my own universe."

"True, however, sometimes teeny tiny subatomic changes can have a domino effect and make drastic changes seen on a larger scale. If you remember your quantum physics classes, an electron can exist in many places at once. If a single electron is dictating whether you wave your left hand or your right hand and it exists in both spots at once, that means you move your left hand and right hand *at the same time*. This is how you have two parallel universes—one in which you're moving your right hand and one where you're moving your left hand."

"And we know that a single electron can exist in multiple locations because of the laws of quantum mechanics?"

"Exactly."

"Okay, so, I'm waving my right hand in my own universe and I'm watching my dumb self wave my left hand. Why do I care?"

"What if in the universe where you're waving your left hand, you suddenly fell and died of a stroke?"

"Why would that happen?"

"I don't know, but it did, you just saw it. You're waving your left hand and you drop dead. Maybe, you'd say to yourself, 'I should just keep on waving my right hand so that I don't die'."

"But that doesn't make any sense. The parallel dimension is separate from my own. Waving my left hand couldn't affect my own reality in the same way."

"Are you sure about that?" Raz said, squinting at him.

Cal paused.

Raz continued. "What if the only thing stopping you from dropping dead is *not* waving your left hand. What if the only difference between the two dimensions is that you waved your left hand instead of the right? That would mean you're witnessing the aftermath of a potential decision that you could make in your native dimension."

"Given that the parallel universe is identical enough to my own."

"Which it is if you're close enough to see it. It would do no good to look into a universe that has diverged so far off from our own that, say, the dinosaurs never went extinct and mammals never evolved into humans. Might be neat to watch, but it gives you no information about your own universe. And that brings me to my next lecture: time slippage."

"Time slippage?"

"There is significant slippage in time that can occur between dimensions, resulting in a minute staggering of timelines. Past and future."

"So, if I can see into another universe that's almost identical to my own and I can see the consequence of something that's different from my own," he thought about watching his own ship disappear into the tunnel of the asteroid, "then I could pretty much—"

"Predict the future," Raz said, finishing the thought. "If you can see all of the possibilities at once and the immediate consequences, you know what the right choice is for your own reality. I knew, Cal, *knew* that if I released the cargo bay at that exact moment, it would surround that X8 and strip off its wings. Why? Because I saw it as one of several hundred possibilities that were right in front of me. I refracted my own reality to get a glimpse into others."

"And since the universes that you're seeing are almost identical to your own—"

"The outcome will be the same in my own universe. *That* is refraction."

"So, you can just look into the mirrors of other realities and see?"

"Well, unfortunately, it's not as convenient as looking into a bunch of mirrors."

"I know what you mean. At the asteroid, it looked like a bunch of shards of shattered glass. Each piece was like a little movie playing out of my own ship."

Raz nodded. "That's refraction. I didn't know you would've done it so effectively by now."

"By now? What do you mean?"

"You haven't yet been formally refracted. It will happen sometime in your future but the effects are timeless, this is why you can already refract reality."

"How do I get refracted?"

"That's a secret that I would like to keep a secret. Look, we're almost there." He slowed the ship to a standstill and then flipped on the underbelly cameras which displayed the terrain beneath on the dashboard. Cal saw that they were still high above the Earth, floating stationary in the sky. Streaks of clouds partially obscured the view of the land but he saw bits of black and gray beneath.

"Where are we?" Cal asked.

"We're above what was once the most powerful city on Earth."

"Are we over America?"

Raz nodded. "Yep, and below us was its main city of power, Washington D.C. It's where the president lived and doled out his decisions, which then rippled throughout the entire planet. One man's thoughts —only men—and his actions instantaneously affected wars, trading policies, and economies. It was an amazing seat of power, unlike anything before it."

Cal squinted at the screen. "I don't really see much down there."

"Let's take a little closer look. Not too close, though." He dropped the ship through the cloud cover, exposing a landscape of ash-gray. Cal saw what had once been a city. Fallen rubble of concrete and wood had stacked along the edge of a center clearing. The debris was clumped at the edges of the city as if it had been blown there like stray twigs in the wind. In the direct middle of the city, there were no buildings left behind. He only saw the faint etchings of city blocks in between roads. It was simply one square of city after another, cleared of all structures like a clean canvass. Further out from the middle point of impact, some buildings still stood, none of them whole. He saw only a single facade of one building still standing, a monolithic reminder of an ancient people.

A large river ran through the heart of the destruction like an artery feeding a dying organ. The land was diseased. Diseased and motionless. Nothing moved—not a car or plane made its way across the city. The size of the city didn't seem nearly as big as Central Cell to Cal but he could only imagine how many people must've been living there when it happened. They had been working, traveling across the city, or eating lunch—minding their own business when they all saw a flash. He imagined an entire city looking at the same place at the exact same time. There would've been a moment of wonder at first, a second where they all tilted their heads, trying to understand what they were looking at. Sheer terror soon followed. The lucky ones would've had a little more time to think before it was over for them. Others, farther from the immediate impact, would have had their bodies torn apart, but not enough to die on impact. *They would've had time*, Cal thought. They would've had time to contemplate their torture and to wonder who had done it to them—who would've finally brought this destruction to their front door. Cal had read about what happened; he had even seen pictures of the destruction but it was nothing like floating in the air above the blackened wasteland.

From above, the city was a black streak of destruction, inset within a browning landscape. There was no life here, no greenery from new plants finding life among the destruction.

It was dead land.

"'Now I am become death, the Destroyer of Worlds'," Raz solemnly stated.

"What?"

"Oppenheimer said that after he saw what a nuclear bomb could do."

"Who's that?"

"One of the men who invented that destruction," Raz said, pointing to the aerial view of the city. "'A few people laughed, a few people cried... most people were silent', he said when they first successfully detonated a nuclear weapon."

"What did he mean?"

"Once he had seen the destruction that his creation was capable of, I don't think Oppenheimer was ever the same man. He had the saddened eyes of someone who was bearing the responsibility of the gods—the ability to destroy with nothing more than the press of a button."

"Why are you showing me this?"

"You need to see the *real* history. Unlike World War One and Two, the Nuclear Night was much shorter. It lasted only a few days and it wasn't fought with soldiers, guns, warships, or fighter jets. No. It was fought by only a handful of men—opportunists who finally saw their chance to change the world—to reorder things how they saw fit. They forgot that they didn't have the power to recreate things. Do you know what 'mutually assured destruction' is?"

"No."

"Once nuclear weapons were invented and most world powers were available to develop them, these countries developed backup systems in their governments. It was essentially supposed to be a deterrent to other countries using nuclear weapons. 'If you bomb me, I'll bomb you back, even if I'm dead', was pretty much the strategy. It was hardwired into most governments to immediately use retaliatory nuclear force if it was used against them first. That right there," he said, tapping on the screen, "is one of thirty-one other cities that look exactly the same."

Cal was speechless.

"In little over forty-eight hours, the capital cities of most world powers were made into ash. Both coasts of what was once America are now nuclear fallout zones. It's amazing that human beings are still even alive. The last American President, Tobias Stroupe, was a deeply flawed man, but I like to believe that he did his best. He tried. He tried to save his country the best he could but everything just got out of his hands." Raz looked down at his lap and clenched his fists.

"Raz," Cal said. He sensed deep sorrow from the man who seemed to make a joke of anything, including barely escaping from Central Air alive. "What are we doing here?"

"The ability that you'll have—that I have. It's very powerful. More than you know right now. I brought you here to show you the wrong thing that history's leaders did with great power. I want you to remember this city full of ash and death from now on. Do you understand?" His eyes quivered as he stared at him.

Cal slowly nodded. "Okay, yes. But... what is it? Why am I this way? Why are you this way?"

"That," Raz said, changing the controls on the dashboard and turning off the underbelly camera, "we're getting to."

"And who or what is *Custos*?" Cal asked, uncertain if he should've even brought up the name.

An immediate look of recognition fell over Raz's face. "Oh. I was hoping you could tell me. I've been wondering about *Custos* my entire life."

PART III
THE PHANTOM OF MARS

CHAPTER 13

JANUARY 11TH, 2155 EARTH RECKONING (ER)

Charlotte watched the gigantic images broadcasted along mammoth screens of the downtown district. They replayed the same disheveled man—his hair hanging over his face as he held a torch to the massive tapestry of the assembly hall. An old fear flickered inside of her, stoked by the fanaticism in his face. His fervor and dedication were entirely new and terrifying to her. The man in the footage believed in something more than hunger or shelter. He believed in an idea; something she had rarely seen in someone from Earth.

The footage then cut to the large, wooden hall filling with smoke as the fancy-looking Martian politicians fled. In the very back corner of the screen—although for only half a second—she saw the robot president that she had met, standing at a podium with his arms crossed. The robot wore a brief expression of shock on his silicone face. The reaction seemed so human to her, *too* human. His expression on the screen vanished as the assembly hall plunged into darkness.

The news footage cut to the hydroelectric plants—a string of bulbous buildings that had been built along the wall of the city canyon, collecting the kinetic energy of millions of tons of water fall.

They looked like cracked eggshells with smoke billowing out as fire consumed their insides. All of them had exploded at once—a coordinated bombing.

She got back to a veggie sandwich that she had been devouring before being distracted by the news streaming all over the city. It was lunch break during her civic duty. She realized "civic duty" was just a term for going out and scrubbing the streets. Beside her sat an employee of the immigration department who went by Elisa as indicated on her colorful name badge. She had the exact smile and asked the same questions as Bernard, the immigration agent who had previously introduced her to the edible gardens of the city. They had both found a bench on the city street to stop for lunch.

"So, you lived around the old Central Cell?" Elisa asked, ignoring the bombing footage that streamed across hundreds of screens through the city street. "I remember hearing about the fall of Central Cell when I was a little girl."

Charlotte wiped her mouth with the side of her hand. "Yep. The huge towers are still there. Dead. Sometimes they collapse. No one goes there."

"Do you speak any other languages?"

"No. Do you have attacks like this often here?" Charlotte pointed at the screen across the street.

Elisa glanced at the footage of one of the hydroelectric plants finally breaking free of its anchoring struts and crashing to the canyon floor below. "Never." She couldn't hide the astonishment in her voice.

"Nothing like this has ever happened?"

"No." Elisa's face was pale. "I've noticed a lot of immigrants from Earth come from around the old Central Cell area lately. Is it dangerous there?"

Charlotte nodded. "Very. It's dangerous around that part—too many factions. It's hard to stay in one spot for too long. Most tribes and villages don't understand other tribes. A lot of fights and wars break out only because they don't understand each other. There must be fifty different languages with fifty different ways of talking. I usually just move around a lot."

Elisa nodded. "Are there people like him? The man with the torch?"

"Maybe."

"What does that mean?"

"There's something new happening there. *Someone* new. You don't want anyone else from Earth coming here."

Elisa wore a surprised look. "Why's that?"

"They're all bad there. You want more of him?" she asked, pointing to the screen which continued to loop the fiery assembly hall footage. "You want that?"

"Well..." she said, considering her words. "I certainly don't want anyone like him. I don't want criminals here."

"Then maybe you shouldn't let anyone else from Earth here."

"I don't think we need to go that far. We want anyone who will come here and contribute to our society. It just takes a willing heart, and anyone who comes will be a citizen. As long as they do their part by cleaning the streets, gardening, volunteering at community centers or hospitals—" She stopped as if realizing the hollow platitudes.

"What about people that won't do any of those things but want to come anyway?"

"Once someone sees the benefits of contributing, they are always willing to do their civic duty. We're not a traditional city, we're a massive cooperative of hundreds of millions of people. If you come and work, you'll have education and healthcare, which then opens the door to employment. New Athens and the colonies are a place where people—*anyone*—can thrive."

"But what if... what if people come and they just want to burn things? Like that guy?" She pointed to the man on the screen again, holding the torch to the tapestry.

"Of course, we don't want people... like him."

"Well, that's what they're all turning into over there and they're all rotten. They're bad. Except the sick ones; they don't hurt anyone. And there are a lot of sick ones."

"You know more people like him? Do you know what he was talking about?"

Charlotte nodded. "Things are changing where I'm from."

"What do you mean?" Elisa leaned forward now.

"Do you hear about the wars on Earth?"

Elisa nodded. "Sometimes."

"What do you hear about them?"

"Oh, I'm not sure. Just that from time to time, the people on Earth will fight. Sometimes a new faction will make the news cycle but they're always replaced by the next one. From what I understand, there doesn't seem to be enough organization on Earth for one nation to even fight against another. There aren't organized states. Correct?"

"There are armies. Couple thousand or more men at a time. They go about, from one settlement to the next trying to make the leaders give up goods or... women. If they don't, they kill whoever's in charge and take what they want. Once they're all nice and settled in, the next army will come in and do the same thing. Been happening my whole life. It's why I usually don't stay in one place at a time. I move. It's the only way to survive. A lot of people don't get to my age because they don't know how to move at the right time."

"How old are you?"

"Thirty-something."

"And you're an older person where you're from?"

"They're lots older but they're all men. Women like me... we don't live long. And things are not getting better."

"How?"

"There's... someone. A man—making promises to everyone. He's stirring them up against Mars—making them think that all of you here owe us something—that you stole the good life from us."

"Who is he?"

Charlotte looked around. A few people strode by on the sidewalk next to the busy road full of speeding aircars. She was hesitant.

"Charlotte, what is it?"

"I don't want to say."

"Why not?"

"Because he *wants* me to tell you."

"He does?"

"He wants the people of New Athens to know his name. He wants you to be scared. He wants us to have this conversation about him."

"Was it that man who burned the assembly hall?"

"No... at least I don't think so. I've never seen his face. But I'm afraid—" she paused.

"What?"

"I'm afraid that if that guy on the news got here, then *he* will come."

"But who *is* he?" Elisa grew uneasy. "Who are you talking about?"

"He's old. I don't know how he survived so long but he came—I... accidentally freed him." Charlotte's heart was pounding as she spoke. "But I'm so far away from him now, right? Mars is like... like a million miles away. I'm free, right?"

Elisa nodded, a weak smile cracking her face. "You're... safe now. We are a very peaceful people."

"How do you know that he's not here already? That guy got into where the president and all your big leaders were having a meeting. Half the city's power is out because of bombs." Charlotte looked back uneasily at the television screens on the side of a building. She watched the Earthman lift the torch as if...

As if heralding a new era.

"Have you ever seen anyone able to do something like that here before?" Charlotte asked.

"No..."

"If someone like him did that in broad daylight, don't you think there might be other people just like him that are already here? They've probably already come through your fancy immigration building. Maybe they're already out there." She pointed out to the city. "Working in your shops and building your roads. How do you know I'm not one of them?"

Elisa nervously cleared her throat. "Does he have weapons and battleships?"

"Weapons, of course. Battleships... I'm not sure. But it doesn't matter, he doesn't even need a single weapon to make people do things. He knows things. He can make anyone do anything with the perfect words."

"Have you told anyone else about this?"

She shook her head. "Been too scared."

"I think we should probably talk to someone else about this. This is something... new."

A terrified look came over Charlotte's face. "No! You can't, it'll get back to me. He'll find me."

"What if I did it anonymously? I could report this to the authorities without anyone knowing it came from you."

"You don't get it. He'll know. He always knows."

"Who?"

"*Him.*"

———

When he opened his porcelain eyes for the first time, Custos assumed he would never have to sleep again. Robots don't need sleep, so why should he? During his first week as a robot, he went about creating artwork. He painted, sculpted, and couldn't be stopped from playing the violin. Thousands came to see the great emergence of genius that was *Custos the Dreamer*. He quickly learned that consciousness—robot or human—demands rest when he fell asleep during his first concert in New Athens. The public, of course, only laughed about how *human* he really was.

When he awoke the day after that ridiculous man with a torch waltzed into his assembly hall, he felt peculiar. Glowing morning light crept into his presidential penthouse at the top of New Athens' tallest building. From the penthouse, one could see all of the city.

But this morning, there was something... off. He quickly looked around the house—checking under the beds, in closets, and all three bathrooms. Nothing seemed out of place but he felt... disturbed. For a moment, he thought he remembered hearing someone near him while he slept. They were... what were they doing? Breathing? He did have dreams, but this seemed somehow different than a dream.

"Douglas?" he called his personal guard into the room.

Douglas, a combat robot fitted with a single firearm at his side, stepped in. His eyes, a single visor, scanned the room. "Yes, sir? You sound distressed."

"No, I'm fine. Did anything unusual happen around the penthouse last night? Security breaches?"

"No, Mr. President. Nothing of the sort. I have been here all night and personally providing security over a team of twenty-five security droids—"

Custos raised his hand. "I understand, just wanted to check."

"Is something wrong, sir?"

"No, nothing."

"Do you have anxiety because of the intruder during the assembly meeting yesterday? Do you have hyper-vigilance because of the power outages and bombing?"

As advanced as his robot counterparts were, they had problems with bluntness. Custos rolled his eyes. "No, Douglas, nothing like that."

"Of course. Shall I leave you, sir?" Douglas asked.

"Yes."

Custos went to his desk and prepared for the day. Besides the obvious distraction, he thought that his legislation to gradually make currency obsolete was received quite well. He knew he only needed a small majority of their support to turn the delegates of the colonies as well. The twelve council member votes in legislation had far more weight than an individual colonial delegate, however, the delegates could outvote council members if they had ten votes to one in opposition.

He knew his plans to phase out currency were still likely too superficial to actually come before the assembly for voting. The talking points he had given the day before needed much more thought-out timelines and a solid framework for implementation. He was confident that he had the majority of the legislation worked out, but he knew it needed something more... It needed style. It needed a name that would encapsulate its purpose. He would have to simplify the concept to avoid public outrage.

He had never before felt such excitement about changing things in New Athens. From all his experience in the government, combined with his encyclopedic knowledge of world economics throughout human history, he was confident. The archaic form of labor-based economics was holding humankind back. All of his calculations, reasoning, and theorizing had led him to this point. As far as he was concerned, there was only one way forward.

"Mr. President?" Douglas' voice erupted from his desk, breaking his concentration.

"Yes, Douglas?"

"I'm sorry, sir, I know it's very unusual to accept visitors at your home—"

"Who is it?"

"Delegate Vana Iberian from the Terrabel Colony is requesting to meet with you this morning."

"Vana Iberian is here? Right now?"

"Yes, sir."

Custos shook his head. "No, that's ridiculous. Tell her to call my office to arrange for a time." He had been hounding the Terrabel delegate for weeks to meet with her but she always managed to slip away. It was her turn to wait.

"Yes, sir."

"No, wait." *Then again,* he thought, *she's trying to make some sort of point by coming here directly. Maybe she's ready to talk about turning her farms over for automation.* "Have her go to the conference room and I'll meet her there in ten minutes."

"Yes, sir."

One calculated hour later, Custos met Miss Vana Iberian in the conference room. She sat, legs crossed and arms resting on the chair, looking up at him. Her red lips were currently puckered in impatience. Without too much haste, she stood and held her hand out. "Mr. President."

"Miss Delegate Iberian, I've been trying to meet with you for months and you come to my home when you feel it's convenient for you?"

"Mr. President..." She still had her hand out.

Custos took her hand. Vana felt the rubbery grips over his finger-pads and slid her fingers along the cool, metallic mesh of his hands. "Do your fingerpads have fingerprints like a human?"

He pulled his hand back. "What can I do for you?"

"Mr. President," she said, throwing up her hands. "Forgive me. I just find you so... fascinating."

"I'm certainly glad that I've satisfied your curiosity but I have a city to run. I don't like having my time wasted."

"You have a city to *protect*," she said, changing her tone, "and my colony would like to know what you're doing to keep us safe."

"Keep you *safe*?"

"Yes, I'd like to know what you're doing to protect us." She crossed her arms.

"I wasn't aware we were unsafe."

"Half the city—and my colony—lost power for half a day because of a terrorist bombing."

"No one should have any reason to feel unsafe."

"Are you kidding?"

"No one was hurt. The man didn't harm anyone at the assembly hall and the hydroelectric plants were one hundred percent unmanned. They are completely automated and controlled remotely. Not a single citizen was hurt."

"No one was harmed because that... man chose not to harm anyone. That wasn't good protection, it was just dumb luck."

"I disagree. We had security detail surrounding him within moments—"

"But not before he set a priceless piece of history on fire. That tapestry was created by the first Martian government!"

He nodded. "The loss of the tapestry is... unfortunate."

"That's putting it mildly."

"The man was apprehended in a timely manner and no one was harmed."

"But the fact that he was able to even enter the building... and with a weapon no less."

"What weapon?"

"That barbaric torch."

"The man didn't possess any firearms."

"The facts are, an unauthorized citizen came to our city, entered a building housing the highest leadership of Mars, and tried to burn that building down. At the same time, there were coordinated and timed explosions in seven hydroelectric plants causing massive power outages."

"The man is a threat, I'll admit. It's regrettable he was able to do what he did. We're reviewing the data from the plants. Explosives were used but the investigation is ongoing. But as far as I'm concerned, that threat is now eliminated. I'll concede we should have tighter security at our assemblies from now on."

Vana sat back down, next to a conference table. "Mr. President, please. Have a seat."

Custos eyed her for a moment and reluctantly sat at the head of the table. He was now much less interested in speaking to the woman. He also couldn't remember the last time someone asked him, the president, to take a seat.

"I believe that you are missing the point, Mr. President."

"Perhaps, Delegate Iberian, you can elucidate that point for me."

Vana looked sideways for a moment. "It's not the threat of the individual man that I'm talking about. Yes, yes, I'm sure you'll place all the appropriate measures in place to make sure that nothing like this happens again at the assembly hall. Anyone can just lock the doors to a building and add a hundred more guards. I'm afraid our problem goes beyond what this one crazed Earthman did during a meeting."

He stared at her, waiting for her point.

"Every citizen of New Athens and the colonies has seen the

footage of that man and the burning tapestry behind him. They're all seeing the destruction of the plants."

"I'm aware, yes."

"Why do you think he did what he did?"

"To scare us."

"Not to scare *us*—not me and you," she said, pointing to herself and him, "but every citizen of Mars."

"People aren't scared of that man."

"They're scared of more men like him."

"There's not going to be anyone else like him."

"Oh, yes, there will. Let me ask you, what is the first thing that refugees from Earth ask for when they come here?"

Custos paused, thinking of that dark-haired woman, Charlotte, he had met in the park a few days earlier. "They ask for food."

"And, did the man yesterday ask for food?"

"You know he didn't."

"When is the last time someone came from Earth, not looking for something to eat?"

"Please, get to your point," he said, looking at the clock.

"There was something more in the man with the torch. We all saw it in his face. He had something in him that made his hunger melt away. It's something that drowned his fear of infiltrating our government building with no regard for his own life. He had *passion*. And passion is dangerous. And whatever, or whoever, he has passion for is clearly a threat to our people. Believe me, there are more like him. Martian people might cozy up to the needy, hungry refugees. That's easy, that's simple. Martians want to feel like they're doing good for their fellow man. But when that person becomes a torch-bearing lunatic that's going to threaten their way of life, the attitude will change in a heartbeat. Now, please, back to my first question. What are you doing to protect your people? And what are you doing to protect the people... from *themselves*?" She pointed her index finger into the table.

Custos looked at her for a moment and then spoke. "Let me explain something to you. For the past twenty years, there have been hundreds of armies, warlords, prophets, gods—whatever—on Earth. We hear their radio transmissions from time to time, talking about how they're making a new and great nation. They'll claim they've built new battle spaceships and that they're forming a fleet that is going to destroy Mars. Amongst these claims, they'll say they've found the lost caches of nuclear weapons from before the Nuclear Night and that they're loading them up into their ships. Do you think I don't know what's happening on Earth? Do you think I'm just sitting in this penthouse all day, twiddling my thumbs?"

Vana didn't answer but screwed her mouth sideways.

"We have thousands of surveillance satellites around Earth. There are no battleships—there are no nuclear stockpiles. What is present is an abundance of shanty towns, nomad encampments, and about two dozen cities that barely qualify to function as third-world countries. There are also a few industrial city-states that produce a lot of ore that we happen to import. There is no organizing force that is coming to destroy our way of life. The day that I see an armada of battleships coming for us, I'll make sure to give you a call."

Vana looked at him for a moment before responding. "With all your wit and... synthetic intelligence, you may not have learned the most important thing about human beings."

"And what is that?"

She pointed a finger at the ceiling. "Passion rules all."

"I'll keep that in mind," he said dismissively as he stood and pointed to the door. "I'm a little disappointed, Miss Delegate Iberian. I had hoped we could discuss what we could do to move our nation forward with progress, not backward with fear."

Vana stood and walked out without saying another word.

Custos joined Dev who had been waiting in the hallway outside.

"She finally decided to take a meeting with you?" he asked, watching her as she walked away.

"Not exactly."

Custos left the building with his administration entourage accompanied by security guards leading them out of the building. He noticed there were twice as many guards than usual. Before he could question why, he was interrupted by a barrage of media press surrounding the entrance to the building. Hundreds of cameras and microphones followed after him as he shuffled his way through the crowd.

"Dev!" Custos yelled ahead as Dev managed to push forward. "What's going on?"

He couldn't hear Dev's response as the voices of reporters filled his ears. "Mr. President, who was the man with the torch? President Custos, is it true that your administration is preparing for imminent attacks? Mr. President, what security measures are you placing to prevent further attacks? Are there more Earth immigrants that could be a potential threat to the city? How many people died in the attack at the assembly yesterday, Mr. President?" Dozens more shouted at him, trying to draw his attention.

Custos and Dev managed to get to their shuttle that was parked in the middle of the street and slam the doors shut against the reporters.

"What's this all about?" Dev asked.

"Nothing. It'll blow over soon," Custos said, checking his calendar.

———

Charlotte had finished a long day of street scrubbing. The ceramic roads developed a thick coating of Martian dust after only a few days. The grime needed to be removed in order for the air traffic to connect with the electromagnetic circuits built into the road. Apparently, both robots and humans shared this duty to 'connect them to the city', or something like that.

She closed the door to her room and sat on one of the most comfortable chairs she had ever experienced. It molded to her body and soothed the dull ache at the small of her back. She didn't care about having to do menial labor if it meant she didn't have to go back to Earth. *I'll work every day for the rest of my life to stay here.*

Surrounded by clean walls, fresh linen, and a desktop computer with access to unlimited information and entertainment, she yearned to relax. Never in her life had she felt that she could finally just let go. Hunger, however, crept in her mind at all times. At that moment, she had already stashed a stack of bread, apples, oranges, and crackers under her bed. Every time she had access to food now, she always took more than she could eat and saved it for later. Although she was currently getting three square meals a day, she knew that could change in an instant. She worried about how the fruit under her bed would quickly go bad. She'd have to stock it often and rotate out the fruit that was turning.

It suddenly dawned on her that she could bathe. Anytime she wanted, there was a shower and sink right next to her bedroom. Before coming to Mars, she had never experienced plumbing. She knew some people on Earth had it—those warlords in their mansions—but she had never felt the warmth of running water. She had already showered but wanted to get in again, still not yet complacent with the novelty of on-demand bathing.

She went to the bathroom and looked in the mirror. Her black hair was so smooth after she had used a beautifully smelling soap earlier. Instead of stiff locks that swayed like clunky rope, there were suave sheets of hair that cascaded through her fingertips. Her face also looked different. There was pinkness in her cheeks, giving her a youthful hue. Her eyes, though, still tilted down at the sides and there were permanent lines around her mouth—etched in from her Earth life. Worst of all were her teeth. She had no idea that the missing incisor and grayed bottom row of teeth were even ugly until she saw the Martians with their beautiful white smiles. She sighed and looked away.

She showered and got into bed—her thoughts giving in to exhaustion. She wasn't sure how long after, but she stirred from sleep and opened her eyes. The room was dark. Dark just as it was when she fell asleep.

But there was something new—there was someone there.

She froze with fear, holding her breath.

A voice cracked through the darkness. "I know you can hear me."

That voice. That crackling rattle over his words. The way he drew out the ends of his sentences. It was *him*. What happened? Did she even come to Mars? *I'm still back there, back on Earth, he never let me go!*

"You can look at me. Don't need to pretend anymore," there was tenderness in his voice.

She dropped the covers from her face and saw his hunched silhouette from a faint light at the window. For a moment, she wondered if her eyes were playing tricks and if she only saw a pile of clothing hung over the back of a chair. *Maybe I'm just hearing his voice in my mind?*

"Why haven't you told them about me?" he asked.

Charlotte tried speaking but only gasped in surprise.

"Sh, sh, sh, no, no, don't cry. I'll let you know when you need to cry. Answer me. Why haven't you told anyone about me?"

"I—" she whispered. "I have, I swear."

"Are you lying to me?" he spoke louder—his tone thickened to a growl.

"They'll... hear you." She looked hopefully at the door.

"Hear me? And you think they will help you if they come running down the hall and into this room? You think they'll stop me?"

Charlotte only answered with a whimper.

"Have you told them my name?" he asked again. "Tell me the truth, my dear."

She shook her head. "No."

"Why not?" he asked with new sincerity. "I asked you to tell them about me."

"Because... I'm scared."

She saw him slowly nod. "Yes, I know. It's because you're scared. Did you not tell them about me because you thought you'd never see me again?"

Charlotte nodded, trying to look away. His face remained darkened.

"Do you see now that you can't hide from me?"

She nodded.

"And that, I'll find you wherever you go?"

She nodded.

"I'm happy for you. I'm happy that you've learned this important lesson. I knew I couldn't teach it to you. I could only show you for you to understand. It doesn't matter if you go to another planet. I'll find you, my dear. My dear, Charlotte. My liberator."

"Yes, I-I understand now, thank you."

"Now, you will tell everyone about me, won't you? You're my liberator—my speaker. They need to know that I'm coming."

"Yes. I'll tell them."

CHAPTER 14

FEBRUARY 15TH, 1989

The Rift opened to Straus.

There was so much data at times that he couldn't write it down fast enough, let alone understand what was streaming through his mind. The math was chopped up and he had no idea how to piece it together. He knew there was information about the Casimir Drive but there was also much more. He saw bits of gravitational field equations that looked familiar but, somehow... out of place. When he tried to connect the expressions together, it turned into mathematical nonsense.

He also saw math that had to do with the thermodynamics of the Casimir Drive but he couldn't make sense of it. He couldn't figure out the correct alloy composition to get the Drive to run for longer than a few seconds. After hours in his basement room, he wasn't getting anywhere. He felt like a baby who'd come across a jigsaw puzzle. He could pick the pieces up but had no idea how it all fit together.

It was familiar but alien at the same time. The Rift had the familiarity of a recent dream but the strangeness of considering the same dream in woken hours. He had only recently stopped wondering where the Rift was and why it had come to him. He was convinced that it was not a coincidence that it had opened to him and not someone else. *Obviously, there is more to this than insanity,* he thought. *Could a crazy person revolutionize an industry?*

Before leaving on his way to work, he slipped into his son's room. He was asleep; his face calm above the blankets of his crib. Straus reached down and felt the smoothness of James' cheek against his hand.

Downstairs, he found Jo sitting at the kitchen table, facing away from him. It had been days since they had even said a word to each other. He looked at the back of her neck and suddenly felt a twinge of guilt. *Is this what great minds throughout history had to sacrifice? Einstein's first marriage certainly ended because of his work.*

"Good morning," Jo said quietly. "Are you heading out?" She brought a cup of coffee to her lips and vacantly looked out the window, away from him.

"Yeah, we've got a lot of work ahead of us today. Like most days, I guess."

"I'm sorry if I've been distant," she said.

Straus was surprised, believing she was about to accuse him of the very thing for which she was apologizing. "It's okay, I have been, too. What we've got going at the lab is too big to slow down."

"Is it bigger than me and James?"

He hesitated, measuring his response. "It's bigger than anyone."

"Do you think it'll be worth it in the end?"

He frowned. "What do you mean?" But he knew exactly what she meant.

"Will it be worth what we're losing? You and I, I mean."

Straus hesitated, trying to avoid an argument as he made for the door. "It might be."

"Tim," she said, finally looking over at him. "Whatever happens, just know that I do everything because I love you and I want you back. I'm doing everything for you."

"You want me back? I'm right here." He gestured to his chest.

"You're a different version of yourself."

He nodded in agreement. "I'm better now... things make sense. I used to be afraid of losing my research or my job—I was convinced that everything I did was a failure. But now, look at what's happening. You're the one who says good things will happen if you give it enough time."

She nodded. "Is a good thing happening to you?"

He opened the door to leave. "I think so."

"I love you," she said to the closed door. Jo stood, placed her coffee on the table, and then headed down to the basement.

"So, what were we talking about yesterday?" Straus asked his class.

Chloe, the most eager girl in the front, spoke up. "Singularity of a black hole."

"Oh, that's right. The singularity. Again, before jumping into the math, let's talk about what it would mean if you or I were hanging around a black hole and what would happen to us once we were at the singularity. Can anyone explain what would happen to you if you fell into a black hole?"

Chloe raised her hand. "You'd be crushed."

"Not exactly. You see, as you get closer and closer to the black hole —once you're well beyond the event horizon—the gradient of gravity across your body gets larger and larger. Meaning, if you're going feet-first toward the singularity, your feet are experiencing a far greater amount of gravity than your head. So, what do you think that would do to your body?"

A student in the back raised his hand. "You'd be stretched."

"That's exactly right. It's actually a very sophisticated word that physicists have come up with called 'spaghettification' because you'd just look like a long noodle." At this, the class laughed. "You're laughing, but this is seriously the term that we use. And, once you reached this point along your journey to the singularity of the black hole, you'd essentially be dead. The molecules of your body would be ripped apart. But what if you were an observer, watching someone fall into a black hole? What would it look like to that person?"

"It would take a really long time to watch them fall," Chloe said.

"Exactly. And why is that?"

"Because time slows down the heavier that gravity gets."

"That is true only to the *observer* sitting outside of the black hole. For the person who actually enters the black hole, their watch would tick away at a normal rate to them, but they would be dead long before getting to the center of the black hole. And while you are stretching into a long spaghetti noodle, to the observer, you'd slowly decay. The molecules of your body would be torn away, one atom at a time until you were nothing but space dust. Now, I want to get into some of the field equations—"

"Dr. Straus?" Chloe said.

"Uh, yes?"

"I was just wondering. Is there anything that is the opposite of a black hole?"

Straus was taken aback, considering her question. "The *opposite*? What do you mean?"

"I don't know. It just seems like, in nature, there are always opposites to everything. Light and dark, hot and cold, negative and positive quantum energy, matter and antimatter—you know, stuff like that."

"It's an interesting question." He rubbed his chin, a creeping uncertainty building as he considered her question. Why did a cold sweat form on his brow? "No, no, there's nothing observable in the universe that behaves as the opposite of a black hole—at least I don't think. But what do you think the opposite thing would do?"

"I guess, instead of time slowing down, it would speed up? Instead of being torn apart you'd be... made whole?"

He snorted. "That all sounds like a nice idea but there's nothing like that. I suppose if there were an opposite of a black hole, it would be... an inverted black hole. It's hard to know what would happen there but it probably wouldn't be anything better than what would happen to you at the center of a black hole. Time would very likely slow down because you'd still be under the influence of a strong gravity force, but—" he paused, thinking, then shook his head. "But the extremes of anything in nature are dangerous whether it's being stretched apart in a black hole or being... I-I uh don't know what would happen in our imaginary inverted black hole—"

What is the opposite of a black hole?

And then his mind flooded with voices.

Wincing, he grabbed a hold of the table while his body shook. The entire class got to their feet.

"Dr. Straus!" Chloe yelled.

"It's okay," he said as he trembled. The voices streamed through his mind at a low pitch but began rising in volume. His head throbbed—he felt like giving in and falling to the floor but he continued standing. Waves of nausea flooded through him and glowing auras surrounded everything in the room.

He closed his eyes and focused.

The chattering in his mind receded away and became refined to only a few voices. They were men. One man was speaking over another man but none of it made any sense. Who were they? What did he have to do with them? He wanted to understand so badly.

"...the Destroyer of Worlds... we've come this far, I'll do whatever it takes... time is a circle, doesn't matter who you are right now... who you are now is who you'll always be... the person within is eternal, you've just broken the surface... the Destroyer of Worlds... help us!"

And then, the numbers and equations streamed into his thoughts.

"Pa-paper!" he yelled out. Chloe rushed to him and handed him a piece of paper. "Give me a pen, dammit!" Trembling, she thrust a pen into his sweaty palm. He wrote it all down, scribbling all over the page. Sweat fell from his face onto the page as he wrote, not even aware of what he was putting down. After another moment, he threw the pen down and grabbed at his temples as the voices subsided. Finally, he opened his eyes to the class of students, mouths gaping.

"I'm s-s-sorry, everyone. That happens to me sometimes," he said, glancing down at the paper. On the paper, he had drawn hundreds of simple circles. Large circles filled with smaller circles. Along the edges of the circles, he had also scrawled math that looked similar to other expressions he had received from the Rift. Only, this time, they made a little more sense when they were lined up along the edges of the circles.

Before he could think more on the matter, he heard a booming voice from the back of the classroom. "Dr. Straus!" It was Jack Van Wert, looming behind the students. "Class, Dr. Straus isn't feeling well. Class is canceled. Please exit."

Straus stood, looking up at Van Wert who wore a flat expression. "Tim, it's happening again."

Straus shook his head. "No, no, I've just been getting really bad migraines lately. It's okay, I've been seeing a neurologist about them," he lied. "They're under control."

Van Wert took a look at the paper covered with circles. "You were in the middle of a brief migraine—which has since magically disappeared—and you were in the mood to do some... sketching?"

Straus wanted to apologize—to revert to his old self—but he resisted. "Hey!" he snapped, "I've been under a lot of stress in the lab. Do you know how much money I've brought into the department? I don't particularly appreciate that you're still spying on my classes—keeping tabs on me. And do you think sending in that... Doctor Holloway into my lab, sniffing around—do you think I wouldn't notice what you're trying to do?"

"Please, Dr. Straus, tell me what it is you think I'm trying to do."

Straus scowled at him. "I'm not going to play a game with you. I've been... cleared by my psychiatrist for work. There is no question about my competency."

Van Wert nodded. "Okay. And on that note, have you been able to figure out which metal alloy will get your Drive to run for more than three seconds?"

"It-it's not that simple. We're working on it."

"Then you won't mind if Dr. Holloway and I join you for your run later today."

Straus thought for a moment. Which alloy were they going to try today? He had put Duke in charge of trying something new but he hadn't even remembered what. "You'd just ignore me if I refused anyway." He collected the sheet of paper from the table, crammed it into his briefcase, and left Van Wert alone in the classroom.

Van Wert tapped his cheek in thought.

Jo was waiting outside of Van Wert's office again, this time, with another stack of papers that she had taken from Straus' locked basement room. Once again, she had moved the storage boxes from the corner of their unfinished basement and crept in. There were even more papers scattered throughout than when she first found the room. A lot of the pages seemed to have repeated math and words written in different directions. To her, it was all nonsense. Jack Van Wert, however, had seemed to take great interest in the papers she was bringing him.

"Mrs. Straus," Van Wert said as he approached his office. "I'm so happy to see you again."

She looked at him sternly. "Can we go into your office, please?" she said quietly. "I don't want anyone to know that I've been meeting with you."

He fumbled with his keys. "I'm so happy that you finally came to me, Mrs. Straus," he said as he sat down, motioning for her to do the same.

"Have you found the papers... helpful?"

"Yes, very helpful."

"For Tim?"

"Oh, yes, absolutely. It's really helped me understand what's going on inside his head. He's not... he's not healthy."

She nodded. "I'm very aware."

"Just now, while he was teaching class, he had another episode."

"Today?"

He closed his eyes and nodded. "Yes."

"I thought that he hadn't had one for a while."

"I thought the same thing, but I saw it. Clear as day. He stopped teaching and almost fell to the ground, the poor man. Even more, this time, he started scribbling a bunch of the same nonsense all over a piece of paper. Right in front of the students!" He thumped his plump fist on the table.

Jo sighed. "I was afraid of it starting up again. He's become more secretive—even with me. Is there some way that we can help him now? Now that we can see his behavior in public?"

"Oh, of course we can help him. We just need to be very careful."

"In what way?"

"Well, Tim commands a certain amount of authority now that he has created so much commotion from the Drive that he's made. And the commotion is well deserved. What he and his lab have created is truly an accomplishment. The problem is that he has become masterful in hiding his mental illness under the cover of his genius. No one but you and I really understand how deep his illness runs."

"I agree."

"And it's complicated because his ingenuity is mixed up within the illness. These... voices he hears and the things that he writes down—they're all connected. It all comes from him but from a sort of shattered version of himself. Sometimes it makes me wonder if he would even have the mathematical brilliance he has if it weren't for a touch of crazy—um..." he looked away, scratching his ear. "I'm sorry, but you know what I mean."

"What makes you say all of this?"

"The papers you've brought me from him have some brilliant derivations, stuff that I've never seen before. But it's all mixed up with some sort of... narrative."

"What do you mean?"

He pulled out the several pages that she had brought him earlier and flipped through them. "There are at least two people, maybe four, that seem to be talking to him. Or maybe they're talking to each other. I think the words that he writes down among the math are pieces of conversations that he... hears—in his mind. Some of it seems fairly grim. There are references to nuclear weapons; sentences about worlds being destroyed, and two voices in particular that seem to be arguing back and forth. These are the classic words of someone with paranoid schizophrenia. For example, there's a sentence right here: 'I'll bring this whole city down myself', or this one, 'the Destroyer of Worlds'. Jo," he took off his glasses, "these are deeply concerning words. Has he been acting violently at all?"

"No."

"Has he ever talked about end-of-world scenarios with you?"

"No—sometimes. He talks about the Soviets a lot—worried that it won't end well. But we really haven't even been talking all that much lately."

"I see. He's just entirely hiding it from everyone now. He probably fears you'll think exactly what we think—that his mental illness is getting worse. Clearly, he's starting to think in apocalyptic terms and I'm very alarmed at how good he is at hiding all of this from everyone."

"So, the papers have been useful? I thought that if I could help you solve his problems in the lab with his notes, it would relieve some of the pressure he's been experiencing. Here, I've brought more."

Van Wert reached out for the papers and quickly flipped through them. "Uh-huh. I see what he's done here. Wow," he said in a whisper.

"Maybe you can show them to his psychiatrist and he can obligate him to come in. I've tried calling Dr. Simmons so many times now that he won't even take my calls."

Van Wert didn't respond but continued going through the new pages as if he were discovering something new.

"Dr. Van Wert?" Jo said.

"Oh," he sat up. "Yes, I'm sorry. Well, this is getting back to our original problem. We can't just point our fingers and start a witch hunt. We need more credibility in order to get him the help that he needs."

"What more is it going to take? I'm getting so—" she sighed again and then stared off. "I'm getting so tired."

"We need his colleagues and students to witness and attest to erratic behavior. Once we build our case more, then we can take action to help him."

"But how are we going to do that? You know, when he's being so careful?"

"We wait."

———

"Okay, Duke, what are we looking at today?" Straus asked as he was putting on his lab coat. The lab was bustling with techs and grad students as they prepared for the day's test of the Casimir Drive. Straus looked over at the miniaturized front end of the mock-Corvette. The Drive, bolted to the back of the plastic Corvette, sat motionless on the circular track. Straus stared at it for a moment, thinking.

"We have a little bit of a problem," Duke said.

"With what?"

"Holloway. Van Wert's stooge."

"Yeah, what about her? You know if she's giving you any trouble, you have my authority to just throw her out of here. I'm the one who's doing Jack a favor by even letting her be here."

Duke shook his head. "I already tried that today. She's been telling me she's been given full access to our lab and data."

"What? By who?"

"The dean."

"Which dean?"

"The *dean*, dean. Of Georgetown."

Straus sighed, peering through the glass of the Drive track and saw the blonde hair of Holloway as she was inspecting the back of the Drive. She wore a sterile mask over her face. "Hey!" he yelled. Holloway couldn't hear him behind the glass.

"She wants to try her own alloy in the Drive today."

"Her own alloy? There is absolutely no way—"

"I'm sorry, I tried getting a hold of you earlier. I couldn't stop her."

Straus scoffed. "She's outta this lab starting right now." He walked directly to the door into the Drive dome and opened it. "Hey!" he yelled, his voice echoing off of the curved walls of the room.

Holloway jerked her head at him. "You need a mask on!" she yelled. She was in the middle of placing a copper-colored metal cassette into the back of the Drive.

"You need to get away from my Drive!" Straus yelled back. "What do you think you're doing?"

"Dr. Straus, can we talk about it away from the Drive so we don't risk contamination?" she said coolly.

"What are you doing?" he continued to argue once she came out of the Drive dome.

"Testing out the new alloy we came up with," she said calmly. "Is there a problem?"

Straus paused in indignation. "You thought you could just make up your own alloy, bring it, plop it into the Drive, and do a run all without telling me? I've never even given you clearance to do any work here. You're just an observer."

She shook her head. "Clearly you haven't touched base with Jack for a few days. I've been given full access to the Drive to run whatever experiments I want. This has become a joint project under the auspices of the university. And the state."

"What're you talking about?"

"Jack Van Wert went to the president and consulted with the department heads. Everyone agreed that the Drive is too important of a project to have just one team working on it. It's really quite a compliment to your work, Dr. Straus."

"You think it's a compliment to walk all over my Drive and my crew?"

"I'm sorry, you're misunderstanding—"

"And what kind of alloy did you even put in there?"

"Copper."

"Copper!" he laughed. "We've tried copper to death. Probably twenty-five different alloy compositions. Copper only runs the Drive for seconds—sometimes milliseconds. We've abandoned copper."

"Dr. Straus," a voice boomed behind him. Van Wert. Again. Straus had grown tired of how an otherwise large man could manage to walk up behind him, unannounced.

"Jack," Straus said. "Please explain to me what she's doing here."

"Just relax. This is now a joint project. We've gained full authorization from the board and the state. We're only here to help move things along."

"I don't believe this," Straus complained, looking at Duke.

"I know it's hard to give up some control over your project, but trust me, in the long run, it's only going to help," Van Wert reassured.

"You cannot put copper into the Drive. It will melt everywhere just like it always does. We've already tried it. Every time a cartridge melts in there, it sets us back a week. You can't do it—I won't allow it."

"Tim," Van Wert said loudly. "You don't have a choice. Dr. Holloway and I have come up with a copper composition that I believe will work."

"Since when have you been working on this?"

"It doesn't matter. We were... going over some of the data recently and I believe we found an excellent alloy composition."

How could Jack Van Wert, a subpar mathematician and physicist who settled for administrative work, possibly come up with something better than himself, the creator of the Casimir Drive?

"If you want to gamble a week's worth of lost lab time, please go ahead. I can't wait to see what's going to happen." Straus laughed and looked over at Duke. "They think that running a couple of numbers for a week will come up with better results than what we've been working on for months—years even. Please, Dr. Van Wert, go right ahead. Run the test." He crossed his arms over his chest.

"I intend to. Duke, please run the protocol," Van Wert said.

Duke looked timidly over at Straus.

"It's okay, Duke, run it," Straus said, nodding. He stared back at Van Wert who hadn't flinched. "This should be entertaining."

The lab crew went into action. A dozen lab technicians stationed themselves at a control panel while Duke and Chou Jia stood at the main controls which consisted of bulky monitors and keyboards. Duke gave a countdown and typed several commands into the computer.

Straus, Van Wert, and Holloway stood in front of the glass windows, looking into the Drive dome. A small hum reverberated beneath their feet which grew stronger each second. The Drive was motionless for a moment but then shuddered and vibrated. Just as before, space began rippling behind the Drive. It swiveled and stretched, extending away from the Drive. The light in the dome room twisted as it spiraled through the distortion. An expected loud *snap* whipped into the air, which could be heard from the other side of the glass. The mock-Corvette thrust forward and quickly spun around the track. It glided effortlessly through the air as it circled around.

Give it another second and this is all over, Straus thought. He looked over at Van Wert where beads of sweat formed around his mustache, revealing his apprehension about the run. *He has no idea what he's doing.*

But the Drive kept running.

It spun around the track, faster and faster to the point that they could no longer track it with the naked eye.

"Fifteen seconds," Duke declared. "Twenty... twenty-one... twenty-two..." he stopped counting as it was clear that the Drive wasn't stopping. Copper didn't melt from the back as Straus expected it would.

Van Wert looked over at Straus after the Drive had been running for well over a minute. "Well, I believe *our* alloy has set a new record for the Drive. I think we've come up with a winner. The Casimir Drive is now functional."

Straus kept a deadpan stare at the Drive.

There's no way.

CHAPTER 15

SEPTEMBER 5TH, 2098

"But what *is* it?" Cal asked after almost an hour of silence. Raz previously pulled the ship away from the blackened city—the nuclear fallout of an old world. They were heading south. "What is it? What is refraction? And why can I—we—do it?"

"It's a complicated question that has taken me a long time to even half answer."

"And?"

"In its simplest sense, refraction is you. It's the sum of all the *yous* that there are."

"And am I just one *me* right now?"

"Yes. You are just one iteration of the numberless versions of you that exist throughout all dimensions. But we are *not* finite beings. Our bodies, yes—but who we are at our fundamental core—that doesn't change. You are Cal Stanger, and you'll always be Cal Stanger. You may have different names and live in different places or galaxies, but who you are—in your core—will never change. Right now, in this reality, you are only one version of an entire composite of the multiverse. You're just a shard of a multidimensional being."

"What makes you believe that?"

"It's something you'll just... get a sense of. You'll see. It's like looking down at a stream flowing over a rock bed. The water is always moving and changing, but that rock bed—it always stays the same. The stream is your corporeal self but the rock bed is the essence of who you are. You following?"

"I think so."

"The person within, the person that you really are—your soul or whatever you want to call it—it doesn't change. Who you are now is who you'll always be. You're as eternal as... as stardust. Everyone is, they just don't know it. Once you break the surface—once you've refracted—then you can see it all. You can see that you are eternal. Before refraction happens to you, it's like you're standing at the edge of a pond, looking at the reflective surface. You can't see anything beneath the water. But if you were to cast a rock in, the ripples would break up the reflecting light, giving you glimpses of the rocks or fish beneath the surface. With refraction, you get a peek into the other dimensions of yourself. When we refract, we're able to see all the different versions of who we are. I can only see my refracted self but I can't see your refracted self."

"So, you wouldn't be able to see what I, Cal Stanger, have done within other dimensions but you can see what you've done?"

"I can see you only as much as you interact with me. And, once you're refracted, you in part become uncoupled from time."

"Uncoupled from time?"

"Your physical body is tacked down to your native dimension and you can never leave it. However, your mind or soul—the essence of who you are—part of it uncouples from time. At least I think it does."

"I can time travel?"

"No. Not exactly. You know all the voices you hear?"

"Yes."

"Do you know who it is that is talking?"

"I've wanted to know that my entire life."

"They're you. Well, some of them at least."

"They're *me*?"

Raz nodded. "You're hearing the echoes of your own voice throughout time and all dimensions."

"It's... *me*? This whole time, I thought I was crazy but I was just hearing my own voice?"

"They are timeless reverberations that flow through your mind. You're hearing your own voice layered over millions of conversations that you've had or will have in other dimensions and also your own native dimension."

"I understand how it's voices from other dimensions, but why from other time periods too?"

"Because, remember, the further you look out past the closest mirrors of your dimensions, you start seeing dimensions that become dissimilar to yours as well. If you look at enough of those parallel dimensions, they will start to look like the future of your native dimension. And some of them will be mere seconds into the future. That's how parallel dimensions work. There are an infinite number and combinations of them, including those that are near identical to your own future but just a few moments ahead or behind from your own timeline."

Cal looked out the window, into the blanket of clouds surrounding the ship. "This is so hard to wrap my mind around."

"I know. That is why I haven't shared everything at once. It's a lot to take in."

"So, how do you know that some of the voices you hear are from the future?"

"Because, sometimes, I'll hear something in my mind—a phrase or a word—and it won't have any meaning until I hear myself say the very thing years after."

Cal laughed in disbelief. "Wow."

"Wow is right. But it's incredibly hard to decipher the meaning of the voices. Some things we hear may just be from other distant dimensions that will never have anything to do with our native dimension. This name, *Custos*—sure I've heard it a lot but it doesn't mean it's a person I'll ever meet. It could be someone in the future, or the past, that is in an incongruous dimension that has nothing to do with my reality. This is what makes it so tremendously difficult to find meaning from the voices—you have no idea what is pertinent to your native reality."

Cal's heart pumped with excitement. It was all becoming clear. He was relieved that he had never told anyone about his 'problem'. Going to a psychiatrist would've gotten him thrown out of the academy. The voices that he heard in his mind throughout his life weren't just symptoms of mental illness.

It was him!

It was himself talking over thousands of dimensions—conversations leaching into his own reality. It made so much sense to him now. The voices always seemed so familiar and unobtrusive, much like his own thoughts, only amplified. For the first time, Cal felt something new about himself. He felt... *special.* His failures as a flight cadet were now nothing to him. He learned for the first time that he existed in an entirely different spectrum of existence than Central Cell Air academy. Captain Kalai, Agent Starken, his mother... they all seemed like little bugs, concerned with trivial things.

"But why are we—why am I like this? Was I born this way?" Cal asked.

Raz didn't answer right away. "It's a difficult question to answer."

"Why?"

"If something is eternal, which I believe we are at our cores, then we don't have beginnings. So, it's hard to say if you've always been this way. What I do know is that your body will undergo a change. I know that you've already made the decision to become refracted."

"I decided to *become* like this?"

"Sometime soon, you're going to be refracted."

"How?"

"I will refract you. It must be me, there's no one else who knows how. The fact that it happens in the future is meaningless. It's already done. This is why you already have the ability of refraction right now."

Cal closed his eyes, wincing at the vagueness. "But how can it be my choice if I already made the decision in the future?"

"Time is an illusion, my friend. You're already showing signs of refracting. What you did at the asteroid belt—you've already decided to have yourself refracted. But soon, you'll undergo a process that will unleash your mind from this reality. The side effects of refraction affect your entire being, past and future. The voices you've heard your whole life—they're a side effect of something you'll decide to do in the future. You've already made the decision, it's just a matter of time until it actually happens. This is why I've explained all of this to you. This is why I've been watching you most of your life—looking for clues that it was happening to you."

"So, I never had a choice?"

"No, you will have the choice, and you will decide to become refracted. It is a certainty."

"But what is this process?"

"I... can't tell you. Not yet, anyway."

"Why not?"

"It's too great a knowledge to just give over to you. The only reason I've told you all of this is because I know you'll be refracted, and when that happens, you'll have a very powerful ability. You'll be able to do what you did at the asteroid belt, but on demand, any moment you want. You'll see all the best possibilities for any situation you're in and be able to *know* with certainty what is the best choice."

"More so than I can now?"

"Yes. At any moment. This is something not to be trifled with. I can't just show you how to gain the ability."

"Anyone can be refracted?"

Raz nodded. "Yes. And the way must be kept secret. The way to refraction is right underneath our noses. I can't let it be common knowledge."

Cal sighed with frustration. "Wait, but why have you suspected that I would be refracted? Why follow *me*, all this time?"

"Because you're my nephew," Raz said casually.

Cal was about to retort but stopped with shock. "I'm your nephew!"

Raz nodded. "Yes."

"B-but, why doesn't my mom know you?"

"Besides being her doorman, we've never met. I was your father's brother before he died in the riots. No one on your mother's side ever met me."

Cal studied Raz's face. They did have some similar features— black hair, a narrow nose within a thin face. His chin was squared at the bottom, like Cal's. Even the man's posture was familiar. "My uncle..."

"What?" Raz asked.

"You always seemed... familiar to me."

"We're family. For a long time, I've suspected that you could refract. Also, hearing your name in my mind for the last couple of years helped convince me. I started to suspect that someone related to me would decide to be refracted. That's why I've been following you all this time. I was waiting for the signs."

"What signs?"

"Distraction, introversion, being misunderstood by others—I started to suspect you were hearing the voices."

"Well, you were right. It feels so good to feel like someone gets me. Makes me realize how little anyone has really understood me."

"Just be understanding of them. How could they know?"

"Wait... Timothy Straus..."

"Ah. Yes. Timothy Straus."

"He wasn't crazy, was he? He could refract."

"Yes."

"If only I had known this whole time. I could've been more open to people. More confident. Jelena... I might've even told my mom if she wasn't so wrapped up in her own world."

"You'll see the beginning at the end."

"What does that mean?"

"You'll understand soon. I'm just trying to protect us."

"Us?"

"All of us. Humanity. We've been in trouble for a long, long time —never really been out of trouble. I'm trying to help but it's been a hard road, Cal. I want you to join me, to change how things are. This isn't about just me or you, it's about all of us."

Cal nodded. "I think I get that."

Raz motioned to the window. "We're almost there."

Cal was so absorbed by Raz's revelations that he forgot to ask where they were going. "Where?" He looked at the dashboard navigation. "Wait, we're back over the Gulf?"

"Yes, but we're not going to Central."

"Where then?"

"Just outside of Central. Ever been?"

"Never."

"I find it amazing that you've been trained to fly among the moon and planets of our solar system but you've never been right next door to your own city."

Cal shrugged. "It's never come up."

"That's by design." Raz brought the ship into a field that was worn to dirt. It was a makeshift landing pad surrounded by lush jungle foliage. Raz undid his harness and leaped out the back of the ship, leaving Cal to stare through the windows at the empty field. Once again, Raz had set Cal's mind on fire. Shaking his head, he followed Raz out into the humid air. There was nothing but jungle. "You wanted to show me *this*?"

"This wasn't always a jungle," Raz said, wistfully. "This part of America used to be dry as a bone. The Nuclear Night threw off the world's climate so much that some dry land became tropical forests and the deserts of Africa turned to a cold tundra."

"What are we doing here?"

"Believe it or not, I didn't escape the clutches of Central Cell just to bring you to an empty field in the middle of the jungle." He crouched above a large backpack full of water bottles and packaged food. "Grab that other pack in the back of the ship. We're going on a hike."

They hiked for three hours through the dense and wet jungle, following a well-trodden path that cut through the ferns and shrubbery. Cal insisted on stopping several times for a drink of water. Raz only waited seconds and then moved on.

"They keep it isolated, geographically," Raz explained. "When you're malnourished, making a three-hour hike through the jungle—even if you are following a trail—becomes impossible. Notice how we haven't even seen anyone yet?"

Cal wiped sweat from his forehead, thinking of his comfortable room at home. They continued on for another hour, Cal making frequent breaks. "Why are we doing this?"

"You can really only understand how the world works when you see it with your own eyes." Raz put his hand on Cal's shoulder. "And walk it with your own feet."

At last, they walked out from beneath the blanketing canopy of the jungle. Before them lay a shallow valley where thousands of shanties sprawled for miles. Each building was a rectangle, about the size of a streamcar in Central Cell. They were packed together tightly, with small paths in between for foot traffic. The valley was blackened from dirt and soot, contrasting against the lush greenery of the surrounding jungle. Cal looked for larger structures in the distance but only saw more shanties covering the entire valley as far as he could see. Between the small homes, there were blackened mounds of what Cal thought was dirt. The mounds were interspersed at random around the valley. *Did they try to build some sort of walls?* Cal thought. There were no downtown buildings, no roads for vehicles, no flying delivery ships. No ships of any sort. The valley looked like a blackened crater that had been blasted right in the middle of the jungle.

"What is this place?"

"This is Earth. Welcome," Raz said, stepping forward down a trail that stooped into the valley.

Cal first noticed the smell. The air was musty with a sweet rot. As they got closer, he was overwhelmed by the odor of raw sewage. Gagging, he wrapped a piece of cloth around his nose. It didn't help. As they approached, the dirt beneath their feet hardened and became black. Cal saw mounds of garbage, heaped on the sides of the widening path. Murders of crows hopped around the garbage mass, picking at plastic bags or pecking into cardboard boxes. Further down, he saw what looked like larger animals, rummaging in the garbage.

"What are those animals?" Cal asked, pointing. As a Central Cell citizen, he hardly encountered many wild animals except at the zoo.

"Those are people, Cal," Raz replied without looking back.

"What?" He squinted and finally understood. They were covered in black grease which made feathers and bits of dirt cling to their skin, camouflaging them against the trash heaps. There were thousands of people searching through the garbage. Many were children. They waddled about slowly, encumbered by heavy layers of clothing. Many had adopted a strategy of tying long cloaks around their shoulders which trailed behind them for several feet. They loaded the back of the cloaks with items that they found and towed them around while they searched.

Some had real shoes but most had mock-sandals fashioned out of plastic cartons, cardboard, or rubber and fastened to their feet with shoestrings. Their most striking feature was the blackness of dirt that marked their faces. Streaks of grease surrounded their eyes but spared the eyelids, making a sunburst pattern of clean skin like a raccoon. They eyed Cal and Raz's approach and backed away. The children fled from their sight.

"I don't understand," Cal said. "Why do they dump their garbage at the front end of their own town and then go searching through it? Someone should tell them how to do it properly."

"You think this is *their* garbage? No, this is *your* garbage. Central Cell dumps here. It's been dumping here for decades."

"What?"

"Where did you think all your garbage actually went?"

"I—"

"Never thought about it?"

Cal remained silent.

Raz continued. "See, in Central, there's an economy of business, trade, medicine, aeronautics, and whatever else. In the rest of the world, though, Central garbage is one of the largest markets. It's mostly garbage trade and mining for everyone else on Earth. People come and scavenge and then barter what they've found at the markets."

"But all these... children. Are there schools?" He looked at the top of a heap where a small girl squatted. Her hair was matted in black grime. She looked at them while chewing on a piece of raw spaghetti. She stole one more look at them and then scampered away.

"Cal," Raz said, "there are no schools outside of Central. These people don't even know what schools are."

"Where do they live?"

"They don't exactly 'live' the same way you think they might. Some people have the strength to defend a little shack but they can never leave it alone. Someone always has to guard a home at all times, otherwise, someone else will just take it over. So, if you're lucky enough to be part of a crew, then you might sleep with a roof over your head—sometimes. Some people are smarter than others, they'll build little lean-tos that can be broken down and moved whenever they need to. People adapt in different ways. Most people don't really have homes, though. The kids least of all. This garbage is that girl's home."

Cal thought about Jelena's parents, who got deported. *Is this where they are? How could Central Cell let people live like this?* He thought about the flights he took during his time at the academy. Central allowed cadets to visit exotic spots—Mount Everest, Machu Picchu, the fjords in Scandinavia. There were, however, strict policies to not visit unapproved sites outside of Central. He now understood the restriction: they didn't want citizens seeing what happens to people outside its walls.

They moved through dozens of rows of garbage heaps, the natives receding and eyeing them suspiciously. The people wore thick clothing even though the air was hot and humid.

"Why wear so much? They must be boiling. Are they... not too smart?"

Raz gave a disapproving grunt. "They don't have a safe place to keep any of their belongings, so they just wear everything. They're not dumb, Cal. They're impoverished."

There were pockets of odors as they moved, releasing from garbage heaps that baked in the sun. After thirty minutes of hiking, the garbage heaps got smaller and the smell weakened. They arrived at the edge of yet another sunken valley. Below them were thousands more of the same shanties, haphazardly built throughout gullies and small streams that traversed the landscape. Throngs of people moved below. They bartered at impromptu markets, haggling over their scavenging finds. Others worked on their homes, plugging roof leaks or digging irrigation. Apparently, there had been a cooperation to divert all refuse and sewage to a mainstream that cut down the middle of town. Instead of a fountain or river at the centerpiece of the town, they had a steady stream of raw sewage. The air was thick with flies.

Never.

Never had Cal imagined that human beings could live in this way.

"This is Copper Mound," Raz said, pointing. "One of thousands of cities like it. Copper Mound is more fortunate than most."

"*More* fortunate?

Raz nodded. "Yes. It gets quite a few runoff resources from being so close to Central Cell. Other cities across old Texas and parts of Europe aren't as lucky. It's hard to find farmable land when so much of the Earth sits in nuclear fallout. Many towns and cities across Earth simply starve. There are towns in Southern Texas that are now graveyards—the cities go extinct from hunger and radiation sickness."

"I thought life could be okay outside of Central. Like in Europe or... or the Mediterranean. They can't all be like this."

Raz shook his head. "I've been to all those places. They're exactly like Copper Mound or worse."

"Doesn't Central help?"

Raz looked at him curiously. "Is that what you believe?"

"I thought we sent relief all over the place."

"Relief! Not only do they not send relief, but they're the reason that all of this is happening. This is the problem. This is why I've brought you here. You need to understand what's going on. Come on, there's more I need to show you."

They walked into the shallow valley and through the bartering markets, people glaring at them with distrust. Cal's clean clothes and shaved face made him stand out against the black grime of the streets and wooden shanties. They drew everyone's attention as they passed but no one came up to beg.

"They're afraid of us?"

Raz nodded. "Yes, they think we're Central authorities who visit all the time. They are not kind."

"It's so quiet," Cal remarked. "No one talks."

"What would you have to talk about if you lived here? There's no politics, no sports, no music or arts. No movies or restaurants. There are no pets—they get eaten—and no other animals around. The wild animals have sense enough to stay away from Copper Mound. There's not much to talk about here."

They left the barter market and squeezed down a narrow alley between a back row of houses and a rusted chain-link fence. Cal's pack felt heavier as the sweat and humidity soaked into his clothes. They shuffled past each home, borrowing glimpses through the loose wood panels. The inside of the homes were bare save for piles of frayed clothing that were converted into bedding. Every home had at least one person within, guarding against potential squatters. Once through the alley, Cal plopped his pack down and sat next to it, exhausted. Looking around, he saw more large, dark mounds surrounding him, but it wasn't trash.

They were bodies.

Cal had never seen a dead body before. "What happened?"

"Nothing happened. This is just a graveyard."

"They just... dump them here?"

"There's no energy or resources for anything, especially not the proper burial of their dead."

Thousands of stacked bodies lay before them. The largest heaps rose dozens of feet high. Legs and arms hung limply from the mass, appearing to not be parts of whole bodies. The decay in the air hit Cal's nostrils. He doubled over to dry heave. It was as if the mounds had formed a singular entity of organic mass, spontaneously sprouting human limbs and heads. In Copper Mound, the individuals had lost identity in death, becoming absorbed within a communal grave of bodies.

Cal heard a man cry out somewhere from within. "Someone's alive!" He leaped to his feet and raced around the nearest mound of bodies, toward the voice. Hollow faces glared back at him as he inspected the mostly nude bodies. Not even death could stop the scavenging of clothing. At last, he found the man, lying alone, in the middle of two body mounds. "Hey!" Cal cried, kneeling at the man's head. Bloodshot eyes stuck out at Cal. A drizzle of blood sprayed from his mouth from a deep cough. His skin was yellow.

"Cal!" Raz yelled after he caught up with him. "You should back away. That man isn't well."

"What's wrong with him?" Cal asked, reluctant to leave the man.

"He's sick."

"Sick? This isn't sick. Sick is getting a cold."

"For you it is. For anyone outside of Central, this is what getting sick is."

"I've never seen anyone like this."

"That's because people who get sick in Central and can't afford to pay for medical bills get sent away. They come here."

"Here?"

"This isn't just a graveyard. It's also their hospital."

"*What?*"

"When you get sick, you get brought here. There's nothing else they can do."

The man breathed heavily and slowly, keeping his eyes open, staring up at Cal. Cal was, at first, repulsed. He wanted to run away. He wanted to get back on the ship and run back to Central. However, the man's eyes pleaded with him, begging him to stay with a beckoning stare.

"No, no, it's okay. It'll be okay." Cal brought the man's head into his lap and placed his hand on his forehead. "Everything is okay."

"Cal..." Raz said. "You can't help him."

"It'll be okay," he repeated to the man, ignoring Raz. Cal didn't know anything else to say so he just kept stroking the man's hair. How could they let a man die alone amongst corpses? How could Central not care about him, a man gasping through bloody coughs? The nameless man couldn't answer Cal's questions—he stopped breathing.

"Hey," Raz said, looking down at him with a cold stare. "Don't you dare tell him it's going to be okay if you're not willing to do anything about it."

"This is the last place I wanted to show you," Raz said. They stood at the edge of a massive gorge in the ground. A steel shaft towered in the middle of the enormous hole where hundreds of steel crates carried up raw copper ore. Long, winding roads snaked down the edge of the mine, littered with cargo trucks and laborers.

Cal was mostly silent since the man had died in his arms a few hours earlier. Raz had shown him so much that day; it was too overwhelming to ask more questions. *Wait,* he thought with optimism, *people are working down there. Some people are employed.*

"Central Cell prisoners," Raz said as if reading his mind. "Do something against Central, and you get sent to the copper mines. Every person you see down there; they were once Central Citizens and now... well, you can see for yourself. Most of them get sentenced to life. If they ever do get out, they don't come back to Central."

"They mine copper for the rest of their lives?" He thought about which was a better existence—the slums of Copper Mound or being a prisoner in the mines.

"Yes, and do you know why Central has them mine copper?"

Cal nodded. He knew that the Casimir Drive used copper cartridges to stabilize their engines. They were the same cartridges that his own ship used.

"This is how we run our city. Off the backs of those people down there. There's enough copper in that mine for a century. It'll never run out."

"How can they do this?"

"What do you mean?"

"How can all of this... the sickness and starvation and lifelong imprisonment happen? How can they allow this to happen?"

"Philosophy."

"What?"

"Men create philosophies—ideologies—as a cloak to veil their tyranny. The true madness of men is the consensus of cruelty. As long as everyone agrees, it must be true. Men manufacture their own versions of truth. Central knows what's going on here—they all know. But they justify it as means to preserve their noble and virtuous way of life."

"I didn't know!"

"No, and most people like you don't know. But those in power... they know. Your mother knows, Cal."

"My mother?"

Raz nodded. "Minzy Stanger and nine other people control the Central Cell government. The heirs of the same ten families who invested all their wealth into Central infrastructure in the very beginning. You're not ruled by kings or monarchs. You're ruled by a board of trustees—a corporate plutocracy. Your mother is part of the ruling class."

"The Straus fortune," Cal said with bitterness.

"That's right. The very man who invented the technology that pushes you around in your spaceship—your great-great-grandfather —the wealth that his name amassed is responsible for everything you see around you."

"But, in Central, it doesn't matter what inheritance you have, you have to have self-sufficient revenue to be a citizen. That's the whole basis of our society."

"Sure, for everyone else. But not for someone like your mother, or even you for that matter. Your family founded Central Cell. It doesn't matter if you even get kicked out of the academy. You'll be just fine. That's one of the reasons I wanted to bring you here now. I needed you to know what complacency does."

"I don't want to be here anymore."

"Then run away. Run back."

"I don't want to be anywhere, anymore." Cal left the railing and sat on the dirt, tears welling up in his eyes.

And then they heard screaming—a voice railing and arguing. "No! You can't do this!" the voice echoed from down the dirt road.

The voice was familiar to Cal. After another moment of yelling and screaming, two Central guards walked down the road, dragging someone by both arms. He was yelling and screaming, kicking at the dust as his feet dragged in the dirt.

A young man.

"You can't do this!" he screamed.

Cal suddenly realized who he was and leaped to his feet.

"Benedito!"

CHAPTER 16

JANUARY 20TH, 2155 EARTH RECKONING (ER)

"We're just not certain that this is the best idea right now, Mr. President," Benjamin Cher insisted in front of the assembly. He was one of the twelve council members of New Athens who voted on legislation. "We applaud you for your creative ideas, however, this council questions our stability to undertake such a dramatic change. Abolishing currency? You must admit, it is a lofty goal. Even for you."

Custos, masterful at controlling his facial expressions, held an inquisitive expression despite the extreme frustration he had for the assembly. He had called for an emergency hearing of the twelve council members to stay ahead of the hysteria of the Earthman with the torch. "In what way are we unstable?" he posited.

"Mr. President, you know what I'm talking about. Just days ago, we had a madman in this chamber, threatening us," Cher said. "We've had massive power outages for days. Terrorists have brought *bombs* to our city."

"I agree, the bombings are alarming—"

"Alarming? Yes, in the least."

"They're alarming. But they're not an excuse to halt decades of unprecedented growth for our city. What I've achieved—what we've achieved—here is unlike anything humanity has been able to accomplish. But we can do so much more. We can attain progress that has never been dared. We're so close."

Cher winced. "While that may be true, we can't ignore what's going on in our streets. Have you heard reports of the graffiti around the city?"

"The vandals painting on the walls? Yes."

"I might be a little too superficial to just call them vandals. This council is very concerned about the content of the message."

"'He is coming'," Custos quoted. "Why should we care? I certainly don't care that he is coming."

"Because *he*—whoever *he* is—clearly can do damage. The council believes we need to focus on our own security first and then we can get back to a regular agenda."

"And what would you have me do?" Custos asked, looking at the other council members.

Anita Linwood, another member of the council, paused with apprehension and then stood. "Close all trading routes to Earth, as a starter." She stopped to swallow. "Stop accepting refugees for a time. We don't know how many people are going to be as extreme as the Earth people that are already here. We'd also like daily intelligence reports about military activity happening in North America. We need to know about his army."

Custos shook his head. "There *is* no army. All of my reports... no satellite data shows any evidence of a new army forming anywhere on Earth. There's no evidence anywhere of militarization whatsoever."

"There are rumors," Linwood said, somewhat embarrassed. "We've all heard about it. A new... general of some sort. People say they've seen him. Even here. In our city."

"What?" Custos said with genuine surprise. "What're you talking about?"

Cher nodded. "People have been talking, Mr. President. People are afraid of him."

Custos stood. "Council members, are we really going to give up in front of these irrational fears? Are we falling for the obvious scare tactics of a fear-monger who has no real power other than to frighten the Martian people? We are safe, I assure you."

Linwood hesitated and then continued, "Safety is in the eye of the beholder, Mr. President. You're the only one who doesn't seem alarmed, Mr. President. People are suggesting—"

"What? That I can't feel fear? Because I'm a robot?"

"Those are not my words or the words of this council," Cher interrupted. "You know that you have our full support. It's just important that you know the mood of the people. There is a certain amount of distrust that we're starting to see."

"I make no excuses for what I am and I don't think I need to."

"Of course not, President Custos." Linwood nodded.

"This meeting is adjourned," Custos announced and then left the podium. The council members muttered amongst themselves while Custos left them behind, joining his security detail.

Dev waited for him at the entrance to the assembly, where the antique tapestry had once hung. "I don't like this," Dev said. "Why've they all changed? I thought they were all going to get on board."

"I don't know, it's strange." Custos nodded, looking back at the council as they dispersed from the table. Secretaries and aides flooded the room, assisting their respective council members out the doors. Custos spotted the dark hair of Vana Iberian. She was speaking softly to three of the council members, including Linwood and Cher. "What is *she* doing here?"

"Who?" Dev looked around and then saw her. "Oh, her. I don't know, she must've been waiting for the meeting to end and dashed in here. I didn't know she was so chummy with the council."

"Neither did I," Custos complained and then stomped out.

They were led by ten bodyguards through the halls of the assembly building and whisked outside into the rain. Hundreds of reporters clogged the steps to the building. Farther out, there were people that Custos had not seen in a very long time.

Protestors.

"What's going on?" Dev asked, opening an umbrella over Custos' head.

Hundreds of protesters marched in circles across the street. They carried signs and yelled chants that Custos couldn't make out among the commotion of the reporters. Some signs read 'Keep Earth Out!', 'Save New Athens', or 'Protect Our Children'. Curiously, Custos saw a few signs that read 'Bring Bacon Back'. There was also another sign that read, 'Only Humans For President'. Confused and overwhelmed by the media force at the steps below him, he almost stepped back into the building.

But then he stepped forward, summoning an audience.

"Ladies and gentlemen," he said, looking into the cameras. "I know we're scared." He lowered the umbrella that Dev held over him. "But we are a brave people. We crossed an ocean of space to arrive here. We escaped nuclear war and the collapse of society on Earth to come to our new home. We've created a near-perfect society. No one is hungry. No one is unemployed. When you're sick, you get better. Every man, woman, and child in this city and our great colonies have roofs over their heads. I'm going to show you that we have nothing to worry about."

He turned to Douglas, his head security robot. "I don't want anyone from security to guard or follow me. Do you understand?"

"Sir?"

"No one, Dev." He put his hand on Dev's shoulder. "Don't follow me."

Custos walked down the steps and through the wall of reporters who hammered him with questions. Ignoring them, he walked through the stomping protesters who yelled in his face. Weaving between bodies, he cleared the protesting mass and continued down the street, alone.

The protesters lowered their signs, confused. The commotion of the reporters died away as every person watched the president walk down the middle of the street. After a moment of hesitation, the mass of people followed him. The protests started back up and the reporters ran to his side.

"Mr. President!" It was Gina Wilder, the reporter with whom he'd had an interview a few weeks prior.

He looked at her, continuing to march.

"Mr. President, what are you doing?" she asked, holding a microphone to his mouth.

"I'm taking a stroll through the safe streets of New Athens," he said, rain pouring down his sleek, metallic back. "From this point on, you'll never see me with a bodyguard again."

The Terrabel Colony was built thirty miles outside of the metropolis of New Athens. Several decades after the founding of New Athens, it became clear that the people would need dedicated farming lands outside of the city to sustain the population boom. New Athens itself was a dense population that built upward with thousand-story structures. The city loomed over the massive waterfall generators, hundreds of feet above the floor of a canyon.

The Terrabel Colony, however, was clustered along the Teeth of Telephus mountains, on the opposite side of New Athens. The colony was a series of thousands of greenhouse domes, scattered throughout the Martian terrain. After terraforming, Mars became subject to all weather types, including cold winters, necessitating greenhouse climate control to sustain year-round crop growth. As the population of New Athens and her surrounding colonies grew, Terrabel built new domes to keep up with growth. There was an enormous central dome where most laborers lived within pockets of smaller domes clustering off and extending wide into the terrain. New greenhouse domes were built at a gradual pace, with a handful popping up every few weeks at pace with general population growth.

Custos looked down from his aircraft at the thousands of biospheres sprawling out over the red and green patchwork of Mars. He flew alone, leaving his security detail and Dev behind in the city. He landed, unannounced, at one of hundreds of outdoor pads and got out and walked steadily to the main dome of the colony, which loomed above him, hundreds of feet in the air. He stood before one of hundreds of double-door gates and pressed the intercom.

"Welcome to Terrabel!" a woman addressed him from an intercom. "How can I make your visit pleasant?"

"Just coming in for a visit to the markets," Custos said.

"Excellent, we have daily farmer's markets to which everyone is welcome. Do you have security clearance?"

"Clearance? What clearance? You don't need clearance to walk into the markets."

"You do now, sir," the woman said, flatly.

"I'm President Custos."

"While you do certainly look like President Custos, I will need some sort of identification."

Custos scoffed, staring at the intercom. "You've got to be—"

"You need clearance, sir."

Without another word, he made a quick call to his office and had them call over to Terrabel security, finding the whole process ridiculous. A blast of air blew out at him as he entered the Terrabel domes, revealing a wide marketplace that extended in all directions. Dozens of shops, intermingled with staircases and elevators rose above him. He saw the curve of the main dome high above the shops. Wisps of clouds clung to the top of the dome. There were no independent vehicles within the main dome, instead, it was mostly local foot traffic and a tube system of individual pods that the people took for longer distances inside of the dome. Hundreds of Terrabellers walked through the market around him. He moved swiftly through the crowds until someone recognized him and called out to everyone else.

"President Custos!" the crowd yelled as it surrounded him.

"Do we have to worry about attacks in our colony?" a woman yelled, while another shouted, "No farm automation!" A teenage boy wiggled through the masses and put his face right next to Custos'. "Who is *he*?" he asked.

Custos walked swiftly through until he made it to a pod at the tubing transit system. He hopped on a private pod. "Colonial Ministry," he said, after which the pod shot away from the market. He got off at the administrative offices of Terrabel, which was a row of buildings on top of the dome's largest hill, connected by a series of skywalks. He marched through the offices, drawing the attention of secretaries everywhere he went. He quickly amassed a crowd of dozens of office workers, wondering and shouting questions at him. Following the signs, he finally made it to the office door that read *Colonial Delegate Vana Iberian*. Without knocking, he opened the door and surprised the woman sitting at her desk.

Nonplussed, she looked up at him. "Mr. President." She didn't stand. "I could've used some advanced notice that you were coming."

"You came to my home unannounced. I thought I'd do you the same." Custos shut the door to the crowd behind.

"I've been watching you on the news, walking through the streets with cameras chasing after you. A little desperate for attention?"

"Spreading rumors amongst the council and throughout your colony will not work," he warned.

"Work? What do you mean it won't 'work'? What do you think I'm trying to do?"

"Manufacture fear."

"I have no idea what you're talking about. I'm justifiably concerned about the safety of our people." She crossed her arms.

"Even if that's true, don't you understand the harm that you're doing? Are you trying to willfully destabilize our society?"

"I understand the harm that *you* are doing. You will not or cannot see the threat that is coming."

"Do you think using fear to galvanize the people is anything new?"

"Does it matter if it's new or not?"

Custos paused, realizing that she made a good point.

"Mr. President," she interrupted his rebuttal. "Have you ever been in love?"

"*What*?"

"You are a self-aware robot, holding all passions of the human heart, correct? I could only assume that love is part of those passions."

Custos thought about the question. No one had dared ask him if he had been in love. The question threw him off—he was expecting a shouting match between himself and the delegate, not such a personal question. She clearly took his hesitation as an answer.

"Hmm, interesting," she said. "You don't have a quick answer for that, do you? I can only assume there has been someone special in the past. I guess he or she never got leaked into the media. Must've been before 'Custos The Dreamer' was plastered all over the press. I do wonder how you've kept it a secret all this time."

Custos regained his confidence. "Now you're just making things up."

"I only asked if you've been in love because being in fear is just like being in love. In both love and fear, a person doesn't think rationally, is terrified of loss, and hangs on every word of their lover or their fears. They do not appeal to a sensible argument. You can't talk someone out of being in fear just as little as you can talk them out of being in love."

"Thank you for the life lessons, but I came here to tell you to stay away from the council members."

"I know why you came. I'm just telling you what you need to hear. I think there's a lot about us human beings that you still haven't figured out yet."

Custos sighed and stared at her as if figuring out how to condescend to her level. "Do you think my metal body prohibits me from understanding you? I know more about humankind than anyone you've ever met."

She gave a mirthless laugh. "There is no way that could possibly be true. You," she said, lips quivering in anger, "are a *robot*."

"A robot is only what you see in front of you."

"Teach me then, robot. Teach me about what you know of humanity."

"All human beings believe themselves to be one thing: an expert. People believe in consensus more than thinking critically. Humans trust orthodoxy over science and data. They believe their opinions to be universal and feel qualified to condemn those that believe differently. They are brave when they have hope in something and afraid when they don't understand. They are at their unhappiest when they desire more than what they have and are the most content with routine. Most of all—above all traits—human beings follow those around them. They are kind when others are kind and cruel when others are cruel. Humanity has gone through endless cycles of economic and technological superiority only to succumb to fear. When we are at our height of tolerance and understanding, we give in to fear of a globalizing community. We are innately terrified of inclusivity. Embracing tribalism is what brought us The Nuclear Night. Most of Earth is in ashes because of fear of the other."

"You said, 'when *we* are at our height of tolerance' as if you, a robot, are one of us."

"Oh," he said with a startle. "Now I understand why you're doing what you do—whispering into the ears of the council."

"Is that right?"

"You're not afraid of a new Earth faction. You're afraid of me. You're afraid of my power."

Iberian paused. "I'm afraid of Earthmen coming for us. I'm afraid of people that have nothing to lose. I am not afraid of *you*, robot."

"New Athens and her colonies are the first successful, multicultural democracy that has ever existed in the history of humankind. I am her steward and I will do whatever it takes to keep us from slipping back to the dark ages."

"The dark ages still exist, we just left it behind. It's people from the dark ages that are coming for us."

He shook his head. "There's no one coming for us. The only thing that's going to stop us is our own misunderstanding." He moved to the door—never having sat—and turned the knob. "I'll be making a surprise visit in the next week to inspect your farms. We will begin full automation within the next six months. You can keep looking back but I'm taking New Athens into the future."

"Oh? You're just going to come into a sovereign colony and do whatever you like?" She stood as he opened the door. "Are you a tyrant or a president?"

"Semantics," he said and then left.

———

At two in the morning, Charlotte waited under a tree in the park where she had once met the robot president. The streets of New Athens were absent of foot traffic but the air was still full of delivery and maintenance drones. There were also thousands of air freighters flowing over the city. Charlotte looked up at the night sky and saw the ships flitting past the small moonlight from one of Mars' moons, Phobos. She had heard that Mars had two moons but hadn't yet seen the second.

A breeze blew past her, shaking the leaves in the trees. She shivered at the sound of the leaves—reminded of the deep scratchy voice from what she hoped were nightmares. *How could he possibly be here?* she thought. *How could he just appear in my bedroom with no one noticing?* For her, the novelty of clean sheets, a new dress, and fresh food every day had worn off. There was only a constant river of fear running through her now.

He followed me.

Followed her from the jungle.

How could he find her?

She heard footsteps from behind and jumped, ready to flee. She relaxed when she recognized the thin figure of Elisa, the immigration officer.

"Hi," Elisa said nervously as she approached the tree. "I hope you don't mind, but I brought someone."

"What? Who?"

A man revealed himself from behind Elisa and waved. "Hi, Charlotte. Remember me?" It was Bernard, the other smiley-faced immigration officer who had taken her to the communal garden for her first breakfast in New Athens.

"You? What're you doing here?"

Elisa spoke up. "He's my friend at the immigration office. We've been talking about the things that you and I have been saying. You know, about how we need to take better control over ourselves with such a big threat at our doorstep. Anyway, Bernard here feels the same way. He wanted to come with me tonight."

Bernard nodded. "Is that okay? I've just been feeling so... anxious about everything that's been going on lately. Everyone is talking about that man with the torch and everything else. The president doesn't seem to care at all. He hasn't even mentioned the man or the Earth threat on the news once. He just keeps talking about 'the path forward'. It's just really frustrating to feel so powerless. And did you see him in front of the protesters today? He just walked right past them; didn't even look at them. It's like that robot doesn't understand what any of us are feeling at all."

"What he means is," Elisa interrupted, "we want to help. You know better than anyone what's happening on Earth and we want to be prepared. The only way we can help everyone is by raising the alarm. Today, me and Bernard got to talking and we both feel like more needs to be done. I also told him about everything you've been telling me about... *Him*."

Charlotte sighed and looked back up at the moon.

"What?" Elisa asked. "Did I say something wrong?"

Charlotte looked at her. "No. It's just... this isn't a game. He is very real and *he's* coming. I know it. I've seen him."

"You've seen *him*?" Bernard asked with wide eyes. "Who is *he*—er —*what* is he?"

"He's angry and he's powerful. And we need to warn everyone."

"Warn them of what?" Elisa asked.

"That if we don't do what he says, he'll destroy this place."

Elisa and Bernard looked at one another. "But how?"

"I'm not sure, but I don't want to find out. We just need to do what he says. Come on." She lifted a backpack over her shoulder and marched away with Elisa and Bernard following. The three moved swiftly across the empty park, Elisa and Bernard looking around anxiously. They arrived at the center of the park where a towering bronze statue of a man in a suit stood. At the foot of the statue was a plaque that read:

We will reach for the stars and find ourselves there.
-Last American President, Tobias Stroupe

Charlotte thought about how her first encounter with anyone on Mars was right at that spot, where she met President Custos. He was so... understanding.

"What're we doing here?" Elisa asked with a puzzled look.

Charlotte squatted over her backpack and rolled out a dozen cans of spray paint. Without answering, she picked up a can of bright orange and climbed the concrete foundation of the statue.

"It's you!" Bernard gasped. "You've been the one spray painting around the city. No, no, no, Elisa," he said, shaking his head. "This is bad. I didn't know we'd be doing something like this."

Charlotte sprayed across the shoulders and torso of the statue and let herself down.

Elisa squinted in the dark light and read aloud, "The Copperhound is coming."

"The Copperhound?" Bernard said.

"Here." Charlotte thrust spray cans in each of their hands. "Go and spray this sentence all over, as much as you can. The people need to know. They need to be ready. The Copperhound is coming."

PART IV
THE COPPERHOUND

CHAPTER 17

SEPTEMBER 5TH, 2098

"Cal!" Benedito yelled as the guards dragged him to the gates of the copper mines. "Cal, help!"

Cal looked at Raz who was just as confused, and then yelled at the guards, "Stop right now! You've made a mistake." The guards threw Benedito to the dirt in front of a steel gate and pressed on the intercom for security to let them in. "Hey!" Cal yelled again, approaching them from behind. "I said stop! You've made some sort of mistake. This is a Central Air Academy cadet that you're about to throw in there. He didn't do anything wrong."

One of the guards looked down at him, a burly woman with thick arms. "Get out of here, copper scum."

Cal looked down at his clothes and realized that he had been covered with the dirt and grime of the trash heaps. The guard smirked as the gates opened.

Benedito pleaded with Cal, "Cal! Tell them! Tell them we didn't work together!"

"*What?*"

"Don't let them throw me in!" The elbows and knees of Benedito's cadet uniform had been dirtied and torn. The guards picked him up by both arms and dragged him through the gates.

Cal looked to Raz. "Help him!"

Raz watched as Benedito was carried away. "You have the power within you to change this situation."

Anger bubbled. Flashes of a man dying in his arms, his mother lounging for days in their penthouse, and a small girl eating food she found in the garbage. *That's my garbage,* he thought. *We're responsible for all of it. I am responsible.* The rage exploded, fueled by guilt.

And then he felt it—a rubbery boundary deep within him.

It was the same surface he felt when they were chased by a fighter ship earlier that same day. Cal pushed against the surface and felt it rebound back at him. Each time he pushed with his mind, it bounced back at him with equal force. Instead of trying to figure out what he was pushing against, he just let go. He let go of concentrating and only felt the weight of the dying man's head in his lap. Anger over his mother and his own ancestry bathed his emotions. The thoughts turned to raw indignation over Central Cell and the misery that he and people like him had caused. Funneling the energy, he released it at the rubber surface within him...

And then the world shattered.

Before him glittered hundreds of slivers of reality, each one a slightly different version of his own reality. In every fracture, Benedito was being carried away by the two guards. Yet, as Cal looked around —even behind him—he saw that some fractures farther away from his native reality changed significantly. Some didn't even show Benedito and the guards, there was only the closed gate. There were the parallel dimensions that were farther away from his own, having less in common with his native, real-time dimension.

Cal focused.

He looked at the center of the fractures, trying to think of a solution. In some of the fractures, he saw that he himself was already dashing through the gates, trying to save Benedito. It was the time slippage to which Raz referred—some of the dimensions were mere seconds ahead in time. In one fracture, he plows into the back of one of the guards, causing him to roll down the road into the copper mines. The other guard, however, unholsters her pistol and immediately shoots Cal in the stomach. In another shard, Cal sees himself pick a large rock off the ground and slam it into one of the guard's heads while the other guard throws Benedito down the central mine shaft to his death. *Nothing works*, he thought as he scanned the fractures. He was running out of time, stalling to watch the fractures. *How does Raz figure it out so fast?* And then he saw it.

Okay. Go!

The gates to the mine began closing behind Benedito as Cal dashed through. He carried his pack with him and held it above his head as he ran at the unaware guards. Benedito saw Cal coming and fought against the guard's hold on him. Cal ran at them, down the hill, and thrust his pack above his head, which soared over the guards. They jumped when they saw the pack fall in front of them. One of them momentarily let go of Benedito's arm as he went for his gun, startled by the motion of the backpack. Benedito fought with the other large woman, who grabbed him with both arms, taking her attention away from the pistol at her belt.

Cal rushed up, unclasped the pistol from her belt, and took it out of the holster.

"Hey!" she yelled, completely letting go of Benedito.

Cal held the pistol to her while Benedito stood and rushed at the other guard, head-butting him in the back. The man fell with outstretched arms, causing him to lose his grip on his pistol which flung from his grasp, into the central shaft of the mine.

"Don't move!" Cal yelled at the guards.

Dazed, Benedito backed away from the guards who now looked at Cal with derision. "You think you're going to get away with this?" the woman asked. "You're going to pay for that, copper scum. Put down the gun right now!"

"Bene, let's go," Cal said calmly.

"Cal!" Benedito said with an edge of shock. "That was incredible."

"We need to get out of here," Cal said as he backed away. The guards watched the two back up and started following them. "Get your hands up and stay put!" Cal yelled. He shot off a bullet into the air. "Get on the ground with faces down." The guards complied and lay on their stomachs with their faces in the dirt. "Come on," Cal whispered, grabbing Benedito's arm. They dashed through the gates of the mine and found Raz waiting patiently, arms folded, leaning against the railing.

"Couldn't bother to help?" Cal asked.

"Looks like you managed just fine without me," Raz said with a grin. "Come on, those guards won't wait long."

"Cal!" Benedito yelled from behind. "What're you doing here? And who is that?" he looked suspiciously at Raz until his face flashed with recognition. "So, it is true! Y-you're... with him, the terrorist!"

"What're you talking about?"

"Children," Raz interrupted. "We need to run."

Cal looked behind and saw the same two guards approaching. The three of them broke into a full sprint, away from the gate of the copper mines and into the jungle. The shouts of men and engines echoed in the distance as Cal followed Raz with Benedito trailing behind. They slipped through muddy gullies and ducked under gigantic plant fronds that sprouted from all directions. Benedito coughed at the humid air while Cal shrugged off his cloying flight jacket. They were soon soaking from the moisture of the jungle and breathing heavily as they moved.

"Wait!" Raz whispered, holding his arm out to stop Cal. "Get down."

The group crouched below the forest plants and waited. Cal looked back at Benedito who scowled back at him. *What's his problem?*

After a moment, a drone plunged through the jungle canopy. It buzzed with several small turbines and carried a myriad of cameras that telescoped in and out, surveying the jungle.

Raz looked back at them and lifted one finger to his lips.

The drone hovered around the trees and vines, searching. It flew around the area except where the three of them crouched. After another moment, it lifted through the canopy to search another area. The group traveled through the wilderness for another hour, periodically stopping to wait for search drones or aircraft overhead. Eventually, they broke through the suffocating foliage of the jungle and emerged to the trash heaps of Copper Mound. The sky had grown dark over the columns of smoke and mounds of trash that surrounded the shanty community.

"What's that smell?" Benedito said, covering his nose.

"It's *your* garbage," Cal responded. "This is how the rest of the world lives, Bene. They eat our garbage."

"What're you talking about—"

"Do you two ever stop talking?" Raz interjected. "Come on. If you see any twigs or wood to burn, pick it up as we move. We're going to need it."

They filed through alleys and crooked paths that had been carved through the garbage heaps. The people of Copper Mound didn't take notice of them anymore—the three were covered in dirt and grease, helping them blend in perfectly with the natives. They found a small clearing at the top of a mound and rested. They threw down the wood and kindle they had gathered while Raz prepared to make a fire.

"You had us collect wood just to make a fire?" Cal asked.

"Of course. What else did you think I was going to do with it? You want to be devoured by mosquitos tonight?"

"Mosquitos?" Benedito asked

"We're sleeping here?" Cal ineptly stacked twigs for the fire.

Raz rolled his eyes. "We need to stay here tonight. Get comfortable."

Benedito cut in, "What are you two even doing out here? And why are you with him?" He pointed at Raz.

"He's my uncle."

"Uncle? What uncle?"

"He's been out here showing me things. Showing me how things really are." He glanced out over the darkened valley.

"Well, while you've been out here missing for two days, you two have become the most wanted men in Central Cell."

"What!" Cal looked at Raz who gave a shrug.

"That's right," Benedito said in a bitter tone. "And they think I'm with you. I had Central police all over my house, asking me all sorts of questions. They know we're best friends from the academy. Cal, they think all the extra flight time we've been logging together was terrorist planning. They played me all these conversations they had recorded, trying to twist the words to make it sound like we were planning something. I kept telling them I didn't know anything so they brought me all the way out here to throw me in those mines."

"I had no idea you'd be dragged into this."

"Relax," Raz said. "Just petty threats. They weren't really going to leave some privileged teenage kid to rot in the copper mines forever. Just Central scare tactics."

"Wait," Cal said. "I don't get it. Why are we wanted?"

Benedito glared, bug-eyed. "Do you remember leaving behind a flaming wreckage of a fighter jet when you left Central? They have the footage from the plane and your faces plastered all over Central news. Everyone knows you're the Straus fortune heir and it's blowing up the media coverage."

"Oh no," Cal whispered.

"Oh no, is right. Look, I know you failed the Jupiter Run and everything, but I didn't expect you to fly off the handle! Some of us actually had a future in Central Air. I beat the highest record for the run!"

"Bene..."

"What am I supposed to do now?"

Raz cut in, "You two, relax."

Benedito glared at Raz. "How am I supposed to relax when I got thrown out of Central and I'm camping out on the top of a pile of garbage? Also—" he suddenly gasped. "Wait! You're Cal's doorman."

Cal nodded. "Yeah, that's true but—"

"And, suddenly, he's your long-lost uncle? Cal, are you crazy? You're listening to this guy? He's not your uncle. He's some crazed fugitive that Central's been looking for, for decades. I know you've been having a hard time lately but this is not the right path to go down."

Cal shot a glance at Raz. "Is that true? Have you been a fugitive for that long?"

Raz, now lying on a blanket that he had unrolled, nodded. "I've assumed several identities throughout the years. Before I was your doorman, I was a waiter, and before that—" he squinted, trying to remember, "I was a delivery man. Before that..." He yawned at the night's sky.

"Why?" Cal asked.

"When you're trying to infiltrate Central Cell and understand all its weaknesses, one needs to fly under the radar and under many identities."

"It's because he's a terrorist, Cal." Benedito threw up his hands. "That's it, I'm outta here."

Cal called after him, "There's nowhere for you to go. They'll just throw you into the mines again if they catch you."

"Not if I give you up." Benedito crossed his arms.

"You'd do that?" Cal asked.

Benedito hesitated and then dropped his arms.

"Bene, I'm sorry this has happened but you need to believe me. Raz *is* my uncle. We are... definitely related and he's shown me what the world is really like. Did you see all these people here as we walked in? Did you see how they live? That's how the entire *world* lives. Central is only a tiny fraction of the world's population but we consume about ninety percent of its resources. Doesn't that bother you?"

"What're you talking about?"

"Ever wonder why the academy has such strict rules about where we can and can't fly?"

"Not really."

"It's because they don't want us to know what we're doing to the rest of the world."

"Whatever, there are still big cities all across Europe that do just fine."

Raz shook his head. "They're all like this village here. They're not all built around Central's junkyard but they're just as poor. Yes, there are a lot of cultures that survived the nuclear war who live in the pacific islands. They easily reverted back to being fisherman and traders. Probably some of the most peaceful people I've ever met."

"Raz has seen it all," Cal said. "The world is suffering while we just fly around, totally oblivious."

Benedito shook his head. "That may be, but I've got to get back home. I'm not cut out for—" he glanced around, able to catch a view of Copper Mound from the top of their campsite. The shallow valley was dark and mostly silent. "I can't live here."

"Don't you two worry," Raz said. "Uncle Raz has got plans for Central."

Benedito, unrelieved but giving in to exhaustion, rolled out one of Raz's canvases and laid down. "Fine, we'll figure it out in the morning." He closed his eyes.

"Hey, Raz," Cal whispered as Benedito fell asleep. "Earlier, at the mines... I refracted. I tried and it just... happened."

Raz looked up at Cal, smiling. "We're finally going to change things. It's been so long."

The next morning, Cal awoke to rain dripping on his face. He got up and found Raz sitting by the extinguished fire, gazing at a small photograph—a family portrait.

"Who's that?" Cal asked, pointing.

Raz, caught unaware, slid the picture into his front pocket. "Um, my family."

"Really?" Cal got excited about meeting a new cousin and aunt.

"No, not anymore. They're gone."

Cal frowned. "What happened?"

"They..." He squinted at Cal, something complex written on his brow. "They've died."

"I'm sorry. I wish I could've known them. Did Central deport them?"

"Not exactly. I had the opportunity to see them more and I didn't. It's a story for another time. Right now, we've got more important things to talk about. We have things to do."

Benedito joined the conversation after returning from a spot at the edge of the campsite that he deemed to be the latrine.

"How does Central Cell stay in power?" Raz questioned them.

Cal looked up, thinking. "It keeps us blind. They stop us from knowing the truth."

Raz nodded. "That's true, but when people don't really care to begin with—when they've ceased to be citizens and have become nothing more than consumers—they don't really care to find out. Commercialism breeds apathy. If people don't ask questions, they don't really have to blind us. Think of how easy it would've been for one of you to fly into Copper Mound and see how these people are living. But you never even thought to do it. And this place is no more than thirty miles outside of Central."

"True," Cal acquiesced.

"How else might they maintain power?" Raz asked.

Benedito spoke up, "They just lie. They kept saying I had something to do with you and Cal but I didn't do anything. They twisted my words and created evidence out of thin air. And then, to get me to talk, they throw me into a mine. They terrorize us."

Raz nodded. "Yes, they only tell the truth if it benefits them, and even then, they reframe or re-contextualize facts to fit a comfortable narrative. They're also not above outright lying. They'll intimidate, bully, and kidnap anyone who threatens the institution. They use the same scare tactics that many world powers have used throughout history. They build walls to keep out the underprivileged. They have strict laws prohibiting their citizens from leaving—maintaining their vetted population. These are all their tactics, but it's not how they keep a stranglehold over the world's resources."

"How then?" Cal asked.

"Exclusivity," Raz simply stated. "To be a citizen, you must make a certain amount of money. If you don't, you get kicked out. They breed elitism by creating a false sense of scarcity. By doing so, the remaining citizens that do qualify, naturally conform without need for coercion. This is where Central is unique. The people become unified by status and the will of the people becomes the will of the government. It becomes a utopian harmony of greed and self-importance. When every citizen feels like a king, they have no need for dissent—no fire within them—that questions the authority. That's because they *are* the authority. They are beautifully complacent."

Benedito hung on Raz's words. "I never thought about it like that."

"Of course you haven't. You're a Central Cell citizen. Or, at least you were."

Benedito looked on, uneasily. "Guess that's right."

"So," Raz continued, "if the foundation of Central's power is maintaining exclusivity, how might we go about undermining that power?"

Cal pondered for a moment. "Take away what it means to be exclusive."

Raz nodded. "Uh-huh... so?"

Cal continued, "You make it so no one knows who has what. You take away what it even means to meet the revenue cutoff for citizenship—"

"By getting rid of how we keep score," Benedito added.

Cal nodded. "Take everyone down to zero. You make it so that, economically, there is no difference between someone outside of Central and inside."

"And what is the only thing that gives a person distinction inside of Central compared to the people out here in Copper Mound?" Raz asked them.

"Brics," Cal said. "It's all about brics. We get rid of the means of measurement."

"Explain how," Raz said.

"Make it worthless," Cal said. "You make brics magically not have any value."

"You boys catch on fast," Raz said. "Now, tell me. Where are all the brics?"

"Where?" Cal asked.

"Yeah. Where are they? Have either of you actually *held* a bric in your hand?"

"What do you mean?" Benedito asked.

"What does a bric look like? What does it feel like? Is it a coin? Is it paper?" Raz questioned.

"It's just digital currency. You buy something by giving your thumbprint and the brics come out of your bank account."

"That's right. Anyone seeing a vulnerability here?" Raz asked.

"Like what?" Cal asked.

"Back before The Nuclear Night, countries like America kept a reserve of gold that gave value to their money. They used the gold standard for a large portion of their existence. They used paper and coins as a surrogate for the worth of the gold reserve. That way, if something like inflation were to happen to their money, the gold that was held still had intrinsic value. Banks and countries used their gold reserves to secure their own currency. The gold was insurance against economic disaster. However, once deflation caught up to them, they just started printing their own money beyond the gold standard. But even then, debt and currency had value within a global economy. Once the economy globalized, the US was able to maintain its currency on more than a gold standard. The US dollar itself had intrinsic value in global exporting and bond auctions. The outside nations gave value to the dollar."

"There's nothing like that at Central," Cal said.

"That's right. Because Central Cell entails the entirety of the global economy. The board of trustees who founded the city never found it necessary to secure their digital currency with intrinsic value or within a larger economic framework. And there is no gold reserve. This is their mistake."

"Why would they not back up the currency?" Benedito asked.

"Again, it's maintaining exclusivity. If a bric is only a figment in a computer, no one outside of Central can ever own a single bric," Raz said. "Money equals citizenship and if all brics are digital, then Central dictates who has money and who doesn't. That way, someone outside of Central can't just stockpile physical brics and buy their way back in. You can't collect and save something that doesn't physically exist. By keeping brics exclusive, they limit citizenship."

"If someone were to wipe the accounts clean—like if they could hack into everyone's accounts and make it so everyone had zero brics —it would cause total chaos," Cal said.

Raz nodded. "Uh-huh, particularly so because Central is not founded on robust public coffers that could potentially stabilize a shock like that. In Central Cell, there is no public money that countries like America relied upon when the corporatists of their day crashed the economy. Central capital is held by a single corporate plutocracy. If all of Central were electronically wiped of brics, Central itself would instantaneously dissolve."

"Wow," Cal said, his mind beginning to work.

"Anyone know where all the financial information is kept?" Raz said with a grin. "Because I do."

The three of them moved through the crowds of Copper Mound. Benedito still hadn't gotten used to the smell and kept one hand to his nose at all times. They blended in with the people despite their newer clothing. The natives assumed them to be recent deportees of Central Cell and didn't give them another thought.

Benedito watched in disgust as he saw two men haggle over the worth of a shoelace. Cal noticed that no food was sold at the market. *They must immediately eat whatever food they find,* he thought. He wished he could bring them truckloads of fresh vegetables and fruit—that he could magically whisk them all to a better place.

They left the bartering alley and filed through a crowd of people that had stopped in between two garbage mounds.

"What're they doing?" Benedito asked.

Up ahead, they saw the reason for the hold-up. Two people, an older man dressed in a thin blue suit, and a woman wearing a flowing orange dress, were standing in the middle of the crowd. The woman was crying while the man stared forward at the crowd, his arm around her.

"Recent deportees," Raz said. "They don't let them take any of their things. Once someone is deported, their property is seized by

Central." He shook his head. "Poor people. They have no idea what they're in for."

"Wait!" Cal said, looking over the heads of the crowd. "That's Jelena's parents!"

"Really?" Benedito bobbed his head back and forth, trying to get a better view.

"It's definitely them. Jelena told me they were getting deported. But she said they were going to stay with relatives in Croatia..."

Raz nodded. "A gentle lie to protect their daughter from worrying," Raz said. He put his hand on Cal's shoulder. "You better not show yourself to them. We don't want to implicate them in anything that we do."

Cal nodded. "Raz, we've gotta do something. We have to change this..." He held his hands out to abject poverty.

"We will. Come on."

They left the crowds and hiked through the outer trash heaps of Copper Mound. The paths wound out of the shallow valley until they could look back and see the town at midday light. It was a valley of garbage and ash. Large freighters flew overhead and dropped down into the valley. Their underbelly doors opened, releasing a flood of fresh garbage down into the heaps.

Cal saw a few drones buzzing about the valley, sweeping down and arching back up repeatedly. "They're still looking for us?" he asked.

Raz nodded. "The son of Minzy Stanger is not a person that will be easily forgotten. They want to find you."

They left the edge of the valley and plunged back into the jungle, Benedito complaining about not having the best shoes for the hike. He also made it very clear how hungry he was. After another hour in the jungle, they stumbled into the open field where Raz's cargo ship sat, undisturbed.

"Good," Raz said. "I was worried they would've found this already and taken it." He looked up at the sky. "Doesn't look like anyone has even been here at all since we landed yesterday."

"So, where are we going?" Cal asked with apprehension.

"Back to Central, of course," Raz said as he crouched at the ship and opened a panel. "We've got some things to take care of. Hey, Benedito," he called out.

"What?" Benedito said while turning his muddy boot upside down.

"You good with navigation recalibration?" Raz asked.

Benedito's face lit up. "Um, yeah, actually. I always do it by hand myself. Most cadets just use auto-calibration."

"Have you ever tried recalibrating using only Earth's magnetic field?" Raz asked.

"What? No, how do you do that?" Benedito's curiosity grew.

"Hop in, I'll show you," Raz said, closing the panel. "We need to recalibrate before we go. Everything is off and my auto-calibration broke."

"Okay!" Benedito lightened up as he climbed into the cockpit of the cargo ship.

"Cal, just wait here. This will only take a second."

Cal nodded.

Raz also climbed into the ship, leaving Cal alone in the field. He sat on the ground, grateful it was dry, and watched as Raz fired up the engines. The main thrusters came on, lifting the ship off the ground. It hovered, motionless for a moment until Raz flipped on the Casimir Drive. A thin, pencil-like funnel shot out from the Drive, distorting light and space behind the engine. The ship lurched forward, pushed by the expanding gravity wave. Instead of flying up like Cal expected, Raz curved the trajectory of the ship and kept it low, hovering only feet off the ground. The ship shot forward, curving around the field, encircling Cal.

"What is he doing?" Cal said aloud as the ship sped up. It circled faster, sweeping across the field and blowing the leaves of the surrounding jungle. Raz continued the ship in a circle around Cal. A powerful wind swept across him, almost knocking him to the ground. Cal rolled his eyes, figuring Raz was trying to impress Benedito with how fast he could go in a circle. The ship started moving so fast around him, Cal noticed that a large circle of bent space was created within the trajectory of the ship. *Wow, I've never seen that before.*

And then a river of voices pounded through his mind. He dropped to his knees as the ship continued to circle around him. His body stretched outward as if each limb was trying to tear away. He curled into a ball as the voices showered over him.

Raz finally slowed the ship down until it came to a stop.

The voices ceased as Cal stood. A silent energy seemed to flow over his skin. *What?* He opened the back cargo door and looked at Raz. "What—" he stopped to catch his breath. "What was that?"

"What?" Raz said, checking the dashboard.

"That circle—I felt like I was going to be ripped apart. It was so... strange." He clenched his fists as if gloves of energy flowed over them.

"That was really cool!" Benedito exclaimed. "I didn't know you could calibrate the system just by going in a circle like that."

Raz nodded. "Neat trick, huh? The navigation system will track the trajectory of the magnetic fields of the planet and triangulate the ship's location. Just a little something I figured out a while ago," he said, giving Cal a furtive glance. "Okay, pals, let's go home."

Slowly, Cal climbed into the cockpit, unsure of Raz's 'recalibration'.

"Let's go and reshuffle things. Again," Raz said.

The ship lifted off the ground and sped away from the jungle, toward Central Cell.

CHAPTER 18

JANUARY 22TH, 2155 EARTH RECKONING (ER)

From his penthouse, Custos saw the vast expanse surrounding New Athens. The colorful plains ran through the desert prairies, The Meadows of Mars, rolling away into the rocky mountains beyond. Terraforming had made it a fertile land. It stretched for thousands of miles in every direction—naked of any human development whatsoever—ripe for humankind. *The seed of New Athens has grown. We can now expand. We can fill every measure of this planet in a unified and beautiful way.* Why couldn't they see his vision?

Solutions to his city's problem were no more complicated than solving a mathematical expression for Custos. The answer was right in front of him but the rest of New Athens couldn't see it. He thought about all the problems that had plagued humankind since history began and how they had all but abolished them in New Athens.

Spoiled. Spoiled and jaded. They don't know how good they have it. But I know. I know what humankind has had to put up with. He sighed, looking out the window. *Patience,* he then told himself. *Be patient with them. How could they possibly know?*

He yearned to gaze over the land of Mars and marvel at the potential of New Athens, but his view was marred. Across the city, he saw an enormous banner that hung from the upper floors of a skyscraper with crude lettering spelling out a simple message:

The Copperhound is coming.

He watched as it was cut down, one edge of the banner folding over itself, obscuring the words.

There was a knock at the door and Dev appeared. "Can I come in?"

"Of course." Custos turned from the window and looked up at his vice president. "Dev, can you answer something for me?"

He looked slightly uneasy. "Yeah..."

"Every time a great world power rises up throughout history, every intellectual of the day probably asked themselves one question. Whether it was Persia, Greece, Rome, America, Central Cell—many others. The philosophers of their days probably all asked themselves 'Are we any different than the past? Have we overcome the follies of men just enough that we will continue in our greatness? Or, will we make the same mistakes, forgetting the lessons of the past, thus perpetuating the same endless cycle?'. These are the questions that every great power has had to ask themselves, and all of them—every single one of them—has been wrong about their own success. They all forgot the lessons from history, and they all fell."

Dev nodded and sat down. "Okay. So, what can I answer for you?"

"We find ourselves at the same precipice as the past world powers. Here we are. We are the leaders and philosophers and we are asking the same questions. Will we finally elevate humanity and continue or will we fall just like everyone before? Are we any different? Can humanity ever escape the cycle?"

Dev let out an awkward laugh. "Jeez, I don't know. That's a pretty heavy question to answer."

"What do you think?"

"Not through all history of mankind has anyone achieved what has been done in New Athens. We are at the apex of civilization."

"Every previous culture has thought that about themselves."

244 | WICK WELKER

"Okay, okay, but we have done more than all of them. We are... great," Dev said, trying to sound confident. "There's no way we could ever fall like anyone before us. We're too stable. But also, maybe..."

"What?"

"Is it the right question to be asking?"

"What do you mean?"

"Your question: are we any different from the past world powers? Does it matter? You're assuming that humanity must always be progressing. And how are you even defining progress? Sure, having everyone in New Athens equally agreeing to clean dirt off the roads is great, but..."

"What?"

"What about everyone else?"

"Who?"

"Earth."

"Oh, of course. Yes. Well, they fit into our plan here as well."

"How?"

"Once we have perfected our society here and created a stable foundation, we will bring all people to Mars."

"And... if that never happens?"

Custos nodded as he listened. "Do you still trust me?"

"How long have we known each other? You met me when I was a coffee-grabbing intern in one of the council members' offices. I'm your friend and your vice president. You have my total trust."

"Good. I think I'll need it more than ever. I think—" the screen on his desk rang.

It was his secretary. "Mr. President?"

"Yes?"

"You have a call from GraviWave lab on Phobos moon."

"Oh." Custos was relieved, thinking it would be someone from the council complaining. "Please, yes, send her through." He clicked off the intercom. "It must be Dr. Farr about the gravitational waves."

Dev sat down. "What do you really think it is? Could it have something to do with... *him*?"

Custos scoffed. "I highly doubt some demagogue from Earth has the power to generate gravitational waves."

Farr's head and shoulders materialized above Custos' desk. "Mr. President, I wanted to thank you for sending the team of cryptologists up to Phobos. They've been tremendously helpful." She stopped in a pregnant pause.

"And?"

"I've got big news for you."

Custos leaned forward. "Please, go ahead."

"We've deciphered much of the waves. It's in English."

"How is that possible?"

Farr just shook her head. "I don't know but there is definitely someone out there sending a message in English through encrypted gravitational waves."

"Maybe it is from him..." Dev said.

Custos threw Dev a frustrated grimace. "What is the message?"

"We only have part of it figured out and we don't even know if it's in order. It's a much more complicated process than you'd think. It's not simply trying to crack a code in the frequency of the waves. Bits of data are scattered throughout the waves, sort of jumbled—"

"Dr. Farr," Custos interrupted. "What does the message say?"

"Oh right, of course. It's only a few words. I'll just display it on the screen so you can read it yourself. Keep in mind, we don't know if this is the right order of the phrases."

Her hologram disappeared and was replaced by text which read:

...trapped... we've created a... weapon... a Destroyer of Worlds but it didn't... deactivate from the outside...

"That's it?" Dev asked.

"'A Destroyer of Worlds'," Custos repeated.

Farr flashed back. "It's... a little disturbing to say the least."

"What do you think it means?" Custos asked.

Farr sighed. "Not sure. Me and my lab have been speculating for days."

"Do you think it's a threat?" Dev asked.

"Not exactly," Farr said. "The word 'trapped' seems to convey vulnerability about the person or people that sent the message."

"'Deactivate from the outside'," Custos repeated. "What do you make of that?"

"Some sort of instruction? Maybe it's about this weapon that they've made. Some of us here have been thinking that, perhaps, the weapon got out of control. Maybe they're warning anyone else who comes across the weapon how to disable it or to prevent something bad that may have happened."

"Maybe..." Custos said.

"Well, we've pinpointed where the transmission is coming from. It's even closer than we originally thought."

"How many light-years?" Custos asked.

"Not even one light-year. It's only about one thousand AUs away."

"How is that possible?"

"It is just beyond Neptune and the Kuiper Belt but we believe it originates between the Solar System and the Oort Cloud, in a space with very little astro activity."

"I can't believe intelligent life has been that close all this time. How could they be there? There aren't any planets or anything else in the Oort Cloud."

"Maybe they've been hiding themselves all this time," Dev suggested.

"But how do we only know about them now?" Custos asked Farr.

"I think they've always been transmitting. It's only with the new gravitational wave arrays that we've been able to detect their transmission. Also, we can't pinpoint exactly where it's coming from—only a general location. It's as if the signal is moving."

"Yes. That makes sense," Custos said.

"It does?"

"Why wouldn't they just use radio wave transmission?" Dev asked.

"I have no idea," Farr said. "We also took a look with our telescopes at the general direction of the transmission."

"And?" Custos said.

"There's nothing there. Well, there's no star there. Your Dyson Sphere theory doesn't make a whole lot of sense now. If there was a covered star, it would have greatly altered the orbits of the planets of our own solar system."

Custos tapped his chin, thinking. "If they're so advanced, why this message? They seem to have a weapon, but the message isn't necessarily threatening. They use the word 'trapped'. What is trapped?"

Farr nodded. "These are the questions me and my lab have been asking ourselves over the last few days."

"Also," Custos continued, "they speak English. How is that even possible?"

"Our radio transmissions have long since swept past that part of space and well beyond the Oort Cloud. We have a bubble of two hundred light-years of radio waves projecting from us. They no doubt learned English from us and our past radio waves. We're still in the initial phase of understanding. We'll get to the bottom of it," Farr reassured.

"Yes," Custos agreed. "We'll figure this out. Can't expect to know everything at once. Is there anything else?"

"No. I mean, we can speculate for hours, but that's all the substantial progress I have for you."

"Needless to say, this information is strictly confidential. I'm placing a gag order over your entire lab. No one is to divulge any of this information to the press, the council of New Athens, or the Chamber of Colonies. This is between my administration and your lab. Is that understood?"

Farr quickly nodded. "Of course, Mr. President."

"Thank you. Please notify me immediately of any new developments." He ended the transmission. Custos looked over at Dev. "What do we do about this right now?"

"Not sure. There's so much going on. Reporters are hounding me constantly. Vandalism is popping up everywhere lately about... about—"

"About what?"

"About... *him.*"

Custos scoffed. "Come on, just say the name."

Dev forced a laugh. "The Copperhound."

"Don't give the name power by avoiding it."

"But who is he?" Dev asked forcefully.

"Does it matter?"

"I think so, yes."

"You've seen the same intelligence reports I have. There are no mobilizing armies. There are no warships. All of North America is a complete wasteland. Most of Earth is barren under nuclear fallout. There are only a few trading cities that actually function and they aren't gearing up for war. If anything, the threat of an Earth faction harming us is at an all-time low. I don't really care who The Copperhound is—if he's even real. If he is a real person, then he's just clever at marketing. Has there been another attack on Martian soil?"

Dev hesitated. "No."

"Then why does it matter who The Copperhound really is?"

"Because people are afraid of him. That's why it matters," Dev asserted.

Custos paused, staring at Dev. "Are you with me, Dev?"

Dev nodded. "Yes."

"I can trust you?"

"Yes."

"Good. I might need your help more than ever."

———

Gina Wilder shuffled through the dense crowd of protesters. They had accumulated over the past several hours at a central crossroads in the middle of downtown New Athens. As she walked, she had a tablet on which she furiously scribbled everything she saw. A small, inconspicuous camera on her breast pocket was also continuously recording. The last several weeks had been a gold mine of reporting for her piece in The New Athens Times. She had followed all recent demonstrations and attended every event she could. It had been decades since the city had seen protesters at all. Her readership increased by two hundred percent. She had grown to love everything about protests and the plunging popularity of the robot president.

She made note of several different chants as she moved along. Most of the protesters yelled about safety and shutting down importing from Earth. It was interesting, however, that the anxiety about New Athens' safety had energized other issues of which she wasn't even aware. Some groups yelled about maintaining human farming while others shouted about having more pork products and abolishing communal gardening. *It's like all these issues were just bubbling underneath the surface, waiting for an excuse to come out,* she thought.

Thousands of protesters filled the crossroads, having shut down traffic many hours ago. All along the sidewalks and walls of the buildings was the same warning that she had seen in various spots in the city. Given the close proximity, style of writing, and spray paint, she guessed it was likely only a small group of people that was actually doing the graffiti.

"Hello?" someone said from behind. Gina felt someone tugging at her shirt. She made room through the elbows and backpacks—pushing signs out of her face. She flipped around and saw a shorter black-haired woman looking up at her. The woman was missing several teeth.

"Yes?" Gina said.

"You're a reporter, right?" the woman asked.

"Yes." She adjusted the camera in her pocket to focus on the woman. "What can I do for you?

"I'm from Earth," she said. "I know what's going on there."

Gina fumbled with her tablet and turned on the voice recorder. "Do you mind if I make video and audio of our conversation?"

"Go ahead," the woman said, nodding.

"Okay, please. What's your name?"

"Charlotte."

"Charlotte, where are you from on Earth?"

"The ruins of Central Cell."

"When did you come to New Athens?"

"Couple of weeks ago."

"Did you see armies gathering? Did you hear of this Copperhound?"

Charlotte nodded. "Yes. He was gathering armies everywhere. Everyone swears allegiance to him there. I had to run and escape from them. They kill people. They kill everyone who doesn't join them."

"And who is he?"

"He's The Copperhound," Charlotte said, staring vacantly for a moment. "And he's angry. Says he's coming to Mars. Says he's going to take back what belongs to the forgotten people of Earth."

"Did you see warships? Are there weapons?"

Charlotte nodded. "Yes, and everyone joins. They join because they're hungry. The Copperhound gives them food and makes them take an oath."

"Do you know where he came from?"

"He says he was born of Earth. Made in her womb and born to redeem her people."

Gina nodded excitedly, already thinking of how she would word her article about this girl. "How did you escape from the armies?"

"I hid away on a freighter—an old TexasH ship that came here. That's how I got here."

"So, you were able to sneak past customs and come here?"

Charlotte nodded. "Uh-huh, the first person I met was President Custos. He gave me food and new clothes. He said I could stay in New Athens for the rest of my life and that I would be safe."

"I see..." Gina made some more notes on her tablet. "Now, tell me, Charlotte—what's wrong?" She noticed Charlotte looking over her head, mouth gaping.

Gina turned around and saw what had caught the woman's attention—an Earth freighter ship was falling from the sky. It careened in between the buildings, swerving around air shuttles and drones. Whoever was flying it was either out of control or knew very little about flying. For a moment, she thought the freighter would simply crash into the streets but it managed to even itself out and slow down. It hovered above the protesters for a moment as the crowds receded. A space among the people was created for the ship before it clunked down, cracking the ceramic road.

A hush fell over the crowds as they watched the now motionless freighter. Confused, the people approached the ship as the back cargo bay opened. Gina peered into the dark bay and saw several figures within, getting to their feet. She adjusted her camera, aiming it right at the shadowy passengers as they emerged at the edge of the ship.

"More people from Earth trying to get in!" someone shouted out, causing a murmuring in the crowd. One of the figures walked to the edge of the cargo bay and then fell out onto the road. Gina and Charlotte inched closer and saw the man rising to his feet. Screams shot out from the crowd. Half of the man's hair was gone, replaced by a bare metal plate which had been screwed into his skull. He wore jeans and a dirtied t-shirt covered with a filthy cloak, full of holes. He got to his feet, eyes turning in all directions, and stumbled toward the crowd. A woman fell out from behind. Her hair was missing and her face had been burned badly, leaving white scar tissue that had consumed most of her facial features. Her arms had lost most muscle and skin from burns as well. Her lower left arm had been entirely replaced by a robotic forearm with a hydraulic piston at the elbow joint and five articulating finger joints that moved erratically. As the crowd receded around them, yet another person fell from the cargo bay who had robotic legs made of rusted iron packed with hydraulics at the knee joint.

"Cyborgs!" someone yelled, causing the protesters to scatter.

"They've finally come to take the city!"

Another shouted, "He's here! The Copperhound is here!" Everyone dropped their signs and scrambled away from the freighter, trying to crawl over one another.

Gina backed away, keeping the camera on the cyborgs. She was nervous, expecting more of them to spill out with weapons. There was more of the same—they fell out the back with various limbs substituted for robotic parts. All of them were clearly malnourished and most of them appeared wildly confused.

"Charlotte!" Gina yelled over to her, she was also backing away from the freighter. "Have you seen people like this before on Earth?"

Charlotte bobbed her head up and down. "Uh-huh."

"Are they dangerous?"

"They can be. But... they're just sick." She turned and ran, wiggling through the crowd.

One of the cyborgs got to his feet, eyes circling in his sockets until they focused on Gina. *Okay, that's enough footage.*

She ran.

———

Custos stared at the middle of two wooden closed doors. He studied the wood grain of the doors and meditated. He was feeling particularly powerless—an emotion that he hadn't experienced in a very long time. He had always been able to study any situation and find the best possible solution—mastering politicking to ascertain an opponent's weak spots and then leveraging their needs into his goals. It had been one big game of chess. *But how do you play an opponent who thinks their own rook is going to slaughter them?* he thought. *How do you reason with the irrational? Do you give in to the fears, gratifying their paranoia? Or do you assert your own power despite the people not understanding why you're doing it? Does it matter if a leader is considered a tyrant if—in the end—he saves his own people from harm?*

He pressed the doors open to an auditorium packed full of the media core comprising hundreds of journalists and cameras. Beyond the media, hundreds more citizens chanted in protest. Custos' presence at the center stage stirred the crowd into a frenzy of unsolicited questions with periodic shouts. He approached the podium and stood alone on stage.

Custos spoke into the microphone. "Ladies and gentlemen of the press and our welcome citizens, I address New Athens and her colonies as your elected president. As your leader, I've been proud of our achievements. We have accomplished unprecedented growth while maintaining sustainable energy practices. We are a celebrated blend of multiple ethnicities and historic Earth nationalities. We have no reason to fear the people of Earth because we all came from Earth once. They are not alien and they will not harm us—"

"Coward!" someone in the backroom shouted.

Custos paused, taken aback by the unprecedented interruption. He lifted up his finger only to be interrupted again by a barrage of questions that erupted from the media crowd.

"Mr. President!" Gina Wilder yelled from the front row. "What will you do to prevent another cyborg attack in the city?"

"It wasn't an attack. No one was harmed—"

"It was an unauthorized freighter full of cyborgs from Earth that landed in the middle of peaceful protests," Gina asserted.

"Yes, but it wasn't an attack." At this, the crowd in the back of the auditorium exploded with angry shouting. "Did you see these alleged cyborgs?"

"I was personally present during the attack, Mr. President. I barely escaped with my life," Gina said as the reporters around her turned to record.

Custos continued, "None of them had weapons and most were too weak to even walk. They were easily apprehended. Most are in the hospital right now."

"They deliberately landed in the middle of the protests to maximize harm," another reporter yelled.

"But they couldn't have harmed anyone even if they tried. Most of them didn't have any idea that they were even on Mars." Custos breathed heavily, fully aware that the press conference had already spiraled out of control. As more reporters fired questions at him, he looked out at the crowds and caught sight of a familiar face.

It was the Earth woman he had met weeks earlier in the park... Charlotte.

He spoke again, trying to steer the conversation away. "We need to stand up to the people that are trying to terrorize our city. We must act rationally in the face of the unknown. Yes, there may be a group of people on Earth that is trying to attack our city, but we've always had enemies there. They are far too weak and unorganized to ever mount an attack and that includes this newest wave of rumors. Most people on Earth are docile and only want to live in peace. They come here out of desperation, only looking for food. The people on Earth are not dangerous. Just the other day, I met a young woman who had recently come to New Athens from Earth." He pointed out to the crowd beyond the reporters. "Her name is Charlotte and she is standing right here among us."

Hundreds of heads turned toward Charlotte who had been standing in the back among the crowd. Every eye and camera was focused on her, broadcasting her face to hundreds of millions.

Custos continued with his arm extended toward her. "Charlotte was desperate for food and shelter. She snuck onto a freighter and arrived here. I promptly arranged for her to be integrated by immigration and I can see that she now looks well and nourished. I ask you, does she seem dangerous to anyone?"

The crowds finally went quiet, expecting Charlotte to make a statement. She looked around at the hundreds of faces, wide-eyed, and shied away.

"Go ahead, my dear," Custos said. "Tell them how life has been now that you've been welcomed into New Athens." Custos' anxiety grew as he fully realized the political gamble he was taking by singling her out. He barely knew a single thing about the woman.

A kaleidoscope of emotion swept her face. Custos saw apprehension wax to fear which then turned to resolve as her lips straightened. She straightened her back and spoke, "The Copperhound is coming."

Custos slumped at the podium.

"I have seen Him," she continued. "He knows who we are. He was born inside Earth and lives in her shadows. He moves as a phantom among us. No walls can hold him. He is coming to New Athens. He is coming soon and we cannot stop him."

The crowd around her, aghast with shock, slowly backed away. Charlotte stood still and looked back up at Custos. Every head turned back toward him.

Custos paused before saying, "Just... just arrest her," and then stomped off the stage.

CHAPTER 19

NOVEMBER 9TH, 1989

I n the early morning, Straus was hidden away in his locked basement room. Dozens of new pages were strewn across the desk, each with new math and scattered sentences. Amongst the math, he had drawn hundreds of circles—thousands even. It wasn't that the Rift had only given him images and math associated with the geometry of a circle, he also *liked* to draw them. Each time he drew a circle, he hoped it would spark new insight into why he was even seeing circles from the Rift. What did a circle have to do with the Casimir Drive and bending space? What was the connection—if any —and why was it coming to him? Clearly, he was already able to build the Casimir Drive with only understanding a fraction of the information that streamed through his mind. *There must be more to the picture,* he thought. *There is so much more that I'm not understanding.*

He had a brief moment of hopelessness. Not only did he not know why or from where the Rift was open to him, but he didn't even know if it had any purpose at all. *Maybe it is just coming from my own mind. My math and physics have just been twisted by my schizophrenia and churned back out to me and I think that it's a mystery to solve.*

Or... the Rift is real.

It opened up to me for some reason and it's instructing me to build the Drive.

But why? What he once believed to be a noble endeavor of building a machine that would connect all of humanity had transformed into an obsession—an obsession tinged with unassailable feelings of dread and... something else. A new fire burned within him. It was a fire of deep resentment—no, not resentment. He knew what it was but didn't want to admit it to himself.

It was hatred.

Hatred for what? Or who?

The feelings were as inexplicable as they were impossible to ignore. Infused with the panicked pressure and indiscriminate hatred, he knew there was more to the Drive. The current Drive seemed so incomplete as if it were just one part of the Rift's riddle to him.

"I'm just sick," he'd say to himself in his lonely room. "It's my head. There's no one out there—no one waiting to get me. There is no enemy." His words always rang hollow to the tidal waves of fear and loathing within. What would Jo think of him if she knew he was building something that wasn't just an engine?

Moreover, the confidence that had bolstered him ever since discovering the Casimir Drive had been deeply shaken by Jack Van Wert. Straus was still fuming that the oaf of a man had figured out the precise copper alloy composition to get the Casimir Drive to run for hours. Ever since Van Wert had been in the lab every day, overseeing all operations and spewing his unsolicited suggestions all over Straus. He had never been overly impressed with Van Wert's skills as a physicist but now the man almost functioned at a similar level to that of Straus. *When did that bastard suddenly get so smart?*

As he tried ignoring the newly troubling thoughts, he fumbled through the pages about the thermal regulation of the Drive. As before, he found bits of the math, broken apart, which seemed to be the answer to the appropriate alloy cartridge for the Drive to run properly. However, he was never able to put it all together before Van Wert did. As he now laid out the pages and considered the math together—now knowing that Van Wert's copper alloy was correct—he saw that it was there, right in his own math. *How did I not see it? Jo's right, sometimes I'm too much of a scatterbrain to see what's right in front of me. That's why she can always beat me at chess.*

"Hey, Jo?" Straus called up the stairs after he had locked his basement room for the day. It was morning and she wasn't in her normal spot in the kitchen. "Jo?" he called again.

"I'm up here, honey," her small voice bounced around the staircase from the second level. "Come up for a minute," she said, almost taunting him.

"I've got to get to the lab. I just need to ask you something."

"Okay, come and ask me up here then."

"Okay," he muttered under his breath, bounding up the stairs. He rounded the corner into the master bedroom. "Have you—" he stopped, finding Jo sitting at her vanity, wearing a silk robe. Her back was facing him as she finished applying makeup. From the mirror, he saw that she wore bright red lipstick with a splash of rouge on her cheeks.

Meeting his eyes from the vanity, she spoke up, "What is it?"

"Um—" he looked away for a moment and then back at her. "Has Jack Van Wert been around?"

"What do you mean?" She finished up with mascara then stood to face him. From her outline in the robe, Straus could tell she wore nothing underneath.

"Has he been around? Like around the house?"

"Don't you think I'd tell you if I had seen him around the house? That man has never once stepped foot in this house before. I think I'd mention it if he had." She went to the bed and sat down, her left bare shoulder slipping out from her robe. She didn't fix it.

"Has anyone from the lab been by at all? Anyone wanting to get into the basement?"

She shook her head and squinted at him. "Of course not."

"Just wanted to make sure. I'm getting a little suspicious that someone is stealing my work." He turned from the bedroom and was about to leave but then asked, "Why are you looking all dressed up?"

She shrugged. "I'm going shopping with my friends. I wanted to look nice."

"Well... you do look nice," he said, giving a formal nod.

She gave a weak smile. "Thanks."

He turned to leave but she stopped him. "Hey," she said, patting the bed next to her.

"I really need to get to the class."

She said nothing but kept tapping the spot right next to her.

He sat.

She slipped her hand into his. "I miss you."

"I miss you too." He looked at her, and for a moment, remembered what it was like to love her. He thought about their first few months of dating. He'd never once been successful with a girl. Jo was different. She was better than him. Where the world saw a hopelessly awkward nerd, Jo saw a tender heart mathematician. She envisioned a strong father and scientist—someone who could change the world with his mind. She was the reason he got tenure at Georgetown and was even the first to push him when he came up with the early math for the Casimir Drive. Who would he even be without her?

Jo was always the optimist. And her optimism went far beyond himself—where the world saw nuclear standoff, Jo saw light on the horizon. She had believed in him. She believed in healing. He wondered why he had resisted her so much over the last few months. A small pit of guilt sunk inside of him. He had changed. He knew it, she knew it, and the guilt finally hit.

And so, he kissed her.

She pulled away after a moment. "Tim..."

"I'm sorry," he said. More of an admission of guilt than an apology.

"I do everything because I love you. I do everything only to help you."

"I know. I've been... awful lately. I really have missed you." He kissed her again. "I do love you."

"You can get better. Everything can get better if you just wait and hope." Tears streamed down her face. "Please, don't forget that. Healing can always happen."

"I won't. I won't forget it ever again," he said, slipping the robe off from her other shoulder.

He was happy as he rode his bike to work. For the first time in a while, he felt what it was like to not be stressed. The anxiety of the lab and Jack Van Wert oozed out of him, leaving his mind slack and carefree. For a moment, he closed his eyes and focused on the wind moving over his skin. He felt peace, ignoring the pit of despair that rotted within him. He didn't even think about the Rift. For the first time in a while, he thought of Jo. What he thought was a source of distraction to his work should've been a well of strength to him. He winced with regret as he locked his bike and went into class.

"So," he began as his class got seated in the auditorium. "As we make it to midterm, I wanted to summarize a lot of the stuff that we've covered this semester to make sure you're all on the same page." The students shuffled with their notebooks, prepared to take notes. "For your exam, you should be going over General and Special Relativity, including gravitational field equations. There will be one derivation question on the exam as well as one essay question."

"Essay question!" someone complained.

"Yes, you're not here just to learn rote mathematics. I want you to think creatively about this stuff too."

"Well... what kind of essay questions will you be asking?" Chloe asked.

"I'll tell you that it will have something to do with our discussions that we've had in class, so if you didn't bother to come, then you're really going to be out of luck. Who can list off some of the things we've talked about?"

A girl in the back raised her hand. "Singularity and event horizon."

Straus nodded. "Yes, what else?"

"We had a day where we just talked about what happens to time in the middle of a black hole," Chloe said.

"That's right. And what was the main point of that discussion?"

She looked at the ceiling for a moment, then responded, "That time stands still for someone in the middle of the black hole."

Straus shook his head. "No, that's what you said last time. That isn't the full picture. Time will *appear* to stand still to an observer *outside* of the black hole. But for you—the person stuck inside the black hole—your watch will move one normal second at a time—you wouldn't be able to tell the difference."

Chloe and a few others nodded. "Oh right."

"But this is given that you would survive being torn apart from the gravitational tidal forces of the black hole, which you wouldn't. You'd be stretched apart. The middle of a black hole is no place for anyone to live."

The class nodded in agreement.

"And what's interesting—and I know this is a little beyond this course—but if you take quantum mechanics and gravitational equations and act like time doesn't exist, something really surprising happens in the math. Under a gravitational force that mimics the singularity of a black hole, with time factored out, material decay ceases."

Chloe raised her hand. "And what does that mean?"

"It means that entropy goes away. It means that the strong nuclear forces persist in perpetuity. Whatever is organized, stays organized. Matter stays bound together under the unique conditions of enormous gravity with time becoming irrelevant. Matter would essentially persist forever."

Chloe raised her hand again. "Um, is what you just said going to be on the essay question?"

Straus shook his head. "No, that was just some bonus stuff. Don't worry, you're not going to be explaining how you can get matter to not decay on the exam. Okay, let's get into some of the math for review—"

But then the Rift opened to him.

Again! Why does it happen so often right in the middle of class? Did their discussion trigger the Rift? He had become skilled at hiding it as throbbing pain instantly split through his head. His eyes teared as he grimaced, trying to compose himself. His vision blurred and he succumbed, bending over and covering his eyes from the blinding light.

"Dr. Straus!" Chloe said. "Is it happening again?"

"Uh—" he didn't respond but only sunk to the floor as the class got to their feet.

The bastard is probably lurking at the back of the class, watching, he thought, looking for Van Wert but doubled over with nausea before he could see.

He waited for the Rift to close but something new happened.

He heard a low voice speaking in his mind. The man's voice rattled like someone speaking with the diseased lungs of a chain smoker. The voice scratched on Straus' feelings, tugging at him, filling him with that dread—that hateful dread. *Who is this?* Straus then heard a phrase that was repeated but couldn't make out the words. A sweat broke over his forehead and a series of chills rolled through him. He was filled with the instinct to flee. He wanted to run and hide—hide from the man with the rattling voice.

Straus, with the help of his students, got to his feet. He trembled, supporting himself on a table. The chanting ran through his mind, people shouting the same phrase over and over again—a phrase he couldn't make out. He freed himself from the supporting arms of the students and tried to run up the auditorium stairs but misplaced a step and slipped, falling down again. Chloe came from behind to try to help him to his feet again, but he pushed her away, making her smack her arm on a chair.

"Ow!" she cried. "My arm!" A handful of students rushed to her while Straus tumbled onto the stairs.

The deep voice kept rattling through him, filling him with panic until he could no longer think straight. He forgot where he was or what he was even doing. The chanting got louder and louder and it suddenly became clear.

He finally screamed, "The Copperhound is coming!"

He looked back at his students, his glasses askew, and blinked. They gawked at him while Chloe held her arm, crying.

The Rift closed and he was left to a cold sweat, lying on the auditorium steps. "I'm sorry, everyone," he said, looking back at them. "I'm not... feeling well."

"Is Dr. Van Wert around?" Straus asked Duke, eyeing the lab.

Duke looked at him suspiciously for a moment. "No, he hasn't been in yet. Why? You seem stressed out."

"No, no, it's nothing. What about Holloway?"

"Yeah, she's here. She's been running the Drive all morning."

Straus squinted into the track room and saw the Casimir Drive —*his* Drive—circling around the track. Holloway was at a computer analyzing data. "How do we get rid of her?"

"Oh, I-I didn't think we needed to. I think she's brought a lot of good thinking to the lab. We wouldn't be near where we are if her and Dr. Van Wert hadn't used their copper cassette."

"What?" Straus was irritated. The episode in class earlier had visibly shaken him. The Rift had opened up to him many times in his life but he had never felt the measure of dread and fear that had overcome him. He was now only processing things in a haze of paranoia. He continued throwing furtive glances around the room. "It was *my* copper alloy, Duke."

Duke grabbed him by the shoulder. "What is going on?"

Straus looked at Duke's hand, resting on his shoulder and then eyed Duke. "Don't."

Duke, unnerved, removed his hand. "S-s-sorry."

Straus backed away, his hair disheveled. "Just listen to me. I've been thinking about it a lot." He tried brushing stray strands of hair back from his eyes but they stuck in place. "We've had everything wrong from the beginning with the Drive."

"What?"

"Come here, come here." He rushed Duke to a lab table where he spoke softly. "The Casimir plates that we made, that was the beginning... that's how we were even able to make gravity waves. But there's something wrong with the application of the Casimir Drive. It's not supposed to be an engine. It's supposed to be something else..."

Duke looked confused. "What do you mean 'supposed to be'? It's not supposed to be anything. We made it. We can do whatever we want with it."

Straus shook his head. "No, no, you don't get it. It's not supposed to be just for transportation. We got something wrong about how to use the Drive." He breathed heavily. "Listen, we need to rethink the whole thing. I have so much unused math. The Drive is just one part of the machine—it's a key part, but it's not the whole thing."

"What machine?"

"I, uh—well, I don't quite know yet." A maniacal grin flitted across his face. "But this whole thing," he said, motioning to the track, "all of this, it's part of something bigger than what we're currently trying to do."

"And what is that?" Duke asked. He began glancing around the lab.

"We're supposed to stop... *Him*," Straus blurted out and then was quickly shocked that he had said it.

"Stop *who?* What are you talking about? Are you feeling okay?"

"I'm fine, I'm fine. I'm not sure who..."

"Dr. Straus," Duke said, scratching his neck, "I gotta say, I'm a little worried about this stuff you're saying."

Straus nodded, his mood jumping from suspicion to agreement. "I know, I know, it all sounds crazy what I'm saying, but it's true. The Drive goes way beyond what we're trying to do to it. And that woman there," he said, pointing to Holloway who now noticed Straus' presence in the lab, "she and Van Wert are going to stop us."

Duke looked back at Holloway and then gave a heavy sigh. "I don't know about any of this."

"You need to trust me. Look how far I've brought you already—"

"Dr. Straus!" the familiar deep voice of Jack Van Wert boomed behind him. This time, his tone was of sheer indignation. "Please step away from Duke."

"What?" Straus turned and saw Van Wert's beet-red face flushing against his white beard. There were two police officers behind him. "Whoa, whoa, whoa, what the hell is going on here?"

"Tim, these officers are going to escort you out of the lab. Please just cooperate," Van Wert warned.

"What are you talking about?" Duke asked, putting his arms on his hips. The rest of the lab crew, including Holloway and Chou Jia, watched from a distance. Holloway wore a look of satisfaction at the sight of the police officers.

"Oh," Straus said, "and where do you think I'm going?"

Van Wert shook his head. "Don't make this harder than it has to be."

"Why am I being escorted out of *my* lab by two police officers?"

Van Wert sighed. "It is even more alarming, Dr. Straus, that you don't even recall that you broke the arm of one of your students no less than an hour ago during your own class."

"What!" Straus exclaimed. Flashes of his student, Chloe, falling to the ground flooded his mind. It was true, he'd completely forgot and would've never guessed that he'd hurt the girl. "I—" he stopped, considering his words.

Van Wert shook his head. "This has been a long time coming, but you finally did yourself in by hurting someone."

"But... but it was an accident."

"It doesn't matter. You were clearly suffering from psychosis in the middle of your classroom. You've demonstrated that you are unsafe to be around. Let's go."

Straus panicked, his hair whipping across his face as he looked around the lab. Everyone was staring at him. "But I need to stay. You don't get it, Jack. Look, I know we've had our differences but things have changed. We need to change the direction that we're heading with the Drive. We need to change the design. We've got it all wrong!"

"Do we, Dr. Straus?" Van Wert said coolly as the police officers walked from behind him.

"Yes, yes, we need to dismantle the Drive—take out the Casimir coils and redesign everything. I think... I think it needs to be circular."

"Circular?" Van Wert asked. "Is that what Custos told you, Jack?"

Straus' heart pounded in his chest. "*Wha—*" He couldn't think straight anymore as sweat dripped into his eyes. *How did he know?* Straus had never uttered that name out loud. Not even he himself knew what the name meant. How could Van Wert know?

And then Straus knew. "Thief!" he cried, pointing at Van Wert. "Thief! You stole my work!"

"Okay, okay," Van Wert said gently, waving his hand. "Let's get him out of here."

The officers seized Straus by the shoulders and handcuffed him while he continued to shout and accuse Van Wert. They hurried him out of the lab, leaving the lab crew behind, staring at each other.

————

Jo Straus walked through the double doors of the hospital, keeping her head low. She checked into the front desk and was told to have a seat in the waiting lounge. She sat, picking a few small holes in the vinyl of the couch cushions and jumped at every person that walked by. She thought about the morning with her husband and how it already felt like it was a lifetime away. She noticed a newspaper on the coffee table and picked it up.

"Jo," she heard a familiar voice down the hallway and quickly recognized Van Wert standing in a doorway. He waved her over.

She rolled the newspaper under her arm and scrambled over to him. "Where is he? Is he okay?"

Van Wert nodded and spoke softly, "He's being taken care of. I personally know some of the psychiatrists here, they're a very good group. He'll get the help he needs."

Jo breathed a sigh of relief. "I'm so..."

Van Wert put his hand on her shoulder. "I know you wanted him to get help. Of course, not like this—not with a student being injured.

But now you know that you were right to want him to be institution-alized. This is the right thing to do."

She nodded. "I hope so."

"And we're happy to continue his work in the lab while he gets better."

"Yes, it'll make him happy to know that his work will go on even while he's here."

"Not that he's particularly thrilled about me now taking over the project. He seems to have projected a lot of his problems onto me."

"I know. Just this morning he was asking if you had been sneaking around the house. He thinks you're stealing from him."

He nodded. "It's a classic sign of paranoid schizophrenia, I'm afraid. Anyway, I think it's time that you bring me the rest of his work that you have at your home as well."

"What?" she looked at him. "Why? I thought most of it was nonsense."

He paused. "Well, yes, a lot of it are his ramblings with several fantastical characters, but there is a significant amount of math that could be helpful." He looked away, attempting to appear casual.

Jo looked at him, wide-eyed. "Is that all you care about? Getting his work?"

Van Wert put up his hands. "No, no, of course not. I've wanted for Tim to get help, just like you. Now, it's undeniable that Tim has a certain mathematical genius when it comes to this particular project. I'm just using whatever means I can to accomplish his own goals."

She saw shame cross his face for only an instant, and she knew. "You... don't care at all about him. You've just been... using me."

"That's simply not true."

"You'll not get another scrap of paper from me." She turned her back to him and said, "I will single-handedly make sure your name is found nowhere on any publication related to the Casimir Drive."

"Jo—Mrs. Straus, that's not how it is," he said weakly as she walked away.

Jo found the psychiatric ward and moved through double security after providing photo identification. She walked into a common room of patients, many of which were rambling to themselves or sitting around a snack table eating graham crackers and staring at the opaque windows. She finally spotted the back of his head sitting in a chair.

She walked over to him and sat at his side without him realizing. He had his eyes closed and was quietly talking to himself. "...if I encircle him, I could...no, no, no, that could backfire. If it's built as a halo, it would have an equal gradient all around. Whatever is in the center would be stable and anything off—anything even a little off-center would be torn apart—at least I think. This could work—"

"Tim," she interrupted his ramblings.

Straus jumped in his chair and looked up at her. "Jo!" He sat up. "Oh, I'm so glad you're here. You need to get me outta here, Jo. There are so many things I need to get to work on. We have everything wrong—so wrong. I need to tell everyone in the lab to change everything."

"Tim..." She held his cheek.

"I'm trying to piece together what it's trying to tell me. The Rift."

"I'm glad you're here now. This is where you need to be. We can get you back on meds and get you back home."

"Jo." He took her hand. "I know it sounds crazy but there is something—someone real who is coming. He's going to destroy us—all of us. We have to stop him. The Rift has been telling me how to do it. This whole time I thought it was trying to get me to build an engine, but it's not, that's only part of it."

Jo looked down.

"It's a design for something big. It's a weapon."

"Why do you want to build a weapon?"

"There is someone coming that's going to destroy us all."

"Who?"

"I... don't want to say."

"Is it the Soviets?"

"What?" He looked at her, surprised. "No, this has nothing to do with them. Although, if this weapon is as big as I'm imagining, we could easily take care of them as well. We could end this whole nuclear standoff."

"Maybe you don't have to." She dropped the day's newspaper in his lap.

Straus picked it up and saw a photo on the front cover. It showed crowds of people assembled at a concrete wall. The middle section of the wall had been torn away; crumbled concrete littered the ground. Atop the wall, a string of people stood, holding hands and raising their fists to the air. The headline above the picture read, *Berlin Wall Tumbles.*

"The Eastern Bloc is over without a single bullet being fired."

He studied the newspaper as if expecting to find it fraudulent.

"Sometimes it just takes a little time, a little patience, and the right thing happens. People can come together. Things *can* work out. You always used to be so optimistic, Tim. At least before you started working on your Drive. It hasn't been healthy for you—it has changed you."

He shook his head. "No, this is different. My weapon is to stop a much bigger threat—"

"The world doesn't need another weapon. It needs courage, humility... kindness. The very qualities that made me fall in love with you in the first place. Come back to us. Your wife needs her husband. Your son needs his father."

"Last Athens needs me."

"Last Athens?"

"Last Athens," he repeated with uncertainty.

She let go of his hand, exhausted. "I've been in your room."

He raised an eyebrow at her. "My room?"

"Your basement room. I've been there. I've seen what you've been doing."

"But... I always keep it locked."

"It doesn't matter how. I've seen your writings and all the hangers you have with math and words all over them. It's not healthy. You're not well. There is no Custos, New Athens—or Last Athens or whatever. None of it is real."

"No, no, no, you don't get it. I do that so I can make connections. Everything you saw in the room—all that math—it's schematics for the weapon—"

"What?"

"Wait—" he said, looking at her with shock. "It was you!"

"What?"

"You've been stealing my math—been giving it to Van Wert!"

She stood from her chair. "Was only trying to help."

"And this morning, you got all dolled up. You were trying to seduce me—"

She held his lips in her hand, stopping him mid-sentence. "You're not yourself, Tim. You're better than this. I *know* there is something beautiful inside of you. Please find it again."

She left him there.

CHAPTER 20

SEPTEMBER 9TH, 2098

C al stood among a bustling crowd. The soaring, vaulted ceilings of the shopping plaza dwarfed the fugitive teenager. He kept his collars up and sunglasses over his eyes as the masses filed around him, hardly noticing the motionless figure. He stared with wonder at them. Before, they were just... people... gazing at their tablets, gossiping about their friends, or buying clothing they didn't need. He never thought anything was wrong with the way Central Cell citizens lived and, to be fair, how could they know better? He fixated on a small child, escorted alone by an automated and locked stroller. Her eyes were placid beneath virtual glasses that displayed thousands of hours of gaming entertainment.

Since returning from Copper Mound, he felt different—he felt *new*. His body hummed with energy and something else...

Power.

Caleb Stanger was now a relic. His mother, Central Academy—all of it was a distant past now. He was an entirely new creature, reborn into something with infinite possibilities. As soon as he boarded Raz's ship as they left Copper Mound, everything about him seemed to have changed. Raz acted aloof but every time Cal looked over at him, his uncle had a flicker of understanding in his eyes. Something had happened. Raz had done something to him. Breath moved through his lungs like fuel, filling his chest with energy. Enriched blood circled through his body, enlightening his mind. A new strength flowed through his tendons, invigorating his muscles with an unbreakable tautness.

He felt himself as a new creature as he studied the people. They were no better than animals following the scent of food—their attention so easily swayed by skewed headlines, shrewd marketers, or beautiful bodies. They were stuck—damned to dwell within the confines of a mind that didn't ask questions.

And then he *refracted*.

It was a mere thought and he shattered the windows of his reality and saw the crowds through hundreds of dimensions. They were all the same—identical to his own. Even those he had admired in his life —Captain Kalai, Professor Hendricks, and many of his cadet friends were nothing more than pawns in the self-imposed prison of Central Cell. They were all complicit in the iron rule Central Cell. Now, grimacing at the crowds of shoppers, he didn't think of them as independent, compassionate human beings. There was only one word to describe them: pathetic. They were pathetic to him.

But things can change, he thought. A Nuclear Night changed the world order in an instant. The masses can readjust if someone just shows them the way. People are inherently good, he reasoned. They just need a beacon, an ensign—a *leader*.

Cal had been many things in his life—a depressed kid and a flight school drop-out. His mother had groomed him to be part of the ruling class, to pass on the torch of subjugation.

Until now.

Cal turned from the crowds, finally deciding who he was meant to be.

———

Minzy Stanger was busy preparing for a dinner party. She had personally inspected both the dining halls, the lounge, the balconies, the rooftop pool patio, and the central mezzanine. The mezzanine had several bridges that ran across, connecting between reflecting pools and surrounding bars. She knew it was her guests' favorite place to congregate and so had swept through the flower beds and tables of the mezzanine, checking for dirt or cluttered cleaning supplies from the servants. It was only an hour before the first guests would arrive and she wanted to single out those of the cleaning staff who hadn't yet finished. She had been patiently waiting to identify who the weakest link was in the household. To her disappointment, everything appeared perfect.

She returned to the kitchen to perform her pre-party ritual—an old bottle of scotch she kept at the back of a cupboard, of which she served herself a single shot before every important dinner party at her home. She hated the taste but the strong drink gave her a quick balance of relaxation and composure that she desperately sought during these occasions. She found her anti-anxiety medication too sedating and that her antidepressants dulled her senses. No, a single shot of scotch always did the trick.

Minzy needed all the luck she could summon for this dinner party. She was going to beg in front of the very board of trustees on which she sat for mercy for her idiot son. For several days straight, dozens of Central agents were in and out of the house, ransacking Cal's room. She shuddered in disgust at the thought of the boy and set the shot glass down after coughing on the hot liquid in her throat.

"How long did you know?" a voice surprised her from behind.

She turned, aghast, and saw Cal standing in the kitchen with her. "Cal!" she yelped after clasping her hand over her open mouth. "How did you—"

"How long did you know?" He looked at her with brooding eyes.

"Know what?"

"How long have you known how much people are suffering because of you?"

"Where the *hell* have you been? Do you have any idea what you've put me through?"

Cal shook with anger. "I've been outside this city's walls. I've been among the people who live in our garbage. They die like animals—cows live better lives than the people outside the walls of Central Cell. I held a man as he died in my arms, surrounded by the corpses of thousands of people who suffered the same fate. All of this happens, all over—just miles away from here—and what do you do? You throw a party for your friends—"

"This isn't just a party. I was trying to ensure safe passage for you back into Central." Her nostrils flared in disgust. "You've never understood everything that I do for you."

"We just go about our days, living our lives of excess," he said as if in soliloquy. "We shop on our phones and buy clothing—buy outfits with money that could feed someone on the outside for years. And you just sit here, in this castle, watching movies about all the poor souls. You *feel* bad for them but you don't do anything for them as long as it threatens your control. You only use them for the emotional catharsis they give you. You use them for the perspective it gives you about how blessed your own life is. Their suffering becomes a shrine to your glut."

Minzy rolled her eyes. "Cal, you're not the first young man who has grown up thinking about these things. Stop being so... idealistic. Are you going to explain what you've been doing the past week?"

"I won't let you invalidate how I feel and what I know. Not this time. Not ever again."

Minzy paused. Something about her son was different. It was his eyes; there was something new in them. She realized it was conviction, something she had never seen in him. "Who have you been talking to?"

"I know what you do," he said dryly. "You sit on the board of trustees. You push the buttons that build the walls and push the people out."

She sighed, measuring her words. "You need to understand, this is how Central works. We survive as a nation because we preserve the best of mankind here, within the walls. You don't know enough about history—about how things were after the war. There were no countries anymore, there weren't any nations of people. We knew it all fell apart because nations expanded out too quickly; they tried to make their economies inclusive to everyone. But there will always be someone to take advantage of the generous—always some country that will be an opportunist and crush their long-time enemies when they sense weakness. This was the world that was created. It was the world that I—as the heir of the Straus fortune—was born into. I knew what needed to be done. We needed to concentrate the world's wealth—the world's talent—and start again. That is what we've done here. Freedom has nothing to with opportunity and has everything to do with preserving existing rights."

Cal sneered at her. "You've condemned the rest of the world by trying to save yourself and your warped sense of freedom. And you... you are responsible for it. You and the rest of the board of trustees of Central Cell. You're responsible for the children starving under our trash. You're responsible for that man who died in my lap. You may not directly be killing them, but your hollow words—your sympathy —don't mean anything if you don't do anything about it. Shaking your head and blaming their suffering on things that happened in the past makes you complicit. It's your fault. It's my fault, too, and I'm sick of being a part of it."

"Cal, sweetie." She moved over to him and brushed his cheek with her thumb. He flinched and pulled away. "We *do* help them. We help them by expecting more from them. We show them the example of what they can become. We don't insult them by simply giving it to them. We can't just open our doors and let the rest of the world flood our streets, and just *dilute* who we are. We need to stand up for what we believe. We are a special people. We've survived a nuclear holo- caust and have achieved technological and economic heights that have never before been seen. We cannot risk having it fall apart by—"

"Caring?" he said, trying to finish her sentence.

"No. We can't give everything to them and expect our city to be the same. We earned this. They didn't. It's not our fault. We can't be blamed."

"Earned it!" He laughed at her. "You think you earned all this?" He held up his arms to the enormous kitchen. "You inherited a fortune all because of some crazy great-great-grandfather who happened to invent something. You didn't even earn the money! Technically, by your own laws, your fortune and your own citizenship is illegal!"

"I keep order!" she yelled, slamming her tiny fist on the counter. "That is how I earned it. Me and the board are the guardians of the best of humanity. Cal... please." Minzy changed from stern to sweet again.

"Your city isn't as great as you think it is. What's the point if we're just letting the rest of the planet die? You're not helping anyone. You're just elitist hypocrites." He walked away from her.

"You, Cal, you are part of the same class. It's in your blood. You are a part of this, too."

"I was," he said, his gaze burning into hers. "Not anymore. Now my eyes are open."

"What're you going to do? Live in the jungle the rest of your life?" She laughed. "Come on, sweetie. We can forget about it. I can pull strings and we can get everything cleared up with Central. I'll just tell them that the crazy doorman that everyone saw you flying with on the news made you do it."

"That crazy doorman is the only person who's ever told me the truth. Raz is the only real family I've ever known."

"I am your *mother. I* am your family."

"I have other family now. I have Raz. He's my uncle."

She shook her head, incredulous. "What are you talking about?"

Cal shrugged. "I guess you are just more clueless than I ever thought."

Minzy simply sighed. "What has that man been telling you? Cal, he is *lying* to you. I swear to you, you do not have an uncle. Your father died a young man with no siblings—I swear to you."

Cal flashed an arrogant smile. "I used to pity you. When I'd come home from school and see you lounging around, eating ice cream and watching movies, I pitied you. I thought you were just a pawn— an unfortunate byproduct of our sad little city. It took me so long to realize that something was wrong. It ate at me, day by day. I could feel it—feel it in my bones—that there was something wrong with the way we lived. There was no meaning, no substance. I thought you were just a tiny cog in the sad machine of Central Cell. But now I know the truth. You're not a cog—you're the mastermind. You and your little board set the revenue cutoffs. You fabricate your lies to the public about what the world is like outside of your paradise. I don't pity you anymore. I don't feel anything for you anymore."

Minzy slowly backed away. "How can you say such terrible things?" she whispered.

He continued as if relishing the new terror that came into his mother's eyes. "I'm going to stop you. You've had your run. Your little board has had its golden age of corruption and greed. It will end soon."

"Cal, you're scaring me." She backed away to the door, secretly pressing a panic button on her watch.

"Good, maybe you'll start to fear the very people you've ignored and condemned to die in your own filth."

Before Cal noticed, two of the house guards ran into the kitchen behind him. "Grab him!" Minzy yelled. A guard, brandishing a gun, pointed it at Cal while another came up from behind and put his hand on Cal's shoulder.

He had handcuffs in his other hand.

———

Cal watched his mother with disdain and then remembered Raz's warning to him:

Don't ever let yourself be chained up or tied down, it doesn't do any good to see into a thousand different dimensions if you're chained up. You might see all the possibilities but you're still not stronger than steel.

Cal laughed at his mother. "You think I wouldn't know you'd just call your guards in? I was hoping for it. I want you to see what I can do now. I want you to know how I'm going to bring this down all around you."

"Just get him out of here!" she yelled at the guards.

278 | WICK WELKER

Cal swiveled around, flinging the guard's hand from him. He then focused inward, pushing against the surface of his dimension, shattering it into thousands of windows of other realities.

He refracted, smiling as he saw the hundreds of ways to escape the two guards playing out, right in front of him. One guard maintained his gun on Cal while the other guard, getting his bearings, produced a club from his belt and moved toward Cal. He swung it sideways, trying to hit Cal in the gut. Cal easily moved ahead of the man's swing, causing him to lose his balance. He pushed the guard, propelling him into the solid, stone island counter in the middle of the kitchen. The guard's head thumped on the stone before he slumped to the ground, unconscious.

"Stop!" the other guard with the gun yelled.

Cal grinned. "Or what?"

"Or I'll shoot you, you idiot!" The guard gestured with his gun. "Get on the ground!"

Cal looked at the man for a moment, ready to move but then relaxed as he watched the refracted windows before him. "No... you won't." He smiled.

"Get down now!" the guard yelled again.

"Cal," Minzy pleaded, "just do what he says! He's going to shoot you."

"No," Cal said, "he won't. Given a thousand opportunities, he's not going to shoot me." He walked up to the guard and put his hand on the barrel of the gun. The guard maintained his grip on the gun despite Cal's approach. "Will you?" Cal taunted.

"Back away or you will be shot!" the guard yelled.

Cal looked into the guard's eyes. "Put the gun down. You're not going to shoot me. Not ever. You don't have it in you."

The guard faltered, loosening his grip. "How—"

"It's okay," Cal said. "I know you can't do it. No version of you can." He stared at the guard with confident but understanding eyes. The guard lowered the gun and Cal took it from him.

"What are you doing!" Minzy yelled, backing away.

The guard looked down at his own hands, shaking.

With both guards subdued, Cal looked at his mother. "Enjoy your party, Mother. It's going to be your last." He put the gun in his waistline and walked out of the kitchen.

———

Jelena sat on the edge of her bed, alone.

For the first time in her life, her home was empty. Usually, when her parents weren't around, there were cleaning staff and door guards that busied themselves around the house. Now that her parents had been deported, she had to lay off the entire house staff, leaving her alone in a mansion that would go up for auction in a few days.

At least I know they are someplace safe. She had begged her father to take her with them, out of Central Cell. Jelena didn't care about being a citizen, she just wanted to be with her parents. As an only child, she'd grown to cherish the closeness that she had with both of her parents. *As soon as I sell the house, I'll follow them to Croatia and use the money to start a life with them there.* She kept rolling the plan around in her mind, *sell the house, quit the academy, flee to Croatia.* The last obstacle was finding where her parents were in Croatia. Her dad had refused to give her any sort of address to discourage her from following.

On top of everything else, she knew she could never convince Central Cell authorities that she had nothing to do with Cal and his terrorist doorman. She had been detained for over a day as they questioned her about their friendship and demanded she tell them everything. She knew they were watching and waiting. The fact that she hadn't been able to get a hold of Benedito for the last day was now too much to bear. She simply pushed everything out of her mind except for the one goal of selling the house and saying goodbye to Central Cell forever.

She looked out her bedroom window, now that the sun had set, and saw the towering skyscrapers twinkling with thousands of lights. The streamcar traffic flowed through the streets like a river, effortless weaving through buildings in coordinated movement. She knew this may be the last night she spent in her childhood home.

She got up from the bed and turned to the darkened hallway but jumped when she saw a silhouetted figure standing in the doorway. The person stepped forward into the city light that came from the window.

"Caleb!" Jelena cried. "What are you doing here?"

He lifted his hand. "It's okay. We need to talk."

"But... but, how—"

"I know there's a lot I need to explain but there's something you need to know before any of that."

She shook her head. "No, no, this isn't good that you're here. They're never going to believe that I had nothing to do with you. How could you do this and come here? Now? I know you were having trouble at the academy, but to run off with a terrorist? Do you have any idea how much trouble you've gotten me into?"

"Yes, and I can explain everything—"

"I can't deal with this right now. I need to go to my parents." She walked to the door, motioning for him to go.

"It's about your parents."

She glanced back at him. "What?"

"Where did you say they would go when they got deported?"

Jelena paused for a moment, trying to guess what he was getting at. "They're in Croatia. I need to go to them."

"They're not in Croatia. They're less than fifty miles outside of Central."

"What are you talking about?"

"Just sit down for a minute."

Cal explained how her parents had been banished to Copper Mound and how they lied to protect her from the truth—that there were no safe cities where anyone could live. He told her about how people outside of Central live and the prisons inside of the mines. He explained that everything was run by a board of trustees on which his mother sat and told her about Raz and their time in the jungle.

Finally, he told her about how they rescued Benedito from being thrown into the copper mines.

"Wait, wait," she interrupted. "If you saw my parents in that slum, then why didn't you stop to help them?"

"Because there's a better way to help them. There's a way that we can help everyone."

"Cal, I don't know what you're getting at. But this is all so weird." She looked up at his inscrutable face. "You seem... different."

"Yes, we could go back to Copper Mound and find your parents there, but what then? You'll never get back into Central. You'll just join them, living on the garbage of the elite. You'd probably die there at a young age. Nothing will change. You're not going to help them by going to them."

"So what? At least I'll be with them."

Cal smiled at her. "This is why I've come back for you."

"Come back for me? You sound like some wannabe superhero. I don't need you to rescue me. And why are you talking like that? All prophetic and creepy. You don't even sound like the same person."

"Things have changed since I saw you last. But I came for you because you're one of the pure ones. You care about people. You care about me. Right?"

"Yes, of course I care about you. But—"

"You're willing to give it up... give this all up just to be with your parents."

"Of course I would. Who wouldn't?"

"Most people wouldn't go after their parents. They'd cry and mourn and act like they care but they'd just stay behind in their comfy mansions and just ignore their guilt until it washed away."

She thought about his words, they touched on feelings she'd had her entire life about Central. It was something she felt deep in her bones. Something was wrong with the way they all lived. "I know what you mean," she said. "So, what are you going to do about it?"

"I came to recruit you."

She looked back up at him, his face shadowed in the dark room. "Recruit me for what?"

"I need two good pilots. I've already got one of them."

"Who?"

"Bene."

"What do you need pilots for?"

He handed her a slip of paper. "If you want to make a difference —not just for your parents but for everyone else—meet me at this location tomorrow morning."

She held the slip of paper.

"You can go and find your parents and be happy with them for a few years and then slowly fade away, or you can change history with me. We can bring all this down and start again—new, but with everyone. We can start a society that cares about everyone. The choice is yours."

He left her, marching down the dark hallway.

———

Benedito leaned back, his feet crossed and propped on the edge of a battered armchair. He crossed his arms behind his head and watched through a small hole in the roof of the warehouse as a pair of exhaust trails stretched across the sky. Central Air fighter jets had been cruising across the city non-stop since they had returned to Central and even more so now that Cal had come back from whatever it was he was doing.

The warehouse was a maze of discarded ship parts. Hulking Casimir engines were stacked all over the floor with chunks of wings, wheels, rubber belts, and chains strewn together, forming a web of mechanical parts. There could've been dozens of people hiding within the warehouse and Benedito would've had no idea. He shrugged, oddly content about where he found himself. His room back home—his sister and parents—crossed his mind, but not as much as he would've thought. He rather enjoyed the current lack of structure, contrasting what had been thrust on him most of his life. There was something about the chaos of not knowing what would happen next that comforted him.

Not only did he escape from being thrown in a labor prison—mining for copper the rest of his life—but he had snuck back into the very place that tried to exile him. He still didn't quite know how Raz had piloted their ship perfectly in between surveillance radars of Central Cell, and he didn't really care.

He was both troubled and intrigued by Cal. He remembered when they first met. Cal was shy and kept to the back of class. The kid wasn't particularly good at pilot simulations and was obviously intimidated by the other cadets. Benedito always felt compelled to help him. He didn't want to see someone drop out who tried so hard. But now things were different. Cal was... confident. He spoke with the tone of a prophet—speaking in metaphors and making vague predictions about what would happen next. Given that he couldn't return to Central Air Academy or to his home, Benedito felt compelled to follow his friend.

On another side of the warehouse, Raz and Cal were hanging out on a few ragged couches surrounded by several stacks of large, spooled copper creating somewhat of a private enclosure. Raz sat quietly, drinking coffee with his eyes closed while Cal watched him apprehensively.

"It already happened, didn't it?" Cal asked.

"What?" Raz said, sipping coffee.

"Refraction. I've been refracted."

"What makes you say that?"

"Because I just refracted on demand and saw you ask that same question in a hundred different universes. Also, I feel like I'm made of gold."

"Made of gold?"

"I feel like I can do anything. It's also like I'm more than one person at once. Much more than I've ever felt. How did it happen?"

"I can't tell you."

"Why not?"

"It's not an ability that I want other people to have without my say."

"Did it happen in the field? Before we came back to Central Cell?"

"I can't say."

"But you did it? It's something that *you* did to *me*?"

"Yes. Being refracted may not have been your choice at that moment in time, but it most definitely is at some time in your existence."

"How do you know that?"

"Because I've been hearing your voice come to me, talking about wanting to be refracted for most of my life. We are bound, me and you."

"Bound? In what way?"

"Our paths are linked. We're both refracted beings and we transcend time... and space."

Cal was silent for a moment. "I like it."

Raz nodded. "I know."

"I feel like I'm above it all. I don't care about my previous life at all. My mother, Central—whatever, it's all so trivial now."

Raz frowned. "You don't care about your mother now?"

"No—I do. I just... see her in a different light now. You know?"

Raz smiled. "I do and I'm happy for you but I'm also happy for me."

"Why?"

Raz sighed. His face softened with sadness which Cal had never seen. Raz looked vulnerable for the first time. "I've been... lonely. I've tried to use my gift on my own and haven't done very well. It's a power that is difficult to wield. Yes, we can see immediate outcomes of what we do. But the long-term effects? No, we don't have the power to see the downstream future of the big decisions we make. Small alterations during critical times can have dramatic effects on the future. I've made mistakes—big mistakes. I need help."

"Oh," Cal said, surprised. He couldn't imagine someone with the ability to refract would ever get lonely. "Is there no one else? I thought you said it runs in the family."

"There's no one else. Not right now, anyway. I watched your mother for a long time, hoping that she would be one I could trust but that didn't work out. I do suspect that Timothy Straus was able to refract as well. He must've felt very lonely with his ability like I have."

"Really? B-but why do you think he—"

"Killed himself? He thought he was crazy, just like everyone else in his life. He probably couldn't understand what refraction even was and it drove him mad. He probably had enough of it."

"How do you even know about refraction in the first place?"

Raz shook his head. "There is so much more to explain. You need to learn to walk before you run. It's not smart to give you too much information too quickly."

"I get that."

"You'll understand someday. There's more you need to know about refraction. There is a certain side effect that I haven't told you about."

"Like what?"

"Things change about you, about your body. You know how you 'feel like gold'?"

"Yeah—" he stopped.

There was a sudden loud thump on the other side of the warehouse. They looked at each other, alarmed.

They dashed out of their mock-living room and found Benedito also perched in his chair. "Did they find us?" he whispered.

The three of them froze.

"We can take 'em," Cal boasted, brandishing a handgun that he kept at his side.

"What're you doing?" Raz asked. "We're not going to kill anyone. Not ever. Where did you get that?"

Cal only smiled. "We're over here, you Central bastards!" he yelled out.

Raz glared at him, shaking his head. "This is not how we do things."

"Are you crazy?" Benedito yelled at Cal.

A single voice called out from the other side of the warehouse. "Yeah, I know. I could smell you dirty boys a mile away."

"Jelena!" Benedito yelled, recognizing her voice.

"Where are you guys?" she shouted, her voice echoing around the vast ceiling.

She eventually made her way through the maze of airplane and spaceship parts and found their living space. She emerged from behind a column of pallets, wearing street clothes with a denim jacket. "Wow," she said, wrinkling her nose, "I was only joking earlier about the smell."

Both Cal and Benedito hugged her. Benedito jabbered on about how they had got there and everything that had happened at Copper Mound.

"Yeah, yeah, Bene, I know. Cal pulled a batman and already visited me in my bedroom last night. I'm pretty much up to speed."

"I'm so glad you came," Cal said.

"Why *did* you come?" Raz, who had been standing with his arms crossed, asked her.

She looked at him for a moment. "The great criminal mastermind who only goes by Raz." She snorted. "You're not as scary as all the Central commercials say. You don't even have a beard anymore."

"Jelena, it's nice to finally meet you as someone other than Cal's doorman," he said and offered her hand.

She reluctantly shook it and then sat down on a rickety chair. "Okay, tell me what you guys are up to."

"Funny you should ask that, I was getting a little antsy myself. I have no idea what we're doing either," Benedito said, looking at Cal.

Raz looked at Jelena. "Jelena, are you really ready to join us? What we're doing—there's no coming back from it. I'm not going to lie, we need another pilot to do what we're going to do. But if you want to stay behind and live in Central, then you should leave now."

Jelena nodded. "I've already committed a crime simply by meeting you here. And I'm already a criminal in Central's eyes just by being Cal's friend. I might as well go all the way and at least hear you out."

Raz nodded. "Fair enough."

He led them back to the secluded area surrounded by copper

spools and sat at a table. The three teenagers pulled up a chair and looked at him.

Raz began. "Do you know why it's called Central Cell? Where do you think the name came from?" Raz asked.

Benedito shrugged. "I dunno, never really thought about it."

"It's not just a name," Raz said. "Central Cell is named after something."

"It is?" Jelena said with surprise.

Raz snorted. "It's named after a central cell."

"What?" Cal said.

Raz continued. "Back when the city was founded, they built a large database of financial information about every person that joined the society. When Central Cell was being founded, wealthy people who had survived the wars would solicit Central, trying to gain citizenship. At the time, no money from any country was worth anything, but because most developed countries were in ruins, no one really had any assets left either. The only thing that the wealthy had to prove they had money was electronic bank statements verifying that they did indeed have monetary value in whatever country they lived. The early Central founders deemed this as initial proof of citizenship, but under the stipulation that once they were granted access to Central, they would need to continue to generate income. This is what started revenue cutoffs that we still see today. And this is why there isn't a treasury that backs up Central money. All the rich people's prior wealth was converted into a new currency, the bric, and they were admitted to take part in Central Cell. Their entire worth is stored as electronic brics with no intrinsic value. The founders of Central didn't think this would be a problem since they had a tight fist on all finances within the city, kind of like a capitalistic dictatorship where individuals are encouraged to make as much money as possible but must disclose everything about their finances to the government. And now, decades later, they've created a major weak spot in their infrastructure."

"What?" Jelena asked, interest growing in her voice.

"Isn't it obvious?" Raz looked around at them. "Everyone's wealth is just a bunch of zeros and ones on a computer somewhere. No one even owns land—Central owns all land and grants land based on income. No one actually has real wealth except defined by a computer."

"Where?" Benedito asked.

"At the central cell," Raz said.

"What?" Cal looked confused.

"It's called Central Cell because there is a central cell database that independently stores all individual financial data. Because it's not on a network, it can't be hacked. It can only be accessed and changed by physically being within the cell. It's there that all financial data is stored by Central."

"So, why do we care about this?" Benedito asked.

"Because if all the data on that database is lost, everyone goes back to zero. There would be no wealth. Economic status would instantly vanish. Everyone's bank accounts would be emptied of brics because there would *be* no brics. The difference between the rich of Central Cell and the poor of Copper Mound will no longer be defined by the bric."

"Hmm," Jelena said. "That means my parents could just stroll back in."

"Not exactly. What I'm proposing won't really have the effect of equalizing."

Cal asked, "It won't?"

"In theory, yes, but not in practice. Equalization is not what's going to happen."

"So, what will happen?" Jelena asked.

"Anarchy."

They sat in silence for a moment.

Raz continued, "Erasing currency will result in chaos. The hope is that through the chaos, there will emerge a restructuring with *everyone* at the table. It's like burning crops to prompt fertile ground for better growth. This is the only option."

"That's... intense," Jelena said.

"It is."

"Who will lead?" Cal asked.

"The people."

"What people?"

"Everyone. For centuries, humankind has worked on the premise that the elite knows what's best, but I've started having this crazy notion that maybe people actually know what's best for themselves."

"But, we'll help, right?" Cal asked. "We'll help lead?"

"Yes. We can give guidance—direction."

"So, where is it?" Cal asked. "Where is the database?"

"At the center of Central Cell. Right in the middle of the city. It's that dark, gray monstrosity right in the middle of the financial district. Tallest thing on the horizon. It has no doors. There are no roads that lead up to it. It is one hundred and fifty stories high but it has no real floors except at the very top. There are no stairs, elevators, or escalators. The entire building is surrounded by thousands of guards and hundreds of fighter ships ready to launch at the drop of a hat. Also, a lot of turrets are planted all over the building."

"Okay, no problem," Benedito said.

"Shush, Bene," Jelena scolded him. "How do we get in?"

Cal glanced at Jelena, surprised at how eager she had become. "Yeah, how?" he asked.

Raz paused, waiting for them.

"We fly to the top of it," Cal answered.

Raz nodded. "The only way in or out of the cell is by a spaceship or helicopter through a portal that opens at the top of the building."

"And we can just waltz right through?" Benedito scoffed.

"Of course not," Raz said. "The portal into the building is heavily guarded. There are turrets mounted all around the skyscraper as well as a squadron of fighter jets parked right on top."

Benedito laughed. "Oh, great. No problem then."

Ignoring him, Cal asked, "How and when does the portal open?"

"I've been studying that for the last year. It opens routinely at eight a.m. every Tuesday morning when the board of trustees enters to update their own financial portfolio. The board makes sure their own finances are up to date and they compare their finances to the other elites of the city. They make sure that they're one step ahead of the aristocracy so they don't get thrown off the board."

"If you're such a great terrorist—" Jelena started.

"The rebellion of the subjugated is often deemed terrorism by the ruling class."

"Okay. If you're such a great—anarchist or whatever—why haven't you infiltrated the central cell yet?"

"I'm one man. I'm nuts, but I'm not crazy. There are too many guards, too many ships, too many possibilities that I can't keep track of all of them at once."

"Of course you couldn't, no one could," Jelena said.

Raz shot a furtive glance at Cal and continued, "I can't do it alone. But now I have three excellent fighter pilots to distract them. Should be a cakewalk."

"We're not fighter pilots," Jelena said.

"We are now," Cal remarked.

Benedito smiled.

"Would the three of you like to change history?" Raz asked.

Cal, Jelena, and Benedito looked at one another.

CHAPTER 21

JANUARY 24TH, 2155 EARTH
RECKONING (ER)

A nd what is it that we know about our current president, anyway? True, he has been a staple of Martian culture for the past twenty years. We all grew up both marveled and entertained by the meteoric rise of 'Custos the Aware' or 'Custos the Dreamer'. We were dazzled by his paintings; how he created beautiful impressionism in a way that no artificial intelligence ever could. We bought his books, captured by the paradox of a robot reflecting on his own humanity. He is a natural violinist. He stole our hearts with several concert series and albums that he produced. It wasn't that he played music with perfect precision—his music has the heart and soul of any human contemporary. He truly is a marvel and one could say is the capstone of man's creation—a perfect reflection of the best of mankind.

But a reflection, nonetheless. Custos is no man.

He is a machine.

Although we've incorporated machines into every part of our lives, including the highest seat of our government, there is still one undeniable fact about them: they were created by someone else. Every robot, including President Custos, had a creator. Machines are not born, they are manufactured by someone with design—someone who had a purpose. I think it's time we ask ourselves, what did Custos' creator have in mind when he made him? Was he really designed just to be a servant bot who happened to spon-

taneously burst into emergent consciousness? Or was the self-awareness of Custos planned? I don't think it's outside the realm of possibility that Custos was designed to be a sleeper cell, a dormant consciousness predestined to emerge as the powerful cultural icon that he is today.

These are important questions to ask given recent events. We have vandals running through our streets at night, spraying their vitriol on our buildings. We have cyborgs descending from the clouds, terrorizing our peaceful protests. We have continual power outages all across the city from terrorist bombings. There are those amongst us who whisper His name, warning that He is coming. It's getting to the point that we can't even trust our neighbors anymore. Anyone could be one of His servants. Who is He? Who is The Copperhound? And more importantly, why doesn't President Custos seem to care about Him?

Is it a coincidence that Custos is a known sympathizer of a woman— The Speaker—who stood in front of a presidential media core and announced to New Athens that He, The Copperhound, is coming for us? Why would Custos point her out in front of all of Mars? What, or who, does Custos know that he's not telling us?

I think the time to demand more from our president is long past due. He certainly likes to give us answers from his own lips, but we need more. We need evidence of who he is. In this time of uncertainty, we need to know more than what he is telling us. I want to know that my president is a true Martian and not a pawn with other motives. It's time to demand to see the full schematics of President Custos. I'm calling him out to make public his entire artificial intelligence core system so that we can all know that he is not an agent himself of The Copperhound. It's time to no longer be afraid, but to be bold in our demands.

Mr. President, show us who you really are.

Custos dropped the tablet that he was reading in disgust. He kicked himself for ever letting Gina Wilder step foot in his office. It was just another consequence in a series of admitted mistakes that he made over the past several months. The greatest of which was taking a gamble and singling out the Earth immigrant who turned out to be one of those fear-mongering sycophants. Worst yet, it had turned out that she was a major leader in New Athens and single-handedly led the campaign of vandalism across the city, recruiting New Athens citizens as she went.

He was grateful for the distraction that came from Phobos moon. He thought about the encrypted message, wrapped up in gravity waves. He rolled the phrase over in his mind:

...trapped... we've created a... weapon... a Destroyer of Worlds but it didn't... turned off from the outside...

There were many unanswered questions.

How did they know English? Did they intentionally send the message to Mars and Earth knowing that someone would likely speak English here? How did they become trapped and what were they trapped in? How could a civilization that was advanced enough to manipulate large gravity waves ever need help from a puny civilization like New Athens? And what was this weapon? Was the entire message a threat to stay away? Maybe it was a warning to stay away or whoever is foolish enough to visit would be trapped. On top of the gravity waves, the growing protests and Vana Iberian blocking him at every corner, he felt like Dev had become more distant from him as well. *Where has he even been today?*

His thoughts were interrupted by the door opening, followed by a young woman escorted by a security guard, her hands cuffed.

Charlotte. Or, as the media would now call her, The Speaker.

She looked down at the floor as the guard brought her to the table where Custos sat. The guard sat her opposite Custos and then looked at the president. "Are you sure about this, sir?"

Custos nodded. "Yes, yes, it's fine. This young woman isn't going to harm me. Are you, my dear?"

Without looking at him, Charlotte shook her head.

"See?" Custos said. "You can leave us. I'll be perfectly safe."

The guard gave him a skeptical look and then chained her hands to the table. He left them alone.

"Charlotte," Custos began. "How are you?"

"Fine." She wouldn't meet his gaze.

"How does he get you to say the things you say?"

At this, she perked up. She swiped her long hair from her face and looked at him. "What're you talking about?"

"The Copperhound. How is he getting you to say and do all these things?"

Charlotte glanced around the room, unsure.

"There's no one else in here," he reassured her. "You can say anything you want."

"The Copperhound is coming," she muttered, looking back in her lap.

"Yes, I've heard. Do you remember when we first met at the fountain?"

She nodded.

"You told me about a man, but at that time, you didn't want to say anything else about him. You just wanted to forget him. But now... now he seems to be all you want to talk about."

"So?"

"Well, what happened in between then and now? You were just a hungry mushroom hunter but now you're the ambassador for a warlord? How did The Copperhound get you to start talking about him? What happened?"

She glanced around the room again.

"I told you, we're alone. There aren't any cameras or recording equipment in here. You can talk freely."

"I—" she hesitated.

"What?"

"The Copperhound is coming," she repeated.

Custos sighed. "I wanted to give you a chance to explain yourself. Do you know of the serious charges that are brought against you now?"

She nodded.

"The Martian council wants to put you in jail for a very long time."

"Did I commit a crime?"

Custos paused. "Maybe."

"Why am I cuffed to this table talking to you?"

"You may have committed sedition."

"Fine. Throw me in prison. He'll just find me there, too."

Custos leaned over the table. "So... he's visited you here?"

"He goes wherever he wants. He's a phantom. None of you have any idea. He's... dancing around you, President robot. He's laughing at you."

Custos sat back in his chair. "What does he look like? How old is he?"

"And when he comes, he's going to take back what was taken from him. He is going to mold this people in the way he sees fit. He will bring the purifier's fire to your people and keep only what survives—"

"Quiet," he chided her.

"He was born in the womb of Mother Earth and sent to redeem her fallen people."

"These aren't your words."

"And you!" she yelled, trying to stand.

"Enough!" he slammed his metal hand on the table. "I don't want to hear anymore."

"You, he will open that metal skull of yours and show the world who you are! He will tear your limbs from your body and melt down your frame. He'll mold the metal of your body and form it into his throne chair when he comes to rule your people!"

Custos clicked an intercom on the desk. "Take her, please," he said, his voice quivering.

Two guards burst into the room and un-cuffed her. Custos expected her to scream and kick but she composed herself once again and gave him an almost imperceptible nod like an actor on a stage finishing a soliloquy. They dragged her away and shut the door behind, leaving Custos alone.

Custos left the prison, which only housed about a thousand prisoners for the entire population of New Athens. He still traveled through the city without a security detail, but this didn't seem to satisfy the protesters who had only grown in number and anger since his botched press conference. They saw him wherever he went, yelling at him and demanding better protection. Custos kept his head down and mostly didn't reply, he had nothing else to tell them.

He returned to the penthouse tower, almost a thousand stories high, and took the elevator to the top floor. The doors opened, revealing his personal guard and assistant robot, Douglas. He frowned at Custos.

"Is everything okay, sir? Were you accosted on the streets?"

Custos waved his hand. "Of course not, I'm fine. Everything is fine. Everything quiet here?"

Douglas nodded. "Yes. Everything's been running as usual at home base."

"Has Dev been by?"

"No, sir."

"Strange. He didn't answer my daily briefing call this morning either." Trying to ignore his annoyance at Dev, he walked past Douglas to his penthouse doors.

Upon opening the doors, he saw that the entire place had been turned inside out. Drawers were ajar or dumped over on the grounds. His mattress was flipped over. Most of his paintings and photographs had been ripped off the walls and thrown across the floor, their frames broken. Several desks were turned over with their contents strewn across the floor. He took a few steps in and noticed the picture of his old family that he kept on his desk. The glass within the frame was shattered.

Quietly, he walked around the destroyed room. The furniture had been gouged with a knife, showing tufts of cotton where the blade had sliced. Anything that had been on a shelf was thrown on the ground and any furniture that was upright had been tipped over. As far as he could tell, nothing was missing. It wasn't a robbery.

It was a message.

He walked to the large window, the same place where he spent hours looking out over the city. Across the window, in large black letters, someone had spray-painted:

I'm coming for you.

He stirred as a very distant feeling blossomed inside of him. He hadn't felt it for a very long time.

Custos was afraid.

———

Dev was breathing heavily under a cloth sack. Sweat stung his eyes as he gasped for air. His feet and hands writhed beneath tight knots of rope as he squirmed in the chair. He couldn't think straight. The terror of being stunned with an electrical weapon and thrown into a ship was entirely surreal. The uncertainty of not knowing where he was shocked him almost to the point of catatonia. He had no idea that someone could even be kidnapped. He heard footsteps next to him. "Who's there?" his voice quivered.

Someone was breathing next to him. The breath rattled in the man's throat followed by a deep cough that rang out in what sounded like a small room. Dev heard the harsh breathing closer now, almost next to his ear.

"Who—" Dev stopped and cringed, feeling the man's hot breath through the cloth sack over his head.

"You know who," the man said. The voice was hoarse and deep as if damaged from smoking.

"Who—"

"You know who I am, Dev," the voice twisted to a higher tone when he said Dev's name.

"Cop—Cop—" Dev shuddered.

"Say it!" he shouted.

"The Copperhound," Dev finally whispered. "Y-y-you're real."

The man let out a gratifying sigh. "I am real."

Dev shuddered and started to sob.

"You see?" The Copperhound said. "You are the product of a pampered people."

Dev continued crying.

"It's not your fault. You've grown up in a bubble. How could you have known that I was in the jungle, waiting? I waited for so long. It was only a matter of time that your people were reminded of their lost brethren on Earth. While your president abandoned us, he tinkered and grew this little utopia. But he didn't know that he was sewing within the fabric of your society the very weaknesses of its undoing. You're an entitled nation—petulant children whose only tribulation has been nothing more than a stubbed toe. You've never learned the wisdom of suffering that builds warriors. You are weak. I will bring you to your knees without firing a single shot."

Dev couldn't respond through his choking sobs.

"Poor Dev. Can't even speak up for himself. He's too afraid. I can smell your fear." Dev heard The Copperhound take in a deep breath and then choke on the air. "Time to be a man. You must address your people, Mr. Vice President."

Suddenly, the cloth sack was ripped from Dev's head. His eyes pricked with pain as they adjusted to a bright light shining right at him from a few feet away. He shut his eyes, trying to pretend none of it was happening.

"Open your eyes," The Copperhound said with surprising gentleness.

The bright light dimmed and Dev opened his eyes to a large silhouette that stood in front of the light.

It was *him*.

He had a bulky build with thick arms and shoulders rounded by muscles. Dev couldn't make out any expression as his face was completely shadowed with only the bright light outlining his form from behind. He closed his eyes again.

"No, no, open your eyes. This is happening. Don't deny it. I'm standing right in front of you. It's time to grow up, child." The brightness of the light came back and Dev opened his eyes. The Copperhound had vanished and a projected screen of words was floating in the air. Dev felt a hand on his shoulder. "You will read these words to your people," The Copperhound said.

"Wha—"

"Go ahead, they're already watching you."

Dev squinted and saw the circular lens of a camera behind the floating, holographic screen. The hand on his shoulder gripped him harder, making him squeal with pain. "Read," The Copperhound said.

Dev focused on the words and read. "Th-The Copperhound is coming. Formed in Earth's core and birthed in her caves. He comes to reclaim her lost children. The Copperhound can be merciful. New Athens is his and he cannot be stopped. He gives the people of New Athens two choices. He will either destroy New Athens and give what's left to the people of Earth, or he will graciously accept the concession of your robot President. You may either support the charlatan robot who has blinded the people of Mars and die, or demand his resignation and live. Custos must submit his neural schematics to the public and step down or the hundreds of millions of you will bear the wrath of The Copperhound." Once he finished this last line, the words disappeared and the camera turned off.

Dev dropped his head and started crying again.

"You did well... for a coward," The Copperhound said.

———

The video had been leaked to the media and immediately blasted on all stations across New Athens. Custos hadn't left his penthouse since he saw it. His phone had been ringing non-stop to the point where he simply turned it off and his email had filled up with thousands of messages within minutes. Every talking head in the news was demanding that Custos release his schematics for the good of the commonwealth of New Athens.

He was startled at a knock at the door and eyed it suspiciously. "What?"

"It's Douglas, sir."

"Yes?"

"May I enter?"

Custos sighed, annoyed at the persistent robot. "Fine." He pressed the door command on his desk and Douglas entered. He looked around the room, it still lay in the chaotic mess from earlier that morning. "Sir, I insist we summon a cleaning crew."

"Don't," Custos said. "It's fine."

"I still insist on my deepest apologies along with the guard detail that an intruder made it into your living quarters with us unaware. We do not know how it was possible. We all understand if you insist on our resignation."

"No, it's fine," Custos said despondently, looking out the window. The spray-painted message was still covering the glass.

Douglas bent down and lifted a photo frame and placed it back on Custos' desk. "Who are the people in this photo, sir?"

"They were my family," Custos said without turning.

"The family that you served before becoming self-aware, much like I am right now?"

Custos nodded.

"Do you still visit with them?"

Custos looked at him. "Not anymore. Things got very complicated. I don't really like to talk about it, Douglas."

Douglas nodded. "I understand, sir."

"I understand that girl now," Custos said, changing the subject.

"Who's that, sir?"

"The Earth girl, Charlotte, from the news conference. She's... terrified. How can you run from someone who watches you while you sleep? You'll do or say anything that person wants. I mean, he's been here, Douglas. He's been right at this spot."

"We don't know if it was him that came, sir."

"It was him. He was here. I know it."

"Perhaps."

"He uses it so well."

"What's that?"

"Um—fear. He is a master of fear. Not a single person has been hurt ever since we started hearing about him. Not a single citizen of Mars has been injured yet we're all panicked. I've never seen anything like it."

"It is a spectacle."

"No, he's more than that. This whole time, I thought I could just ignore him. I wanted to pretend that he wasn't real, that it was just a coincidence."

"What coincidence?"

"Every other week we hear about a new army rising up but nothing ever happened. But this man—this monster—is actually real. All satellite and drone reconnaissance confirms that he has no army on Earth. There are no warships. There isn't anything out there powerful enough to hurt us. I know this and he knows this. So, instead, he's corrupting us from the inside out. He placed a wedge of doubt and keeps driving it deeper with each new public display of fear. And all of this," he pointed to the ransacked room, "are his theatrics. I've been a fool to underestimate him."

"We all make mistakes, sir."

Custos stood and scraped some of the spray paint off of the window. "I suppose it's human."

"Only, you're not human."

"Right..."

"Why don't you just show the people that you made a mistake?"

"No, I-I can't."

"With all due respect, sir, it seems like a simple solution. As a robot myself, I would have no problem if someone were to peruse my schematics. I'll show them to you right now."

"I know, Douglas. But I can't do it. People wouldn't understand."

"Understand what, sir?"

"People are afraid of what they don't understand."

"Honesty can be the most disarming of weapons."

Custos shook his head. "No, not all the time." His phone rang for the hundredth time. He silenced it. "Douglas, could you leave me alone for a bit?"

"Oh, course, sir." Douglas left unceremoniously.

Custos went to his bed, brushed off the shards of broken glass, and laid down. Instantly, his watch rang—it was a message from his secretary with a high-priority flag.

"What?" he snapped.

"Sir, your presence is needed in an emergency assembly meeting."

"What're you talking about? I didn't call a meeting."

"The council has called the meeting."

"They can't—" he realized that the council had evoked the rare majority rule right to call an emergency assembly, a clause that he had helped write. "When do they want to meet?"

"Now. Right now."

"Fine, tell them I'll be there within the hour." He sat up and leaned over, looking down at his hands. For the first time, he wished he hadn't sworn off the security guards.

The streets were boiling over with people. All surface traffic had been shut down as Custos' building had become a magnet for protesters. The skyscraper was an island in a sea of angry people marching, shouting, and chanting. The video of their kidnapped vice president was the last straw. Custos cringed as he looked out, wondering what would happen if the people finally snapped and became violent. It was obvious from the sheer mass of people that there would never be enough police to handle a violent outbreak.

As he threaded through the crowd, they reached out at him, knocking on his metal body and shouting. A scrawny teenage boy plowed through several bodies until he reached Custos. The boy cocked his head at Custos and then hit him over the head with his fist. "What's in that head of yours, robot?" the boy said. Custos fell from the assault but got back to his feet. Giving no attention to the boy, he cut through the crowds, suffering mild attacks and projectiles, and made it to the park where he had met Charlotte. He marveled at how much had changed since that encounter. He moved quickly, arriving to the other side of the park where the assembly building stood.

Inside, dozens of security guards stood along the long hallway that led to the assembly hall. The men and women, brandishing rifles and earpieces, eyed Custos. He waved and smiled as he walked, but wasn't answered with friendly faces. He entered the hall and looked down the deep purple carpet path, bordered by marbled rock. The path cut through the auditorium seating of the colonial delegate and pointed straight at the semi-circle of desks where each of the twelve council members of New Athens sat.

He ran his fingers along the yellow Martian wood paneling of the walls and looked up at the tapestries that hung around the hall. He saw where the burned tapestry had hung and regretted that he hadn't had the time to have it replaced. He thought of that antique tapestry with Mars glowing against the sun with their nation's motto: *Live on, Our Hope of the Risen Red.*

Custos walked past the dozens of colonial delegates and created a stir among them once they realized he was present. The twelve council members swiveled around at his approach. Most of them wore frowns. Paying them no attention, Custos made his way to the central podium and clicked on the microphone. He was taken aback that all twelve council members and the full complement of colonial delegates were present despite the assembly being called emergently.

"Ladies and gentlemen of the assembly," he said, waiting for the crowd to quiet down. The people whispered to one another while only giving him brief glances. His presence at the podium only stirred them more to commotion. Almost everyone was in heated but quiet conversation except for one person—Vana Iberian. Her pearly, smooth skin glowed in the lighting of the assembly hall. She was staring directly at Custos. "Excuse me," Custos said. "The President of New Athens is going to address his legislators."

Anita Linwood, a councilwoman seated in front of him spoke into her microphone. "Mr. President, thank you for coming." Finally, the delegates went silent. "As I'm sure you have matters to bring to the council and colonial delegates, I remind you that this is an emergency assembly called by the council members, evoking clause twelve-point-two in our constitution. Under such a clause, the council controls the assembly and sets the agenda in an emergency setting. Is that understood?"

Custos nodded. He was well aware of every constitutional clause and already didn't like where this was going. "Go ahead."

Linwood continued, "It has been the concern of this council, considering recent terrorist attacks and in light of the recent circumstances, there has been considerable skepticism raised not only among the delegates but this council about your fitness to continue your administration."

"May I hear the specific complaints?"

Cher spoke up, losing his formal tone, "Inaction, hesitation, second-guessing—you know what the news is saying about you and it is the same thing that this entire body of government thinks as well."

"Oh, did you want me to declare war on Earth?"

Artru, another councilman spoke up, "You're being facetious, Custos, but many people have brought up that very action."

Custos nodded. "And who would you declare war on? The thousands of non-existent armies? The hundreds of warships that the news keeps talking about? It's hard to declare war on something that doesn't exist. How about the millions of starving people that live there?"

"The Copperhound," Cher blurted. "You need to do something about him!"

"Ah, so you want me to dedicate the resources of our entire city to go to war with one man—one coward who plays his games from the shadows. Is that it?"

"You do nothing, Mr. President," Linwood said. "Even now. Your vice president is in the clutches of that madman, yet y-you do nothing."

"Dev will be found safely, I assure you."

"Are you going to release your schematics?" Artru asked.

"Of course not."

"It would be an act of good faith and a boost to your public image if you did," Linwood said.

"No, it would just be giving into fear and the demands of a terrorist. I won't be doing that."

"The people don't trust you anymore," Cher said.

"*You* don't trust me anymore."

Linwood spoke, "Mr. President, this council would now like to evoke the third sub-clause of paragraph eleven of clause twenty-one. With a petition signed by half of the councils and two-thirds of the colonial delegates, we are able to bring a vote for your expulsion from the presidency at this time."

Custos slumped at the podium.

Linwood continued, "I present the signed petition to the assembly hereby forcing a vote from the twelve members of the assembly. A unanimous vote from all twelve members is required for the expulsion of the sitting president. We will now proceed with voting with a verbal yea for expulsion or nay to deny the expulsion."

She looked at councilman Cher, who then stood, "I will read off each council member's name, which will then follow with their verbal vote." One by one, he called off the council member's names, each followed by a 'yea'. "I, councilman Benjamin Cher, give my vote as yea for expulsion." He sat down, his face red.

Linwood stood, "Custos, with a unanimous vote from the council of New Athens, I hereby expel you from the office of President of New Athens and her colonies. You are excused from the podium and may watch the proceeding as a citizen of New Athens."

Just like that.

Custos the Dreamer was no longer the president. He pushed away from the central podium, looking out over the delegates. Vana Iberia hadn't taken her eyes off of him. She then smiled and nodded.

Councilwoman Linwood walked up to the main podium. "In the current state of emergency, and without proper time for an election process, I now move to nominate Terrabel delegate, Vana Iberian, as acting President of New Athens until a proper election. Miss Iberian, would you please stand?"

Vana stood, brushing her black hair from her eyes. Her gaze left Custos, who was now walking out of the assembly. She smiled at the council.

"We move to vote, requiring a unanimous vote from the council to place Vana Iberian as acting president of New Athens," Linwood said.

Councilman Cher stood to once again take votes. As Custos shuffled out of the assembly, he heard "yea" from every council member, followed by uproarious applause from the assembly as Vana made her way to the central podium to accept the interim presidency.

Before he left, Custos turned and spoke, shouting over Vana as she started what was clearly a prepared acceptance speech. "She didn't win," he said. "The Copperhound did."

No one heard him.

CHAPTER 22

NOVEMBER 29, 1989

Straus pushed against something in his mind. It felt *rubbery*.
He pushed again and felt it bounce back. For a moment, he thought he was dreaming but the whirring ceiling fan above his bed reminded him of his new reality in the psychiatric ward. He closed his eyes, feeling the same rubbery plane. In his mind, he dragged his finger along its surface and then pushed, testing its give. The more he pushed, the more the surface resisted his effort and snapped back into place.

He left whatever this was inside of him and returned to the task at hand. Now that he had been isolated for a few weeks, he had become skilled at opening his mind to the Rift. Complete sentences and mathematical expressions streamed through him, although he understood very little. Three days earlier, he had frantically searched his room and the patient commons for a pen but they didn't just leave a small, penetrating object around a psychotic, paranoid schizophrenic. Fortunately, he had managed to procure a miniature set of crayons that he found at the bottom of a Cracker Jack box.

He kept a careful record on rolled-up toilet paper. Hidden like ancient parchment, he kept his writings within a makeshift pocket in

308 | WICK WELKER

his mattress where the fabric had been torn open. Laying in bed, he had unfurled the toilet paper and was reviewing his latest entry:

...much more advanced weapons than we have. Our last option is a trick—a trap—something to lure his forces in... see there is no gradient of gravity in the direct center, this makes positioning of the halo extremely important... it's too late...

Under this writing, he had new math pieced together. It agreed with the conversations that came from the Rift. *We have it all wrong,* he thought. *Our design has to be circular. It's the only way to stop him.* He still had no idea who The Copperhound was but he felt nothing but abject terror at the thought of him.

Amidst the stream of voices, images, and numbers, he managed to have lucid thoughts. He had very carefully considered the likeliest scenario of his own insanity. He had resisted it for years until he was finally thrown into a hospital with a man he met on his first day who believed himself to be Ronald Reagan.

Yet the Rift was more open to him than ever. He couldn't deny it.

Besides the Rift, he continually focused on one question that his student, Chloe, had posed to him several weeks earlier. He winced, thinking of her broken arm. *What is the opposite of a black hole?* He wrote this sentence on his toilet paper. There was something so familiar about the concept. He wished he had more mental energy to understand what it was. Instead of returning the toilet paper to the mattress, he stuffed it in his robe pocket and got out of bed.

Before moving, he felt for the rubbery wall again, this time, it was more pliable—easier to manipulate. It was as if the wall had always been there, hiding in his existence but which he only now noticed. He felt on the verge of breaking through. He couldn't deny the Rift. And the fact that the math was real and resulted in a space-bending engine only bolstered his confidence that what he was attempting was correct. Somehow, he was going to change everything... and stop The Copperhound.

He only needed to get out of the hospital.

"Snack time," a flat voice called through the overhead speakers.

He found the door to his room unlocked and so shuffled to the communal area, cringing at the folding table brimming with paper cups of Tang and graham crackers. He unwrapped the crackers and munched on them while staring at the floor, trying to appear inconspicuous.

"Tim!" someone said behind him.

"Hi," Straus said, ignoring the person's approach.

"You don't need to call me Mr. President, Ronald is fine. Sometimes I just like to go by Ronnie," the man said, cracker falling from his mouth. He wore pajamas and a long bathrobe.

"Okay, Ronnie." Straus looked over at the front desk, which sat behind a wall of windows. A narrow corridor led from the communal area to the front desk and the rest of the hospital. The door was always locked and controlled electronically by whoever was at the front desk. He learned that guests visited patients in the communal area once they were buzzed in, briefly opening the security door.

Ronnie noticed Straus' gaze. "Don't try it, Tim. I've been here for a while and I've seen the escape attempts. The Secret Service runs a tight ship around here for me. I saw a guy get past that locked door when it opened up once, but he didn't make it far. You got the whole rest of the White House to get through, too. Even if you do make it out there, they'll just call the rest of the agents all over the building to bring you back in. Not worth it, my friend. Besides, you should just stay. I need a new appointment for Secretary of the State and you're definitely on my shortlist."

Straus looked at Ronnie and considered his point. "I need to get out of here, Ronnie. The fate of millions of people depends on me building a weapon."

Ronnie laughed. "Timothy, come on, do you hear yourself?"

Straus did consider what he said and then was embarrassed that a man who believed himself to be Ronald Reagan was trying to convince him that he was crazy.

"Now, as president, I do understand the responsibility of millions of lives resting on my shoulders."

Straus watched as visitors were buzzed through the security doors.

"And I've learned a lot over the years, dealing with the Soviets," Ronnie continued. "Nuclear deterrence, of course, is a strong motivator to prevent attacks on our country. But it's gotten away from us, Timothy—it's gotten out of hand. We build them and then the Russians build them and then we build them... it doesn't end. And where does it get us? Puts us back at square one—equal footing. Only now, no one talks, and we could all be annihilated. We build walls higher and higher, making ourselves our own prisoners with every brick laid."

Straus looked at Ronnie for a moment, surprised by the man's insight.

"And the higher the walls go and the bigger the mounds of nuclear weapons get and all it takes is a little match—a spark—and everyone goes up in flames. No, Timothy," Ronnie said, shaking his head, "you don't need to build your weapon. You just need to talk. And anyways," he looked at the security doors, "there's no way out. I even try to get out sometimes and I'm the president! Sometimes I think they forget who's running things. Ooh, Twinkies!" he shrieked, abandoning Straus for a newly arrived tray of pastries. Patients swarmed the snack table.

Straus inched toward the security door and sat on the tiled floor. The snacks were devoured while he remained, legs crossed, on the floor. Passing nurses eyed him in silence but didn't bother him. He stayed on the floor for the rest of the afternoon, watching the security doors. Several visitors had come and gone. Each time they walked through the secure hallway as one door was opened and then locked behind them. The visitors waited for the inner door to be buzzed and then they entered the patient area. There was an average five-second window where both security doors were open while visitors walked through the corridor. *It's too quick,* he thought. He would have to be standing at the door—without drawing attention—wait for a visitor to come through the first security door, then wait for the click of the inner door to open and burst through the corridor, knocking over whoever was inside and move fast enough to the outer door before it locked.

There was no way.

He closed his eyes, remembering his chess game with Jo. She had always beaten him, except for a few months ago, where he beat her several times in a row. He was now wise enough to know that it wasn't his cunning that had won the game. He *saw* the best option right in front of his eyes. Moreover, the fewer pieces there were on the board, the easier it was to see the best option. *The fewer variables there are, the fewer possibilities to keep track of.*

"Give it up, Timothy," Ronnie said.

Straus flinched but didn't look up. "Leave me alone."

"Why don't you just go back to your room?" Ronnie nudged Straus' hip.

"Please, just leave me alone."

Ronnie gaffed with outrage.

A passing nurse took notice. "Okay, you two, no bickering. Time to take a break and go to your rooms."

"You heard my Chief of Staff," Ronnie said, nudging Straus again. "Get going."

Straus reflexively jerked his elbow into Ronnie's thigh.

"Hey! How dare you!"

The nurse rolled up his sleeves. "Get up, Tim. Your communal privileges are revoked for the rest of the day."

Straus closed his eyes and sighed. The rubber surface was inside him now, almost vibrating. He pushed it.

"Let's go!" Ronnie yelled.

The nurse shook his head. "Ronnie, give it a rest."

Straus didn't move.

"Tim." The nurse lost all patience. "Up. Now."

Straus pushed into the surface, but instead of letting go against its force, he pushed harder. Sweat beaded over his eyes as he shuddered.

"Fine then," the nurse grabbed Straus by the armpits and boosted him to his feet. "We're done messing around." Straus got to his feet then rested in a sloppy stance within the nurse's arms. "Stand up straight!"

Ignoring him, Straus shut his eyes and bore into the rubber surface. He trembled, focusing on a single point of pressure, feeling the opposition pressing back against him. At the moment he thought it would knock him back, he finally tore through, shattering the entire surface.

Straus opened his eyes.

Cascading scenes of himself struggling with the nurse played in front of him. The images danced within refracted windows. It was only after he broke this surface within that he realized what happened.

I... broke reality.

In one window, he continued to struggle with the nurse until he was knocked out with a sedative. In another, he struggled until the nurse broke his arm. Several times, he freed himself from the nurse by stomping on his foot and ran through the open security door as more nurses rushed in. In these realities, however, he was tackled within the security corridor. *I can see what's going to happen.* He swiveled his head, studying each shard of reality. Now, standing within an auditorium of thousands of alternative realities, he knew what he should do.

He lunged at the ceiling and stomped on the nurse's foot. Howling in pain, the man stumbled from Straus and loosened his grip. Straus bolted toward the security door, but rather than going for the handle, he crouched to the side, waiting. Another split second later, and the security door burst open with two guards brandishing nightsticks. Bewildered, they stared at the nurse, splayed on the floor and then crouched to help.

"No!" the nurse yelled. "He's right behind you!"

Straus had already slipped behind the guards and through the security door, pushing it closed and triggering the locking mechanism. He dashed within the corridor and caught the outer door on its way shut, slipping in an index finger to stop it. Wincing, he thrust the door open and ran into the lobby, startling a couple who was standing in line to visit. Without a second thought, he ran through the lobby and out into the expanse of the hospital, bathrobe flapping behind. An overhead voice boomed down the hall as he walked swiftly, trying to avoid a suspicious full-out sprint. "All available staff, Code Gray, psychiatric wing." He didn't know what a Code Gray was, but he knew it had to do with him.

The kaleidoscope of realities still swirled around him. He discovered that he could transiently focus on his own central reality, pushing the others aside while still being able to consult them and make decisions that were happening only seconds later in parallel dimensions. *Of course, they're parallel dimensions,* he thought. *It explains so much! That's where the voices are coming from—it's where the math is from. It's coming from other versions of myself! I'm not crazy!*

He stopped fast, seeing that there were three policemen that would come around the corner any second. Across from their approach was a man walking, clutching a bunch of *Get Well* balloons that trailed behind. Straus crept toward the man and matched his footsteps, keeping himself obscured by the floating balloons as the policemen turned the corner. Straus continued with the man and then ducked into a utility hallway, following overhead pipes that led to an exit sign.

The hospital never recovered the fugitive patient.

The back door of the Straus home creaked inward. Straus paused at the threshold, listening. Through the crack in the door, he watched for movement but dust motes slowly gliding through rays of light indicated a kitchen undisturbed. A thin film of dust also covered the kitchen counter. He stopped to think—how long had he been at the hospital? Three weeks? A month? Where had Jo been? *She must've gone to her mother's.*

He shrugged the thought off and stomped through the kitchen, confident that there wasn't anyone to hear him. Giving into hunger, he paused at the fridge only to find old milk and condiments. Settling for stale crackers in the cupboard, he headed to the basement. He needed his secret room more than ever. The padlock was still in place over the door. He patted his hospital robe as if he somehow would've had the keys there and then threw up his arms. Examining the flimsy sheetrock, he remembered that he never finished extending the walls to the foundation of the home and that it left a small opening where the walls meet. After moving aside the boxes that covered the opening, he noticed a piece of cloth—a piece of clothing—clung to a stray nail in the bare scaffolds of the wall. He recognized it from a dress that Jo wore often. A flash of anger passed through him as he crossed into his secret room, knowing that it had been violated. He sighed in relief seeing all his work—thousands of papers and lines of coat hangers hanging from the ceiling with math plastered all over the wall, just as he had left it. Anxiety washed out of him as he sat down in the central chair.

He was finally home.

Without lingering too much longer, he took down all the papers hanging from the ceiling and threw them on the table, ripping them from the yarn he used to hang them. Even the hundreds of discarded pages in the corner of the room drew his attention and he brought them over to the table.

Over the next several hours, he meticulously searched the stacks of papers that had accumulated over the last year. Choosing to ignore the math, he cut out every piece of dialogue and sentence he could find and assembled them on the floor. Soon, the concrete floor was covered in small scraps of paper, each with a snippet of his writing that had been hastily jotted down during moments that the Rift was open to him. Many slips of paper had repeated words and—placing them side by side—they formed complete sentences. On hands and knees, he hovered over the slips of words until he organized them into piles of similar words. He realized each pile were fragments of sentences from an entire paragraph, with each pile representing a unique paragraph. Who was the author? Was it one person? Aside from the more organized piles, he kept a large pile of miscellaneous fragments that seemed to be more random parts of speech between people.

With aching knees, he finally formed a whole paragraph and transcribed it onto a separate page. Although it still appeared incomplete, the paragraph appeared to be a manifesto:

...much more advanced weapons than we have—a Destroyer of Worlds—our last option is a trick—a trap... see there is no gradient of gravity in the direct center, this makes positioning of the halo extremely important... created a bubble... The Halo opened up... please... Last Athens... I know you, Custos... He is coming!

He moved to the pile of paper slips containing all the math that he hadn't used in creating the Casimir Drive. He clicked on the hanging bare lightbulb as daylight faded from the window well. After piling the similar scraps of paper together, he got rid of the extraneous math and began making connections between the separate expressions. Words from the Rift helped him as he arranged them on the ground, shuffling them into various permutations. He began to see that there was math concerning the angular velocity of the Casimir Drive, clearly referencing a circular structure. Moreover, it became clear that the halo wasn't supposed to have just one Casimir Drive but *many* Drives running at the same time. Also, it was supposed to be bigger.

Much bigger—astronomically bigger.

But why?

He slapped pages all over the floor and began scribbling over them, connecting the expressions in an attempt to have a unified derivation of the engineering and mathematics that would go into making the Halo weapon. He knew that the small Drive that he created at Georgetown was nothing—trivial compared to what the Halo was supposed to be.

Night fell but he didn't sleep.

He continued to work, sweating over the pages and never stopping to eat or drink. He blinked at the dawn light as it crept back through the basement. The night had been a brilliant flash of one breakthrough after another. He stood, examining the new math that he had discovered. He smiled over the pages like a god pleased with his own creation. After a deep breath, he picked up a bag of tools and left.

His car was missing from the driveway. Across the cul-de-sac was a neighbor's old truck parked in a driveway. He peered in at the ignition—no keys. He had no idea how to hotwire a car but got in anyway after discovering the door was unlocked. Thinking about how he escaped the hospital, he pushed against the surface of reality and broke it into pieces.

There were thousands of windows of himself trying to get the engine to start. He struggled in most and saw red and blue lights suddenly flashing around him in many of the dimensions as police surrounded the truck. Quickly, he looked through the windows, dismissing the dimensions where he was clearly struggling. He watched a refracted window as his hands dismantled the ignition manifold, unfurled blue and green wires, snipped the rubber coating, and then twisted them together. The windshield wipers moved but the engine didn't start. Tossing the scenario aside, he found a similar dimension in which he twisted a red and green wire together. In this dimension, the engine started. He followed the same actions with precision, taking off the ignition manifold, finding the red and green wires, cutting away the insulation, and twisting the exposed wires together. The truck started. He backed out and peeled off down the street.

Easy.

After pulling into a hardware store, he walked in, heart pumping as he explored every aisle. He threw nuts, bolts, pliers, and wrenches into the flatbed shopping cart. He wound through the hardware section and had a confused employee help him load a table saw onto the cart.

"Copper wiring—do you have copper spools?"

"We have copper piping," the man responded. "What kind of project are you working on?"

Straus rubbed his chin. "That'll work. Do you have anything I can cut the pipes with?"

The man helped him select the copper as well as two dozen two-by-four planks. They now had enough material to fill two flatbed carts.

"Do you need help getting all this stuff out?" the employee eyed the massive piles of hardware and tools.

"No, no. Just leave it here. I'm going to go look at some other things in the store..."

"Okay..."

"Thanks for the help!"

The employee slinked away.

With no way to pay for the thousands of dollars' worth of supplies, Straus refracted reality once more. While pushing one cart and pulling the other behind, he made his way toward the checkout where three cashiers were helping other customers. He watched the dimensions, taking small steps as they turned their heads away from them. He knew the exact moments they would look away. He saw other versions of himself step too soon in many of the dimensions; after which they were caught as a shoplifter. He simply did the opposite of those dimensions, which refined the possibilities of escape into fewer splintered dimensions. Soon, the possibilities became fewer and the path out of the hardware store was obvious. He crept toward the entrance with precision, avoiding detection. After loading everything in the back of the truck, he twisted the battery and ignition wires together again and sped out of the parking lot.

Easy.

———

Jo opened the backdoor into the kitchen. Dozens of opened cans of chili, cracker wrappers, and empty cereal boxes littered across the floor and over the counter. Given that she left the kitchen completely clean before leaving to her mother's weeks ago, she was more than startled. Grateful that she didn't have James with her, she rushed to the cabinets above the fridge and blindly fished around until she found it—the cold steel of a crowbar. She had always kept it there in case of an intruder.

Creeping lightly, she came into the living room and saw evidence of a squatter—pillows, blankets, more food wrappers, and garbage strewn throughout. With her home close to the Georgetown University district, there were constant break-ins of addicts in the area. She quietly investigated, surprised not to find hypodermic needles. She picked up the phone to call the police but the line was dead: the bill hadn't been paid since she left with James over a month ago. She turned and saw the door to the basement was ajar.

"Tim?" she called quietly. There was no response. "I know you ran away from the hospital. We can talk about it."

She clutched the crowbar and headed down the stairs. In the unfinished basement, the air was dank and chilly. Dread washed over her when she saw Straus' secret room. The padlocked door was slightly open.

"Are you there?" No one responded from the secret room. *No, it can't end like this,* she thought, her hand on the door. Paranoia pushed her through the door where she expected to find the final resting place of her husband. She sighed with relief. Straus wasn't there but the room had utterly *transformed.*

In place of his chair surrounded by hanging pages of math, there was a circular, wooden apparatus the size of a hot tub. It looked like someone had constructed a wooden water well in the middle of the floor. Thin metal sheets ran along the top edge of the structure as if intended to be a circular track. Atop the large wooden well sat a metallic box. Inside, there was an intricate grid network of thin sheets of metal. At the back edge of the box was a coppery cartridge that had been jammed into a crudely cut slot. She noticed the box had six wheels and that it sat on top of the track like it was a cart on a miniature roller coaster. At the bottom sides of the wooden well, hundreds of electrical wires quested along the wood, connecting from a row of batteries up to the metal track. Dozens more car batteries were scattered across the floor, reaching to the edge of the wall. A crudely-constructed shelf consisting of two wooden planks suspended even more batteries above the ground. There must've been three dozen car batteries in total.

Jo gripped the crowbar and walked through the chaos of metal shrapnel and wiring that covered the floor. She peered at the workbench at the edge of the room and found it covered with hundreds of handwritten pages. On closer inspection, she saw that Straus' infantile circles that she'd previously seen had matured. The sketchings contained detailed schematics of some sort of circular machine with various compartments and electric boards. She picked up the schematic and inched closer to the wood and metal monstrosity in the middle of the room.

She sighed. He had finally done it.

He had built his weapon.

Everything she tried—pleading with him and loving him—it couldn't stop his fictitious obsession. Going behind his back to Van Wert to get him committed only fueled his machinations to build a weapon—*his* weapon. She had even been naive enough to hope that showing him the newspaper with the crumbling Berlin Wall would fight his pessimism—break him free of the hopelessness that he not only had for the world but for himself, too. The man she married was gone, replaced by the irrational ravings of a man divorced from reality.

"It will work," a voice spoke behind her.

It was Tim.

She dropped the crowbar to the ground and embraced him. "I was so worried," she said, sobbing on his shoulder. But he stood motionless, like a statue.

"I have a lot of work to do before this is done. This is just the beginning—just a mock-up of what I have to build."

With tears spilling down her face, she looked into his eyes. "You don't have to do this."

"I know you can't understand what I'm doing. No one can. But this is more important than you and I. The fate of humanity depends on me building this."

"And... what are you building, my love?"

"I'm building freedom. I'm building redemption. I'm building emancipation."

She looked at the machine and then back at him, rubbing the scruff on his chin. "You have a son. You have a wife who loves you."

"I know. But I must go down this path. It's more important than us."

She let go of him. "The world has all the bombs and weapons it can take, Tim. It doesn't need yours."

He swallowed. "I don't expect you to understand."

She left him, standing there at the bottom of the stairs. "I don't think you understand, Tim. You don't understand that weapons are more powerful when they're destroyed."

She walked up the stairs, alone, and called the hospital.

CHAPTER 23

SEPTEMBER 29TH, 2098

Cal ran his hand over the glossy finish of his aero8 ship, wiping away droplets of new rain. The red and blue streaks of paint ran down the fuselage and turned to a burst of bright yellow around the Casimir Drive. He remembered the first time he had flown it—the exhilaration of falling through clouds and soaring over oceans—it now seemed like a long time ago. Just days ago, he never imagined he would see the ship again, but here it was, parked in its usual spot on the launch pad at Central Academy. A blanket of rolling gray clouds moved above.

"Cal, how did you do that?" Benedito whispered, out of breath.

"That was... weird," Jelena added. "We should've been caught a thousand different times. How did you know when to move and when to hide?"

Cal smirked. "I can see things that you can't."

She recoiled. "That's... weird."

Cal looked at the gray clouds. "I've changed. I'm... different now."

"Different how?"

"I know where people are going to be and what they're going to do. You can trust in me. We will only succeed if you do everything I say. Do you two understand?"

Benedito looked, mouth gaping, at Jelena. "Who is this guy?"

"Just do what I say," Cal insisted. "I will keep us safe. I promise."

"Fine, we get it," Jelena said, annoyed. She tied her hair up in a bun. "I just wish you weren't acting so different."

"Are there any questions about what we're doing?" Cal asked.

Jelena shook her head. "We're the distraction, Raz is the payload. We stir up enough dust so that the central cell tower will temporarily be without its defense ships. When the board of trustees enter the portal in the tower at nine, Raz will sneak in behind them. But I still don't get—" She glanced away.

"What?" Cal asked.

"How are we supposed to get these ships off the ground without the Central Cell Air noticing?"

"Oh, they'll notice."

"Then how are we going to get to the central cell tower if they send ships after us? You think they'll let us just fly away with their ships?"

"Did you not just see how we evaded dozens of guards, each of them who personally know our faces? You still question how we're going to get past a couple of ships?"

"It's not a dumb question," Benedito said. "It's not like we're going on another Jupiter Run—we could be killed."

Cal shook his head. "No one is going to get hurt. I won't let that happen." He peeked over his shoulder, through the air control towers of Central Academy. Beyond the hundreds of launch pads rested the city horizon beneath a rolling cloud cover.

"Okay, fine." Jelena put her hand on Cal's shoulder and squeezed. "This is your show. We trust you... and your weird uncle. Let's do it." She pulled a red helmet over her head. "Let's change things."

Cal placed his hand over hers and met her eyes. It finally felt so right. So many things were going to be different when they were done. He felt a thrill thrum inside him as he closed his eyes and pushed against reality. A kaleidoscope of scenarios broke open. Hundreds of views of the vast launch pad hung before him with various guards and cadets scurrying over the asphalt. He peered into the shards of realities that were staggered in time just ahead of his native reality. Enough trivial differences of events in almost identical parallel universes resulted in a slippage of time. Some universes were a few moments ahead of his own while others were moments behind. He viewed the snapshots of his crew's potential actions. Several times, the three of them get caught immediately as Jelena tries dashing to her own ship. If they rush out at that moment toward the nose of his ship, they would be seen. But by whom?

Cal nudged Jelena. "If you go that way, they won't see you." He pointed toward the tail of his ship. "There must be security cameras the other way."

"Are you sure?" she asked.

Cal stared but he wasn't looking at her at all. He was making small mental notes. "Go. In six seconds. Move."

"Where?"

"To your ship. It's still at your usual launch pad. Make sure you crouch the entire way. You'll stay under the view of the security cameras the whole time."

"Okay, but—"

"Go now!"

Jelena moved, crouching along Cal's ship and then dashed across the launch area to her own aero8 ship.

"You'll do the same in about five seconds. No one will see you," Cal said to Benedito.

Benedito squinted at Jelena, who was now dozens of yards away, crouching along her own ship. No one had noticed her. "Yes, sir," he said, his voice infused with fresh confidence.

"Go," Cal commanded.

Benedito crawled to his own ship and flashed a wave, signifying that he was in place. Cal stood and pressed the release for the burner glass on his ship which sprung open, exposing the cockpit. He hopped in, thinking of the last time he was in the ship—the Jupiter Run—and how quickly he had honed his refraction abilities since his encounter at the asteroid. It wasn't that he had improved his ability to refract, he *was* refraction. Whatever Raz had done to him outside of Copper Mound had completely changed Cal.

As he passed his hand over the controls, a flood of voices filled his head. The same pain pounded between his temples. Instead of succumbing to the pain, he focused on the voices—teasing out the strongest. Like tuning a radio to match a frequency, he heard a man speaking above the chatter:

...I know who you are, Custos... we were going to change mankind! It doesn't have to be like this... we were going to change mankind! It doesn't have to be like this...

The voices ceased. Cal gasped, sweat beading on his face. Rather than dismissing the voices, he brooded. Raz had spoken about the voices—assured him that they were only a side effect of refraction. But where did they come from? Who was speaking and who was this Custos? The creeping uncertainty of betrayal clouded his thoughts. Was it smart to trust everything Raz had told him? Who even *is* Raz?

"Cal!" Jelena yelled, bringing Cal from his stupor. "Can we get out of here now?"

"Yeah, hang on." He refracted, checked to see that they could escape once they launched, and nodded. "Ready your engines, we're getting outta here."

The three warmed up their Casimir Drives and punched on the upward thrusters. As they hovered momentarily, their headsets burst with angry voices from a control tower, warning them that they didn't have authority to launch.

"Don't respond," Cal warned. "Let's go."

They burned their thrusters and punched up through the sky, the ground shrinking to miniature city street blocks. The sun peaked out over a blanket of clouds on the horizon, the glow of the downtown buildings bleeding out over Central Cell.

"Damn, it feels good to be up here again," Benedito said, bringing his ship in between Cal and Jelena.

Cal surveyed the landscape, focusing on the jungle surrounding the dense city. "Jelena, your parents are out there, living on garbage. Bene, that's where you were doomed to live the rest of your days—digging up copper until you die. This is what this city—that board of trustees—does to people. We're going to change things. Today is the beginning of a new era. After today, everyone will know our names."

Jelena was silent for a moment. "I trust you, Caleb."

Those words from Jelena sang inside of him.

"Let's do this!" Benedito cried out as if in a war cry. "Cal, do your magic."

The frantic voice of a man at the control tower burst into their ears. "Cadets, you have illegally launched against Central Cell Air command and regulations. Ground your ships immediately. I repeat, ground your ships immediately. Central Air squad is en route to your position to ensure grounding."

Cal flipped on his comm to all frequencies. "This is fugitive Caleb Stanger, son of Minzy Stanger, heiress to the Straus fortune."

"Please hold," the man replied.

"Hold for what?" Jelena asked.

"Cal?" a familiar voice came into their headsets. "Bring the ship back. We can work this out," it was Captain Kalai. The last time Cal had heard his voice was when he was yelling at him about his failed Jupiter Run. "We just want you to be safe." There was a new softness in his voice that Cal had never heard before, reeking of a trap.

"That's not going to happen, Captain. Your cadets are done being the pawns of Central Cell. After today, you're no longer going to just spit out automatons ready to enforce your subjugation."

"Cal, land your ship. We'll call this a... peaceful surrender."

Cal scoffed. "There will be a surrender today, but not by us." He flipped off open comm and cut outside transmissions. "You guys ready?" he asked only Jelena and Benedito.

"Yes," they said in unison.

"Follow me and listen to everything I tell you to perfection. You'll be safe if you do exactly what I say. We need them to chase us for long enough to distract them. There's going to be a lot of them."

"How will we know when Raz has made it into the central cell?" Jelena crackled in his ears.

Before Cal could answer, four fighter ships shot up between them. Their back thrusters pumped white billows of exhaust into the sky, clouding their view. Cal flipped on thermal sensors and refracted, seeing another four ships burst through their exhaust cloud before they even arrived.

"Cal!" Jelena yelled over the hailing attempts of the ships. "What do we do?"

Benedito's crackling voice betrayed his confidence, "They're just going to shoot us right out of the sky. What do we do?" As four more ships crossed through them, another four formed a circle pattern around the fugitives. With the arrival of four more ships, two below and two above them. "I-I think I'm done here, man."

"Just wait," Cal reassured them. "Wait."

"Wait? Wait for what?" Jelena complained. Her voice was cool but with a frantic edge.

"Just. Wait."

The fighter ships assumed a spherical pattern around them.

"What're they waiting for?" Benedito asked.

"My mom," said Cal with an expectant smile. "She's been told that we've been found and she's told them to try to get us down peacefully."

Jelena peered through her cockpit into Cal's. "Your move, Cal."

Cal was continually refracting. Every attempt they made to flee resulted in at least two of them being shot out of the sky. He saw his own body flung from his ruptured cockpit, bursting in flames. Thinking back about how Raz had masterfully fled from Central Air fighter ships, he imagined what he would do. Frantically, he went from one shard of reality to the next, searching for the best outcome but only saw them being grounded or shot down in an attempt to escape. The confidence that emboldened him since his ability to refract melted away. Maybe refracting wasn't as easy as it seemed?

"Cal!" Jelena yelled. "They're going to shoot us out of the sky! Do something!"

Frantic, Cal saw a Central Air pilot shaking his head through the clouds. With his eyes stinging from sweat, he surveyed the refracted landscape again and then froze. "Bene, on the count of three—no, five—on the count of five, you fly at the northern ship. Jelena, you do the same but fly at the southern ship. Play chicken with them."

"What!" Jelena cried.

"Just do it. One—"

"You sure about this?" Benedito said in a quiet voice.

"Two... three... four—"

"We're trusting you, Cal."

"Five. Go!"

Jelena and Benedito brought the nose of their ships one-eighty from one another, facing opposing Central Air ships.

"Don't stop," Cal commanded.

Jelena and Benedito picked up speed and headed for the ships as the Central Air squad fired up their turrets. Jelena and Benedito disappeared from Cal's cockpit view, but he saw them through the parallel worlds—he saw what was going to happen.

"Jelena, veer up. Bene, down. Now!" Cal commanded.

Jelena swooped her ship up and over the Central ship moments before it fired its turrets. In that instant, Benedito sank just below the Central ship facing him, which also fired its turrets. Cal, seeing the end before it happened, shot straight up through the sky, leaving empty space between the two attacking Central ships. Their bullets tore into one another, dropping the two firing Central ships from the sky.

"Whoa!" Benedito called.

"What did you do, Cal? They killed each other!" Jelena yelled.

"They'll be safe," Cal said moments before the two pilots emergently ejected from their falling ships. "No more talking, we're heading downtown," Cal instructed.

The three shot out from the cluster of Central ships, trailing whorls of clouds behind them. The Central ships snapped into formation and pursued. The three teenage fugitives shot across the sky in a V-pattern as dozens more ships cropped up from the ground. It only took a minute for Central to double their ships in pursuit.

Following Cal's orders with perfection, Jelena broke off from the group and fired her Casimir Drive, bolting the ship up through the stratosphere. A moment later, Benedito did the same in the opposite direction. The Central pursuers followed suit—a third breaking off to follow Jelena, a third to follow Benedito—the rest stayed on Cal as he headed straight toward downtown Central.

Cal shrieked through the sky, bursting through the rainy cloud cover. Streamcars swarmed beneath like ants along the roads, weaving through tunnels and overpasses. Delivery trucks, drones, helicopters, and the mindless foot traffic of pedestrians did not notice the storm of fighter ships that was descending over the city. A cloud of metal, wings, thrusters, and warming turrets brewed behind the single dot of a cadet ship that plunged to the ground. Cal wore a smirk as he sunk through the clouds. The hundreds of skyscrapers— plump like a diamond set within the surrounded green of the jungle —transformed from a foreboding authority into a plaything well within Cal's grasp. For a moment, he wondered what he would rename Central Cell once he was done dismantling it.

His ship roared and then lowered to just hundreds of feet above the city. Onlookers finally took notice of the massive fleet of ships that now spanned the sky. The streamcar passengers cranked their necks through the windows, offering confused looks to one another. The armada of ships lowered to Cal's level and kept their distance from him, forming a noticeable gap between them and the fugitive.

"Jelena, report," Cal said.

"There's a ton of them behind me."

"Are they shooting?"

"No. Nothing. They're just following behind. They've stopped trying to get me on the radio. It's just silence."

"Same here. I want you to keep circling around up there. I'll let you know when I want you down."

"Got it."

Cal radioed Benedito and received a similar report of Central Cell Air ships coasting behind him as if silently awaiting a change in orders. "I'm already over Brazil," Benedito complained. "How far do you want me to go?"

"Don't stop until you see snow."

"Roger that."

"Jelena?" Cal said.

"Heading north. Riding along the pacific coast," Jelena said.

"Circle back to the east. Make them think you may be heading back toward Central."

"Got it."

"Time to stir up the hive," Cal said.

———

"Mrs. Stanger, the fugitive's ship has been spotted circling around the central cell. Are you sure about this?" the pilot's voice bubbled out of the intercom.

Minzy Stanger glanced down the luxury aircar, lined with the board of trustees who tossed suspicious looks her way. She suspected that some of them believed she was attempting a power play—having her son gallivant across the sky, distracting security at the central cell in order to fabricate her own financial data. *If only Cal were that obedient,* she thought.

"We should probably postpone the exchange for another day," a board member remarked. He looked out the window as the aircar lifted above the streamcars of the city. "Miss Stanger's son needs to be grounded first."

Minzy flinched. "Mr. Burrough, if you're suggesting they shoot my son out of the sky, then may I posit that we reopen your daughter's embezzlement case that was conveniently dismissed?"

Burrough snorted in derision and looked back out the window.

Minzy glared at the board. "All of us have had to look the other way when it has come to certain indiscretions. My son's happens to be a little more public than everyone else's. You can see he's not hurting anyone."

"Only because we've agreed to your order to not shoot your son," a slender woman said. Her manicured face barely moved as she spoke. "*We're* the ones stopping the violence."

Minzy rolled her eyes. "My point is, this is not unprecedented. We've all made concessions to preserve the integrity of the board and of this city. Today is no different."

Another man in a soft blue suit spoke while looking down at a tablet. "I'm now just reading reports of a few crashed ships. Central Air ships, they're stating." He lifted an eyebrow to Minzy.

Minzy clenched her jaw. "What's your point, Mr. Harris?"

"Seems that we should cancel our transactions today. We have half of Central Air chasing your son around the city. You're not just asking us to make a concession, you're asking us to risk our lives to enter the central cell."

Minzy knew Mr. Harris was trying to stall the transaction. It wasn't a secret that he had lost a considerable amount of brics in the market only days before. She knew it would greatly benefit him to recoup as much of his losses as possible before updating his finances at the central cell tower. "As the board of trustees of Central Cell, have we ever not updated the central cell every Tuesday?"

The board said nothing.

"The integrity of our city and the fabric of our society rests on a clear economic hierarchy. This hierarchy needs to consistently be established and updated. You all know as well as I do that if we allow financial power to leak outside of the board, we could easily slip into an uncontrolled market. Do you want average citizens owning Central Cell? We'd fall back into a pre-war economy. I'm not going to let that happen just because my son decided to play fugitive for a day. Mr. Harris, you're absolutely right that I'm asking you to risk your lives. Central Cell depends on us getting to that tower."

The gaunt women who struggled to make facial expressions nodded. "Minzy—Mrs. Stanger is right. We need to get to the central cell. We always need to update our finances. Otherwise, when someone does decide to parade around the city as a fugitive without the board of trustees on firm financial grounds, they really *could* cause a revolt. For all we know, Minzy's son is actively *trying* to get us not to enter the central cell."

Minzy was satisfied as the board nodded in agreement. "I will deal with my son. I assure you he will be punished. Even if that means spending a decade in the copper mines. He will be punished but I will not have his blood spilled across the city. The Straus family has worked too hard for Central to face such a disgrace." She spoke back to the pilot, "Proceed to the central cell tower."

"What of your son's—uh—compatriots flying with him?" Mr. Harris asked. "They're leading the rest of Central Air fleet across North and South America."

"My son will not be harmed. As for his friends, do whatever you want with them, Mr. Harris. They are terrorists. I leave that decision to the Central Air command."

"I see," Mr. Harris said. He looked at the rest of the board who nodded in return and then typed onto a tablet.

———

Cal darted toward the towers of downtown and weaved between their glittering facades. The Central Cell Air fleet broke off and effortlessly streamed between the buildings, keeping in close pursuit. He half hoped for the sounds of collisions in his wake and frowned when he saw the ships moving in neat, single-file on his radar. Shaking off the unsettling thought, he twirled his ship and swooped down above the streamcars, both dazzling and frightening the confused masses.

The squatty, gray buildings of the financial district flitted beside him. He cocked his head, trying to get his bearings until he saw the highest tower of the city—the central cell, the hardwired database of all financial information of every citizen. The tower winked at him through the slits of the skyscrapers. He launched himself above the buildings and headed straight for the central cell tower. The Central fleet followed suit as if acting like an escort rather than a hostile force.

Cal ran straight at the central cell tower and pulled up hard before slamming into the building. Hundreds of turrets on its facade activated and followed his trajectory—none fired. The top of the tower—which had been built with multiple launch pads—roared into life. Dozens of small bursts of fire licked out of fighter ships as they joined the pursuit of the fugitive. Cal circled the tower three more times, corralling more of the tower's defense ships. He now counted over one hundred ships following him as he circled the tower.

After circling for the fifth time, he pulled away from the central cell tower and weaved back through the skyscrapers, leading the fleet of ships away. *Alright, Raz,* he thought, *they're all watching me now. Do your thing.*

"Bene, report." He was answered by static. "Bene?"

"Cal—started to fire." Benedito's voice was panicked. "They're shooting!"

"*What*? Jelena, are you there?" His breath quickened. "Jelena, come in. Jelena?"

Jelena's voice crackled. "Cal. Under fire!"

"They can't hurt you. I won't let them." He punched the Casimir Drive and soared north. Toward Jelena.

PART V
HELIANTHUS

CHAPTER 24

MARCH 21TH, 2155 EARTH
RECKONING (ER)

"You have a visitor," the guard said.

Charlotte rolled over in her prison cot and looked through the small window of the cell. The guard's face was framed by the thick window.

"Approach the door."

Charlotte sat up, her black locks of hair falling off her shoulders. "Who?"

"Approach the door," the guard repeated.

The cell door opened and Charlotte was placed in handcuffs. Bewildered, she was led down a narrow corridor. Charlotte was an immigrant—now terrorist—to New Athens. She didn't have a single friend on the entire planet. Who would come to visit her? It couldn't be *him*. No, no, he lives in the shadows. He doesn't make open prison visits in the middle of the day. The guard escorted her to a glass partition. On the other side sat Elisa, Charlotte's immigration agent.

"*You?*" Charlotte said. "What are you doing here?"

The woman waited for the guard to leave them. "We need you."

"Need me for what?"

"You've... started something. People are gathering."

"Who is?"

"The graffiti we did. It spread. It caught on. I don't know how, but hundreds more have popped up. People are starting to embrace The Copperhound. Have you been organizing the movement from prison?"

Charlotte shook her head. "No. It was just me and you. Well, and Bernard."

"You haven't been doing it with others?"

"No."

Elisa nodded as if confirming suspicions. "It's really happening. There's a movement now. In the city. There are those of us who *want* The Copperhound to come. Just like you. We're waiting now. People have been vandalizing and writing his name all over the place. And now that he has the vice president, we expect any day for him to come."

Charlotte only nodded, scared that The Copperhound could be watching her that exact moment. For all she knew, Elisa was an agent of The Copperhound.

"So?" Elisa said, expectantly.

"So..."

"So, what?"

"When is he coming?"

"I don't know."

"But you're his Speaker."

Charlotte cringed at the moniker. She just wanted to be done with Him. "No, I'm—" *Careful. He could show up in your prison cell tonight, kill you, and leave without anyone knowing.* "I-I don't know."

Elisa frowned. "You don't? We need him now. With that tyrant Iberian taking over, there is no one to trust. No confidence anywhere in the council. We need him now, Speaker. The people need someone to *rule*."

"I don't know where he is."

"Then tell us what we're supposed to do."

Charlotte dropped her face into her hands. "How is it that you're looking to me to know what to do?"

"Because—"

"*You're* supposed to be the ones who know what they're doing."

"Us?"

"Mars. New Athens. The wonderful and happy people of the terraformed world. How is it that me, a stupid Earth woman, is supposed to have the answers to everything? What's wrong with this place?"

Elisa did not have much response to this. "It's that..."

"That what?"

"That there's never been anything to be afraid of. Never had a reason to think we weren't safe. Until now."

"But the very person that is threatening you is who you're now looking to rescue you."

"The Copperhound is strong. He will take care of us. Isn't this your message? Aren't you the Speaker?"

"I—"

"Where is he?"

"I don't know."

"Help us, Speaker. We're looking to you now."

"I don't know what to do!"

Elisa gazed through the glass. "You must instruct us. We will follow you."

"Guard!" Charlotte stood.

Elisa stood, looking through the glass at Charlotte. "Where are you going? We *need* you."

Charlotte gave the woman a sidelong glance. "I'm going back to my cell. I think you should go back to yours."

———

The protests didn't stop.

Despite the advice of his advisors to withdraw from the streets— to step away from the public eye—Custos found himself shuffling down the street. He admired the interactive navigational maps built within the sidewalk. Blinking lights and tracings followed along with each pedestrian, giving suggestions and directions about where a person may be heading. The sidewalk sensed footsteps, recognizing the individual's distinct pressure pattern and tailor-made every walking experience for the hundreds of millions of people that ventured out every day across New Athens. The sidewalk alone was an advanced artificial intelligence way beyond any technology that Earth had ever seen.

Most people didn't even notice it.

Almost every aspect of Mars life has been advanced with artificial intelligence down to the ground beneath our feet. Even the surface of New Athens has its own nervous system. But, apparently, human beings haven't made the same advancements.

Many people across the city had stopped going to work. Initially, to join the protests, but soon to align themselves with parties and—what appeared to Custos—the beginnings of factions. Much to Custos' shock, there were several parties that claimed allegiance to him and hinted toward him returning to power with a coup despite himself publicly condemning any such government takeover. His own words were soon overtaken by new demagogues, claiming to act in his name, out crying every signature act of the acting president, Vana Iberian.

The skies above New Athens streamed with fighter jets while all import freighters from Earth were emergently prohibited. There were rumors of food shortages as the Terrabel Colony went on strike with limited produce and animal products arriving. Since a large majority of civic services like waste management, sewage, medical care, and building maintenance was done by civil cooperation, most city services had been wholly abandoned, heavily shifting the burden to the now understaffed city robots.

Despite violent utterances against him, Custos still chose to walk without a bodyguard. Trash fluttered down the sidewalk as he overheard quickened conversations. They reasoned that everything was temporary—as soon as we figure out who's in power, everything will be up and running again. Some were delighted at the Earth embargo while others condemned it as crimes against humanity. Within only a few steps, Custos heard an entire polarizing spectrum of opinions, all substantiated by nothing but speculation. All events had turned into one mass Rorschach test—everyone saw what they wanted to see.

All it took was a small crack, he thought. *A single crack of distrust to expose the weaknesses and insecurities that I've bred into them. They jump at ghosts who aren't there and decry conspiracies that dissolve and reform almost daily.* He wondered what he could've done differently. *How many times does it take to get it right?* Too much change, too quickly is what he finally decided was his latest mistake. *When we have war, we kill each other to prove who's righteous, and when we have peace, our paranoia convinces us of an enemy, even if that enemy is ourselves. We wipe out nations—entire cultures because of misunderstandings and then implode from the unrest of peace. War almost wiped humankind from the face of Earth, but peace will make us finally wilt away on this red planet.* He marveled at the paradox of humankind that had so quickly boiled to the surface again. Mostly, he was tired. His metal joints moved effortlessly but his mind was ragged with grief over his people.

"Hey! Robot!" someone shouted behind him.

Custos knew well enough to not turn around. He bolted down an alleyway, leaping over heaps of garbage. Pursuing footsteps echoed from more than one person. Easily, he made it to the other end of the open alley but was stopped by a group of teenagers, most brandishing crude weapons—splintered table legs, and crowbars—which shifted menacingly between their hands. Custos stopped and stared down the boys as the group from behind caught up. Evidently, they had followed him, planning the trap.

"Please move," Custos said, waving his hand.

A scrawny boy with a ring of sweat around his neck butted his face through the crowd. "Didn't hear the news, robot? You're not president anymore."

Custos sighed. "Do you know what I've seen in my life?"

"I wonder what he's got in there," another boy said, tapping his baseball bat on Custos' metallic head. "Maybe we should finally find out for everyone."

Ignoring the encircling gang, Custos looked up through the buildings and into the blue Martian sky. "To succumb to some petty criminals in an alleyway seems like a good punishment for me. I did... nothing with my gift—squandered every chance and everyone I love. I've been foolish to think I could change anything."

"What's he saying?"

Custos looked at the boys. "I could disarm you all in seconds. I could have you begging for relief in moments."

"He's lost his bolts now."

"But it goes nowhere," Custos said, looking beyond the gang. "My gift has only made things worse. I am the reason for all of this. Humankind would've done better without me."

"You got that right," a boy said and cracked his baseball bat over Custos' head. Custos fell to his knees as laughter filled his ears. "We're gonna find out what's in his head and spray it all over the cameras. Then maybe The Copperhound will leave Mars."

Custos didn't fight.

He didn't dampen the neural feedback from the blows to his body. He wanted to feel the crowbars and baseball bats as best he could as a distraction from his own self-torture. *No physical pain could ever match my failures.* He wept, not for his life but for the lives of the people he had let down or sacrificed for his own self-righteous journey.

Several more blows followed and Custos found it fit that after all he had been through, a darkened alley is where it would end. It wasn't pain that kept him on the ground, it was hopelessness. Hopelessness for himself, New Athens, and also for the young men that delighted in beating a conscious being to death. He laughed within himself, embarrassed at his own naivety in thinking that the people of New Athens no longer thrived on violence. Violence wasn't an Earth thing—it was a human thing. It had just been dormant in New Athens. *History doesn't repeat itself but it often rhymes.*

"Hey!" a voice sprang from the mouth of the alleyway. The gang turned in surprise and scattered as a shot was fired into the air.

"Custos!" a familiar voice approached him. Custos looked up and saw the battered face of his vice president.

"Dev! Y-you're here. What about—"

"I escaped from him this morning, been out all day looking for you, following the news feed about sightings of you. You look—" Dev tried to hide the shock in his face. "Those bastard kids. I can't believe they would do this!" He grimaced, taking in the dents and scrapes that covered Custos' head and torso. Custos realized that Dev had probably never witnessed a violent act. The robot still managed a weak smile from his silicon face.

Custos stood while Dev yelled back to the police officer who stood with his gun. "Go after them!" The cop wiped the perplexed look off his face and ran after the gang. "Are you okay? I've got a lot to tell you. The Copperhound is planning—"

"Wait, wait, how did you get away from him?"

"I just... slipped away. I overheard all his plans. He kept me in a shed on a farm in Terrabel. I only saw him come in and out but he always had the lights off—would never show his face."

Custos shuddered. "I never thought he would come, Dev. I never really thought he was real. It's why I didn't do anything. I didn't want to believe... all these years, I never thought—"

"He's here. And he's very real."

"I know now." Custos' mind flashed to his destroyed penthouse. The Copperhound had been there.

"Listen, I overheard him talking to someone on the phone outside the shed. It's really bad."

"More so than right now?"

"The Copperhound planned Vana Iberian to get into power. He wanted her to take over the Presidency."

"No surprise there. The man's power comes from driving up the people's fear. Vana Iberian captures that fear and leverages it into power."

Dev shook his head. "No, no, it's different than that. I think him and her were in on it together."

"Why would you think that?"

"It was the way he talked over the phone. He was talking to someone important—someone who was in the government. The Copperhound was receiving detailed information from someone high up. I think she helped him hide away in Terrabel and that the two were working together to get her in power. He does all the theatrics that whipped up the people in a frenzy and she swooped in and stole the presidency from you. I think they're working together."

"Hmm." Custos considered his words as Dev spoke with a new confidence that he hadn't before seen in his friend. Maybe facing a little fear did some good for Dev.

"There's more."

"What else?"

"I overheard him talking about a cache of nuclear weapons," Dev said with wide eyes. "And they are in Terrabel."

White fear bloomed inside Custos.

"He's been stockpiling ancient nuclear weapons brought from Earth. I overheard him talking about specific shipments with someone. He already has thousands hidden in the farmland in Terrabel."

"But how?"

"All the freighters from Earth, that's how. The thing is, I don't think Vana knows about any of this."

Custos sat on the concrete and considered Dev's words. What could possibly convince Iberian to collude with a maniac from Earth? How could a lone man get that many nuclear weapons from Earth to Mars? How stable would century-old nuclear weapons be? Could they spontaneously explode any minute? Everything seemed so ludicrous, but considering how everything else was crumbling beneath his feet, he knew he needed to accept the absurd. "You didn't see what he looked like?"

Dev shook his head. "Never saw his face."

"But you were in the same room with him, right? What was he like?"

"Big man. Angry, but also..."

"What?"

"Gentle, somehow. He's smart—complex I should say."

"Did you hear what his plans are with the nuclear weapons?"

"No, but could it be anything good? The man has publicly said he's going to destroy New Athens."

"But why wait? Why wouldn't he have done it already?"

Dev shrugged, wincing at the pain in his shoulder.

"Something is off about this. Are you okay? What did he put you through?"

"He kicked me around a bit but not much more."

"You seem... different, Dev." Custos somehow felt better talking to Dev—lifted from the hopelessness.

"I escaped from The Copperhound. I *feel* different." He nodded proudly.

"How did you get away?"

"I wriggled out of my ties and ran out of the unlocked shed. No one was around."

"That's strange. Too easy."

"It doesn't matter now. Look, The Copperhound is just a man, he's not a ghost."

"Men are worse than ghosts. But we can stop him."

"How? We're not exactly in a position of power anymore. Do you still have any contacts with the council? I know there's a ton of colonial delegates that would still support you."

Custos waved his hand. "No, no, it's all corrupted now. We can't risk trusting anyone. For all we know, Vana is well aware of the nuclear stockpile and would try to have us eliminated if she found out that we knew." He stared vacantly at the brick wall of the alley. "We can't use diplomacy anymore. It's time we stop trying to outsmart The Copperhound."

"So, what do we do?"

Custos stood, supporting himself with Dev's arm. He looked at his vice president, his friend for over ten years, and admired him. "Thank you for finding me, Dev. I needed you more than you could know."

Dev shrugged. "Of course, Mr. President."

"It's time for us to start doing the manipulating." He limped out of the alley as Dev stood, puzzled.

Phobos moon looked like a brown, oblong pebble floating above the atmosphere of Mars. Dev had to squint to distinguish the speck of a moon against the streaks of marbleized greenery and rusty soil of Mars. Phobos was pockmarked with thousands of craters—suffering an eon of asteroid bombardments but nevertheless undaunted in its endless march around its planet. The moon glided through space as if oblivious and uncaring about the New Athens turmoil happening beneath its orbit. As their ship approached, Dev spied small sprouts of research labs on the underbelly of Phobos. Various domes with connecting causeways became larger through his small window.

"How long has the GraviWave lab been up here?" Dev asked.

Custos looked up from a few pages on which he was scribbling calculations. "About fifteen years. They first tried to set up triangulating stations on the highest peaks of Mars but seismic activity prohibited good results. I helped renew funding for their station here on Phobos just a few years ago. Probably one of the biggest reasons I had the backing of the scientific community during my election."

"I remember it. The council thought it was pointless to sink so much money into it, but with the backing of 'Custos the Dreamer', they gave in."

"I've been thinking about the message they sent."

"Who?"

"The gravity wave beings. Whoever they are."

"Right, the 'Destroyer of Worlds' people. They sound very hospitable."

"Do you know where that line comes from?"

"What line?"

"'The 'Destroyer of Worlds'."

"No."

"It's from a Hindu sacred text but it was made famous by Robert Oppenheimer, the man who helped create the atomic bomb. He marveled on mankind's new destructive capability after seeing what his own creation could do."

"And these gravity people are what, quoting him?"

Custos tapped his chin. "That's the question. Why would they use that phrase in particular? There's some sort of connection to me—to us, I mean."

"What connection?"

"I intend to ask them."

Their ship approached Phobos and lowered toward the Gravi-Wave lab. A small docking bay accepted them after Custos confirmed who he was. He heard a commotion over the radio as the lab scrambled to accommodate their unexpected guests. A woman with thin-rimmed glasses and sandy-blonde hair inched toward them as Custos and Dev came down the docking ramp. It was Dr. Farr. Dev tried picking up the pace but stumbled with his footsteps, unused to the light gravity on the moon.

"Mr. President!" she said, extending her hand. Her face soured when she saw the dents that riddled his body. "What happened to you, Mr. President?"

"Oh, I'm not sure how much you've been keeping up on New Athens' events, but I'm not the president anymore."

"You're still *my* president. Are you okay?"

Custos looked down at the dents in his body and shrugged. "I'm fine, just got into a sticky situation with some kids."

Farr's face turned pale. "Are things really getting so bad? People actually... did that damage to you?"

Custos nodded. "We need your help."

"I'll do anything." Shock still flooded her face.

"I'm sorry we've arrived unannounced. I needed to talk in person about the gravity waves."

Farr put up her hand. "No need to apologize. I'm glad you're here. There's more I need to tell you, too. Come with me." She abruptly turned, leading Custos and Dev to a pod vehicle that zipped around on tracks along the moon station. They sailed through long hallways with small windows showing the rough surface of the moon.

They entered an extensive laboratory full of people looking up from control comm stations or toying with electronic arrays that spanned dozens of feet. Workbenches were scattered with thousands of electronic components, gears, coiled wires with twisted metal covering the floor. The entire lab barely stopped working to notice the new guests.

Farr gave a polite laugh. "Sorry, things here are kind of crazy at the moment. I've had every available person working on the gravity wave message. No idea is a bad idea to decipher the message."

Custos asked, "Have you deciphered the whole thing?"

Farr scoffed. "Yes and no. I realized just a few days ago that the problem isn't that we haven't arranged the message in the right order, it's that we don't even have the full message. The majority of it has been lost on its way here. Bits of the message dissipated by the time they reached Phobos. It took our cryptologists weeks to even realize that they were trying to decipher parts of the message that weren't even there."

"What more of the message do you have?"

"I'm glad you asked. We've finally finished an algorithm that has pieced together the entire gravity wave message. Everything we've received has been deciphered. I've been trying to get a hold of you for the past two days to let you know."

Custos' face grew concerned. "Did you tell Vana Iberian about this?"

Farr shook her head. "Of course not. I wouldn't trust that charlatan as far as I could throw her."

"Good. Well, let's see the message."

"Absolutely." She led them around a conference table, partitioned from the rest of the lab by glass walls and dimmed the lights. She typed into a computer panel on the wall, prompting a display in the middle of the table. It was the decrypted message.

"Keep in mind, we've only received bits and pieces of the original message and we have no idea if it's even in the correct order."

Custos read the words floating in front of them:

...much more advanced weapons than we have—a Destroyer of Worlds— Our last option is a trick—a trap—something to lure his forces in... see there is no gradient of gravity in the direct center, this makes positioning of the halo extremely important... it's too late... it was a mistake, but we were

so desperate. I designed the Halo with one purpose—the Halo opened up... but it's too late... please...

Custos stared at the words for a moment, lost in thought. "Halo..."

"Mr. President?" Farr said carefully.

He looked up at her, his porcelain eyes wide in their metal sockets. "Halo..." he repeated.

Dev nudged him and said, "This doesn't make any sense. Why would they send an incomplete message through gravity waves? Why not just normal radio waves? They could've sent us—or whoever—a complete message easily by radio."

"We have no idea," Farr said. "It is incredibly bizarre."

"Is that all there is?" Custos asked.

Farr nodded in silence.

"And what is this about... a halo?"

"We're not sure, but it likely has something to do with whatever weapon is also referenced in the message."

"How are they creating these gravity waves?" Dev asked.

"We don't know."

"What about Casimir Drives? They bend space," Custos said.

"Casimir Drives? True, the Casimir effect can, on a small scale, bend space. But the bending is short-lived and doesn't create a rippling effect at such long distances."

"If they're trapped and have the potential to destroy worlds, why would anyone want to help them?" Dev posited.

"The message isn't necessarily a threat," Farr said. "In addition, there is a single word at the end: 'please'. I think whoever these people are, they are in a position of vulnerability."

"This algorithm that you've figured out for decrypting the waves, can I use it?"

"Well, yes."

"Is it a safe assumption that the closer one got to the source of the waves, the more of the message would still be intact within the waves?"

"Yes, we've been working on that assumption. We were planning, in fact, on asking for a grant soon to get closer to the waves to obtain more of the message."

Custos stood. "That won't be necessary. I'll be going to the source myself."

"You *will*?"

Custos nodded. "Can you outfit my ship with the gravity wave algorithm? I may have to do some more translating on the fly as I get closer to the source."

"Mr. President, we were planning on sending an entire team but we've barely planned anything out right now—"

"No. I'll be going alone. And I'm not the president anymore. You need to recognize that you're giving state secrets to someone who may be considered a traitor very soon. Your acts will be considered treason."

Dev stood. "What the hell are you talking about?"

"I'm going to take control of this weapon," Custos said coolly.

"Take control?" Farr asked.

"We don't even know what it is, or who this is—"

"It's a week's journey. I'm going to go and take this weapon and stop The Copperhound. Once I'm there, I'd like you to make it public that I am in control of a world-destroying weapon. New Athens is imploding in on itself all while a madman may or may not wipe us off the face of Mars in a single nuclear detonation. We have to do something. I'm going to take control of this Destroyer of Worlds."

Dev shook his head. "And do what with it?"

"Threaten The Copperhound." Custos walked to the glass doorway.

"Threaten him with what? That lunatic just wants to burn everything down."

"What is the one thing that we know he cares about?"

Dev shrugged.

"Earth," Custos said. "He cares about Earth."

CHAPTER 25

SEPTEMBER 29TH, 2098

C al's Casimir Drive shrieked across the sky.

"Jelena!" he yelled into the radio. "Jelena, report!"

"—firing at me, Cal—" It wasn't static that broke up the communication, it was gunfire.

"I'm coming!" He knew he would get there. He *had* to.

A Central Cell fleet followed Cal as he rocketed away from the city, in hot pursuit of the Straus-heir fugitive. He headed north, over old Texas, and then to the yellowed plains of the Midwest. His eyes stung with sweat as he checked the navigation guidance system. His mind went back to the asteroid belt during the Jupiter Run. He had been marooned inside a gigantic rock in the middle of the solar system. There was no one to save him—not his mother, not Bene, not Captain Kalai, not even Raz. It was Jelena. She looked after him, cared for him. She invited him out, made sure he felt like he was part of the circle even though he really wasn't. There was no one else like her in his life. She was there at the asteroid and he would be there for her now. There were so many things he was going to tell her.

"Jelena," Cal radioed. "Hang on, I'm coming."

"Come quick!" she yelled. "They're firing at me!"

Central ships flanked him on all sides. They began streaking across the sky in front of him, trying to get him to veer off course. He looked out the cockpit and saw dozens of thruster engines surrounding his ship. The ships shot in front and slowed, prompting him to dive down and then careen back up. He was constantly making course corrections to avoid collisions, slowing his approach to Jelena. His heart hammered in his ears as he gripped the sweaty controls. *I'm not going to make it to her. Unless...*

And then he smiled.

He refracted, shattering the sky.

He became the wind, knowing where to move in the instantaneous moment that the enemy pilots tried to block him. The ships became small pawns to him. It was like playing chess with someone who knew their opponent's moves before they did.

He moved like a phantom.

The Central pilots crisscrossed in a panicked frenzy, unsure of how to react. They undoubtedly had orders from Central instructing them to not fire. Cal looked into a refracted shard in which he killed a pilot with gunfire. In that universe, his ship was quickly torn apart by return fire. Apparently, orders didn't matter when the rich brat started killing good pilots. So, Cal fired his turrets carefully, shearing the wings off the ships ahead just enough to make them plummet from the sky without exploding. The precision of his shots would have normally been near impossible. He saw the pilots safely eject before their ships exploded on the flat terrain below. If they stayed alive, he stayed alive.

And then he saw the armada of ships ahead that had followed Jelena. He soared toward them, his back sinking into the seat and his knees bouncing with the shuddering of his aero8. Jelena's pinpoint ship—a red dot—was weaving through clouds, desperately avoiding gunfire. A black trail of smoke spiraled from her ship.

"Jelena, I see you."

"I'm hit! Clipped wing—losing altitude."

"Thrusters okay?"

"I can still land."

"Corkscrew down. I'll have your six."

"Roger."

Cal slammed through the armada, refracting as he went. He played chicken with them, knowing that every single time, the Central pilots would veer out his way. They fired warning shots, some glanced off his hull but didn't penetrate. He fired back, taunting them with precision shots that punched holes through their wings. He weaved through the ships, advancing on Jelena's position until he saw her below the armada now, descending to the ground. He punched downward and saw a white trail flash across his cockpit. What was that...

A missile!

"Jelena! Bogie on your six!" But it was already okay, through time slippage of the refracted realities, he already saw her safely eject before the missile even hit. And it was a direct hit, turning Jelena's aero8 into a fireball of metal shrapnel in less than a second. Just as he predicted, Jelena was safely parachuting away from the wreckage as it plummeted to the plains.

Rage flared within him. *They don't know what I am. But they will. Things will change. And they're going to change* now. *Raz is wrong. We can't just empty their bank accounts. We must destroy the elites and those that defend them. They must be wiped from memory.*

He spun around, facing the ships that studded the sky above him. In the refracted shards, he saw them scatter from the gunfire he was about to release. For a ship in flight, it was a trivial thing to dodge gunfire from a stationary enemy. They could simply see when he fired and then moved out of the way.

So, Cal fired to where they were *going* to be.

He fired ahead of their trajectories, connecting bullet to hull. Over and over—direct hit to wings, cockpit, engines, and fuel tanks. Explosions littered the sky. A barrage of angry voices flooded his headpiece. So, he took it off. Hot metal rained through the clouds. He was a one-man fleet, throwing bullets where they shouldn't have been. He was a statistical anomaly, predicting with one hundred percent accuracy where all his enemies would be. The shards of refraction opened to him, exposing his enemy to him. The Central

352 | WICK WELKER

ships fled through the chaos, not understanding the barrage of impossible hits that beset them on all sides.

Rage burned.

And Cal kept firing.

His thumbs worked the knobs, firing and cooling, waiting for ammunition exchange and then releasing hellfire again. Minzy, Bene, Kalai—faces flashed through his mind. Timothy Straus' face, projected up in class for everyone to see. Maybe he wasn't crazy, he just didn't understand what he had. But Cal understood. He had *power*. Power to make whoever he wished to drop from the sky. Power to banish the Central elites to the copper mines. Power to bring justice to the world.

And then he remembered Jelena.

Molten metal rained from the sky as he watched the cowards flee in parachutes. Just like that, the armada was gone. Wiped out. He thought about the blackened city Raz had shown him. He felt sick at how easily he could've killed them all, but then sneered. They tried to kill her. They deserved death.

They all did.

He dived to the ground, to Jelena, to rescue her. Flipping on the belly cameras, he pinpointed her small dot of a parachute as it landed on the ground. He sunk his ship down, after her. Nothing would stop him, and nothing could. There were no more Central ships. He plummeted after her, feeling both sick and satisfied at the same time. He was a new creature. One who watches the masses. One who judges the rulers. One to bring justice to the people of Earth.

A new ruler for a new time.

The voices bubbled in his mind, bolstering the thick sense of control running through his hands. They clamored for his attention —voices spanning dimensions and times, iteration after iteration of himself throughout eternity. One voice fought for prominence, teasing itself from the echoes. Cal focused, bringing the man's voice to the surface:

Cal... it's us.

What?

It's us?

There is no *us*. There's only Cal and Central Cell. Cal and the world.

He landed.

The burner shield of the cockpit opened and he leaped out. She was there, laying in the dead grass. It had wilted—yellowed by the sun since the Nuclear Night. He ran to her. She was so small in her cadet uniform.

"Jelena!" He knelt at her side.

Her face was turned from him, her hair fraying from the bun that she had tied. Her helmet, gone.

There was blood.

"Jelena!" He grabbed her shoulders and dragged her head into his lap. "No," he said, weakness in his voice. A streak of blood painted the side of her face—a gash suffered sometime on the way down.

"Wait. Just wait," he told her, "I can fix it." He refracted and looked into the shards of realities. Only...

Every reality was the same—Jelena in his arms, her glassy eyes on the sky.

———

The long aircar lifted from the stream and glided through the downtown buildings. The board of trustees maintained silence, staring at their cell phones as the streamcar soared above the buildings and entered the financial district. The cityscape of glittering commercial towers was littered with dozens of squatty Central Cell administration buildings. Minzy peered through the cockpit at the front of the aircar and saw the central cell tower straight ahead. There were now no ships in sight. She cast her wayward son from her mind and focused on the previous week's gains she knew she would have to log as precisely as possible. If she reported too little or too much, the

Central auditors would quickly expose it as fraud, even if it were accidental.

She sighed, briefly exhausted from the banality of power.

The aircar sailed toward the tower that had no bottom floors. It had no roads that led to the entrance and it had no windows. It was a monolithic block of metal and concrete, outfitted with turrets that studded each facade. The hundreds of launch pads at the top, normally ready to mount a defense, had vacated in pursuit of Cal. Minzy didn't see a single ship across the entire city. Cal had led them away.

At the top of the central cell tower, a solitary portal in the side of the building remained closed. As their aircar approached, each member of the board took out a security tablet and placed their thumbs on the tablets at the same time, identifying themselves as the board of Central Cell. The portal of the tower shuttered open like a camera lens and they passed through. Before the portal closed, Minzy heard a rumbling sound outside and looked around the cabin, perplexed.

"What was that?" she asked.

"It sounded like a ship just outside. Can anyone see anything?" Mr. Harris remarked, squinting through the windows. Their view was mostly obstructed by the metal struts of the docking platform.

"Did someone else come through the portal?" one of the board members shouted at the pilot.

The pilot shook his head, annoyed. "Impossible, I didn't pick anything up on the radar."

Minzy scoffed, unsatisfied. "Radars can be tampered with. Get me outta this car."

After they docked, Minzy looked out the windows to the bare insides of the central cell. No decorations, carpet, or comfortable furniture adorned the place, reflecting the cold indifference of a warehouse. The walls ran up for a hundred feet, accommodating the vast stores of hard drive towers where all financial records were stored. The room was large enough to be an airplane hangar. In the middle of the spacious floor was a massive computer the size of a bus with a single terminal where the board would enter their financial statements, one by one. The board of trustees sighed with relief that they were finally in the tower with the air chase happening elsewhere in the skies. They filed out of the aircar and stopped.

They'd stepped into a scene of total chaos.

Dozens of guards were preoccupied with a single man who had just moments before emerged from a small commuter ship that had crash-landed into a wall. The man was weaving through the guards, dropping them with a taser in one hand or buckling their knees with a baton in the other hand. He ran straight at a guard who lifted his rifle and let out a shot, but not before the intruder slid to one knee and smacked his baton into the guard's knee cap. Another guard, seeing the intruder preoccupied, dashed behind him and lifted his rifle for a blunt strike. Without looking up, the intruder swung his torso away from the guard and swiveled his hips, slamming his feet into the guard's legs, toppling him. The intruder then kicked the guard square in the face and leaped to his feet again.

As more guards filed in, the intruder moved to the side of the spacious floor, flipping switches, prompting every door to the central cell to slam shut before dozens of more guards could pile into the room. The guards fired their rifles, their bullets scattering around the concrete enclosure. Every time they fired, the intruder was only inches away from their bullets, running unscathed from the firestorm that had the board of trustees scattering. The intruder moved methodically, swinging his baton—not where a guard was—but to where a guard would be. To Minzy, it looked as if the guards were deliberately meeting their faces to his baton as if *helping* the intruder to dispose of them.

Confusion reigned as the man circled around the computer cell, tasering the guards he had previously dropped and swinging his baton at the newcomers. After several successions of shots, the guards checked their rifles, certain of malfunction, while the intruder dispatched them as well. Only moments later, every guard lay unconscious at the intruder's feet. He breathed heavily, his gaze finding the cowering board of trustees.

"None of them are dead," the man remarked. "But they will have bruises." A tuft of black hair swung over his forehead. His face glowed with rage but tempered by patience.

Minzy, infuriated, stood and pointed at the man. "What do you think you're doing? Do you know who we are?"

"Yes," he said delicately. "I know who you are, Minzy Stanger. Great-granddaughter and heiress of Timothy Straus, the psychotic inventor of the Casimir Drive. You are the mother of fugitive Caleb Stanger. You sit on the board of trustees of Central Cell. You live in the Straus Tower on the hundred and eleventh floor. You drink your coffee with three packets of sugar and lick your lips after every sip. You say you prefer wine—Chardonnay to be specific—but you keep a bottle of scotch in the small cupboard next to your refrigerator to relax your nerves before company comes. You're fidgety—can't keep your hands still. You're rarely alone, and when you are, you must preoccupy yourself with movies or chat online with girlfriends."

"How—"

"You're not particularly bright or creative but you believe in meritocracy. You rest on the laurels of good fortune and believe you have some sort of right to rule the people of Central Cell. Timothy Straus would be ashamed to know that you are of his bloodline and fortune. You've earned nothing yet believe you are entitled to what was given to you. The rest of the world smolders in disease, poverty, and misery while you have enough money to literally relieve the suffering of *billions*. You're a disgrace and your time to rule is over."

She crossed her arms and screwed her lips. "Who *are* you?"

"Oh," he said with a twinkle in his eye, "you're also terrible with faces. I'm Raz, your doorman."

"How did you—"

"Know all that about you? I've been watching you since you were a little girl, Minzy. Hoping, waiting for you to become more—to become someone who could change things with me. Turns out, I was waiting for your son."

"You'll hang for this," Mr. Harris yelled.

Raz gave a mirthless laugh. "No, I won't hang. I'll live. I'll live the way I've always lived. In the shadows, working the controls, twisting the arms. I'll continue to be the custodian. And you'll live too, we'll *all* live. I just couldn't let it go on like this anymore. No time since the history of humankind has there ever been such economic disparity as your little board of trustees has inflicted. This must end. Change is coming, but no one will be hurt. We'll give power once more to the people... start again, see where we can get." Raz walked to the middle of the room, where the central cell computer sat and moved his finger along the edge of the keyboard. "This... this must go. Time to send everyone back to zero."

"You can't!" Minzy yelled. "Everything is in there. The entire basis of our society—the foundation of who we are—is preserved here."

Raz nodded. "I'm painfully aware of that." He jerked as something heavy slammed on the other side of the security doors—more guards. "I don't think we have too much more time. The rest of the guards are getting antsy. I suggest you all get back on that pretty luxury ship you came on. Go home and prepare for what's next." He flipped a small cube from his pocket and twisted it open, revealing a tiny cartridge. "As soon as this is downloaded into the central cell, the bric will no longer exist."

He stepped toward the console but ducked when another large crash resonated around the cell, but it wasn't the security guards. Bullets tore through the closed portal door where the board of trustees had first entered. They moved away from the portal as it exploded, spewing flames and smoke into the central cell. Raz scrambled with the board of trustees, most of whom were too overwhelmed with shock to register what was happening.

The thundering of an aero8 Central Cell academy ship drowned their shouts. Twisting metal shrieked as the ship rammed through the blown-out portal. Through the haze of smoke, Raz saw an indignant face inside the cockpit.

Cal Stanger.

"Oh no," Raz said, getting to his feet. "Cal, no!" He waved his hands. "Get outta here!"

Undaunted, Cal brought his ship through, rattled past the luxury aircar, and landed on the concrete floor. The cockpit glass flipped and Cal appeared.

Rage flickered in the boy's eyes.

"What are you *doing!*" Raz yelled. "Get the hell outta here, Cal! This isn't part of the plan."

Cal walked at Raz, looking down at the board of trustees. He surveyed them as if ascertaining the extent of an infestation. He snapped back to Raz. "Th-they're gone."

Raz's mouth widened. "Who?"

"Jelena. Bene."

"What do you mean?"

"They got shot down."

"No..." Raz's shoulders slumped.

"It was them," Cal said, pointing at the board. His eyes met his mother's. "It was *her.*"

Minzy stood. She looked at the smoking hole that her son had just blown through the building and, for the first time, was afraid of him. "C-Cal. I'm so sorry that your friends—"

"You won't be speaking." Cal put up his hand. "She was the only person that even cared about me. To everyone else, I'm just a pawn— a loser. There's no more explanations. Only punishment now." He unholstered a pistol that was fastened to his thigh.

Raz shook his head. "What're you doing!"

Tears welled in Cal's eyes. "I couldn't save her, Raz. She was... gone. Gone in every dimension."

"What—"

"I thought I could do anything with it!" he yelled, blinking away tears. "You told me refraction was the most powerful force on the planet. But she was only dead—there weren't any other possibilities."

"Refraction isn't magic. You can't turn back time with it. I've tried to teach you—"

"You haven't told me anything! You just keep holding things back! What else haven't you told me, huh? What about that 'side effect' you've been waiting to spring on me?"

Minzy held up her hands. "Cal—"

Cal gripped the gun in his hand. He pointed it at the board members as they scrambled for cover behind the central cell. "Don't take another step!"

"Cal, we're not killers," Raz said as if repeating a mantra.

"That rule went out the window when they shot her down." He held back sobs.

Raz stepped closer. "No one needs to die."

"They do. Our revolt starts with getting rid of them." He lifted his gun.

———

Raz refracted. "No..."

Cal noticed the vacant gaze of Raz. "What're you doing? Refracting to stop me?" Cal refracted and, through the slippage of dimensional time, saw Raz lunge at him, knocking the gun out of his hand and stunning him with his taser. Yet, as he saw himself crumpled to the ground in many of the dimensions, something happened —a shift in the potentials. In the shards, before Raz attacked with a taser, Cal sidestepped him and brought the butt of his gun into the back of Raz's head. Most of the dimensions shifted to Cal having the advantage as he could now predict Raz's actions.

Raz noticed the shift in outcomes. As soon as he observed it, there was yet another shift. Raz ducks as Cal tries to hit him with the butt of his gun. He then spins backwards and kicks Cal in the gut as they both topple to the ground. Raz then slams his taser into Cal's neck, disabling him.

"I don't think so," Cal said, now seeing the new shift. "Traitor!"

As the two refracted beings watched the myriad of dimensions before them, their foreknowledge continuously changed the outcomes of the parallel dimensions. As they took turns having the advantage, one would see the outcome and change his plan, resulting in new, alternative realities. It was a dynamic flow of potential futures —a constant flux of change subject to two interdimensional beings.

"Stop!" Cal yelled in frustration.

"I can't let you shoot them!" Raz yelled. A static background of white noise flooded their ears. It got louder as the entire compound of the central cell got brighter.

"But—" Cal squinted as white light flooded his eyes. The air warmed as if someone put a heat lamp over him.

"We need to... we need to stop—" Raz spoke through labored breathing as sweat poured down his face. A wave of heat washed over them followed by a crack of what sounded like thunder. As they both buckled to their knees, the locked security doors burst open followed by a stream of armored guards. The board of trustees scattered while Raz and Cal both released from refraction, overwhelmed by exhaustion. Swarms of guards filled the chamber, protecting the central cell and the board of trustees behind them.

"Kill that man, but do not hurt my son!" Minzy shrieked as the guards opened fire at Raz.

Dazed, Raz opened his eyes and saw the guards pointing their rifles at him. He looked at Cal who was lying motionless on the ground, his chest heaving with slow breaths. He refracted, this time without Cal's refraction clouding the dimensions. He dashed across the compound as the guards opened fire. He died in several realities —bleeding out next to Cal. However, he timed his steps to the luxury aircar, narrowly escaping the bullets. He climbed into the cockpit and hit reverse thrusters, slamming the ship against the docking arms but releasing it into free air. He got one last look as the guards slapped handcuffs on Cal before backing through the blown-out portal at a neck-breaking speed. With rain pouring over the cockpit, Raz flipped to forward thrusters and escaped the central cell tower which remained intact, in power, and with his protégée in custody.

Again, Raz thought, *it falls apart again.*

He felt tremendously old and lonely.

CHAPTER 26

NOVEMBER 30TH, 1989

At 2 a.m., long since Duke had left the lab, the lights blinked on. Straus stuffed his security badge into his pocket, bewildered that it still granted him access to the lab. He went to a coat rack and touched the hem of his white lab coat. Slowly, he put it on, smoothing out the wrinkles. He missed the coat like he missed his lab. He admired the coffee stains as if each one told the long history of his work with the Casimir Drive—back from when they almost got all funding cut up until the state poured money into development.

He didn't know why he was here, but he suspected something dark at the back of his mind—previously hidden but emerging forward like the tide.

Jo had called the hospital, and the hospital had sent the police, so Straus fled. He had left the notes from the Rift behind and was certain that she probably destroyed them. It would take him years to collect and transcribe the same data from the Rift as it trickled in. The instructions to build the Halo weapon were gone. The math and design were far too advanced for him to have remembered. Losing everything he had worked for had spiraled him into a cavern of depression.

He was drawn to his lab now. The Rift was wide open—almost a continual stream of voices, math, ideas, and designs flooded through him. Along with the Rift, he felt different. Ever since he had broken the rules of reality at the hospital, he could actually see into other versions of his own reality in fleeting moments. In the back of his mind, a rational voice did still whisper to him, "*You're crazy, you've abandoned your family, there is no weapon, you need to go back to the hospital...*"

His mind was a clutter of shame and wild excitement. A mixture of emotional extremes that finally made him collapse on the lab floor and sob. *What am I doing? I have a son. I have a good job. I have a beautiful wife. But he is coming and he must be stopped.*

He suddenly missed his students. It wasn't until that moment that he realized teaching class wasn't a necessary burden—he really did enjoy hearing questions from the undergrads. Their novice understanding of theoretical physics helped him to step back and vicariously see things with new eyes.

What is the opposite of a black hole?

He still ruminated on this question. He felt connected to the question that his student, Chloe, asked. *Maybe she was right. There must be an opposite to everything in nature. And what else could be the opposite to a dense sphere of gravity than a dense halo of gravity?* Why did he dwell on this question more than others? Is it because he only internalized it into his schizophrenic psychosis or is it because it actually mirrored something in reality? He had grown exhausted at posing these same questions to himself over and over again.

He was splitting in two.

One half was a theoretical physicist. He had a devoted wife and child and had developed a revolutionary technology. This man also suffered from schizophrenia for most of his life, decided to go off of his medications, and was currently suffering from full-blown psychosis.

The other half was a seer—receiving voices, advanced math, and schematics from a hidden realm. It helped him develop a new technology with the aim of creating a massive weapon that was used to destroy an enemy that no one had ever heard of. The influence from the other realm —The Rift—granted his abilities. Gifts to peer into other dimensions, to see multiple iterations of his own reality. It was a gift to discern the immediate future and to make the wisest possible choice. If it were real, what would a person do with such a gift? *They could easily place themselves in positions of power and change the world—change the future of humankind.*

As he slumped into a chair, wondering which of these two versions of himself was the most likely to be the truth. He knew the answer. He also knew that he could no longer continue living two opposing versions of himself. He felt the Rift open with a chatter of voices flooding his mind. Instead of grasping for a pen and paper, he leaned on his knees, his palms pressing into his face until the voices ceased. He felt the rubbery plane of his own reality thicken within him. Seeing it in his mind's eye and experiencing a visceral feel was now only convincing him of his own virtual insanity. He realized that it had reached a point where his whole body believed in the machinations of his splintered mind. It was only in this moment he realized how insidious his disease had been.

He toyed with the rubbery plane of reality and pushed it. It broke apart easily this time, shattering once again into a waterfall of realities. Small polygons of multiple slideshows bore their scenarios— their versions of him. In every shard of existence, he only saw himself, alone, sitting in the same chair in which he sat. Despite seeing so many versions of himself at once, he had never felt so alone. The multiple worlds shrunk and expanded away from him, leaving him alone in his own native reality.

"I know you, Custos," he said aloud, monotone, to nobody. "We were going to change things... I know you, Custos. It doesn't have to be like this." He sighed, saddened that he would never understand these words that he'd been hearing for years. "Time is a circle, doesn't matter who you are right now." His voice echoed off the sterile walls. "You've just broken the surface."

He looked into the Casimir Drive track. The front end of a mock-Corvette shined under the fluorescent lights. He laughed to himself, admiring Duke's quirks that insisted he design his own fiberglass front for the Drive. He would miss his friend.

He looked over the lab table and saw handwritten pages scrawled in meticulous handwriting. They were Chou Jia's notes. There were circles and math bearing the work of someone with a superficial understanding of the physics of the Drive. *She's just been copying the work of a madman.* He bowed his head, ashamed that he had let his illness infect the mind of a young physicist at the beginning of her career. He took a piece of paper and pen and inscribed circles all over the page in black ink. He drew one halo after another, finding comfort in the repetition. With every circle drawn, he felt a connection to the Rift—as if he were completing some part of the design.

Finally, he shook his head and wrote a message over the circles:

Van Wert. I know you'll be a man of your word and ensure that my wife and son are the main beneficiaries of whatever profit comes from the commercialization of the Casimir Drive. Hopefully, the Straus name will live in honor despite my mistakes. I'm sorry I didn't get the help I needed.

Jo, it will be hard for a while, but things will get better. You were right, weapons are more effective when they're destroyed. You were the only light in my life. I love you forever.

-Tim

He left the paper on the table and stood, staring down at his note covered with his circles and shame. He felt an urge to rip it up and run out of the lab—to go and live in a remote beach cave somewhere and gather his calculations once again from the Rift. The compulsion to build the clandestine weapon filled him for a final moment until he finally let it go. *There is no weapon, there is no enemy.*

There's only my sick mind!

He left the note and went rummaging through the lab, searching through vials and tubs of powders. He had grouped together arsenic, sodium cyanide, hydrochloric acid, hydrogen peroxide, ethylene glycol, and a few others which he sat on a table. He considered them for a moment wondering what it would feel like to mix them together and swallow the deadly concoction at once. He screwed the top off of the cyanide and peered into the white dust at the bottom of the bottle.

Powdered death.

Just one whiff and it would be over. But how quickly? He screwed the top back on and stood, afraid of suffering a prolonged death. He looked over his shoulder, again at the Casimir Drive, a single powerful engine on a circular track.

His creation.

The fastest record they had so far was over three hundred miles per hour. He thought about the fantastic force a collision the Drive would make if it hit a human body. He flipped on the controls to the Casimir Drive as the warning lights within the glass room flickered, indicating the initiation of a test run. After dialing in a speed of two hundred miles an hour, he watched the thin swivel of bent space extend from the back of the engine. Light refracted through the crack in space, distorting the floor beneath. The bending thinned out until it almost vanished, followed by a loud *crack* of space expanding back out. The singular expansion instantly thrust the engine forward, flinging the mock-Corvette around the track. The Drive quickly met the selected speed, stayed in motion as a red blur, and then slowed with the friction of the track.

Straus dialed in another run, this time at three hundred miles an hour and watched as the Drive hurled around the track in a circular blur. It slowed down and stopped. He looked down at the monitor and paused, his hands above the keyboard. He dialed in five hundred miles per hour—more than they had ever done. His hand hovered over the launch button in hesitation for half a second before he slammed it down. Just as before, the bent wave of gravity contracted space and then expanded outward, forcing the Drive forward.

But this time was different.

This time, the Casimir Drive stayed active as the Corvette moved forward, resulting in a trail of bent space following after.

"Whoa," he said to the empty lab.

Normally, the Casimir Drive contracted space using the negative energy of the Casimir plates. As the Drive slowed, the contraction would cease and the space expanded back outward, producing the force that moved the entire engine around the track. In every run before, space was no longer bent behind the Drive as it moved—it just coasted on the momentum of the singular expansion of space at the beginning of each launch. This last run, however, was much different. Straus saw with his naked eye that space continued to bend as the Drive moved.

It must be because I set it to run at a higher speed. The Casimir Drive must have still been actively bending space even after the Drive was in motion, creating an angular momentum of bent space. They had never run the engine at five hundred miles per hour and had thus never noticed the phenomenon. Van Wert had argued that the copper coiling wouldn't have the heat capacitance. Up until now, Straus had always agreed.

Forgetting about images of his body being pulverized by the Drive, he dialed it into five hundred and fifty miles an hour and hit the launch button without hesitation. Space swiveled and writhed like a worm at the back of the engine—thrashing like a serpent's tongue. The Drive burst forward on the track with a tail of bending space whipping back and forth. The Drive, circling around the track, caught up to the bending space and moved through it. The Casimir Drive itself was still running, creating more bending and adding to the distorted tail, magnifying the bending of space. The Drive accelerated while the snake of distorted space became a unified circle around the track—floating independently of the Drive's location.

It looked... like a *halo.*

Straus watched in awe for one brief moment until the engine cut off, the Drive slowed down and the halo of bent space evaporated. He looked around the lab and then back at the now silent Drive. Was his halo, the weapon—the Destroyer of Worlds—right here in the lab the whole time?

"We weren't running it fast enough."

It wasn't that he was supposed to build a circular engine like the one he crafted in his basement—it was to make the engine run fast enough to *create* a circle of bent space. But it didn't seem like a weapon as nothing was destroyed. *But nothing was in with the halo to be destroyed,* he thought. This whole time, was it possible that the Rift *had* sent the right schematics for the weapon but that he just didn't know how to use it?

Once again, his mind cycled over the obvious reality that the Rift didn't really exist—that it was merely a manifestation of his illness to himself. The Rift was just a mental construct of his mathematical mind—an interpreter that translated the raw data of his mind into the executive functions in his frontal lobe. The schizophrenia then created the narrative that the Casimir Drive was a weapon of mass destruction designed to specifically stop a terrorist that didn't exist. *Yes,* he thought, *this is the explanation. This is the only thing that makes sense.*

He glanced at his bar of poisons again, his eyes favoring cyanide. He wanted to reach for the bottle but, at the same time, had an irresistible urge to do another run of the Drive. Paralyzed between the two choices, he collapsed on the ground, sobbing. An overwhelming sense of worthlessness consumed him.

"He is coming," he said through sobs. "I know you, Custos... I know you..." He finally felt his mind stretch to its breaking point. Nothing was real anymore. Jo's face was a shadow in his mind—he couldn't even remember his son's name. He didn't know the last time he had slept or even ate. Van Wert was a figment of his nightmares. His crying was punctuated by high-pitched laughter as he gasped for air, consumed by panic and anxiety.

His world had finally shattered.

Standing, he lurched to the cyanide bottle and clumsily grasped it in his hands. He unscrewed the top and looked down again into the powder. Just one snort and it would be over—he could dump the bottle over his head and breath it in. That's all it would take. He gave one last look at the Casimir Drive—the creation of his demented mind—and dialed in one thousand miles an hour.

If he was going to die, he wanted to die with his life's work.

He rushed into the Drive room before the Drive fired up. An alarm blared in his ear, warning of the impending test drive. He stepped over the tracks and stood in the middle of the circular test room, surrounded by windows. Moving the bottle of cyanide from one hand to the other, he admired the Casimir engine. He thought about its first prototype—a series of thousands of plates stacked across an entire lab. Now, they had engineered it into a compact coil, powerful enough to produce enough negative quantum energy to bend the fabric of space itself.

The tail of bending gravity formed at the back of the Drive and expanded, clapping at his eardrums, nearly causing him to stumble to the ground. The Drive whipped around the track, an immediate blur before him. The tail of bending gravity overlapped the track, forming a solid halo of warped space that floated now, independent of the Drive or the track. Closing his eyes, he saw it, the same halo—the Destroyer of Worlds, the weapon to stop *him*. Some unseen obsession from another world consumed him. He needed to stop him but he didn't know from what realm or reality the yearning came.

He brought the cyanide to his face but held his breath, thinking of the scene that the lab scientists would find in a mere three hours—Timothy Straus lying dead at the feet of his own machine of madness. One draw from the bottle and it would be over.

Before taking a last breath of poison, he saw the halo of gravity tighten around him. Something—death perhaps—washed over his body.

What's the opposite of a black hole?

CHAPTER 27

MARCH 21TH, 2155 EARTH RECKONING (ER)

"Dev, have you heard of Timothy Straus?" Custos asked as he strapped into the flight deck.

Dev squinted, strapping a harness over his chest. "Scientist. Before the nuclear wars on Earth."

"That's right. We're about to travel a distance through space that would have never been achieved without Timothy Straus. He invented the Casimir Drive."

"I thought they stopped making those."

"They did. They became too costly to mass-produce on Mars. Turns out that copper is a necessary part of the engine. It can't run without it. Mars, unfortunately, has no raw copper to mine."

"Couldn't just import the copper from Earth?"

Custos shook his head. "No, no one there mines it anymore. It doesn't matter anyway. With the scarcity of copper and the decreased interest in intergalactic travel, the New Athens market weeded the Casimir Drive out. It's no longer produced. It's mostly a vintage engine now. People will parade them through the sky, showing off their retro tastes in old Earth culture."

"I'm guessing this ship has the Casimir Drive?"

"Yes. It's the only way we can make it to the source of gravity wave communication. If we tried to use a traditional ship—like an old TexasH Earth freighter ship—it would take decades."

"Wow," Dev said, placating him.

"You don't find that amazing?"

"No, no, I do."

Custos stared at him for a moment, realizing that Dev represented a deep flaw in New Athens culture. He was from a generation born in the cradle of automation. He had no appreciation for technology as it was as ubiquitous as the air he breathed.

"You've had this ship this whole time?" He looked out the windows at the craters that sprawled across the surface of Phobos.

Custos nodded. "Yes. I built it."

"You *built* it?"

"Little hobby of mine. I have several old Earth vehicles that I keep on my property in the city."

Dev threw up his hands. "To this day, you surprise me. You're a strange one, Mr. President." He slapped his hand on the comm dash. "Bet you never thought you'd be using it for traveling way outside the solar system to visit these gravity beings."

"Not exactly."

"Custos," Dev said, changing the tone. "What're we doing?" He looked over at him from his flight chair. The cockpit of the ship had two chairs for command control in which the pilots floated in zero gravity, only held down by harnesses. Behind the cockpit, the rest of the ship was a torus, a rotating hull creating centripetal acceleration —artificial gravity for the passengers. Two rows of chairs followed from the cockpit into the torus of the ship. Beyond, there were dormitories, a bathroom with a shower, and a small kitchen area. A small ladder in the back led to a cargo area below the main deck of the ship.

"What do you mean?" Custos didn't look at him, but double-checked the sleek command panel before him. He had downloaded Dr. Farr's star charts into the system's navigation and was surveying the location from which the gravity waves were transmitting.

Dev looked uneasy. "We're going way out there to hope that we find a massive weapon to kill The Copperhound?"

"No, not exactly."

"The Copperhound is in New Athens, not out there."

"I know where The Copperhound is. There's nothing we can do to stop him on Mars. His fear has control there now. It's poison. We need to draw him out. It's time to give him what he wants."

"And what is that?"

"A war."

A chilled silence sat between them.

"I don't like this," Dev said. "You're not..."

"Wha—"

"—not acting like yourself. You would never consider something like this." Dev looked out the window.

"I know."

"You don't even know if there is a weapon. And if there is a weapon, how will you bring it back? In this ship?" He elbowed the hull.

Custos sat silent for a moment. "I've downloaded Dr. Farr's algorithm to translate the gravitational waves. As we approach, the quality of the waves will likely be better than it is here on Phobos. We can get a better idea of what is actually out there the closer we get. If it turns out to be bogus—a hoax, whatever—we'll turn around and start back at square one. What we're doing may be dangerous. Our lives are probably at risk. I understand if you want to get off this ship."

Dev looked at Custos' porcelain eyes. "Why don't you have the lab just send a probe? Why go ourselves?"

"I have to get to the halo."

"What halo?"

"From the transmission. It mentioned a halo. I—we—have to find this weapon. If we don't get there first, The Copperhound might." Custos looked down at his hands. "You don't have to come. In fact, maybe you shouldn't."

Dev shook his head. "No. I'm ready. Can't be afraid."

. . .

Custos called out a farewell to Phobos after Dr. Farr uploaded a few more data points about the gravity waves into their ship's computer. They undocked from the GraviWave lab and lifted from the oblong moon, burning their thrusters. The ship glided toward Mars for a moment, its red and green landmass filling the cockpit. Dev gazed at the deep blue oceans that contoured around several continents and said, "It's not every day that I see Mars from space."

Custos, too, looked longingly at the unadulterated wilderness of the Martian plains. "All that water was once underground glaciers. The terraforming heated the atmosphere and melted the glaciers, creating oceans where there were once canyons." Thousands of miles of untouched, terraformed land hugged the planet. The Meadows of Mars were a beautiful swirl of colors next to New Athens, the small metropolitan jewel at the base of a mountain range. Custos thought of all the animals—bears, gorillas, antelope, raccoons, and panthers that had been brought from Earth when the mass exodus of the fallen Central Cell happened. Mars now bore the fruit of a retired Earth—the unexpected stepchild of humankind to heal the burden of humanity's mistakes. "We can do it right this time. Again."

"Do what right?"

Custos looked at him. "Everything. We started again here on Mars and I won't allow us to make the same mistakes. We're not coming back until we finally get rid of that man." Custos dialed in the coordinates from Dr. Farr and adjusted the controls, prompting the ship to move away from Mars, bringing the expanse of space in front of them. The ship burst forward, leaving Phobos and Mars behind. Dev clutched his chair and looked disconcertedly at Custos.

"Relax," Custos said. "We've got to really get moving before we turn on the Casimir Drive or else the acceleration would tear us apart." As the ship gained more speed, Custos spent several more minutes going over his math and then eyed a large switch on the top of the console. "Ready?"

Dev grimaced. "I think so."

Custos flipped the switch and a low shudder vibrated through the ship. Several Casimir coils flickered with life in the heart of the engine, drawing out negative quantum energy from empty space. A well of gravity dimpled space behind the ship. It concentrated into a pinpoint, drawing in bent rays of starlight. The Casimir coils cut out and the well of distorted space expanded, catapulting the ship. A cry died in Dev's throat before it could escape. The pinpoints of starlight became jagged blurs—rays of streaked light across the spill of space. Mars—their home—vanished behind them.

The vagrant rocks of the asteroid belt were a small blip on the navigation array as they swept by. Jupiter was nowhere to be seen, cruising on the other side of the solar system, but Saturn winked at them like a cat's yellow eye as they flitted by. The smaller gaseous planets were inconsequential bodies of their journey. Custos tensed for a moment as the alarms detected the Kuiper Belt dead ahead. Although he previously charted a course through the lightest possible spots, he knew it would only take a pebble to tear through their ship. They both breathed a sigh of relief as they passed safely through, leaving the outer limits of the solar system behind them. They had reached the dead space between the Kuiper Belt and the Oort Cloud that surrounded the solar system like a shell of gas and rock. After another hour, the ship finally stopped accelerating and Dev unbuckled his harness.

"Steady state now—about 29 AUs an hour," Custos declared. "That's how powerful the Casimir Drive is." Custos continued studying the star charts, fretting about many missing holes in their course to the gravity waves. "Wait, I forgot something." He reached down into his bag and pulled out a white chess piece that he used to keep on his desk.

"Ah, your chess piece. Do you know how many times reporters have mentioned that thing in articles? They're obsessed with the mystery of the 'white queen'. Why'd you bring it?"

Custos shrugged. "It's always been a source of hope for me, reminding me of a better time." He stuck it on the console.

Dev got up and stepped from the zero-gravity cockpit into the rotating torus. He fell forward into the main cabin and stumbled to his knees as he adjusted to the gravity. He went to lay down when something thumped at his feet, stopping him in his tracks. It repeated a few more times and stopped.

Custos looked over his shoulder. "What was that?"

Dev shrugged. "Falling cargo?"

"Maybe, but we're not accelerating anymore and the torus isn't either." He scanned the console and didn't see any lapses in the integrity of the hull. "Everything looks good here. No breaches." He ran a system diagnostic. "Can you go down below and check it out while I see if anything looks wrong?"

"Yeah, yeah, I'll check it out." Dev went to the back of the ship, opened a hatch to the cargo storage below, and disappeared down the latter. Custos surveyed the immediate sector of space with infrared and laser sensors and only found limited space debris—they were flying through a cloud of fine dust with very little relative velocity to theirs. The planets of the solar system were far behind them with the closest star system—the Centauri stars—being well over three light-years away. Their journey wouldn't take them to any known celestial body. As far as Custos could tell from the data Dr. Farr provided, the location of the gravity wave message was in the middle of nowhere. He had a brief moment of doubt about his plan. A blanket of fatigue fell over him.

"Nothing," Dev announced, climbing back up to the deck of the ship. "All supplies were still stacked and buckled down. I don't know what it was."

Custos got up and made it to the back quarters, where a small bed was built into the hull. "Would you mind taking the helm while I get some rest?"

"Take the helm? I don't know how to fly this thing."

"Just wake me up if anything beeps."

Custos found the bed, closed his eyes, and fell asleep to dreams of shouting voices.

After several days, the two travelers grew weary of space. The cock-pit's view was a face of thousands of dim eyes drowning in an ocean of blackness. Dev spoke longingly about his small explorations of Martian terrain—the wonders of the vegetation and animals that sprung up on the immature, terraformed soil. Traveling through space was a vacant journey, void of color and life, stretching on forever with featureless vistas. The supernovae, star clusters, hatcheries, and pulsars of astronomy were rare phenomena in a black desert of nothing.

The boredom of the journey coaxed Dev to speculate wildly about The Copperhound—that he had become a phantom in their minds—a menace of only their dreams who couldn't possibly have any bearing on them in the deepness of space. At one time, he convinced himself that The Copperhound was just an invention of Vana Iberian—a political ploy to get Custos out of power. Maybe she even put Dr. Farr up to fabricating data. What if they got to the gravitational wave source and found nothing?

"He's real, Dev. You saw him."

"But that could've been an actor. Part of the conspiracy."

"He's real."

"But how do you know?"

"I know. I tried to deny he was real for a very long time. But he's very real."

The walls of the ship pressed in on them with each passing day, as if every hour of their flight distorted space itself around them. Several times a day, the same small thumps vibrated through the ship's hull —ostensibly from the cargo bay below. Dev inspected the area several times and found nothing, although he commented about how the air smelled of garbage.

Custos' fastidious attention to detail had slackened by the fifth day of travel, his mind dulled by the monotony of space. The only thing that held his focus was checking the star chart and the course of their navigation. The source of the gravity waves was getting closer to them despite the endless treadmill of space around them.

"It's hard to imagine New Athens even exists when we're this far away," Dev said while looking out a small window. "There's just so much nothing. It's only been a few days but I'd kill to see a sunrise, a cloud, a raindrop—anything to show me I'm on a planet and not some lifeboat in the middle of space. Do you think we're further than anyone has ever been?"

"No. Back when Central Cell was in power, they chartered very far out. Why do you think we have the star charts that we already do have?"

Ignoring his answer, Dev didn't move from the window. "The emptiness makes me wonder if anything we do is even worth it. Someday, we'll all just end up like what's out there—particles in empty space."

"It's always worth it. Even when we fail. Every time we fail, it always matters. That's how humanity keeps surviving. Not because of successes, but because of failures."

Dev flashed a skeptical brow. "Sounds like a hollow platitude at this point."

"Get some rest, I think you're getting a little delirious, Dev."

They passed the next day in mostly silence. Dev was too tired to talk and Custos was too obsessed with checking the gravity wave transducer to see if new messages were arriving. So far, it was the same broken message they had on Phobos.

On their sixth day, Custos grunted at the console. Dev looked at him. "What?"

"The gravity waves—something's weird."

"What?"

"The signal... it's moving."

"*Moving?*"

"It's moving. The gravity wave source is moving much faster than a planet or star would move through the galaxy. I think we can only detect its trajectory now that we're getting closer."

"Moving like it's coming from a ship?"

"Impossible. A starship couldn't create gravity waves like this. Hey!" The console lit up. "The signal is strengthening. Dr. Farr's translator is interpreting new data! Look!" He pointed at the console.

"What's it saying?"

"Hang on, it's still translating." The console lit up with streams of data and encryption algorithms that transduced the imperceptible gravity waves passing through their ship into words. "Here—yes, this is all new. I think it's more of the original message they got at Phobos."

"What's it say?" Dev snapped, disinhibited by cabin fever.

Custos was about to read the words but held his breath. "Wait, it's audio... we must be so close to the source that more complex encryptions are still stable." He flipped on the speakers and played the file.

It was a man's voice. He spoke slowly and with clear enunciation but with intermittent static:

"Whatever is in the exact middle... is equally pulled on all sides, preserving the matter in the equidistant center. However, anything outside... torn apart by uneven tidal forces... this was the trap... unpredictable results."

Dev looked at Custos. "Is that it?"

"'Unpredictable results...'" Custos repeated the final line.

"Does this sound like a weapon to you?"

"Something that can create uneven gravitational tidal forces could rip apart anything."

"So, it's a weapon?"

Custos nodded. "A very powerful weapon."

CHAPTER 28

DECEMBER 1ST, 1989

Timothy Straus—no, someone once named Timothy Straus—
stood outside a window, watching Jo.

She had taken the news about his death with constraint—with bravery. Her face was taut, jaw set, as the police stood at her doorway. He watched her now, her chest breathing deeply as she lay on their yellow couch. Instead of her usual place at the edge, perched forward and thinking, she had sunk into the couch as if... unburdened. Yet, her fingers moved over the edge of the couch cushion, picking frantically at yellow foam that she'd exposed with incessant picking. At her feet were numerous piles of paper strips and torn fabric. Watching her releasing neurotic energy into the couch with a nervous tick gave Straus the full story.

He was toxic to Jo.

Fatigued by worry and burdened with responsibility, Straus had broken her. A part of him wanted to open the door, leap into their home, and wrap her in his arms. It was all a bad dream—his death, his broken mind, his psychosis. He could pick up where he left off before it all fell apart. He could be a husband, a father—someone *normal*.

But it was better for Jo that her husband was gone.

And everything was different now. *He* was different. He felt like gold. His skin and sinews were firm, stronger. He made a fist and felt his heart pumping within his hand. His body teemed with energy from head to foot. He'd changed. How long would this change last? Days? Years?

All he knew is that the Casimir Drive had *changed* him. Fundamentally.

The halo was underneath his nose the entire time. Its energy—its gravity—changing the essence of his body. It made so much sense now: a halo of gravity—the inversion of a point of gravity—changed the spin of the atoms of his body. Just as a black hole would stretch and obliterate a person, the opposite would condense and preserve matter. He was not human any longer, he was... *refracted.*

And not only his body, but his mind.

He could refract reality at the drop of a hat, exploring the multiverse as if turning the pages of a book. Every possibility was open to him. He could do anything he wanted.

Anything.

He could slip into a bank like a ghost, duck and bob as every head turned at the precise moment. He could win every lottery anywhere at any moment. He could slip into any museum and steal famous artwork from any wall. He could feign that he knew everything at any moment—seeing every correct answer in the slippage of the dimensions.

But no, refraction was not for himself. It was a power far too potent for the abuse of a single person.

It was for people like Jo.

Jo always hoped for the better—believing that the good will always eclipse the bad. That the Cold War could end—that walls could crumble. Hope guided her. She even held out hope for Timothy Straus, *believing* he could be healed, *knowing* that there was hope for his sick mind. He could take her hope now. He could refract the world with the hope and love that Jo had given him.

Refraction could be for the world—a gift for the future. He could use his powers to guide nations, counseling and leading to the best possible outcomes and compromises. He could extinguish fears and promise hope by directing nations to the correct choices. With the snap of his fingers, he could heal his country of the Cold War, guiding the leaders into the correct discourse for diplomacy. Knowing reactions before they occurred, a refracted being could always know what to say to anyone, including the leaders of the world.

This was his path now.

He was no longer Timothy Straus. He would become the custodian of mankind—guiding, prodding, teaching, and urging. And if necessary, *leading*. Jo *could* be right about the world. He *could* make things better.

As he watched her, the ocean of voices still lapped on his mind but it gave him solace, not despair. He knew who the voices were—afterthoughts, forethoughts, wakes of future selves and past timelines all mixing around in the boundless eternity; his mind a conduit of all times and possible realities. His refraction was a singular moment at the Drive, but it echoed through him, into the past. He supposed it was meant to be—it was a certainty that he would step into that Drive room, between suicide and eternity, and start the Drive. Even though it was in the future, it affected his past.

Timothy Straus was poison to Jo. But she could heal now. She could be set free and raise their son with financial security.

Hopefully, I saved you, my love.

Voices bubbled up inside him, the seas of time spilling through him.

He is coming!

There was no weapon. There was no Copperhound. At least not for him. At least not right now. They were for another time.

...I know you, Custos...

There were worlds wrapped inside worlds, wrapped inside worlds... telescoping forever.

...weapons are more powerful destroyed...

Which voices were for his time? For his world?

...this was the trap I set...

He could at least start with his own world.

...Cal, it's us...

Try. Try to make it better.

...Ah Sun-flower! weary of time...

Could he change humankind?

...Who countest the steps of the sun...

Could he do it alone?

...Seeking after that sweet golden clime...

Or would he need help?

CHAPTER 29

MARCH 21TH, 2155 EARTH RECKONING (ER)

"Dev?" Custos squinted through the cabin, standing in the back bedroom. "I thought I heard you coughing. Everything good?" He saw Dev sitting in the cockpit. He nodded. Custos plopped himself into one of the passenger seats in the rotating torus.

"Any new gravity wave transmissions?" Custos asked, looking past the cockpit and into space. It was the same curtain of blackness with a glittering sequin of stars. Dev didn't respond. "Everything okay? Look, I know it's been a while cooped up here, but—"

A raspy voice seeped out from the cockpit. "I know you, Custos..."

It was not Dev.

"I know who you *are*." The voice grated down Custos' spine. It was oddly tender with an erratic pitch.

A mass of hulking shoulders stood from the flight chair. The man turned, his face emerging from the dimness of the cockpit as the torus rotated. He ducked under the threshold and stepped into the torus, toward Custos. His face—alive with fire and eyes bright with understanding—was a spectrum of expressions—stoned grimace, awaited delight. His scalp was shorn with evidence of black stubble fighting through scar tissue. The man's face was poked with scarring down the cheeks. Despite the rough skin, he maintained a youthful countenance—a knowing flicker in his eyes. His sharp nose extended from bushy eyebrows and his lips were taut with white anger. His bulky physique suggested an athletic vitality yet his face smoldered with the weather and experience of age. His eyes became placid as he beheld the robot. "Do you know who *I* am?" he asked.

Custos crossed his arms.

"Do I look familiar to you?"

"I wasn't sure. I didn't know if you—"

"Were meant for your time? Oh, yes, robot. We were bound for one another. Right here. In *this* time. In *this* dimension. In *this* moment."

Custos nodded. "For a long time, I didn't want to believe it."

"Yes, yes, that sweet, intoxicating denial. You couldn't face the storm that's been bearing down on you since that day so long ago. Now, say it. Who am I?"

"You are The Copperhound."

The Copperhound shook his head. "No. Not to you, robot. Look *closer.*"

In a flash of panic, Custos thought of Dev and looked around the cabin. "Dev—"

"Don't worry about your lap dog. Look at my face, robot. Who am I?"

Custos stood but was instantly seized by The Copperhound and thrust back into his chair. The Copperhound hunched over in a coughing fit as he wagged his finger at Custos. "I'm sorry about all the noise I've been making down below. Your boy, Dev, performed a diligent search for the source of the sound down there but he could never see me—not in a million dimensions. Do you know why? Do you know how I get around? How I could waltz into your penthouse and rummage through your things? How I found the picture of your family?" He gestured for Custos to answer. "Do you know how I figured out the enigma of 'Custos the Dreamer'?"

Custos bowed his head. "I know."

The Copperhound continued, "Although it was a bit more challenging for the Phantom of Mars to stay so hidden on a small ship. I have a nasty cough. You see, I have a lung condition. It causes quite a bit of coughing. I had to mask it with some noise or I was afraid you'd discover me before the great reveal. Do you know how I got my lung condition?" The Copperhound peered down at Custos. He reached his meaty hands to Custos and touched the side of his head, feeling the glossy metal with his fingertips. "Custos the Dreamer. Custos the Hypocrite. Custos the *Liar*. It's not just nuts and bolts ticking away in that metal head of yours, is it? 'The only self-aware robot?' That's a nice trick—a nice story you wove for your sheep. How is it none of them demanded to understand what you are? You bred a generation of mindless children, robot. They're weak and stupid. All it took to bring chaos to New Athens was a handful of starving people from Earth to spread rumors. Them and my 'cyborgs', people with medieval diseases—tuberculosis and malaria—and burn victims with cybernetic implants. Do you think your lap dog could escape me without me knowing? As if that boy could just slip away.

"It's your meddling—your castration of their innate drive to think for themselves that made them into pawns. You raised them to be controlled and then you made yourself robot king. A king who stopped being clever long ago. All it takes is a well-planted lie about a nuclear weapons cache in Terrabel and you go gallivanting into deep space. And no one—except until I came along—questioned what you have in that skull of yours. Now it would appear that they're trying to tear that human mind right out of your metal head." He gestured to the large dents that littered Custos' head and metal frame.

Custos brought his palm to his chin, thinking.

"You're no machine."

Custos looked down at his arms and legs. "No."

The Copperhound let out a long laugh followed by another fit of wet coughs. He brought a handkerchief from his pocket and spat blood into it. "Let me tell you about my cough, robot."

"I can't imagine what you've been through. If only I'd known..."

A flash of rage crossed The Copperhound's eyes. "You... don't talk to me about hardship! You know nothing! I wish—" he paused, thinking. "I wish you had told me about the side effects a little sooner."

"I can only say that I'm sorry. I didn't know this was going to be real, for me—for *us*."

"I'm *very* real, robot. Not just some dimensional echo. I'm afraid it would have saved me a little trouble had I known what that little side effect was. I would've killed myself when I had the chance—that would've ended things nicely. But no, I had the false hope of escape after they threw me into the copper mines. I bided my time, waiting for the perfect scenario to escape. The only problem is, in Central, they chain every prisoner to a block of stone. Did you know that? Remember when you told me 'it doesn't matter how many dimensions you see, it doesn't make a difference if you're tied up. You're still not stronger than steel'? Well, I learned that lesson—over and over again. When I refracted, I watched myself escape a thousand different ways, but it never happened for me. Not once did they undo my chains." He extended his hands, revealing circumferential scars that tightened around his wrists. "For the first few weeks, I knew you'd come for me. I knew you wouldn't abandon me. It was this hope that moved me through the copper tunnels. Their little whips on my back didn't matter—my friend and mentor—*my uncle*—would rescue me from hell."

Custos closed his eyes.

"I even enjoyed the practice of refracting. Each morning the guards woke me up—used a small forklift to dump my chained boulder into a cart—and then we were off looking for copper. I saw myself in hundreds of parallel dimensions, finding the richest veins of ore. Without fail, every day, I led the excavation teams to vast caverns of copper ore—more than they had ever seen. Do you know what they called me?"

Custos tried to respond but remained speechless.

"The Copperhound!" he hissed, "The Copperhound!" he cried, thumping his fist on the hull. "I was a dog to them! A loyal dog to fetch their precious metal to run their ships and keep their thumb on the world as it sank into madness. Like a bloodhound, I found their copper. I allowed them to treat me like an animal because I had hope, robot." He nodded and pointed at Custos. "I had hope that my friend would come for me."

Custos looked out a side portal window and stared into the black ink of space, his mind dark. The Copperhound paced down the ship, stifling coughs and sputtering saliva as he spoke. A dirty poncho of coarse wool clung to his shoulders, swaying with his movements. The man smelled of refuse. "No, my friend didn't come for me. The hope took far longer than I thought to die. I dug copper for three years until I knew you weren't coming for me. It happened one day when a sliver of copper sliced my eyelid that I knew you were gone. Look at my face." He leaned into Custos, his eyes wide. "Every divot and scar —that's what mining copper does to the human body. It gets into the *lungs*," he said, taking a deep breath. The air he drew wheezed through scarred air sacs. He choked on the air and hunched over, hacking at phlegm. "The copper dust gets into your lungs, your eyes, your dreams—drives all the prisoners mad. And that's how they die. You see, going to the copper mines isn't a life sentence—it's a death sentence. Central Cell knew that the copper kills.

"And that would've been fine with me. Dying alone, chained to a block of stone the size of a gorilla, stewing in my fits of rage and fantasies of revenge. That would've been a happy death—a lovely way to die. But that's not what happened to me, robot, is it?" He peered down at Custos. "Do you know why?"

"Yes."

"Why?"

"The side effect of refraction."

The Copperhound dropped to his knees and bowed before Custos in mock worship. He looked up, his face alive with crazed glee. "That little side effect that you forgot to tell me about." He stood back up again, hands behind his back. "I worked. I worked for years. I worked until Central Cell imploded on itself. Turns out our half-baked idea to delete the central cell wasn't needed all along. So much for the merits of dictatorial capitalism—the entire city crumbled with revolt without our help! We... we didn't need to do any of that rebel nonsense! It only got me thrown into a labor prison!" He pounded his fist on the hull. "And I worked. And I worked. And I worked until my guards were gone. One day, I woke up and there was... no one. 'Okay then,' I told myself, 'I will starve, chained up to my only friend—the giant stone'. That would've been just fine, just fine, but it didn't happen." The Copperhound sat down, out of breath from movement. He pointed a finger at Custos. "I lived, and I lived... and I kept on living."

Custos looked at the floor.

"And I lived. And I lived. I wasn't immortal, I needed food, but not much. Just a few mushrooms that grew about once every two weeks is all I needed to keep these bones going. Finding grubs every now and then was also a nice treat. But it's not like I'm the spry nineteen-year-old kid you knew. I've aged. But I don't exactly look like I'm almost eighty years old, do I? And apparently, there's a... limit to the preservation?" He looked Custos up and down. "Your older body ran out on you, didn't it? Figured out a way of getting that brain of yours into that shell of a machine? The irony! The irony that a society that was so afraid of diseased cyborgs had one as their own president. Right, *Raz*?"

Custos flinched at the name. "I'm... sorry."

"Raz, mind if I call you by your real name?"

Custos shook his head.

"Do you know what kept me alive all those years in that abandoned copper mine? I mean, besides the mushrooms and runoff water?"

"The thought of killing me."

The Copperhound pursed his lips, pondering. "Well, yes, of course, I want revenge. But to live all that time just to—I don't know —strangle you in your sleep? So fleeting. Yes, I wanted revenge, but not with your blood. I did some research—did some stalking. As the only self-aware robot, you drew too much attention to your forgotten enemy. After snooping around for only a few weeks using refraction, I learned who you were. Remember that photo of your family you kept in your wallet? You've got the same one on your office desk, robot. I remember that pretty wife and cute little boy of yours. After I knew who you were and saw the paradise you created, I wanted to destroy it—tear apart everything you stood for and do it in a way that would be incomprehensible to you. I want New Athens. I want to take it from you, show you that you are a failure, not only in taking down Central Cell, but in creating your little intellectual haven on your utopian planet. I want to remind you of the people... the people of Copper Mound—me, Bene... Jelena." He stopped as tears brimmed his eyelids. "Their blood is on your hands. That's why I'm here. That brings me to today, to right now—"

"We were supposed to change things!" Custos erupted at him.

The Copperhound was startled by the outburst.

"We were supposed to change things, Cal."

"That is not my name anymore."

"You lay all the blame on me, but what about what you did wrong? What about blasting into the central cell to kill the board of trustees? Do you remember pointing a gun at your mother? Did your hate for me make you forget what *you* did wrong?"

"They weren't supposed to die. Bene and Jelena. We were all supposed to get out alive. Like you said. And you... *left* me."

"My mistake was trusting you. Had I known that you'd let your anger control you—as it does to this day—I never would've trusted you. We were supposed to change Central Cell and free the people of Copper Mound and the rest of the world. It was directly because of your anger that we failed. I was right on the point of deleting the financial data from the cell before you blasted in."

"I never would've been refracted if you had told me that it made me virtually immortal. You started the domino fall of events."

Custos shook his head. "You don't understand. You never did. The person that you are—the fundamental eternal you—already made the decision. Do you think all those versions you see of yourself in other dimensions are distinct from you? They are *all* you. Every person is eternal, each split reality is just a singular manifestation of our eternal selves. You are responsible for all of your actions because they all come from the same source. You had already decided to be refracted—I knew this—and so I did it."

"How? When? Tell me!" There was pleading in the man's voice.

Custos paused and then glanced at The Copperhound. "Do you know what happens inside of a black hole?"

"What're you talking about?" His voice was softer.

"Do you want to know why you are the way you are?"

The Copperhound rubbed the scruff on his chin. "Speak, robot."

"Inside of a black hole," he continued, relieved that he had The Copperhound distracted, "where gravity compresses to a singular point, matter is stretched and time stands still. In the opposite of a black hole—an inverted black hole—time stands still because matter is *preserved*."

The Copperhound scoffed.

"Listen, it's taken me three lifetimes to figure out the math behind this. If a person were to be sucked into the singularity of a black hole, their matter compresses into the normally unobservable micro-dimensions of the fabric of space-time. Their matter is obliterated—gone from three-dimensional space. But if a person were to stand in the center of a *ring* of gravity, their matter is *unfolded* and strung out through the unlimited dimensions that make up reality. Their atoms slow down—their spin violating the normal laws of quantum mechanics. Their bodies aren't immortal, but their decay is attenuated."

"What does that mean?"

"When you refracted—when I refracted—our minds and bodies went through a prism that opened the window to our own concurrent parallel dimensions. We already existed in all dimensions at once, but refraction allowed us to see them. You are the same person, no matter what reality you live in. Our minds or spirit or whatever you want to call it was unleashed into all the mirrors of reality, only our physical bodies stayed tethered here."

The Copperhound bowed his head in thought.

"And similar to the effect of gravity in a black hole, the effect of inverted gravity caused the atoms of our bodies to decay at a slower rate. We're not immortal, we just age slower. You said it yourself, you're not the spry nineteen-year-old that I knew. And me... well," he looked down at his metallic arms and legs, "my body gave out about forty years ago. I would've died if I hadn't put myself into this body with the cover story that I was a spontaneously self-aware artificial intelligence. It was the only explanation that people would accept."

"Custos the Liar."

Custos nodded in agreement. "I've never said I wasn't a liar."

"But you refracted me without me knowing. You made the decision for me."

"You had already made the decision. You'd been having side effects of the refraction your whole life, long before I ever came along. Cal, listen to the words coming out of our mouths. Don't they sound familiar to you?"

The Copperhound nodded.

"Isn't it obvious that there is a part of our minds that exists outside of linear time? I've been hearing this conversation in my mind ever since I taught—ever since I can remember. Up until now, I had hoped it was just spilling over from other dimensions that didn't have anything to do with my own. I was in denial after I heard that man in the New Athens assembly hall announce that you were coming. Even after that, I convinced myself that you weren't going to be a threat in my native dimension." Custos looked away, distracted by his thoughts. He focused on The Copperhound, wondering about all the time he spent chained in a cave. "Our bodies are bound to this existence but our minds see every parallel dimension. I thought it was a gift when I discovered it. I thought..."

"What?"

"I thought I could change the world. Make it better. I tried and failed so many times for so long before I met you. I thought, with two of us, we could start over again and free the world from its repeated pattern of wealth and destruction. But you were... you were just too angry to change anything."

The Copperhound stood, his mind brooding and his jaw slack. "How did you refract me? You told me that it was right underneath our noses. What is it?" He cast an unrelenting glare at Custos.

Custos stood without response and thought of the lies, patience, and hatred that led The Copperhound to him at that moment. He sensed a softening in the man, but more than anything, he felt a trap. The Copperhound bore years trapped in a cave to plan his revenge. Custos had long ago grown tired of the art of war. He hadn't even refracted in several years, considering himself above the practice. He was afraid of The Copperhound, not because he was a phantom, but because perhaps his pupil had grown smarter. "If I didn't tell you back then, what makes you think I'd tell you now?"

"Wrong answer, robot."

"I will never give that power to another person. Particularly not a terrorist who's vowed to destroy the only remaining city of the human species. The secret to refraction will die with me."

The Copperhound's lips unfurled into a smile, his eyes transfixed. "Can you see it, Raz?"

"Wha—"

"Can you see me killing you?" The Copperhound was refracting, teasing apart the potentials of their reality. "It looks so... easy."

Custos flinched, jumped back from his chair and refracted.

The Copperhound's face tightened. "No—"

"Not quite the same outcomes now that I can see what you see, is it?"

As soon as Custos refracted, he reset the parallel dimensions. He saw moments into the near future, affecting all potentials. In one shard of reality, Custos saw The Copperhound brandish a gun from beneath his poncho. He fires it just moments before Custos leaps out of the way with foreknowledge of the attack. In another fragment, The Copperhound lunges at Custos, but falls to the ground as Custos sidesteps. In hundreds of other dimensions, each attempt by The Copperhound to kill or seize Custos results in Custos easily escaping.

Yet, as the moments passed, the shards of reality shifted. Once The Copperhound observes himself failing at every attempt, he no longer tries to attack. When Custos sees The Copperhound no longer attacking, he goes on the offensive—darting at the hulking man and struggling to strangle him with his powerful robotic grip. But The Copperhound, refracting in every dimension, easily foresees the counteroffensive and dodges out of the way. In several dimensions, he accidentally shoots a hole through the glass panels, depressurizing the ship and killing himself.

As each new shift in possibilities refracted through their minds, they changed their potential actions which reset the dimensions. After a few more seconds, a loop of possibilities fluttered over them in which each one of them tries disposing of the other while their opponent changes strategies based on new knowledge gained from refracted reality, resetting the possibilities.

Every window of reality became a still picture—a robot and a scarred man standing motionless, gazing at one another. For the first time in their lives, neither one of them had the upper hand.

"The first to stop refracting—" Custos said.

"The first to die."

They stood motionless in a stalemate.

They stood in an auditorium full of worlds without number. Each fragment, a distinct dimension where Custos and The Copperhound found themselves in the same predicament—holding one another hostage by canceling out their respective abilities to glimpse potential possibilities. Their mutual foreknowledge perpetually stopped one another from having the upper hand. Every breath and shuffle of the feet was amplified a million-fold instantly into their native reality. The same actions took place in countless dimensions. They stood between an infinity of mirrors, each reflecting back every movement and sound.

"Do you remember when you took me over the nuclear fallout?" The Copperhound asked. Thousands of echoes of his own voice, repeating the same words, flooded his ears. Every refracted dimension was a perfect mirror of their current reality—a standstill of possibilities as the two refracted beings studied each other.

"What're you saying?" Custos winced as a shockwave of his own voice crashed into his mind. Custos knew what was happening... the multiverse was converging at their singular location.

The Copperhound squinted through the dimensional interference. "We flew above the nuclear fallout—you showed me the destroyed city from the nuclear war."

"Y-yes."

"You told me to never forget the destruction of misused power." He shuddered from the feedback of sound.

"You didn't... learn... the lesson."

The Copperhound tried to laugh but stopped when the echo hammered in his ears. "Neither did you, robot. Why did you come all the way out here? You want the weapon—'the Destroyer of Worlds'."

"I never wanted the weapon, Cal."

"You didn't?"

"No. But I know that you do. I knew you were listening and following me. I knew you had stowed away on the ship. I meant to bring you here."

"Why?"

"To end this. To end you. To end me. Away from my people." Custos fell to his knees, overwhelmed by the reverberations of his own voice. It wasn't just the echoing of sound—the inside of the ship was filling with bright light. "I've sacrificed everything to create New Athens. My family... even you. I've lived through wars, hunger, famine, and wealth. I watched Earth descend into the madness of nuclear war. I've lived for... so long. Do you know what that does to the human mind? Do you understand the tortured wisdom gained from watching human civilization unravel and destroy itself? Do you know what it's like to live through all that and be completely helpless? But none of it matters because I keep failing. I'm done failing. I've put myself as the guardian, the custodian of mankind, but I never earned that right. The fall of New Athens shows how I've only papered over the inherent human flaws that make our world. You, Cal, you are the embodiment of everything I've done wrong. I forgot about you for the same reason I abandoned Earth—I thought you were hopeless. I came back for you after Central Cell fell but I couldn't find you, Cal. I'm sorry that you were... chained up for so long. I didn't know."

"You came back?" The Copperhound said with genuine surprise. Custos nodded.

The Copperhound shook his head. "Your words don't matter anymore. I'm going to do what you did to me and then destroy everything you love. I'll bring your whole city down myself!" The Copperhound stood but quickly shielded his eyes as the ship filled with blinding white light. "What's happening?"

"It's a dimensional feedback loop. It is going to destroy us," Custos yelled, "this is the only way." He closed his eyes against the light.

Their concurrent refraction created a nexus between all parallel dimensions, paralyzing every version of them. Rather than energy being dissipated evenly through the diversity of possibilities throughout the dimensions, it crystallized from every parallel dimension at once. The sound, light, and energy from every dimension became identical and amplified together into their native reality.

"Stop!" The Copperhound cried.

"It must end, Cal. *We* must end. We've brought nothing but misery to humankind. We've... we've solved *nothing*."

An oppressive heat grasped them like a giant fist. The Copperhound cried out as his skin singed. Custos' metal frame charred from the positive feedback loop of raw energy that entered their dimension with a thunderous clap, shaking the hull of the ship. A shockwave of energy thundered through time and space.

Then blackness.

CHAPTER 30

MARCH 24TH, 2155 EARTH RECKONING (ER)

V ana Iberian stood at the lectern at the great assembly hall of New Athens. It had been built over the precise location where the first Council of the early Martian colonists had taken place, where a mysterious old man appeared and revealed the thoughts and intents of the council. The stranger's revelations of their mutual treachery instantly leveled the playing field, creating fresh earth for the budding colony to grow into what would become the glory of New Athens.

She glanced up at the back of the assembly hall and winced. The remains of the original council's tapestry clung to the ceiling, frayed and blackened by fire. The first council had commissioned it as a symbol of unity. The Copperhound had commanded its destruction.

She gazed over the lectern. There were four council members.

Four.

She, the newly appointed interim president of New Athens, didn't even have half of a full quorum to conduct city business. Most of them hadn't responded to her request for a council meeting. The ones who did dignify her response cited concerns over their own personal safety.

"Should we really be here right now?" Anita Linwood whined.

Tendrils of unkempt hair frayed above her exhausted eyes. "What kind of business could we possibly have to conduct right now?"

Benjamin Cher nodded. He had a habit of wasting council time with his frequent and unsolicited opinions, but today, he was unusually reticent. "Yes, Miss President. I'm wondering that myself. What's the point of calling the council now? It's chaos outside."

"You're referring to the protesters?" Iberian responded from over the lectern, maintaining her poise. "They're always out there. What I want to know—"

"Protesters? Those people aren't protesters anymore."

"Please explain to me what they are then, council member Cher."

"They're anarchists. They're the Cabal of The Cop—"

"The Copperhound," Iberian finished. "Yes, I've heard of them."

"Yes, the Cabal of The Copperhound. Are you aware they have been running the streets anywhere east of the river? A competing government is out there right now!"

"So," Iberian said, sidestepping his question, "you validate his faction by calling it by its name? They are not a legitimate political entity in New Athens and are not recognized by this assembly."

Cher paused and then sighed in exhaustion. "It doesn't matter if you recognize them or not. They're out there right now. This isn't about politics anymore. Politics are for peacetime. I don't care what you want to call them. The fact is that there is a large group of our own people who are calling for The Copperhound to show his face— to actually *come* to the city and save them."

"I know the facts, councilman Cher."

"And do you know that they're right on the other side of those doors? They've taken over entire city blocks. And you call us here to conduct *city business*?"

"Our army is right outside the chambers, protecting us. *I* made sure of that. There is not a single ship in our skies from Earth. Not a single new refugee out there, poisoning our people."

"They're already poisoned," Linwood said. "We don't have control anymore. Half the city is shut down. You, Miss President, have failed."

"That," Iberian said, pointing at Linwood, "is exactly why we're meeting right now."

Cher suddenly stood. "I'm leaving. I did come here today to entertain your ideas, Miss President, but it's clear you have nothing. I propose we evacuate to the outer colonies."

Iberian folded her arms. "Following the lead of your former president? Abandoning the city—just like Custos?"

Cher scowled at her. "I'm no coward. I just know when the time for talking has ended. Didn't we appoint you because you would act?"

"I've protected our people!" Iberian snapped.

"But," Linwood said, also standing, "you haven't protected us from *ourselves*. Our own people are tearing the city apart."

Iberian wavered. "I didn't... I wasn't—"

"Do you know why The Copperhound had that man, that Earthman, come to these chambers and burn that tapestry?" Linwood asked. "The Copperhound understands words and symbols. He knew that destroying perception of safety is the same thing as destroying safety itself. Who needs to attack with an army when you can get your opponent's people to rot from within? A free people can only operate within mutual cooperation and consent. The Copperhound stole that from us."

"I—"

"And," Cher interrupted, "where are his armies? Where are his battleships? You're the one who said we needed to protect ourselves from The Copperhound. It's the entire reason we have you standing here today. But where *is* he, Miss President? It would appear you've protected us from a phantom."

Iberian placed her hands on the lectern, composing her thoughts. "Sit down, councilman Cher, or I will relieve you of your appointment."

"We don't even have a city council anymore. Go ahead, relieve me."

"Either sit down and be a part of solving this problem or leave now."

Cher looked at Linwood and the other council members. They

exchanged grim looks. "Certainly, Miss President." Cher sat. "What is on the agenda this afternoon? I would love to know."

With the council finally silent, she continued, "Custos waited too long. He needed to act at the first sign of that terrorist—the man who dared come into these sacred halls. Instead of trying to eliminate currency, Custos should've closed the skies to Earth. The damage he did was already done by the time I took office. We can no longer wait for offenders, whether Martian or Earthmen, to commit crimes. We can't only punish the offenders. The state of our city is beyond that. We must go on the offensive. I can't go back and prevent Custos' mistakes. I can only attempt to... course correct."

"And where would you like to guide this sinking ship?" Cher asked.

"We take control. More control."

"Let me guess. Arrest all the protesters? Throw anyone on the streets in prison? Martial law? Miss President, don't fool yourself into thinking we didn't know what you were when we ousted Custos and plopped you right in his place."

"Hmph." Iberian stalled, "Explain to me what I am, sir."

"You." He pointed at her. "You are a despot."

Flustered, she looked at the other council members. "A despot? Does this reflect the belief of the rest of the council?"

The council members nodded.

"We know what you are, Vana. It's why we appointed you. Did you think it was your clever politicking that got you at that presidential lectern?"

Iberian was speechless—confidence vanishing.

Cher continued, "You're the iron fist. You run the same game that mankind has run for a *very* long time. From the Persians to the Russians to Central Cell. You, Miss President, are an authoritarian."

"If this is what you thought, then why on earth did you appoint me?"

"Because fear and uncertainty need authority. It *craves* control. We thought you were the best thing for control over New Athens." Cher continued, "When times are good, we need a Custos—a dreamer, an Aristotle. But when fear seizes the people, we need dominance—we need a Caesar. Central Cell was the best thing for control on Earth after the Nuclear Night. Custos was the best thing for control as a would-be utopian statesman selling his ideas of consensual progress to the masses. And when The Copperhound brought instability, you were the best thing to prevent the people from actually acting for themselves."

"So... it's all about maintaining control for you? By whatever means are effective?"

"Of course! Whatever the form of government, the goal is always the same—stop the people from taking control."

"And... and now?"

"Nothing," Linwood said. "You said it yourself. It's too late."

"Now," Cher said with disgust, "the *people* are the only ones who control the people. The people took over Central Cell once they outgrew the authority. We thought we could quickly slip back into state control by appointing you. But it's too late. The people already usurped us."

Iberian was taken aback by this cutting insight. The council had always been... the council—subject to the whims of the president. She never knew they could be so... Machiavellian. "So, who takes control now?"

"Only the people."

"How do we get them to do what we want?"

"We can't. That would be like telling lightning where to strike. Only the people will decide what the people will do. The people will decide what kind of nation they want to be."

"It can't be—"

And as if on cue, a roar erupted from the chamber doors.

It was *the people*.

The people had come. They had changed—metamorphosed. The people had grown from the chrysalis of the industrious citizen. They inched their way into the sanctimonious protester—oblivious to the consequences of swift change. And finally, they'd become indignation incarnate: the uprising.

The chamber doors splintered into fragments as the people pulled their axes and crowbars from wood. They had blood in their eyes.

Iberian staggered back. "Guards!"

"Don't," Cher yelled over the shouts of the crowd, keeping calm. "They aren't your guards anymore."

The masses weaved through the chambers, wielding cudgels and table legs. They swung their crude weapons, splintering the Martian wood fixtures that lined the assembly hall. They flooded the expanse of the chambers, climbing over chairs and knocking over anything that was standing. Hundreds more poured through the doors—a deluge of angst and anger. They didn't know what they wanted, but they didn't want whoever was in the assembly hall to rule them anymore.

Iberian stood motionless, petrified.

"Go!" Cher yelled at her, "you don't have to die here!" He'd led the council members to the opposite end of the chamber, away from the mob.

Iberian followed the council out through a passageway at the back end of the chambers that she didn't even know existed. Her feet stumbled down the darkened passage, her mind raced, realizing her delusions.

Her power—something she didn't understand in the first place —evaporated.

One last infuriating thought tugged at her... where was Custos?

CHAPTER 31

MARCH 24TH, 2155 EARTH RECKONING (ER)

S moke filled the ship.

The flight seats frowned with rapid melting—the fabric was singed and stoked with smoke. The inside of the torus looked as if a fire tornado had briefly raged through, sweeping aside papers, flatware, clothing, and stationary, leaving the inside of the ship like a burnt-out husk.

"Custos?" A muffled voice called from below the deck.

Dev peeked above the floorboard from the cargo bay, his head throbbing from where The Copperhound had struck him. He crept up and found the remains of what was once the inside of a normal spaceship. On the floor lay Custos—his entire metal frame blackened and twisted from heat. A rainbow sheen covered his body from where the gloss and plastic finishing had melted. Dev gasped. The robot's silicon face had completely melted away, exposing the thousands of arms that controlled his facial expressions. It was like looking at the innards of an old typewriter. His porcelain eyes sat motionless in their metal sockets, scorched to black. Beyond the miniature hydraulics and gears of his face, Dev saw a transparent casing that contained something gray and fatty. On hands and knees, Dev peered closer into his friend's unmasked face and saw what appeared to be a preserved human brain within the metal skull.

"Custos?" he said again, touching his hand.

The robot didn't move.

Dev looked over at the hulking mass of The Copperhound—his face and arms bubbled with fresh blisters. Dev shuffled over to him and nudged his chest with his foot, waiting. The Copperhound lay motionless. "Just a man," Dev declared, turning back to his friend.

In a heartbeat, Dev was seized from behind—a thick arm snaking around his neck. "No, no, no, little Dev. The Copperhound was born in the womb of Earth, taught by her darkness and thrust forth from her jungles by the ire of the people. The Copperhound does not die." The Copperhound's face was a writhing mass of blisters, swollen and glistening.

"No!" Dev cried.

The Copperhound retrieved the gun he had hidden under his scorched poncho. Small flames still licked up his clothing as he brought the gun to Dev's head. "Do you think your robot master lives?"

"Custos!" Dev yelled, stomping his feet.

Custos' face, now devoid of facial expression, sprung into life as the thousands of arms flailed within like insect legs. His eyes swiveled in their sockets for a moment until they focused on the struggle before him. Staggering, he slowly got to his feet, resting on the hull of the ship. The cockpit behind him beeped with alarms—the console flashing with lights.

"Cal! Cal, stop!" Custos' mechanical joints squealed with movement, now dry of lubrication. He reached his hands out to Dev; his rubber fingertips had melted away, exposing sharp divots in the metal.

Dazed, The Copperhound squinted through blistered eyelids. "Not until—" he stopped, his eyes widening. He gazed over Custos' shoulder, through the cockpit, and into space.

Custos turned and saw what had caught The Copperhound's attention. Their journey was over. At first glimpse, they had arrived at a gigantic space hub, alive with thousands of spaceships racing across space. Streams of fighter ships sped along, intermingled with larger ships—cruisers from which other fighter ships deployed. There were blasts from explosions and trails of lasers crisscrossing across the stars. Debris from destroyed ships scattered throughout what appeared to be an ongoing battle. There were clear, elongated beams of laser fire that stretched throughout the battle and then curved around it as if running along a spherical border that surrounded the entire battle scene.

"Impossible," Custos said.

"What, robot?" The Copperhound asked.

"We shouldn't be able to see laser light like that with the naked eye."

Custos followed the laser beams and saw that they indeed circled around the battle as if circumscribing an unseen border. Looking around the edges, he saw that none of the ships—no debris or scattered gunfire—reached beyond this border. Streams of laser energy and gunfire stopped short and disappeared at an invisible edge.

"What is it?" The Copperhound asked with unease rising in his voice.

"It's... it's a bubble of war," Custos declared, stepping into the cockpit where he magnified the view of the battle. In what appeared to be the exact middle of the bubble was an asteroid that had been constructed with multiple space stations, gun turrets, observatories, and many other buildings outfitted with antennas and telescopes. It was a small city built on the surface of an asteroid that Custos estimated to be the size of a small moon. It was clear that the asteroid was the focus of the attack of an armada of battleships. A shimmering line of silver light cut across the bubble like a belt. After scanning the area with even more magnification, he realized that it was a thin halo that surrounded the entire bubble in one plane. It looked as if the halo was distorting the space around it, bending the surrounding starlight.

"It's th-the halo," Custos said. "I've been chasing after this my entire life—even tried to build it myself."

404 | WICK WELKER

"Is anyone hailing us?" Dev asked, also too enchanted by the scene to let The Copperhound's grip around his neck bother him.

Custos looked down at the console. "No. Not only are they not hailing us, but none of our sensors are even detecting that anything is *even there*. Wait, this isn't right. Not a single ship is showing up on radar or IR and there isn't a single radio transmission out there."

"Among that many ships?" Dev asked, bewildered.

Custos shrugged. "Nothing—wait, hold on. What—"

The entire battle froze in place.

Every ship and stray light of laser came to a stop and then spontaneously reversed in motion. Ships flew backwards; bullets and laser light flew back into turrets and mounted machine guns. The asteroid moved backwards away from the battle while the enormous battleship cruisers backed out of the scene. There was a jittery streak of movement as the scene played out in forward time again, and then hiccupped and went back into reverse. Custos felt like someone had their hand on the toggle of a video feed—playing and rewinding footage.

"What is happening?" The Copperhound snapped, incensed as if sensing a trap.

Before Custos responded, the bubble shifted again with frenetic flashes. The asteroid city was still, humming with light while the battleship cruisers orbited the rock at a distance. There were no battles or firefights ensuing around the asteroid—the entire bubble was a peaceful snapshot. Custos magnified the asteroid and saw trains, spacelifts, drones, and ships commuting around the asteroid city. The bubble flashed again, returning to the original scenes of battling starships. The entire scene was within the confines of the thin, iridescent halo that surrounded the sphere.

Dev stepped away from The Copperhound, whose grip had loosened. "Custos, what are we looking at?"

"It's... it's some sort of time loop. There's a colonized city on an asteroid that looks like it's being attacked by an armada, but then it cuts out and it seems like the battle ends with the colony and the invaders no longer in a battle."

"But how? What *is* this?" Dev asked.

The Copperhound grabbed Dev back into his grasp and stuck a gun into his back. "Pull the ship closer, robot."

Custos sat in the pilot's chair and brought the ship closer to the bubble as it continued to shift and reset through multiple series of loops, appearing at random. The bubble grew in the cockpit view as they approached. It was a massive globe of turbulent movement of ships and debris. A fighter ship, at the periphery of the bubble, burst open from turret bullets shot from the asteroid base. The ship blew apart, flinging the pilot and bits of the ship into space. Custos watched as the events reversed back in time—the destroyed hull of the ship collecting itself back together, forming an un-breached ship. With no radio transmission whatsoever, the scene played out as if by ghosts of some forgotten time.

They arrived at the edge of the partitioned bubble, which Custos estimated had one-quarter of the diameter of Mars. The colonized asteroid itself couldn't have been much bigger than Earth's moon. He saw the halo, a thin belt of warped energy that wrapped around the bubble like a belt. It became clear that the halo itself defined the boundaries of the bubble that housed the chaotic world of fragmented time. The halo circled around like a ring with two fixed points along its course, equidistant from one another, where a long series of massive coils, tubing, and boxy structures hugged the halo. As he magnified the images, he saw that the halo itself glittered with light because something was moving along its track. The halo wasn't a structure at all, but a band of energy traveling between two coiled structures that sat along the halo, opposite one another.

"There's some radiation coming in," Custos said. "Whatever that halo is, it's kicking off a lot of energy."

"At least we know we aren't looking at something that isn't even there," Dev remarked.

Suddenly, their ship lurched backward, knocking The Copperhound and Dev to their knees. Custos held onto the console as the ship spun sideways. He kicked on the manual controls and steadied the ship again, bringing it back next to the halo. The Copperhound

406 | WICK WELKER

grappled for a moment with Dev, who barely resisted him until he had a gun sticking once again into his back.

"Do not try that again," The Copperhound warned.

Custos turned and looked at him, his caved-in face even causing The Copperhound to recoil. "You think that was me?"

The cockpit console erupted with beeping. "It was a gravity wave!" Custos said, looking down as new data streamed onto the screens. "It's the message... more is coming in. It looks like it's all here; there aren't any fragments in the data. It's a complete audio file." He looked back at Dev, the tiny arms of his face dancing.

"Well? Let's hear it," Dev said.

A small but hurried voice issued from the speakers:

"I am Custos, defender of Last Athens. We need help. It's been... so long, an eternity. I can't explain everything but I made a mistake—so many mistakes—and I take full responsibility. We are trapped inside a shard of frozen time. I created a powerful weapon—a Destroyer of Worlds—The Halo. I know it was a mistake, but we were a desperate people. He chased us out here... to the outer realms of our solar system, with nowhere else to go but to build a colony on an asteroid that we've named Last Athens. He—The Copperhound—made our people outcasts of our own planet after he went to war with New Athens over half a century ago.

Earth and Mars have been at war ever since The Copperhound arose from the ashes of Earth and deceived the people of New Athens. Since then, both Earth and Mars have colonized dozens of moons and built thousands of warships, trying to destroy each other. We've fought for decades until his forces finally overcame the colonies and outposts of New Athens. He has destroyed all of our forces—New Athens, the apex of human civilization—now sits in ruins. The year we went to our final battle, here at Last Athens, was 2210.

We knew he would come to attack us at Last Athens—to finally destroy the Martian people. I designed the Halo with one purpose—to lure his forces in and destroy them. The Halo is a ring of gravity formed by thousands of Casimir Drives that I've built with our asteroid in the exact center. According to my math, whatever is in the epicenter of the Halo is equally pulled on all sides by the gravity of the Casimir Drive Halo, preserving the matter. However, anything outside of the perfect center is torn apart by uneven tidal forces from the Halo. This was the trap I set to draw in his armies and ships around this asteroid and then to turn on the Drives and completely tear his forces apart. It was so simple—such an elegant solution to finally rid us of him.

I knew there was much more of the physics that I needed to work out. I ignored the bending effects on spacetime. We ran out of time and knew The Copperhound had finally located our hidden asteroid. We knew he was coming to destroy us. And this—my haste to destroy my enemy—was the biggest mistake of my very long life.

Once his forces arrived, they immediately went to battle with us, firing on our asteroid. I wasted no time and turned on the Halo and waited for the uneven gravitational forces to tear them apart. Only, it didn't happen. What I've now learned since that day—and we have no idea when that day was—we don't know the year or if there are years anymore! We only know that we don't age and we don't die. What I learned that day is that the Halo acted as the opposite of a black hole. By creating a ring of gravity, we slowed time down to a standstill, and instead of destroying the matter within the Halo, it is perfectly preserved. We created a bubble of frozen time that can never end. It transformed the matter of our bodies into perfect vessels with perpetual quantum spin. We cannot decay and our minds... our minds see everything.

The Halo opened up the eternities to us. Like pages of a book, we can flip through the infinite dimensions of ourselves. We've learned that the membranes between dimensions are a flimsy, temporal construct and that we exist in all realities at once. I now know that the actions that I've done here—the creation of the Halo—has leaked out through time and space and doesn't just influence one temporal dimension—it influences all. The creation of the Halo is what started the events that led to its very creation. It is a paradox that I haven't even tried to understand. It has crossed the borders of eternity. I finally understand why I am the way I am—why I was who I was. But it's too late...

The Halo has two opposing arrays from which thousands of Casimir

Drives circle through. It is the circular path of the Casimir Drives that creates the gravitational Halo. If you turn off the arrays, the Drives will no longer run. We cannot turn them off from the inside. The two arrays must be turned off at once, in synchrony, or else it will create uneven gravitational tides which truly will tear us apart.

Please, whoever is hearing this message—and I suspect that I know who you are—please, turn off the Halo. I never learned the lesson that Jo tried to teach me: a weapon is most powerful when it's destroyed. But you can. You can destroy it before it even exists. Save us from this existence so that we can leave this space that is only meant for gods. We should never have meddled with these things.

Please, free us."

The transmission terminated.

Custos stood in silence and looked at The Copperhound. "It never ends, Cal."

The Copperhound relaxed his squeeze on Dev.

"Me and you—this vendetta. It led us there." He turned and pointed at the Halo. "Trapped."

The Copperhound opened his mouth to speak, but nothing came.

"Cal," Custos continued. "I've been seeing that Halo ever since I was Timothy Straus. I built a mock version of this very Halo weapon in my basement. I had no idea what I was doing at the time. And here we are. I finally built the damn thing. I didn't listen to her—didn't listen to Jo."

The Copperhound nodded with understanding. "So, you *are* Timothy Straus. Not my uncle. Yet another lie."

"The Halo is the source of everything. It is the reason we are the way we are. When I was Tim, I saw this Halo and I knew it was a weapon but I didn't know it wasn't for my time in the 1980s. Not only did I see the Halo, but the math—the very mathematics that I create in the future—leached back through the ages of time into my mind. That's what refraction does, it creates a seamless conduit of one person throughout all dimensions and time. That is how we are standing right here, right now. That math came to me—scattered and at random—but it came into my mind and so I did what a scientist does. I built the Casimir Drive, even though I had no idea what it was. I didn't know what its purpose was. I didn't know it was a relic of the future; a weapon that was used to destroy you—a descendant that didn't even exist when I was Timothy Straus. Me and everyone I knew thought I had schizophrenia, but I didn't. I almost killed myself trying to understand this mystery and this is it. I-I left my family behind in the dust because of this future madness. It's because of me and you."

"But—"

"I had always thought that refraction may have been something in my genes—something that ran in the family. I observed my son, James, from afar—as a stranger—as he grew older and had a family. I kept track of my descendants, wondering if any had the gift. But they all lived normal, beautiful lives. I could hear the voices in my head. I knew there was someone else close to me who would one day join me in refraction. I was so happy when I discovered you. You were the missing person—the one to finally help me change things in the world—to overthrow Central Cell. But our plan was... stupid. I should've given you more time to learn about yourself and the world. Your passion to help rotted into vengeance. Everything happened too quickly, and then I left you. Cal, I know you hate me, but take a look; we keep fighting until we end up in this—this prison of eternity. You must be in that Halo with me. It did the same thing to you that it did to me. This is why you've always heard voices."

"But you refracted me!" The Copperhound yelled. "It's something you did to *me*. It doesn't just happen in the future in that... that bubble. I will not be tricked by your pseudoscience nonsense!"

"Remember when I said the key to refraction is under our noses? It's the Casimir Drive. Do you remember outside of Copper Mound, before we returned back to Central Cell to start our revolution? Do you remember how I left you alone in that field while I calibrated my ship with Benedito with me?"

"What?"

"Just think."

The Copperhound's eyes flashed with realization. "You circled around me with the ship—a ship that had its Casimir Drive running."

Custos nodded. "I built a prototype of the Casimir Drive when I was Timothy Straus. I built it using the math that crossed all dimensions and time. It flooded my mind. I ran it on the track, faster than I ever had and I stood directly in the center, moments before I planned to kill myself. Something happened to me. Something changed. I stepped out of my lab a new creature. A creature that I knew could never go back to being Timothy Straus. I had a new gift, and with this gift, I decided to finally try and do some good in the world. I was going to change things.

"The circular path of the Casimir Drive creates a ring of gravity that acts like an inverted black hole. It slows down the decay and atomic spin of whatever matter is within the center. This is why we age slower. The Halo of the future broke our minds free from our singular dimensions and the Casimir Drive changed the matter of our bodies. It's the same reason that they, at Last Athens, are living forever. It's the same effect on our prolonged bodies but on a much larger scale than a single Casimir Drive. The Halo around Last Athens was so powerful, it ripped a hole right through spacetime and created a bubble that exists independent of all dimensions. We can see it in our dimension and I suspect that it can be seen in every dimension. And this is why the Custos of the future couldn't send radio waves," Custos added. "Nothing but gravity can escape the Halo. He's in there right now communicating his message through gravity waves. I think the light we see from the bubble is just a holographic imprint in space—it's not real-time, just a shadow."

Custos refracted for a brief moment and saw it. He saw the three of them standing on that ship having the same conversation. In many of the dimensions, they fought, and in many more, he saw both himself and The Copperhound die. He saw their ship explode in many of the shards of time. He stopped refracting and looked at The Copperhound. "Take a look for yourself, Cal. We can't get past this moment."

The Copperhound refracted and looked back at Custos. He said nothing.

"We can either keep fighting each other—keep refracting until we blow ourselves up with the positive feedback of dimensional energy. We can destroy each other, yes, we can. You can have your vengeance. Or we can turn off *that*." Custos pointed over his shoulder at the Halo. "And end this thing for good."

The Copperhound looked over Custos' shoulder. "There's a ship coming."

Custos whipped around and saw a small ship, not a fighter ship, but what looked like a domestic commuter ship within the Halo. It was flying toward them. As it approached, Custos realized it was flying toward the Casimir array which constantly flung thousands of Casimir Drives from a tunnel of coils—a process that created the Halo. The ship docked at the array, the side that faced inside of the bubble, and two figures emerged from the ship. For a split second, the figures and the ship vanished but then materialized again. They were temporarily replaced by a dog fight between two ships which then disappeared. It was like trying to watch a television show that was constantly interrupted by static interference. The figures, donned in trim spacesuits, walked along the Casimir array, inspecting and opening panels on their side of the bubble. They walked to the edge of the bubble, the confines of the Halo track, and looked out into space. It was as if their gaze was fixed on Custos and the ship.

"Do they see us?" Dev asked.

"I don't think they can see anything," Custos said. "They exist in their own space. The Halo created a new dimension within an ocean of dimensions. They're probably looking at their own reflection." Custos magnified the two figures on the display looking out into the universe. He toggled a joystick and focused on their faces and then took a step back. Beneath their transparent helmets was the silicone face of a robot and a man with deep divots, riveted by scars running down his cheeks.

"Cal," Custos whispered. "It's *us*."

The Copperhound looked at his own desperate face on the

screen. "Looks like we're trying to figure out how to turn off the Casimir array from the inside." His voice softened—not the twisted tenderness he used to scare people—but a tone of earnestness.

"We're not trying to kill each other, Cal. After your forces attack, I turn on the Halo and it traps us together. Somewhere along the line, we get over ourselves and try to get out." After another moment, the figures vanish and the original battle ensues across the bubble as the random scenes of time play out.

"How long? How long have we been stuck in there?" The Copperhound asked, finally unhanding Dev.

"Impossible to know. It exists outside of time."

"Are we the first ones to see this?" Dev asked.

"I don't know," Custos said, "but we can be the last." He left the cockpit and went to the back of the ship. The Copperhound watched him, unguarded, while Custos rummaged in the back of the ship. "I only hope it's still intact after the energy feedback that went through the ship," Custos said as he emerged in the main cabin. He wore a spacesuit, intended to fit the much fuller physique of a human being. The sleek fabric bagged under his shoulders and around his hips. The back of the suit was outfitted with a small thruster capable of deep space jettison. He stuck a helmet over his head and locked it into the suit.

"What're you doing?" Dev asked.

"I'm flying out in this suit. I'm going out there, to the Casimir array, and I'm going to shut it off."

The Copperhound stood, looking down at Custos. His face drooped with blisters and his eyes had become vacant vessels of uncertainty.

"What're you going to do, Cal?" Custos asked.

Dev cleared his throat. "Why do you keep calling him Cal?"

Custos nodded. "We've known each other a very long time. We've both made mistakes but I think we can get over it. Apparently, we can in at least *one* dimension. I think that we can heal and help the people of Mars *and* Earth. I've been a fool to think I had to perfect the people of Mars before I could bring the people of Earth. It doesn't matter if one people is thriving if the other half of humanity is suffering. We have to do it together—and that's what matters most—all people must progress together at whatever pace they can. It's what I somehow could never accomplish over three lifetimes." He pointed through the cockpit at the Halo. "We've got to turn the two arrays off at the same time, or else it'll destroy whatever matter is within the Halo with unequal tidal waves of gravity. I'll fly out from here. You two, take the ship to the other array on the other side of the Halo and we'll coordinate the shutdown. Let me know when you're in place." He spoke as if it was a mutually agreed-upon plan. He moved to the airlock at the side of the cabin and turned to The Copperhound. "Cal, I'll understand if you don't come back for me. Revenge is yours if you still want it."

Custos left through the airlock and plunged into the black well of space. He clung to the side of the ship for a moment, wondering if he'd ever see New Athens again—if he'd ever see the inside of the ship again.

He flipped a switch on his suit which prompted two control arms to extend from the small engine at the back of his suit. The pads fit neatly into his grip. Small thrusters burst into life at his back, pushing him away from the ship and toward the glassy sphere of frozen time that consumed his view. Flashes of explosions from railguns and high-energy particle beams danced across his helmet as he barreled toward the Casimir array. The resetting and looping of time that jittered through the bubble had a dizzying effect as he tried to keep the array in line with his trajectory. He let out a sigh of relief as he saw his ship fly away and head over to the opposing side of the Halo, where the other array was running. The Copperhound could at least see the logic in freeing his future self from the prison of time.

The Casimir array, a boxy structure the size of a massive skyscraper turned on its side, filled his view. It was studded with thousands of copper coils and wires that floated freely in space as if the entire structure was hastily made. *There was no time to give it a proper encasing*. He felt the fear of his future self as he ordered the construction of the weapon. It was a fear that had filled him his entire life—a fear that once had him committed to a psychiatric ward. A fear that had chased him away from Jo. It was a fear that he was grateful to now understand.

He slowed his velocity as he approached the array and flipped on magnetized boots. Tucking his feet in front, he slammed down onto a strut that crisscrossed over thousands of rows of wiring and cables. After getting his bearings, he looked up and saw the machine beneath his feet stretching on for hundreds of miles in every direction. It was as if he were on an entire planet whose terrain was endless rows of copper coiling. The array hummed under his boots as he wearily walked along the surface.

The scanner on his wrist vibrated, indicating a hollowed-out space within the array that was a few hundred miles away from his current location. He flipped on thrusters and blasted high above the array while his sensors narrowed in the exact location of what appeared to be a room within the array.

A voice flickered in his ears. "Custos," Dev said quickly. "You doing okay?"

"Yes, are you at the other array?"

"Uh, yes, he... uh, just got behind the controls and brought us here. Our scanners have found a main engineering room within the array that's located near the center. Assuming that both arrays are identical, you can get to it too. It's accessible from the outside. I'll send the details to you."

"Thank you, Dev. Let me know when you've gotten inside and we can coordinate the shutdown." Custos found the engineering room and flew back down at the array. A singular hatch was built within the metal coils. The hatch gently opened without a burst of pressurized air. Inside, a dark corridor led to a modest control room fixed with a row of chairs and several consoles. The seats were empty. Apparently, the array was able to run in perpetuity without maintenance and without needing new copper coils. *Everything that inverted gravity touches becomes ageless,* he realized. He studied the room, sweeping a flashlight across the control panel until he found what he was looking for: a single glass cube. Peering into the cube, he saw a large, red lever and the words *Emergency Shutdown* stenciled below it. His mind flashed back to centuries ago when he was a man named Timothy Straus, standing at the control panel of the Casimir Drive, thinking of how he would kill himself.

"Dev," he radioed over.

"I found it," The Copperhound's raspy voice trickled into his ears.

"The shut-off?" Custos asked, looking down at the panel.

"I'm here," The Copperhound said, voice inscrutable. "I'm in the twin array, standing at the shut-off."

Custos shattered the box with an emergency hammer, glass shards erupted throughout the control room and floated away. "Are you ready?"

"Yes," The Copperhound croaked. "Count off, robot."

Custos, ignoring the chill of The Copperhound's voice, gripped the lever. "Shutdown in five... four... three... two... one."

He flipped the lever and closed his eyes.

The control room was gone.

The massive Casimir array was gone.

The Halo vanished, and with it, the frozen bubble of time. Last Athens, the last bastion of future Martian life, was gone.

Custos found himself floating alone in empty space.

A single flicker of light danced amongst the stars. It twinkled with a brighter light than the panoply of stars behind.

His ship.

"Cal!" he yelled. "It worked! It's over. The Halo must've returned back to its original time. They're—we're free! I think I can see your ship. Are you getting my signal?" His words were only met by silence. "Cal?" He waited but no one answered. "Dev?"

He watched as the bright twinkle of light lit brighter with the flames of thrusters and then disappeared into the abyss of space.

The Copperhound had left him.

. . .

The voices were gone.

Custos had no idea how accustomed he became to the river of voices that ran in the background of his mind. The static was there ever since he taught in a classroom over a century ago. The voices had become a companion—a witness of his gift. Now, adrift in the life raft of a spacesuit, his mind was terrifyingly silent.

It didn't take long to feel like a ghost. The panoramic black screen of nothing began at his mind and ran away with infinity. Custos waved his hands in front of his eyes—barely reflecting light—to assure himself that he still existed. After five hours marooned in space, he stopped checking. A sense of loathing for having a physical body—be it metal and a human brain—set in. He resented the disorientation and longed to be rid of the now obsolete senses of a terrestrial being. His thoughts blurred with the faded starlight, extinguishing not only the hope of rescue, but an entire sense of self-identity. He was now just a vague sentience adrift in space.

And soon, he would be nothing.

With only breath sounds from a world now far away, he melted into the black ink. There were no nearby celestial bodies to coax him with glimmers of hope. He was consumed by the nothing. After one more draw of oxygen, his last breath would bring the life out of his body with it. But the condensed oxygen in his suit could last several days—especially for Custos—a robot whose only oxygenated tissue was a single human brain.

After the rational thoughts—how far was his ship now? Was Dev alive? What would happen to New Athens?—delirium set in. Scattered memories streamed through his mind. He saw Jo—her crafty smile hovering above a chess board. Van Wert glaring at him from the top of his classroom. Cal opened a door into the foyer, concern for his doorman in his face. Cal came again; a picture of rage as he pointed a gun at a huddled crowd. There was Jelena and Benedito, impossibly young, looking at him with unsure faces as they hatched a plan in an abandoned warehouse.

Custos hadn't cried in a lifetime. He made sure that his robotic body—his own design—lacked the capability of shedding tears. Perhaps he had ignored too many of his human emotions, believing them to be vestiges of an archaic version of himself. He could've shared the fear of his people—would've protected better against The Copperhound. He'd become so disconnected by an agenda of progress that he forgot that he cannot force the human mind. He'd forgotten that human beings were both beautifully flawed and terrifyingly optimistic. They can be nudged, but they cannot be forced without total social collapse.

And now, swallowed in the mouth of space, his heart finally wept with loss. Not just the loss of Jelena and Benedito, but the loss of Jo. He lost her to his madness. Not the sickness of schizophrenia, but the insanity of trying to change the worlds by himself. He left her there that last night, alone in their home, believing her husband was gone.

He cried for Cal—a protégé to mold into a tool of change who became nothing but his own foil. Custos never knew he would be the unwitting designer of his own destruction. But was it really The Copperhound who was responsible, or was it himself? After all, he had engineered a society that fell apart at the hands of one man with nothing but a small bag of lies and a handful of terrified peons.

Voices returned but they weren't from the Rift, they were the embittered specters of his memories. Flashes of his past chanted and scorned him. They slandered him with accusations of self-righteousness and called for justice. He was the criminal—guilty of leading humankind astray. How could a single flawed man such as him think to take the wheels of time and steer them where he saw fit? The vitriol built within him and condensed into a single message:

He deserved this end.

The Copperhound's vengeance was just.

I deserve this grave of space.

Custos shut his mind to the voices and shame and finally gave way to despair. He grasped onto the seal of his helmet, found the latch, and unclasped the lock. He knew he didn't deserve a swift death. He deserved half a century floating in space just as The

Copperhound had smoldered with rage in the copper mines—becoming a timeless vessel of wrath. Justice would be a long suffering in space, but he couldn't bear it anymore. He held the rim of the helmet and thought back to his first lab—The Casimir Drive. He wasn't even the brilliant mathematician that changed transportation forever, he was a fluke. Happenstance crept back in time from the Custos of Last Athens and filled his mind with the math. The Drive was never meant for Timothy Straus. It was meant to destroy an enemy who was created by the very existence of the Drive itself. He winced at the paradox and let go of understanding.

I should've done it back then; that one night at the lab with the cyanide. Should've ended it there. The world would've been better off without Timothy Straus the physicist, Tobias Stroupe the last American President, Raz the Anarchist, and Custos the Dreamer.

Custos ripped off his helmet and took a frozen breath of space through his mechanical lungs. Internal sensors went wild with depressurization and hypoxic air. The exposed, dreadful face of space glared back at him. His joints froze and his mind slowed to a sluggish blur. As the freeze crept toward his brain, his porcelain eyes rounded wildly in their sockets until they fixated on one last point of light.

A blinking light.

A growing light.

A ship.

———

"Custos?"

Custos gasped for air.

"Custos?" Dev looked down at him.

He tried opening his eyes.

Cal knelt over Custos' body, looking into his eyes. "I'm sorry for leaving you. I'm sorry for everything. Things will be different now; we can finally change things, Raz. Just like we wanted to. We can put it behind us." The voice of a nineteen-year-old was mixed with the hoarseness of age and suffering.

Custos' eyes rolled back as he gasped for air. "I—"

"Raz?" Cal said like a child at his parents' deathbed. "Raz... I'm sorry. Let's go back to Earth—back to Mars. Me and you together can bridge the rift. We can fix it. Everything you've done, you've done it because you care. You cared about me and about everyone. You're not a failure. Please..."

"Ca-Cal," Custos said through labored breaths. "Save them..."

"Save them?"

"Save my people... with your people." His eyes closed.

"Raz?"

Cal held Timothy Straus' hand as his grip loosened.

CHAPTER 32

APRIL 27TH, 2155 EARTH
RECKONING (ER)

G arbage streamed like confetti through the air.
The Teeth of Telephus loomed over the city beneath a darkened Martian sun. The heavens, typically full of millions of delivery drones, were void save for a blanket of smoke. Fires dotted the city, licking up glittering skyscrapers and carving through parks and edible gardens. Streetlights flickered after the hydro generators were abandoned. At the first sign of power outages, the people panicked, killing and salvaging robots for their core batteries—their metal bodies littered the streets.

After Iberian placed a mandatory curfew on the city, rioting broke out in sheer defiance. Where there was once little social class distinction, the people of New Athens had quickly split into two: the hoarders and the scavengers. The majority of the millions of people of the city stayed at home with their children while hosts of people took to the streets, tearing apart machines for metal and energy sources. Factions sprouted at dozens of parks around the city, trying to claim a stake of land in a new and uncertain world order.

The Terrabel Colony, uncertain about receiving compensation for its produce, wheat, and flour, shut off its trade and stopped admittance of anyone from outside its biospheres. Fearing contagion of rioting, all surrounding colonies of New Athens shut their borders. Markets, warehouses, deliveries, and telecommunications ceased to function. The majesty and streamlined efficiency of the great New Athens had deteriorated into tribalism in less than a month after former President Custos had mysteriously vanished.

The council had to move from the assembly hall as it had been taken over by the Cabal of The Copperhound. Iberian held ineffectual emergency meetings with what remained of the city council in Custos' penthouse. The Cabal barred off the assembly chamber, claiming to have become the stewards of the city until The Copperhound came. They would've been smoked out and arrested if half of the police force didn't support them and bring them daily food supplies. The Cabal had condemned Iberian's Earth embargo and immigration freeze as The Copperhound himself—the great revolutionary—was an Earthman.

Conversely, in New Athens' central park, an enclave of tents had formed around the statue of Tobias Stroupe, the American president who sent the first colony to Mars. Hundreds of thousands sprawled out from the park, calling themselves the Call of Custos. They squatted amongst the streets and abandoned traffic. With both fear and faith, they awaited the return of President Custos. Many rumors abounded—he'd left to kill The Copperhound himself or that he still lived among the people, waiting to reveal himself. The Call of Custos also loathed President Iberian's travel restrictions.

There was distrust in the air. Worse, there was malaise in the air. Uncertainty and fatigue grinding the people into complacency. Fearful eyes surveyed the streets from boarded windows. A frenzy of anti-robotic sentiment flooded the streets. Many homes, in the least, deactivated most of their in-home automation and domestic robots. There was talk of AI uprising catalyzed by rumors of the cyborgs of Earth who would burst from the clouds at any moment. People talked less and stuck to their factions—neither willing to talk nor patient enough to listen.

The days of discourse had swiftly come and gone.

———

Charlotte awoke to a figure standing in the open doorway of her prison cell. She jumped, thinking that The Copperhound—the phantom from the caves in the jungle—had returned to torment her again. It had been months since he had crept into her bedroom or even here—a prison cell—to remind her that he was watching. Hoping him dead, she had finally found some peace, albeit in a prison. She enjoyed the scheduled meals and warm bed. It's all she ever really wanted.

But now a figure stood there, watching her.

"No..." she whimpered, "Don't—"

The person emerged from the shadow. It was a woman who wore a grim expression. Elisa. "It's her," she said, looking over her shoulder. More people crowded into the small prison room and gawked as Charlotte stood, perplexed.

"What's going on?" Charlotte asked, rubbing her eyes.

"We've come to liberate you, Speaker." Elisa wore faded clothing, worn thin into holes.

"What?"

"You're the one who announced his arrival in front of the president. We have a place for you. We want you to lead us." The group behind her nodded.

"Lead you where?"

"We're from the Cabal. We're here to free you, Speaker."

"What? No, I'm happy right here."

"We have a camp in the city and a place for you there. We need you to come." Elisa gestured to the doorway.

"Why?"

"Because he won't come unless his Speaker is free—free to usher in his reign in New Athens."

"How did you get in here?"

"The prison is unguarded. Has been for days."

Charlotte considered this news, realizing that a guard hadn't come to her for some time. She hardly noticed, given that meals automatically appeared in a slot in the wall three times a day. "So, I can just leave?"

Elisa stepped aside. "After you, Speaker."

Charlotte brushed past the group, who watched her every movement. Unwittingly, she led them to a guard breakroom that had been left in disarray with toppled furniture and a flooded floor. As she crammed a few granola bars into her pocket, she jumped when she saw a robot guard sitting silently in a chair. She fled to the door but crept back when she realized she wasn't pursued. On closer inspection, the robot's neck had been hacked open, showing wayward wires. The machine's eyes were closed.

"The machines won't hurt you," Elisa said. The group continued to watch her as she swept down the hallways of the prisons, finding only empty cells. It reminded her of the jungle mine—full of prison cells—where she had found The Copperhound bound to a boulder. She remembered the thin smile stretched across his face when she hacked the chains from his wrists. It was a smile of rage... of anticipation.

Meeting no resistance, she stumbled out of the prison and into the streets where the sewers had overcome their gutters and poured their contents over the road. There were no floating cars, carplanes, city robots, or pedestrians. For a city that, at first, dazzled her with its cleanliness and shimmering surfaces, it had become a dysfunctional failed state overnight. For the first time since arriving on Mars, she felt like she was back on Earth. It turned out that people were the same, whether on Earth or Mars—you can't change human nature.

"Speaker," Elisa called from behind. "Follow us, we'll take care of you."

Charlotte turned, her black hair blowing with the wind. "Just stop."

Elisa shook her head. "You first showed me the inevitability of The Copperhound. And now we need your help. There are a lot of people waiting for you."

"The Copperhound is gone."

"How do you know?"

"I haven't seen him in over a month. He would've visited me."

"So... he *does* visit you."

Charlotte nodded. "He gets around—goes wherever he wants. Seeing what has happened here..." She gestured to the street. "He would've taken control already. I don't think he's coming. All he wanted was chaos."

Elisa was dumbfounded. "But... but I thought you were his Speaker. How could you say that?"

"I was only his messenger because he controlled me—threatened me to spread his fear everywhere. I was a pawn, just like all of you. He's not going to make things better. He works in the dark. He was nothing. A bitter man trapped in a cave. I never should have freed him, he was just so... helpless."

Elisa looked at her, crestfallen. "But we're organizing into a movement. We're going to take control soon, we just need someone—you, a recognizable face that can finally move the encampment forward. We can get rid of Iberian and finally change things."

"It looks like you've changed things enough," Charlotte said, holding her hands up to the chaos of the street.

Elisa and her motley group looked back at Charlotte with the eyes of children.

"Just go," Charlotte said. She bent over and picked up a piece of long, twisted shrapnel that had come from a crashed carplane that left a deep crater in the ceramic road. She hefted the weight in her hands and gave it a practice swing, satisfied with the makeshift weapon. After walking down the street, however, she dropped the club of twisted metal and put her hands in her pockets.

A narrow park sat between two towering skyscrapers that had remained unscathed of crashed ships, fire, or squatters. Charlotte reflexively sniffed the wind, thinking about her life as a mushroom hunter, stepping through the jungles on Earth. It seemed like another lifetime. She looked up at a row of banana trees but saw they had already been picked clean. She felt like she was back on Earth, wandering aimlessly, looking for food. Perhaps she would build a lean-to in the park tonight and sleep with her eyes on the Martian starscape. She would have to learn orienteering with an entirely new sky.

Finding no fruit in the park, she was about to move on but heard a commotion behind. It was Elisa and her group, they had followed her and had grown in number. Dozens of people stood and watched Charlotte. She saw many more people streaming in through the park to join them, murmuring about the Speaker.

"What are you doing?" she yelled.

"Look up," Elisa yelled.

Charlotte craned her neck up.

Hundreds of ships filled the sky.

They streamed through thin morning clouds, flowing in the same direction over the city. They looked like small boxes against the sky, marching along to a shared destination. Charlotte squinted, unable to discern if they were fighter ships or otherwise. "What's going on?"

"The Copperhound is here," Elisa said. "You need to go meet him. We support you, Speaker. We'll follow you."

Charlotte angrily left the crowd and ran through the park. She heard cries of panic and saw groups of people scattering as they feared the approach of the ships. The ships didn't seem to be landing in the city itself but, instead, flowed to some point just beyond. Charlotte craned her neck to the sky, watching the direction of the ships as more and more added to the congregation from space beyond. The stream of ships became so great, they turned into a banner of metal across the sky, darkening the sun. There was no gunfire, only a frenzy of shadows that flitted across the city as the ships soared.

The streets eventually became silent as Charlotte moved, following the ships. The only sound was the shuffling of footsteps behind her. She turned and saw that Elisa's group had grown into the hundreds with hundreds more streaming in through alleys and streets. A crowd was amassing behind her but didn't overtake her pace.

They followed the unspoken leader. They followed the Speaker.

She ran from the crowd, sprinting through city parks, running by abandoned buildings and ignoring the throngs of people behind her.

The crowd bottle-necked as she crossed a river bridge but the people stayed in pursuit of her; never overtaking and keeping a short distance from the solitary woman. The crowd snowballed into thousands as individuals joined. They didn't understand what was happening, but felt safe in numbers as an unknown fleet of ships soared above them.

Charlotte ran for miles through the city, following the armada of ships. Finally, over the tops of buildings, she saw them descend to the surface, arching down to a place outside of the city limits. She trooped on through the silent city, surprised by the lack of gunfire and anarchy—the presence of the fleet had brought a paradoxical calm to the people. After an hour of walking through the streets of New Athens, she saw that the ships had never ceased to arrive from space. It was an endless stream, landing somewhere beyond the city. As they spiraled down, she saw that they were boxy ships, old with faded wording and colors on their sides.

They were freighters—the old TexasH ships from Earth.

An ocean of people followed her as she wound through residential blocks of the outer districts of the city. She ducked through another park and finally arrived at the red plains of the Martian landscape that rolled on into the base of The Teeth of Telephus mountain range.

The red soil was dotted everywhere with plant life. Yellow and purple wildflowers had burst from cracks in Martian boulders. Trails of cosmos danced with blades of grass. Dandelions and honeysuckles grew along small creek beds that zigzagged across the cracked desert floor. Ribbons of pink heather ran through red boulders that towered like the remains of an ancient city. Sprouts of hyacinth and gladiolus were littered throughout a short underbrush of ivy. Out to her right, by the edge of the canyon, fields of lavender flickered with a distant breeze. As she meandered out into the wild desert, she brushed her fingers by a row of peonies that greeted her along a bank of red rock.

Sunflowers had scattered everywhere and were the most pervasive species that had come to touch the alien soil—species that had been brought by the first colonizers. Their seeds were stored away for decades, awaiting the newly fertile soil of a terraformed land. The landscape was a blend of the once barren rust of Mars with the vibrant touch of earthly plant life that rolled out like a tongue of unstoppable foliage. Charlotte had never known the wilderness of Mars was so beautiful.

It was The Meadows of Mars—a hybrid of two worlds that now grew together.

Charlotte, led by the trail of landing ships, marched on through the meadow with a concourse of the human population that swelled behind her. No one overtook her approach. She was the unspoken frontwoman. The crowds were silent. Some carried weapons; all of them full of uncertainty. She made her way through gullies and small ravines, crossing the desert plain. As she got closer, she saw the unmistakable look of the Earth freighters—much like the one she stowed away on when she first arrived in New Athens. Most of the ships were missing cosmetic parts and all appeared to be decades old. There were no warships. After the people of New Athens marched through the meadow, Charlotte stopped at the edge of a vast valley, speechless.

She discovered the landing spot of the ships. Thousands of freighters were scattered in the Martian flower meadow with hundreds of thousands of people that had de-boarded. It was a crater full of humanity. It reminded her of the Copper Mound on Earth. She saw the same Earth people but instead of milling inside of a blackened valley of refuse and sickness, they were in a vibrant valley of wild colors.

As she came down the shallow valley walls, the Martian crowd followed behind, spilling over the mouth of the valley. The invaders from the freight ships stood motionless at the wall of people that descended on them. Above, the ships didn't cease to arrive. One by one, each ship found a spot to land in the meadow plains which stretched on for hundreds of miles, flanked on the north by mountains, and on the south by canyons. The freighters landed and expelled their cargo—refugees of Earth.

Charlotte recognized the clothing of the invaders. They looked

428 | WICK WELKER

like her when she first arrived. They wore long, draped clothing full of holes and filth. The people were gaunt—their cheeks hollow and limbs wasted down to bones. Many of them had mechanical body parts or complete amputations. There were entire groups covered in scarred skin; their facial features having been consumed in fire. Scores of them sat motionless in wheelchairs or stretchers. They held no weapons, only pleading eyes. Their gazes were glued on the impending Martian natives.

At the edge of the invading Earth people, a large boulder stuck up from the ground, dozens of feet into the air. Atop the boulder stood two figures.

Charlotte crossed the valley; a pebble in front of an avalanche of people. She squinted as she approached the boulder. It was meant to be a platform. She saw two people standing on top of the boulder with something—an oblong box—that laid at their knees. As the unwitting leader of the New Athens people, she was the first to approach the feet of the boulder. The indistinguishable figures peered down at her. Charlotte stopped and looked up at them as the concourse behind her slowed in waves and came to a stop. The Earth invaders stood motionless in their throngs of groups and families.

The two masses of people stood in silence, uncertain if a battle was about to ensue.

Before a single word was uttered, a gigantic holographic image sprung up from the boulder, displaying the unforgettable face of Devium Alexander, the former Vice President of New Athens. A roar of excitement erupted from the Martian people at his visage that was displayed for every eye in the valley.

"People of New Athens," Dev said. "I return to you, your president."

The projected holographic feed switched to a wooden box, draped in yellow in the shape of a person lying on their back. Dev removed the drape, revealing the body of Custos. His face, once the perfect composite of silicone polymer to stretch as naturally as any human, was gone. Inside the metal cavity of his face was an arrangement of wild flowers. A small border of dandelions was inset with ranunculus which swirled together with baby's-breath. Two sunflowers, the helianthus, were placed where his porcelain eyes once gazed out over New Athens. A white queen chess piece had been placed in his dead grasp.

Dev spoke as the masses gazed at the flowered face of their president. He read from a slip of paper:

> "Ah Sun-flower! weary of time,
> Who countest the steps of the Sun:
> Seeking after that sweet golden clime."

He smiled and continued, "He was the wise one. A man of the ages. He is the face of timeless optimism. He was the nameless servant of humankind. He was never truly known, but he knew us all. He died as the protector of Mars and the custodian of the people. He was Custos the Dreamer."

A roaring gasp escaped the crowds.

The holographic video feed switched back to Dev, who wore a smile. "I now introduce to you, people of Mars, Caleb Stanger of Earth. A man known and loved by Custos."

A bulky man with a blistered face appeared above the crowds. His brow was tilted with contrition. "The Copperhound is no more. He is gone and can no longer terrorize the people of New Athens. There are no armies—no uprising. He was... a coward and will no longer bother the people of Mars. The only armies of Earth are the armies of the hungry, the sick, and the impoverished that you see before you that have come to meet you in this desert meadow. We come to you, not with threats, but with hopes. We hope that we can stay and share this new world with you. We want you to see that we are not a separate people, we are not your enemy. We... are *you*."

The hologram disappeared as Charlotte's heart pounded in her chest. Although he had never revealed his face, she knew those shoulders—she knew that voice. It was *him!* It was his tricks—his manipulation. She wanted to run and hide from the phantom but she knew he would always find her.

And then he appeared in the desert meadow; the mass of Earth people inching behind him. The people of Earth followed behind, marveling at the crowds of Mars beyond. Cal gently stepped toward Charlotte, being careful to not trample the wild flowers as he plucked a sunflower from the ground. He wore the face of a man once tortured by hate but reformed by forgiveness.

He stood, face to face with her. "Charlotte?" his voice was hoarse but tender.

"Wha—what?"

"Can you forgive me?" He held the sunflower out to her.

EPILOGUE

J o Straus tended a pot of boiling potatoes.

Despite a bank account with more money than they could spend in ten lifetimes, she never hired a maid. She never even bought a new house—at least not a house that she hadn't lived in before. She sold the house with the secret room and bought the apartment that she and Tim lived in before things went bad. She enjoyed the small alcove that overlooked the Georgetown campus. She also longed for good memories.

Her crying days had ended. She had taken the fresh grief of losing her husband and turned it into a memorial. Every time the words of his last written note came to her, her thoughts shifted to their first date, their first song, or to their vacations at Lake Tahoe. She pictured his slanted smile or the way he frenetically brushed his black hair out of his eyes. Every day, she wondered what he could have accomplished if he hadn't had to bear the cross of mental illness. *The world would've been a different place,* she thought. *Timothy Straus could've moved the stars. If only he had the chance.*

She poured the potatoes into a strainer and then back into the pot, ready for mashing. After the cream and butter, she whipped the potatoes vigorously until they thinned into a paste.

James clapped with excitement as his mother brought him the mashed potatoes.

"Who's hungry?" she asked, putting a bowl in front of him, grateful that there was still a part of her husband that would remain in the world. She brushed his hair from his eyes and thought about the future.

After dinner, she took James to his room to play. As she passed back through the living room, the chess board on the coffee table caught her eye. She had kept the board, set with all pieces, up on the table since the news of Tim's death. It was as if he would walk into the room at any moment, ready to play.

She stooped out onto the balcony and looked at his telescope, thinking about the comet he studied that had come a few years ago. She looked up, thinking it would be there but the sky only twinkled with pinpoint stars. The comet had vanished along with her husband. She resigned to the night as the shadows lengthened in the streets and her eyes became heavy. She stepped back inside, ready for bed, but let out a yelp. The chess board, originally set out with a full complement of pieces had changed.

It was now missing the white queen.

AFTERWORD

Thank you for reading my science fiction debut, *Refraction*. I started writing this book in 2014 and finished the first manuscript in 2018. I had some initial ideas about where I wanted the book to go but it kind of took off on me and was certainly molded by current day events of social unrest and uncertainty. I learned a lot of important lessons writing *Refraction*, the chief of which is that human behavior doesn't really change but that doesn't mean we should stop trying. The only thing that matters is how we treat one another, everything else is just details.

I would like to offer a HUGE thanks to my beta readers: DC Allen (who has read everything I've ever written), Ashley Pyne, Austin Welker, David Wang, Tim Maher, Brian Shelby, Danny DeCillis and Monica Reads. Special thank you to my editor Laura Wilkinson.

REVIEWS MATTER!

Books can't go anywhere without reviews. If you enjoyed *Refraction*, please leave a review on Amazon, Goodreads or wherever you spend time on social media. I read a ton of fiction and non-fiction and make sure to leave a review for every book. I read every review written for my books and respond to reader feedback. Feel free to follow me on Goodreads. Thank you!

SNEAK PEEK

Check out a sneak peek of Wick Welker's new science fiction trilogy!
Coming Winter 2021:

Dark Theory

Chapter 1

Miree was supposed to have robbed a castle, bought a mountain of gold and lived on it alone and forever, the end. Already several weeks behind schedule, she was still slumming it up in Korthe, picking over battery casings and stumbling over dumb, dead robots. She'd damn near tripped over another bot that somehow hadn't already been eviscerated of its parts and sold off. The blue bot was sprawled in the dirt, its back resting against a rusted safe. She nudged the bot with her boot. "You alive?" It jerked its head, locking a hollow gaze on her, eyes flickering with indigo light. "You in there, idiot?"

Its eyes shuttered and went dead.

"What did you find over there?" Lucindi called from behind towers of twisted metal and arching shafts of discarded mechanical arms.

"Another dead bot. Might still have parts." Miree finished searching a rusted safe ready to turn into fine red dust at the next cross wind. She found the husk of a dead battery, popped out the corroded metal and stuffed it into her wool satchel.

Lucindi skirted the junk ridge, taking careful steps down the hill toward Miree. After discovering the motionless robot, she met Miree's eyes. "It's so sweet looking."

"Robots cannot be cute. But it is sweet—sweet for parts." Miree wrung her greasy hands in a dramatic show. "There's got to be a fusion core in that chest worth a small fortune." She flipped a screwdriver from her satchel and ran her eyes along the bot's casing.

"Wait!" Lucindi swatted her screwdriver away. "I just saw it move." She touched the robot's hand. The wrist was a metal cuff that held a stainless steel ball composing the palm. Extending out from the swiveling ball were four fingers and a thumb that articulated with the spherical palm by way of magnetism. "I've seen this design before. An older type—quite rare. How did we not see it here before? We were here just two days ago..."

Miree studied the robot's metal shell, noting small specks of sparkling light within its bluish metal. "If it's old—why is it... sparkling?"

"Dunno. Never seen skin like that on a bot."

"Sounds rare—sounds valuable."

"I *told* you I just saw it move—saw a little light flash in its eyes, too."

Miree gave the bot a gentle slap across its rounded cheek. It didn't move. "Looks dead to me." The robot's face was mostly metallic save for silicon edges around the mouth—ostensibly to simulate lip movement. Its eyes were shuttered tight. Miree shot Lucindi a sidelong glance. "How long do we have to wait?"

"For what?"

Miree crossed her arms. "How long do we need to wait from the time it was moving till we pronounce it dead and take it apart?"

"Five point eight minutes. After that, then you can deem the poor thing dead and sell it off."

"Are you hungry? Are all your street kids hungry?"

She narrowed her eyes at Miree.

"We could eat for two weeks off the scrap alone—more if the thing has a fusion core. Speaking of which—" She flipped out a wiry wand consisting of a metal prong with a meter stuck to the handle and studied the meter for a moment. "Looks good. No radio decay. If it has a fusion reactor, it's still insulated." She clipped the detector to her belt and dropped a satchel to the ground, producing implements for robot butchery: tin snips, wire cutters, wrench, screwdriver and bolt cutters. After donning a pair of thick gloves, she looked to Lucindi, tongue working at the side of her mouth.

Lucindi flicked her wrist. "Fine. Do what you want."

Miree knelt over the small bot methodically tapping on its chest and feeling for hollow spots. After exposing tiny compartments that housed screws which she removed, she freed a front plate of metal that covered the bot's abdomen and chest.

"But don't you think it would be worth more if it were still functioning?"

"Not if it's self-aware. No market in any fiefdom in a million klicks wants a self-aware bot. How many times do you see a farming bot out in the fields philosophizing about its own existence? The only bot a fief Lords want is one that works the fields, cleans latrines and cooks him and his harem dinner. No one wants a thinker—they're worthless."

"Just get on with it."

Miree lifted the metal covering off the bot, exposing a host of wires, circuitry and small filaments. "Uh huh." She followed the filaments up the abdomen and into the chest. A cylinder of dark metal occupied where a heart would be in a human. After ten minutes of banging on the cylinder and freeing up large bolts around its base, she lifted off slats of lead shielding. "What is all this?"

Lucindi peered over her shoulder. "That's vapor microtubing. A network of millions of filaments that carry water vapor from the reactor. The filaments spread throughout the entire body of the bot, serving as a highway of kinetic vapor energy fueling hydraulic joints, servos, neural networks—-stuff like that. It's like what a human heart does when it pumps blood to the body. And... that's a brand new fusion reactor," she said, puzzled.

"So?"

"It's a new reactor in an old model bot. And it's suddenly here? Just sitting in the junkyard?"

Miree stifled her excitement at the prospect of selling off the core for a decent bit of gold leaves. Maybe she could get back on schedule for her castle-robbing-living-on-a-mountain-alone-forever scheme. Once again, she inspected the reactor and checked the radioactivity and then sized her tools to the struts that held the reactor in place, planning the extraction.

"You don't think it's weird that someone went through the effort to build a brand new reactor into an old robot and then just dump it in a junkyard?"

A wrench clanked to the ground as Miree shot her a sharp look. "I don't ask questions that don't need to be answered."

Lucindi opened her mouth but went wide-eyed as the fusion reactor spontaneously activated, flickering with a neon green. "Get the lead!"

Miree clamped the lead shield back around the bot's reactor and backed away. The bot's eyelids sprung open revealing blue orbs of light. Its rubbery lips quivered. With twitching joints and wriggling fingers, circular shutters relaxed within its indigo eyes like pupils dilating. Its gaze caught Lucindi's.

It spoke. "My name is Beetro."

After replacing the bot's chest plate, Miree threw her tools back into her satchel, making sure Lucindi could hear them clank together. If Lucindi hadn't wasted time wondering about the life of a stupid robot in a junkyard, she'd already have a fusion reactor to hawk at the market.

"Water," the bot declared.

"Here." Lucindi handed it a skin flask. "You're weak aren't you? Need to refresh your water reserves."

"Yes," Beetro said, voice innocuous. The bot's eyes spun around the mounds of metal and trash. "Who—who am I?"

"I told you!" Miree's voice rattled down the trash heap. She had already scurried away to continue scavenging but watched from above. "It's using the *I* word—self-aware and totally worthless." Her voice cut away in the expanse of the plains beyond.

"Who—who am..." It looked up at Miree with something akin to shame.

"Don't listen to her," Lucindi said. "It's okay. You can refer to yourself as *I*." She patted the bot's hand. "Bots are always a little confused after reboot. You'll be fine."

Beetro fell silent.

"Do you know where you came from? You're an interesting model..."

"I don't know—oh!" His gaze widened.

"What?"

"I have a directive."

"See? You're figuring out who you are already. What is it?"

"I need to find Galiaro."

"Who's that?"

"I have no idea."

"It'll come to you." She peered down at the bot. "Are you a boy or a girl?"

"I'm a man," he answered.

"There we go. There's another thing you know about yourself."

"You're a girl," he remarked, as if only confirming to himself that he preserved some prowess of observation.

"Yes I am. Very good."

Beetro nodded and then stood, his head only arriving at Lucindi's sternum. The filaments leading to his joints kicked in with new water vapor. Joint servos popped with burgeoning energy, stabilizing his initial unsteady stance. Through twin heaps of garbage, he studied a faint mountain range in the distance which flanked a vast valley. Lazy slopes of yellow undulated across the vista.

"Feels... empty," he said.

Miree scoffed from above. "Tell me more about how you *feel*."

Lucindi glared at Miree. "Ignore her. It's nice to meet you, Beetro."

Beetro had no idea who he was. Where did he come from? Where even was *here*? Was he supposed to know? "Where is this?" He gestured to the junkyard.

"Junkyard. Korthe of the Helian fiefdom."

He nodded in understanding despite understanding nothing. He inspected Lucindi discovering a young woman with brown skin and kinky hair—face gaunt, arms knotty. She wore torn, brown trousers, intended for a large man and outfitted with dozens of customized pockets with skewed stitching suggesting she'd made them herself. The pockets were stuffed full making her waddle as she began scavenging the garbage heaps. Beetro noticed blackened grease along her hands and arms but her face was clean.

"You're hungry," he declared.

Tiny wrinkles crinkled at her eyes as she smiled. Beetro liked that. "Yes," she said.

"I am Beetro."

She nodded as if placating a child. "Yes, I know."

"I need to find Galiaro."

"You told me. Sounds like he's your engineer?"

"Can you take me to Galiaro?"

"I don't know who he is."

"Oh."

"You're a strange little bot. I like you." She had moved away and up a heap where Miree had disappeared.

Beetro followed. Over the next several hours, he watched the two humans collect metal shrapnel, wiring, bits of rubber shards and strips of fabric. They brought the scavenged items to a wooden wagon they had parked at the edge of the junkyard.

Beetro helped.

In what became a speechless effort, Lucindi pointed to items that clung at the top of a junk stack which Beetro retrieved. He was lighter than the humans and had smaller feet, affording him easy purchase on otherwise teetering stacks of garbage and metal.

"Dumb thing moves around like a mountain goat," Miree remarked. The comment made Beetro want to run and hide from her.

After the wagon had been stacked high, Lucindi smirked at Miree and nodded toward Beetro. "Not a bad find after all."

Miree shrugged.

They arrived at the market to barter where Miree scoffed at the single cup of flour and gallon of water they received. Korthe was a sleepy town appearing to offer little in terms of a robust trading market. Complaints about an unseasonable drought floated between conversations. Beetro studied the faces of the townsfolk: tired and drooping with their gazes mostly on the ground. Children littered the streets, without family or home and begging food from even Lucindi and Miree, clearly women of no means. They seemed to not notice the strange looking robot in tow.

"Are there other robots here?" Beetro asked Lucindi as they left the trading markets.

"Not many. Bots don't find much use being in small towns like Korthe. Those that can think for themselves usually go to bigger cities like Orion. Those that are owned stay in the country, tending farms."

"Check out Crow," Miree interrupted, nudging Lucindi.

Beetro saw an old man slumped against a squatty shack: mouth ajar, tongue listing to the corner. He slept with a plastic bottle of amber colored liquor in his hand. Beetro quickly learned how the man had earned his moniker: a murder of crows trooped around him, picking crumbs off his clothing.

Lucindi stopped for a moment, made sure the man was still breathing and kept moving. "He's okay."

"Better to have him passed out cold then rambling about how the galaxy is dying," Miree said, a coldness in her voice. Beetro didn't like it—he was overall quite terrified of the dark-haired girl.

Beetro followed the women to the edge of Korthe to a shallow cave dug into the back of a dirt mound. They'd managed a deft attempt at camouflage by planting bushes over the entrance of the cave. Miree crammed the rest of the scavenge that they couldn't sell into the cave and the humans shared a little water and crackers after which Lucindi got to work making dough from the flour they'd bought. She told him it was enough to feed them for two days, give or take how much they shared with the street kids—a topic of much debate between the two humans.

As night approached, Miree squinted at the enormous valley that rolled away from their shaggy, dirt cave. "No storms brewing, let's sleep under the stars tonight," she declared. She then whipped out a tattered blanket, stitched with several generations of patchwork fabric, and lay down. Lucindi pulled out a thatched bed of hay and cotton and placed it over a worn, rectangular patch in the grass.

"Lonely over there?" Miree asked Lucindi.

"Not particularly."

Their snoring was consent enough for Beetro to stay and curl up next to a nearby tree. Before powering down, he looked up into the night sky and saw the stars.

There were only five.

Chapter 2

Who am I?

"Don't know what we did till you came along," Lucindi told Beetro after a few more days of working in the junkyard.

Beetro found he had a great eye for rubber and aluminum, two items of scrap that always fetched a decent price. He was agile—easily treading up junk heaps to pluck anything they asked. His ball-in-socket-joints offered excellent dexterity enabling him to tear open machinery or sort through refuse more nimbly than the humans. He helped them and received their tacit endorsement that he could stay with them in return. Despite the welcome camaraderie, he was profoundly confused about where Korthe was and—

Who he even was.

Lucindi explained that the mystery would unravel as his neural network returned after the hard reboot, but nothing came. His memory was just... gone.

Gone or deleted.

"Who was it you had asked for again?" Lucindi asked.

Beetro was hefting a bolt the size of a tree stump into the salvage wagon—his hydraulic joints affording excellent lifting power. He slammed the bolt into the wagon.

"When we found you, you said you needed to find someone... "

"Galiaro."

"Do you remember anything else yet?"

Beetro looked away, uneasy. "No... "

"Who is Galiaro?"

"I don't know."

"Don't you have any residual programming?"

"Just firmware for basic robotic survival and a single subroutine."

"What is it?"

"Find Galiaro."

"That's it?"

Beetro nodded, chasing a worried look off his face.

"Why hang around here then?" She gestured to the junkyard.

"Do you not like me? Should I leave now?" He stood as if ready to depart.

A high-pitched gasp escaped her. "No, no, no. We really like having you with us. I've actually never met a self-aware bot before. Most bots in these parts are just mindless machines with no awareness. Miree says bots like you are a dime a dozen in Orion. But to me you're so... "

"What?"

"Human."

"Thank you?"

"I'm just saying if you're bothered by not knowing much about yourself, hanging around Korthe probably won't get you any answers. This Galiaro is the one that probably programmed you—the program to go find him is probably an emergency protocol after a hard reboot."

"I just feel so blind—it's like I'm... "

"Lost."

He nodded. "I know basic things: a cup holds liquid, a hammer hits nails—not much more."

"You're learning from us, aren't you? Is that why you stay."

"I guess so. But I also like you. Miree doesn't seem to like me though."

448 | WICK WELKER

"Be patient with that one. She's been through more than most. Girls like her just need time—they need love."

For the rest of the day Lucindi casually chatted about the land around Korthe as Beetro fortified his memory with the new information like a baby laying down neural synapses. She explained the loose feudal system that dominated the region of Helian, extending from the feet of Meteor Mountains in the east to Carister, the nearest town to the west. The fief Lord lived at Peles Castle a few kilometers away from which he spewed his onerous decrees. Every couple of years, some entitled neighboring fief Lord would bring his mercenaries and try to scoop the region of Helian under his control. The last time it happened, the town barely stood to greet the newest brigade of soldiers that came for the perfunctory tax collection.

Miree blathered about some city called Orion. All Beetro gleaned from the brief descriptions was that it was a harbor city far away— way better than anything Korthe or the region of Helian had to offer. Orion was *happening*. It was there Beetro would find all of his stupid robot friends and where they could talk about the meaning of their own pointless existence, etcetera. It was a place for poets, musicians, artists and the rich human merchants that supported them. There weren't any Lords or Kings that tried to take over the city—it was ruled by the merchants and the markets. Beetro was confused by almost everything Miree said about the place.

"Why are you here then?" Beetro asked after hearing Miree's descriptions of Orion. She paused, acting like she was distracted by a rusted scythe that had been broken in half and left in the dirt. Lucindi's ears perked at this query.

"Had to leave," Miree demurred.

"Oh." Beetro learned the social cue of someone discreetly changing subject and looked away, feigning distraction. Yet he persisted. "Why though?"

"Why would I tell you, robot?"

"Why would you not tell me?" he asked, earnest.

"You don't just go around telling everyone you meet everything about your life. Got it?"

"Did you know Lucindi before you came here?"

"You don't learn do you?"

"Just curious. You don't have to tell me."

"We met scavenging. Thought it would be better to pool resources." She shared a glance with Lucindi.

Beetro spied several gigantic rubber tires atop a particularly precarious tower of trash. "Have you seen those?"

"Yeah, too high. That whole thing would collapse—well maybe not if you—"

"Not even Beetro could get up there safely," Lucindi interrupted.

"Too bad, could get a lot of trade for all that rubber," Miree said, morose.

"I'll try if you want... " Beetro said.

Lucindi shook her head. "No, no, you might get hurt."

Beetro might get hurt... and this would bother Lucindi. He let this concept roll in his head for a moment.

On their way back to their dirt cave, they saw Crow leaning against a shack, snoring so loud it was hard to believe it was not intentional. Lucindi gave him a gentle pat on the leg, stirring him awake. She placed a bread cake on his knee, gave a small wave and kept on. Crow shoved the bread in his mouth and pulled his stout cap over his eyes. Beetro wasn't sure if the man even knew where the food came from. "Bah! The galaxy is dying anyway... " he heard the old man's mutterings which went ignored.

Several of the street children seemed to have noticed the small, blue-tinted robot that trailed after Lucindi and Miree for the past few days. Assuming he'd be as generous as Lucindi often was, they surrounded him with outstretched hands. He apologized and weaved through the crowds, catching up to the wagon that Miree was towing. He felt a knock on his back and turned to see an impossibly small girl with brown eyes—skeletal with starvation.

"I don't have anything," he told her.

Lucindi approached the small girl. "Nothing today, Ribcage. Sorry. Just gave the last of my batch to Crow."

"Ribcage?" Beetro asked. "Is that a normal human name?"

Lucindi shrugged. "It's what all the other children call her. She's more ribcage than anything else. I guess the name stuck."

"Who's the bot?" Ribcage asked Lucindi. She inspected his blue metal and tapped on his leg.

"Stop that," Beetro complained.

"He's just a new friend. Helps out. He really likes to be tapped like that."

"What?" Beetro turned to Lucindi. "No. I do not. This bothers me."

"Oh yeah?" Ribcage said, giving Beetro several taps up the side of his metal skin.

Beetro swatted her hand away. "No, I *don't* like that." He looked at Lucindi, confused. "Why would you tell her that I would like this?"

"It's a joke you dumbass robot," Ribcage said before running off down an alley.

Beetro and Lucindi followed Miree around the corner into the markets where she hawked an old hammer for half a gallon of water and nothing else.

"Isn't there a river near town?" Beetro asked, recalling seeing a sliver of sunlight bouncing off a strip of water in the distance.

Miree shook her head. "Radioactive—poisoned. Don't drink any natural water without using one of these." She slipped the radioswitch from her belt. "Well... I guess the water wouldn't hurt *you*, but it kills humans in a few days. I've seen the Poisoning out on the plains a couple times. They get lost, run out of water and get desperate, especially if it hasn't rained in awhile like how it's been lately. They come across a river and guzzle it down. A few days later, blood is pouring from mouth and ass. They really should just do themselves a favor and end it before they drink it. Less pain."

Lucindi caught up with them after stopping to talk to some of the children. "What are you two talking about?"

"She hasn't seen it," Miree continued speaking to Beetro as if she hadn't joined the conversation. "She's been here," she gestured to the dusty town, "most of her life—doesn't know what it's like out there on the plains. Lucindi was one of them." She nodded behind, at the street children who'd returned back to their alleyways or secret rooftop spots.

Lucindi's shoulders slumped at this remark, her gaze falling to the ground.

"But that's okay, too," Miree said, making a belated attempt at backpedaling.

The three returned to their dirt cave. There wasn't any food that night for the humans. Lucindi gave the last couple of bread cakes to some children. Miree retired to her blanket early, either out of hunger or shame for bringing Lucindi to a silent sulking.

"It isn't like I haven't been outside of Korthe, *ever*," Lucindi remarked to Beetro as she tried to sleep. "I've been out in the fields— used to work them until the fief Lord got even cheaper labor than a Korthe street kid. I used to go to Carister every few weeks with a cara-van, too. I met different bots and people from all over. That's where I learned a lot about men. I learned a lot of hard lessons. That's where I also learned about bot designs, too... " She looked over at Beetro.

Beetro finally understood Lucindi's expression—she had flashed it every now and then when she was thinking. "You're confused."

She studied Beetro for a moment. "It's just a little strange. You're an old bot—well I guess all bots are old—no one makes them anymore. But you're short, you have rounded shoulders, cylindrical torso... "

"Why is that strange?"

"Usually when I see bots like you, they *look* old. They're rusted— have faded panels and replacement parts all over. But you're whole— intact. You look newer but you were probably made a century ago."

"Have I been... preserved?"

"Not sure. I'd like to meet this Galiaro and ask."

Beetro awoke in the middle of the night with an idea.

He had powered down next to Lucindi; she slept softly with

something like serenity in her face. He'd begun to worry about her nutrition: she had knotty arms and grooves along her tendons where healthy muscle should be.

So he crept along the thick grass, careful not to wake Miree, and wriggled into their dirt cave. It was lined with junk: watches, strips of leather, stacks of fabric, tin cans and a host of Miree's tools. There was an organization to the chaos: shelves dug into the cave walls and plastic boxes within for storage. Beetro inspected the drawers, disappointed. He noticed a tunnel that led away from the entrance and crawled through, following the narrow path into a smaller room. It was pitch black. He enhanced his vision, changing his view to a dim green.

The room was full of batteries of all types. Boxed and cylindrical. He inspected them one by one, discovering many of them to be dead. After digging through them, he realized they were *all* dead. Why would they keep a roomful of dead batteries? He noticed a fresh spot of dirt that had clearly been recently unearthed and covered and crept closer.

"What are you doing in here?" a voice broke from behind.

Beetro whipped around feeling... guilt, apparently. "I'm sorry?"

"Why are you here?" It was Miree, quite unenthused.

"I was looking for tools."

"Why?" She was wearing tough, canvas trousers, no shoes and a tank top. Needle-like scars ran the length of her exposed forearms— wisps of scar tissue like gossamer on her skin, too numerous to count.

"Why do you have those scars?"

"I'm asking the questions. Why were you looking for tools, *robot*?"

There was something about the way she said 'robot'. It was an accurate description, but why did it make him feel like a big nothing? Beetro held out his hands, each a suspended ball with five perfectly polished metallic fingers floating in the air. "I wanted to demagnetize my hands."

Miree's face changed from suspicion to genuine confusion. "The hell are you talking about?"

"You could use the metal from my fingers once I get them out of the magnetic field of my hands. Probably trade it in for a couple months of food. You and Lucindi could eat—wouldn't have to dig in the junkyard. Not for awhile at least."

The woman's face turned to something like shock. "That's... That's fucking crazy."

"Oh, I'm sorry. I didn't know."

"You need your *hands*, idiot."

"Right." He turned to leave the tiny room.

"And don't come back in here. This is *my* stuff."

Beetro nodded and found his way next to Lucindi.

He powered down.

———

Miree hated caring.

But she hated apologizing even more.

After the rage of discovering that candy-ass robot rummaging through her stuff subsided, she couldn't sleep—couldn't stop caring. That hurt look in Lucindi's face—her shattered expression after Miree had belittled her for being a back-water Korthe street rat.

She couldn't get Lucindi out of her mind.

Miree stood, shuffling through the grass under the slivered moon. She watched Lucindi sleeping next to the robot, her chest rising and falling—somehow sleeping serenely. *Who sleeps peacefully?* With all the pain, corruption and turmoil throughout literally every surface on the planet, how can Lucindi sleep as if she could die tomorrow without a single regret? Also, who has the audacity to feed children when they can barely feed themselves? Miree was both annoyed and exhilarated by the girl she had met only weeks before.

Miree grunted in frustration, watching Lucindi sleeping. She wanted to pack everything up forever and never come back. But she also wanted to go over there and kiss her on the mouth and apologize and confess to everything she'd done wrong in her entire life.

She did neither.

"Fuck."

She returned to bed. *Rob a castle. Mountain of gold. Alone forever.* She repeated the mantra, finally finding sleep.

OTHER BOOKS AVAILABLE FROM DEMODOCUS PUBLISHING

Creatrix of Strife, by DC Allen: "Stand in Hell, But Reach For Heaven."

Rekha is a Disciple of Obcasus: science-worshiping zealots who live deep beneath a poisonous volcano and await the sign to arise and conquer the world. While her fellow Disciples are content to recite violent oaths and practice a form of combat based on instantaneous genetic modifications, Rekha is consumed with doubts. After she instigates a mêlée that goes horribly awry, she is cast out. Now separated from the only life she knows, the young heretic stumbles into the heart of a mystery seven generations in the making, and the reckoning that follows. If the Obcasian Death Cult's apocalyptic dogma is true, what comes next?

CREATRIX OF STRIFE is a literary anthem realized in lyrical, mind-bending, and brutal prose. Set in an arcane, minutely detailed world where troglodytic saints weaponize their own DNA and the main defense against volcanic death is a massive clockwork defense system, Rekha's tale is a thrilling science fiction adventure, but also the account of an outcast channeling her frustration into strength and finding purpose in a storm of uncertainty

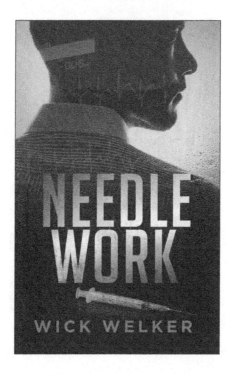

Needle Work, by Wick Welker: Dr. Rosen never lost his demons. They were only waiting.

As a seasoned trauma anesthesiologist in Seattle, Doctor Jude Rosen takes his coffee black with gangland shootouts and vehicular dismemberment. When his best friend, Farrah Abdi, suffers from breast cancer, Jude sheds the carefully cultivated safeguards of a family man to help his dying friend. After being slapped with a malpractice suit and having no recourse to provide for his daughters, Jude embraces what he thought he'd abandoned: his haunted past. Once the criminal underground catches up to him, Jude realizes he can no longer play the game, he can only change the rules—on the operating table.

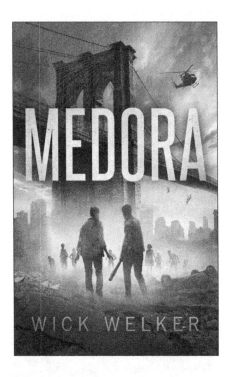

Medora, by Wick Welker: Welcome to Medora, population zero and counting.

As the uprising of the undead sweeps the streets of New York City, a small family fights through skyscrapers and schools to find one another. A special-ops military unit discovers that the cover-up of a chemotherapy nanovirus experiment has gone awry. As a disgraced researcher becomes entangled in the mystery of Medora, North Dakota, the President fights off a modern age of imperialism. As policemen flee from children and mothers brandish hacksaws, the country's fate will depend on the civil war between humankind and the dead. Welcome to Medora, population zero and spreading.

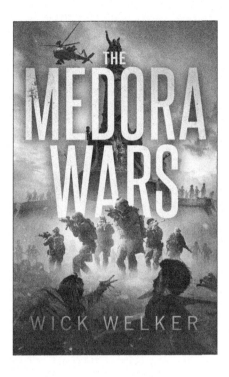

The Medora Wars, by Wick Welker: Die today, fight tomorrow .

Two years after the New York outbreak in Medora, masked terrorists unleash the undead at a mall in Mexico City. Infected bodies fall from unmarked planes over D.C., Seoul and Jerusalem. A terrorist leader, known only as The Sirr, claims responsibility as he rises up with his brotherhood to cleanse mankind with the nanovirus scourge. The fate of the world depends on an elite infectious operations team and one CIA operative whose loyalties have blurred. As the military defends the world with electromagnetic weapons, they soon discover the enemy's secret: the undead have evolved.

ABOUT THE AUTHOR

Wick Welker writes in multiple genres including medicine, post-apocalyptic and science fiction. He is also a medical doctor who practices critical care medicine and anesthesiology. He currently writes and practices medicine in Minnesota. He is supported by an amazing cat and an incredible wife.

Made in the USA
Coppell, TX
03 September 2021